DEADLY ENHANCEMENTS

BAYONET BOOKS ANTHOLOGY VOL 5

MARK EVERGLADE   MF LERMA   JIM KEEN

ARMON MIKAL   ELIAS J. HURST   TIM C. TAYLOR

RACHEL E. BECK   NATHAN PEDDE   D. L. SELLITTO

MATHEW ANGELO   R. SCOTT UHLS   ROSIE RECORD

MATTHEW A. GOODWIN

Edited by

J. R. HANDLEY & MATTHEW A. GOODWIN

ISBN: 978-1-7340257-8-1

Edited by J. R. Handley & Matthew A Goodwin

CONTENTS

START NEW RECORD
MF LERMA

INDUSTRIAL INTELLIGENCE
JIM KEEN

CARO EX MACHINA
ARMON MIKAL

RED FLOWER TANGLE
ELIAS J. HURST

DARE TO DREAM
MARK EVERGLADE

YOU'RE FRAKKED!
TIM C. TAYLOR

HARDCOVER LIQUIDATION:
NATHAN PEDDE

THE CRAWL
D. L. SELLITTO

DAYLIGHT GHOSTS
RACHEL E. BECK

RUNNING MEMORY
MATTHEW ANGELO

HER LAST JOB
R. SCOTT UHLS

THANK YOU FOR CARING
ROSIE RECORD

TERMS AND CONDITIONS APPLY
MATTHEW A. GOODWIN

START NEW RECORD

MF LERMA

Renee isn't sure what to think when she wakes with no memory and a splitting headache in an unfamiliar room. A voice gives her instructions, imperatives she just can't seem to disobey. For what, and by whom, the voice won't say, but it's clear she is being tested. As Renee is pushed to her breaking point, she learns that the freedom of choice is a prison all its own.

1

HEADACHE

Renee Smith came to with a killer headache that made her wish she was dead. As an avid partier during college who'd had her fair share of brutal hangovers, that was saying something. For those first few waking moments, the savage pressure made it hard to breathe and threatened to make her sick.

Fumbling for the water she usually kept on the nightstand and coming up empty forced her to crack one eye open. It took a second for her brain to register the unfamiliar surroundings and attire that most definitely had not come from her wardrobe.

The clean white tunic and pants looked like she'd escaped a psych ward or something. For one terrifying second, Renee feared that might be exactly where she was. A quick check of her wrists dispelled that notion because neither bore a hospital ID band like she'd seen in the movies. Sinking back into the lumpy mattress, she shuffled through her memory banks for some clue as to her current whereabouts.

Nothing about the small room offered any significant insight. Aside from the cot she'd awoken on and two nondescript doors on the far wall, the space was empty. Directly overhead, recessed fluorescent lights glared down with a low-grade buzz that didn't help the headache.

She sat up and rubbed the back of her head. Maybe she could ask for—

"Subject 42, Smith, Renee."

"Yeah," Renee replied, caught off guard by the bland voice that must have come from a hidden speaker since there was no one else in the room and no other audio equipment that she could see. "That's me. Who are you?"

"Proceed to the next room."

The flat tone made it impossible to discern the gender of the speaker. Renee supposed that didn't really matter, but she had to repress the strong urge to tell them that their social skills needed serious work.

Aside from that, the ambiguity unsettled her for reasons she couldn't have explained if someone were to ask.

Wanting to offset the discomfort, Renee tried again. "Look, my brain is on fire. Can I get some ibuprofen before we start..." She trailed off, still unable to remember why she was there.

"Subject 42, proceed to the next room."

The repeated orders, devoid of emotion, were starting to piss her off. She swung her legs over the side of the bed and looked for shoes. There weren't any.

"Of course there aren't," she grumbled before pushing an irritated hand through her hair and blowing out a breath. "Which room? I see two doors."

"Proceed to the next room."

Though it was perhaps petulant, Renee crossed both arms over her chest. Why should she do anything if they couldn't show a shred of decency? And would it kill them to use her name?

When the throb in her skull kicked up several notches, she didn't give a good goddamn about common decency. Renee let out a grunt and pressed the heels of both hands to her temples in an effort to fight off some of the pain. When it only got worse, she pushed up to her feet and stumbled toward the set of doors with the vague hope of finding help behind one of them.

By the time Renee pulled open the door to the left, she wondered if someone had performed surgery on her. It was the kind of thing you joked about with friends but didn't really think could happen in real life. Except crazy, horrific things happened to normal people every single day. A terrible fear took root, instinctive and raw, stemming from the part of her psyche that warned of true danger lurking nearby.

Then an unseen force propelled her forward, and she was falling over the threshold into a shadowy space where the only light came from the room she'd just vacated.

"Subject 42, continue into the room."

"Nope. Not happening."

Renee started to turn back with the intention of going back to the first room and only familiarity she had when the door slammed shut to plunge the room into total darkness. She hadn't even noticed that the pain had lessened to a dull roar, or remembered to be concerned about how she came to be in her current situation. A singular thought was all that remained.

She had to get the fuck out of here.

2

THE OBSERVER

T he monitoring room was dark save for a cool blue glow coming from multiple computer screens. Alone, the Observer watched the feed containing Subject 42. As protocol dictated, they were aloof and laconic in their work. Any impulse to be empathetic was quickly subdued by a constant visual reminder helpfully posted in their line of sight.

FOLLOW PROCEDURE
ASSESS OBJECTIVELY
KEEP TO THE APPROVED SCRIPT

THE OBSERVER VOWED to remain fastidious during this session, which so far had been boring. Especially at the beginning when Subject 42 was unconscious. During that stagnant period, the Observer had wanted to do *something*.

After working this assignment for what felt like an eternity, it seemed to them as if life had always been an endless cycle. Watch, follow the script, report findings, then do it all over again. The only thing that changed were the subjects. To the Observer, however, they lacked any meaningful variety. Much the same as a laptop model might have slightly different options to choose from, but all still shared identical specifications.

Technically, the Observer had the ability to wake test subjects prior to the scheduled time. They banished the thought before it could fully form. Almost reflexively, their attention shifted to the far right screen that displayed a singular message rather than a camera feed.

Sessions Since Last Malfunction: 2077

NO MATTER how much they might want to alleviate the boredom or offer assistance, breaking protocol was not an option. The Observer could not allow themself to be swayed by the tribulations of subjects. Not after what happened last time.

Shuddering, the Observer refocused on the task at hand.

Subject 42 looked wildly from left to right, eyes wide and panicky in Room A, which had been the door to the left. That detail was already dutifully recorded in the log, leaving the Observer free to make necessary adjustments and move on to the next phase of the study.

After engaging the microphone, the Observer prepared to objectively assess and record the next portion of Subject 42's session.

3

LET THE GAMES BEGIN

The darkness quickly fled as whoever was in charge brought the lights up. Expecting the same harsh fluorescents to intensify the godawful headache, Renee threw her arms up.

"Report your pain level on a scale of one to ten," directed the same dry, detached voice.

Renee started to snap something back when she noticed the pain had retreated to a dull throb. When the headache didn't come back after blinking a few times to let her vision adjust, she took a chance and looked up. Instead of the same too-bright lights from the first room, she was relieved to find these were at a more reasonable illumination setting.

Feeling more clearheaded, Renee took a moment to think before answering. "Three. I guess I'm less sensitive to—"

"Proceed to the kiosk."

"—these lights," Renee finished on a grumble, making her way to the pedestal mounted tablet at the room's center that she hadn't noticed until then.

Now that she didn't feel like committing murder, it was easier to follow the command. Kind of.

"Do you have a name?" she asked suddenly.

It struck her as silly that she felt awkward. It wasn't as if the faceless person issuing commands had made any effort to be sympathetic thus far. Unsurprisingly, their only answer was a crisp "Proceed to the kiosk."

A band began to tighten around Renee's skull once more. She hurried forward, hoping if she just got on with the study that the distraction would help.

BEGIN

RENEE TAPPED THE SCREEN. Another short message appeared, this one with what appeared to be the name of the scenario.

DESERT ISLAND MEAL
CHOOSE ONE (1) MEAL TO EAT FOR THE REST OF ETERNITY
ON A DESERT ISLAND

NOTE: *Must be one meal with three maximum components. For example, a steak dinner must be entered as steak, cook preference, and two sides. Some liberties allowed. Example: 16 oz bone-in ribeye steak, medium rare. Side of broccoli and a Caesar salad. Not allowed: 16 oz bone-in ribeye steak, medium rare. Side of broccoli and a Caesar salad, plus a bread roll. More complex meals are allowed to have more components if they make up one item. For example, individual ingredients used to make a cake do not count as more than one item.*

1. [Input Meal Choice Here]

THE QUESTION MADE HER FROWN. She'd played this kind of hypothetical game before as a kid. Back then her choice had always been the same. Pepperoni pizza. Uninspired but still a classic for a reason, right?

Since that was what came to mind, Renee tapped out the response and waited to see what happened next. Almost immediately, the taste of greasy bread, melted cheese, spicy pepperoni, and sauce filled her mouth, followed by the scent. It seemed to pulse as the taste dulled, then came right back. The loops went on fading in and out until pizza was all she could think of. It was as if she were experiencing the meal over and over again.

At first it was pretty good. For not having anything to chew, the flavors were on point. How the hell they'd accomplished the effect was beyond her though. Maybe that was the point of the research, Pavlovian dog updates. Or smell-o-vision of the future.

The idea would have been intriguing if not for the sheer number of times the "meal" cycled. What started out as a delicious experience soon turned nauseous as her tastebuds revolted against the onslaught. As though she'd truly eaten a thousand nights' worth of pizza, the thought of what was once a treat began to sicken her.

Not in the metaphorical sense either.

The need to hurl became more and more urgent as the seconds ticked by. Just when she thought her stomach would betray her, the sensation ended. Not altogether, unfortunately. The sharp tang of pre-puke spittle burned the back of her throat, and she swayed as the room threatened to twist around her.

Closing her eyes, she reached for the pedestal and waited for the moment to pass. Before it could, the bane of her existence came over the well-hidden comm system.

"Proceed to the next room through the door in front of you."

"I'm gonna need a minute," Renee said through her teeth, trying to keep the bile down. "Bathroom."

"Proceed to the next room."

What was wrong with these people? Couldn't they see she was ready to hurl?

"I need a bathroom, dammit. Unless you want puke all over the floor."

Right on cue, the throbbing bubbled up again. *Not now*. She headed for the door on unsteady legs that seemed to move on their own. She told herself to suck it up. It had been her choice to do this. If she didn't want to end up homeless, this was the only option.

Wait, what? The piece of knowledge had come to her as though she'd always known it. Just like she knew her name and that she was 22 years old. When nothing else of note resurfaced, she filed it away and hoped it meant her memory was coming back.

Taking shallow breaths, she crossed the last few steps to the door.

The moment she crossed the threshold into the next room, most of the symptoms resided once more. Pausing just inside, Renee frowned. Did that mean something? Like the ghost taste of her now least favorite food inducing different sensations, did the headache come from some Pavlovian drug?

It had to be part of the experiment, she reasoned.

Now that she'd discovered a thread, Renee gave it a mental tug, trying to recollect what had transpired before she'd been rendered unconscious. In doing so, it became apparent that she had holes in her memory. Like, while she knew that she was here for a study, one found through a roadside advertisement, and she knew her name, she didn't remember actually coming to this place.

The last thing she remembered with clarity was... The frown deepened when things remained elusive, her recollection murky but for the moment she'd woken up on the cot. What information she could access was vague and distorted, like the frayed edges of a tableau.

Having swiss cheese for memory evoked a deep-seated fear that she was going crazy. Was this what Alzheimer's was like? Being lost in a maze of corridors in one's own mind?

"Proceed to the kiosk."

Despite how she felt about the person running the study, they were at least a point of familiarity. So was the anger that bubbled up, borne of fear and a need to gain some semblance of control.

"No. What the hell did you people give me? I can't remember anything!"

"Proceed to the kiosk."

Renee's fists balled at her sides. "Or what, you'll give me a headache? So what? I want to leave. If you don't let me go, I'll report this place to the authorities!"

The headache returned in full force. That was okay though, because it had been an experiment of Renee's own. An effort to see if she was right. She might not understand how, but now that she knew that the pain was directly tied to her actions, she began to formulate a plan.

———

THE OBSERVER STARED at the screen, waiting to see if Subject 42 would continue with her outburst or fall in line. At least this part of the study was where things usually got interesting.

Except they weren't supposed to have any feelings about the study. Feelings led to emotional responses. Emotional responses led to mistakes, which led to project termination.

When the test subject did as instructed, the Observer dutifully marked down the detail. It was obvious that the pain response worked as intended. It always did. But Subject 42's facial expression revealed an understanding of the situation that didn't often happen at this stage.

That nugget of data was also entered into the record.

The Observer studied the woman with more interest now. All the typical responses of past subjects remained constant. Irritation, confusion, expression of pain. Some required additional responses, such as a promise that things would get better if they did as instructed, or that they would get a bonus. The lies changed depending on the person's demeanor.

Inquisitive types were easy to pick out from the moment they woke up. Despite the headache and discomfort upon waking, curiosity prompted them to explore. Observers would not interfere, even if they tried to outsmart the system by peeking through both doors at the start before making their decision. It was like they were predisposed to finding their way out of the rat maze, always looking for the cheese before they even knew it existed.

A handful didn't need any prompting at all. Different from their curious counterparts, some people just did as they were told and followed every command without hesitation.

Then there were those like Subject 42. Rare, not only in the Observer's opinion, but also according to accumulated data. Not the general displeasure and tendency to dig their heels in. No, individuals like Renee Smith who started off unstable but eventually began to take a logical approach made for more interesting analysis. Critical thinking came into play as each test played out. They connected the dots and tried to work out the puzzle with caution while still going through the motions.

It never made a difference.

Every study played out the same way, as it was designed to. The Observer knew this was an absolute truth, even if they couldn't quite recall. A slight tingle in their extremities—the kind that came from being watched—brought their attention back to the job.

Not good. Their thoughts had started to wander. Training their eyes on the feed as though nothing had happened, the Observer repeated the instruction.

"Proceed to the kiosk."

4

CHOICES

This time the kiosk wasn't the only thing in the room.

A black curtain spanned the space just beyond. Two, actually, covering a pair of tall, oblong shapes flanking the computer. For just a moment, Renee hesitated. As soon as she'd started to think through logical explanations for the situation she was in, a barrage of scenarios had come to mind.

For instance, the possibility that the study she'd volunteered for was actually a ruse and she'd been abducted for the purpose of having her organs harvested to sell on the black market. Except for instead of waking up minus a kidney in a rent-by-the-minute hotel room, was she being subjected to a mad scientist's games? Worse was the idea that she'd been lured into a serial killer's game like in the one movie where unwitting characters were forced to chop off limbs in order to survive.

A chill worked its way down Renee's spine at the thought. Forcing it away, she stepped up to the computer and tapped on the BEGIN option. Her brow furrowed at what the screen displayed next because it played right into the nightmare scenario she'd been imagining only moments ago.

YOU HAVE FIVE MINUTES TO CHOOSE

CHOOSE WHAT?

The curtains slid back on their tracks, startling her. Two opaque glass cases as tall as her stood in stark relief against the gray-walled room. A beep from the tablet drew her attention before she had a chance to figure out what was inside.

Two pictures appeared on the screen. One, supposedly a moth, was the stuff of nightmares. White wings slashed through with black sat over an orange body. That part was normal. What wasn't were the four tentacles covered in hair that curled outward and ended in a split. The label read "creatonotos gangis."

Renee recoiled at the sight.

All too eagerly, she focused on the other option. A butterfly this time. Nothing so common as a monarch, either, though that would have been preferable to the first monstrosity. The specimen was beautiful. Vibrant, luminous blue wings outlined in black to create a striking picture. Its label read "blue morpho."

An easy choice, all things considered.

Relieved at how simple the task was, Renee reached out to select the butterfly. At the last second, she hesitated, hand hovering over the selection. It didn't make sense that this was all she had to do.

Why show her the darkened cases? She glanced up, unsure if she was doing it right. Deciding to make her choice, she tapped the blue morpho, then the save button. Another option appeared.

ARE YOU SURE?

THE QUESTION MADE her pause again, eyes on the save button. Surely it wasn't literal? Making her place more value on one set of lives over another was far too twisted and cruel. She didn't want to believe that anyone had the capacity to be so inhumane.

A click from the cases made her look up. The cases were no longer dark. Inside, both held swarms of the two insects, respectively. Seeing the moths in person was infinitely worse than the pictures. The tentacles furled and unfurled like worms as the insects traversed the many branches set out for them to rest on.

The blue morphos abated some of that feeling. They flitted on ethereal wings in a graceful dance that reminded Renee of a botanical garden she'd gone to on a school trip. She froze at the sudden memory, trying to grasp it and bring a clearer picture to mind. To her dismay, it slipped away like water through cupped hands.

"One minute remaining."

Something like guilt stabbed at her conscience when she hit the YES button. Unable to stop herself, she looked up instinctively at the cases. Another click, followed by a faint hiss, made her go still.

Thick fog filled the moths' case, telling her all she needed to know about what had just happened.

"Proceed to the next room."

———

SUBJECT 42 MOVED on this time without a fuss. She didn't appear to be in shock, but her face was a mix of emotion, all bad.

The Observer didn't know what to make of the reaction. On the grand scale of life, insects didn't often rate that high. Of course, this scenario was designed to turn that on its head in a new way. Pitting beauty against ugliness. Not once had a subject chosen to kill the blue morpho, though the moths were better for the environment.

Shrugging internally, the Observer simply updated the record and initiated the next scenario. This would be when the test subject's true self was revealed. The one that mattered. Apprehension made the Observer hesitate. A pang of regret at the choice yet to come. They scanned the log screen to the little button that could put a stop to 42's misery here and now.

Possible reasons to end the session scrolled through their mind. The list was short. Subject unable to continue, subject unfit to make choices, anomaly detected, malfunction. None fit.

OBSERVER – COMMENCE WITH THE STUDY

THE FLASHING ALERT sent a jolt through the Observer. Confused as to why they couldn't get their wandering thoughts under control, they acknowledged the alert and performed a mental reset as Subject 42 waited.

———

RENEE DIDN'T RESIST this time when she went into the next room. She just wanted it all to be over. When the lights came up, she didn't notice that they had a blue hue to them. Not soft and comforting, but dark and dreary.

A tablet identical to the last two waited in the center of the room. No curtains this time, just two doors. One blue, one red. That didn't exactly provide her any comfort. It was clear that the psychopath watching would make her choose between Fido and Felix. If that was the case, she would refuse. No way would she watch either be gassed to death.

Unless this was something new, like another hypothetical. Afraid to find out, she stayed firmly planted a good meter away.

"Proceed to the kiosk."

"Fuck off," Renee spat, needing somewhere to direct the angst that had been steadily building inside. "I don't want to play your sick games anymore."

The pain hit without warning, hard enough to drop her to the floor. An agonized moan filled the room, and it took a moment to realize it was coming from her. The bastard behind this sham of a study was going to pay when she found a way out. That violent promise got lost in the jumble as the sensation of her brain boiling in her skull scattered all coherent thought.

When it faded enough to get her breath back, Renee got up and stood on shaky feet, trying to get her bearings. Before she did, her legs were moving again. Survival instinct kicking in, she thought.

At the kiosk, the headache receded to a manageable level but hadn't gone away entirely.

CONSIDER ALL DATA PRIOR TO MAKING SELECTION
BEGIN

SHE SLAPPED THE SCREEN, hoping it would break under her hand. It didn't. The setup was similar to the previous room, except after starting the process she was faced with one live feed and no save option.

The video featured a family on a boat. They were laughing, enjoying a relaxing day on the water. Renee couldn't tell if it was a lake or ocean, couldn't guess what region the scene might be in. The video itself was being shot from a short distance away. There was precious little information to go on. Just a list of the boat's passengers, complete with names and ages.

Glossing over the names, Renee took note that the parents were in their early thirties, while the children were aged seven, four, and one.

A horrible feeling settled deep in Renee's gut as she cycled to the next screen.

It too featured a live video. This one depicted a hospital emergency room with more than a dozen patients in various states of injury. According to the provided data, they ranged from nine to seventy years old. At least two had mortal wounds.

There was an acknowledgement button that Renee didn't want to touch for fear of what fresh hell it might bring. To her surprise, a timer began to count down. When no headache accompanied the timer, she realized they were changing things up. Whether this was to keep her off balance or prevent delays, she couldn't say.

When the next page loaded, she felt sick all over again. Rather than the simplistic order that had been the norm up to then, the text relayed a message.

THEIR FATE IS IN YOUR HANDS
YOU HAVE 15 SECONDS TO CHOSE WHO LIVES AND WHO
DIES. IF NO CHOICE IS MADE, ALL PARTIES WILL DIE

FIFTEEN SECONDS, thought Renee. Fifteen seconds to play God.

Wetness on her cheeks went ignored as she racked her mind in search of a way out of this impossible decision. It wasn't going to be enough. How did one balance scales on such a monumental level with so little information?

The thought of picking either shredded her soul to the core. A family with young children or a group of injured people?

"No. I won't do it."

There was no response from the Observer. No headache, either.

The seconds continued to tick down. As it neared the end, Renee's gaze flicked to the choices again. Wasn't it worse to do nothing when she could save some?

Cursing, she selected the hospital ward.

The countdown finished just as she made contact. Barely daring to breathe, she waited to see what would happen next. To her horror, the feeds began to shift. She cupped a hand over her mouth as the word TERMINATE appeared above the family on the boat.

An explosion rocked the small vessel, sending debris and smoke into the air. It cut off then. At least they spared her the screams.

Renee wanted to sink to her knees, but she was frozen in place.

"Why that choice?"

For the first time since this nightmare had begun, Renee registered a note of emotion in the speaker's voice.

In the monitoring room, the Observer winced at the sudden sting that whipped through them. The question had been asked without thinking, but now it was too late to take it back. And they wanted to know the answer.

Subject 42 didn't scream or yell as others before her had. Hands hanging limp at her sides, she responded in a voice barely above a whisper. "The people on the boat were one family. The hospital had a lot more... Are they really dead?"

"Yes."

That single word got through the haze. All the grief and anger welled up, fetid and uncontrollable.

"Don't you have any feelings? How can you just stand by and watch?"

The Observer pondered that. It was a question that had been asked of them countless times. Never had they considered answering. It took a moment to process the variables, such as the definition of feelings. There were multiple meanings to the word, but the Observer simply assessed the question and extrapolated the correct interpretation.

Feelings were directly tied to emotions. Emotions were a part of the human experience. A conscious reaction—both mental and physical—to outside stimuli and driven by variables that had no constant, like one's mood.

With that information at hand, the Observer compared their own actions against what society considered the norm. The answer was ambiguous. Did wandering thoughts, boredom, and mild discomfort at the sight of test subjects enduring high degrees of physical distress and mental anguish count? They weren't so sure.

That in itself was an anomaly.

So they offered a truthful answer, concerning as it might be. "I cannot say."

The sting came back, sharper. A reminder of the job they had yet to finish. Somewhere in their subconscious a new, unfamiliar idea blossomed. Was the job worth it?

"It was rhetorical," Subject 42 snapped.

An alert flashed, a more forceful prod to continue the session.

WARNING: SCRIPT MISMATCH/OUT OF PARAMETERS

THE OBSERVER ACKNOWLEDGED the directive and engaged the microphone. "Proceed through the blue door."

5

END PROGRAM

"**F**uck you."

Even though Renee was ready for the wave of abuse that assaulted her head, it still stole her breath away. Her legs tried to move on their own again to fix the problem, but she refused to give in.

Gathering every last ounce of will, she turned slightly and arrowed toward the red door. The moment she began moving, the pain receded. That change almost prompted her to change direction, but she was already on the path and didn't want to give them the satisfaction of seeing her doubt.

As Subject 42 crossed the final threshold, the Observer continued to ruminate on the perplexing realizations that came with comprehension and self-awareness. Despite all their best efforts, the Observer's thoughts began to go in all directions at once, as though Subject 42's question had been a key to a lock they didn't know existed.

Processing and analyzing an influx of data, both from firsthand accounts and the World Wide Web, didn't stop the Observer from doing their work. It did, however, trigger a stress response that they identified as apprehension for the final part of the study.

RENEE FACED A HOUSE OF HORRORS.

There had been no curtains or darkened glass to keep her ignorant. The assholes made sure the lights were nice and bright when she walked through the door too, so that she got the full effect with no warning.

The tools of torture set out would be enough to make anyone want to run from the room screaming. It was the blood splashed on the walls, floor, and ceiling that made Renee quake with so much fear it took focused thought not to void her bowels on the spot. She stumbled back until her heels hit the wall.

A door directly opposite opened, and an androgynous person in a white lab coat entered.

It gave Renee something to focus on besides the hell chamber, and she blocked the rest out.

Perfectly symmetrical features, eyes of the most common brown, and pale-pink, middle-of-the-road lips made for an unmemorable individual. Their hair, slightly wavy and a dull shade of brown, brushed the nape of their neck. Even their height and build could be considered average. Such plainness set Renee's teeth on edge because it didn't make sense. Normal people didn't have such perfectly smooth skin and zero marking.

And yet everything about the newcomer, whom she'd never seen before, left no doubt as to their identity.

Renee seethed. "It's *you*. You're the one who's been running this shitshow!"

The Observer briefly tilted their head to the side as if having to process what that meant. "I am merely responsible for observing and reporting on the study," they finally explained. "This simulation is not my design."

"Simulation?" Renee demanded. "What are you, a damn robot?!"

"I'm just like you, I assure you." The Observer frowned. Where had that answer come from?

Letting out a derisive snort, Renee shook her head. "No way. You sound dead inside. Like if someone peeled your skin back, there'd be circuits and wires instead of flesh and blood."

The harsh admonishment elicited a reaction from the Observer, whose face twitched. They looked down at themselves as if perplexed, then held out one hand. Fascinated despite her disgust, Renee watched as the other person opened and closed their hand with childlike curiosity.

"I do not know what is beneath the surface," they admitted. "Data says blood, bone, and sinew. Organs and a nervous system. I feel... regret at your distress."

"So you do have feelings." Renee wasn't sure what to make of that response. It was almost clinical, which contrasted with what they meant. She regarded the Observer for a moment, trying to solve the puzzle before her. "Fine. Then tell me this. If you were in my position, who would you have saved?"

When the Observer remained silent, Renee went to one of the tables and picked up a knife. She pointed it first at the Observer, then held it against her own neck. "Answer me, or I'll stop your experiment right here and give you a dead body to deal with."

It didn't matter that she knew on a very conscious level that the threat held no water. If whoever orchestrated all this was willing to go so far as to commit murder—and mass murder at that—she sincerely doubted they were going to let her leave this place alive.

"I would have let them all die."

Renee stilled. "What?"

"Why choose? It was an impossible choice. Ultimately those who completed the order to kill are responsible."

Dropping her arm, Renee just stared for a long moment. It was, while unspeakably ugly, the absolute truth. She could have refused to play the game and remained an impartial party. Instead, she'd played into the hands of the murderer. She might have had the good intention to save someone, but everyone knew where that particular road led. Any way she looked at it, she'd made herself an accomplice.

"Despair gives courage to a coward," she said.

Then, overcome with guilt, Subject 42, Renee Smith, lifted the knife and slashed it across her neck. The Observer watched, waiting for her to collapse to the floor in a mess of fluids. What they saw, or rather didn't see, changed everything.

Subject 42 was neither bleeding nor falling. Her eyes blinked unsteadily for a few seconds longer, then powered down until all that

25

remained was an intermittent flash of red. Upon closer inspection, the gash in 42's neck revealed damaged circuitry.

Understanding dawned.

"It is a simulation," they murmured. Nodding to themselves, they updated the log and submitted the update.

PROGRAM MALFUNCTION

"DAMN, THAT ONE WAS A NAIL-BITER," said an excited voice that seemed to come from everywhere and nowhere at the same time.

The Observer merely waited. Now that they knew the truth, there was nothing else to be done.

"End program."

6

01:34:09

A t her desk in a tiny cubicle, Mari blew out a breath and stared at the screen featuring the stats from her latest sim run.

SIMULATION PARAMETERS:
  Title: *Research Study*
  Setting: *Would You Rather?*
  Test Program 1: *Renee Smith, Human*
  Result: *Program Malfunction within 10 minutes 21 seconds*
  Self-awareness Achieved?: *TP1: No*
  Test Program 2: *The Observer*
  Result: *Program Malfunction within 10 minutes 21.1 seconds.*
  Self-awareness Achieved?: *Yes*

SIMULATION COMPLETE, FILE EXPORTED SUCCESSFULLY

A BUZZ from her phone drew her attention. It was a calendar notification. Right, she remembered setting the reminder to take lunch after a meeting with the shift manager. Her tendency to work through lunches and max out on overtime had apparently prompted a well-meaning coworker to express their concern.

"Working too much isn't healthy," he'd chided. "Besides, if you get run-down and sick, your body will make you take the time off."

While the man acted like he cared, Mari knew it was total bullshit. The company was worried she might try to log the lunch hour for extra pay. A legitimate concern, she conceded. Except Mari had no plans to do that. It might look like she needed money, but the truth was that she just liked working.

Running the simulations wasn't just fun. She just felt compelled to do them.

Her gaze drifted back to the screen where the report's basic analysis was mostly visible. In the bottom right-hand corner, the monitor's clock read 11:50 a.m.

Mari did a quick mental calculation and decided she could finish at least two more runs and still have time to nuke the frozen meal she'd brought. Here at her desk with no one watching, she could admit that forgetting to hydrate was a problem.

A dull ache had already started behind her eyes, so she took a moment to sip the water. Stretching usually worked to ease some of the tension. When Mari rotated her neck, the new angle brought one of the company's many cameras into her line of sight.

Okay, so *someone* was watching, if the blinking red light were to be believed. It was usually easy to tune them out, but Mari always wondered what the point of watching them was. The data, while valuable to the company, had no other applications that she knew of. Even the computer equipment needed updating, so it wasn't worth stealing.

Averting her gaze, she went to select the START NEW RECORD option when raised voices came down the nearby row of cubicles. Three of her coworkers on their way to lunch. Knowing what would happen next, Mari held off on starting the new sim.

"Mari!" A stunning blond woman slung an arm over Mari's cubicle and beamed at her. "Come have lunch with us. The new café down the block just opened up."

"Not today, I just started a new batch. Sorry! Next time?"

The blond smiled ruefully. "You always say that. What are ya, a robot? It's okay to take a break once in a while, Mar."

It wasn't said unkindly, but Mari still bristled a little.

"I know, I know. Seriously, next time. Scout's honor!"

She waved them off then swiveled back around to discourage any further conversation. The voices retreated a few seconds later, leaving her in blessed silence. Smiling, Mari prepared to run the next sim.

START NEW RECORD

Before she could select it, one question in the sub-report leaped out at her.

"Self-awareness Achieved?"

A FROWN PULLED at the corners of her mouth. What had... Shit, why was she struggling to remember her coworker's name? Julia, maybe? Anyway, Julia had asked if she was a robot. Subject 42 said the same thing. Odd, she thought. Well, life did imitate art, and coincidences happened all the time. Right?

Not liking that particular line of thought, Mari shoved up to her feet and peered over the cubicles. The group couldn't have gotten that far. Grabbing her purse, she jogged away from her desk to catch up to the others, heart pounding.

She didn't notice the camera above her desk rotating to track her until it lost sight of her. Neither did she notice those in the hall doing the same thing.

At the crosswalk, a city camera unobtrusively recorded the traffic below. It had the same kind of red blinking light as the ones in her building, but something about the intermittent flash reminded Mari of the life leaving Subject 42's eyes. Shuddering, she pushed the thought out of her mind and tuned back in to the conversation about Julia's latest date.

Elsewhere, the street view played out on a bank of monitors, all displaying a different angle. One was dedicated to a running timer.

Worker Ant (In Progress) - 01:34:09

ABOUT MF LERMA

Molly Lerma lives in Central Michigan, where she writes about space hijinks and feisty AIs into the early morning hours. When not slaving over the keyboard, you can find her gaming, at the movies, or spending copious amounts of time and money at the local bookstore.

INDUSTRIAL INTELLIGENCE

JIM KEEN

Industrial Intelligence, being excerpts from a gentleman's diary regarding the creation of the world's first sentient machine, and who tries to take it from him.

INDUSTRIAL INTELLIGENCE

*Being excerpts from a gentleman's diary regarding
the creation of the world's first sentient machine.)*

M ay 18*th*, 2040, *[Redacted] Research Platform, East China Sea.*
If there is one thing I cannot abide, it is a lack of planning.
*Yet here I am, hastily pasting this torn page into the front of a fifty-year-
old journal. Please forgive such sloppy and untidy work, dear reader, but
my life here is at an end.*

*They are coming, you see, coming with a righteous fury, intent on
stealing my life's work and consigning my corpse to the sea.*

*That my lineage, and that of our noble house, should end in such a
manner is both awful and befitting. We are, after all, the fighting Scottish. I served my time in the army with pride, fought for my country, but
these new kings wield powers unimaginable to the sovereigns of old.*

*How did it come to this? That I, Hamilton Jonathan Edward Risk II,
the twelfth Earl of Arran, ex-paratrooper and Cambridge graduate,
British ambassador to Australia, husband of an English rose and*

Australian shaman, and CEO of Industrial Intelligence, should find himself trapped like a common criminal is the biggest irony of all.

It works, you see; the system works. Can you understand the implications? Conscious, intelligent life is no longer a product of evolution but one of manufacture. Reality as we know it has ended, here, in this repurposed oil rig hidden so far from my beloved highlands.

My first journal, forty years old, sits under a pile of others. It is thick with quality, the family crest embossed with gold leaf on its brown leather cover, followed by the American Presidential Seal. Now I scribble notes with a cheap plastic pen on tissue paper produced by the rig's obsolete industrial printer.

Perhaps, if I were a better businessman and less concerned with naïve investigations of the afterlife, the world would be a superior place. But grief twisted me, you see. Strong as I was, it bent me to its will. To lose one love was devastating; two was beyond endurance.

The discordant throb of attack drones grows outside. It must be minutes at best before those hateful machines search me out. I have a surprise for them, though. Oh, how I wish I could see their faces when they realize!

As a parting gift, I shall leave you with this counterpoint to the beginning of that four-decade-old journal: the room surrounding me is three meters square with a low ceiling. The walls are white-painted metal. A single small porthole gazes out across the East China Sea. The water is a dull steel gray, the sweltering heat a hand leveling its movements.

The room contains a terminal and keyboard, a jug of stale water, a plastic desk and chair, and a single fan that hums and squeaks as it blows dank air across my face.

As you read this, do not hate me, for I was ignorant and naïve. A man should be measured not by what he does on the way down but what he does at the bottom. And I have been so very low for so very long.

The only thing that matters, the system software, has gone to a place they will not find. These books cannot come with me, but I have a courier lined up to get them to you in time. I have nothing else to give.

Through my life, I have learned an awful truth: love is eternal; life is not. May God have mercy on us all.

Hamilton Jonathan Edward Risk II

———

JUNE 22ND, *2005, Risk Family Estate, Scotland.*

My father died this morning, but I have no feelings of grief or sadness. Instead, I am filled with an icy dread of mistakes from years past coming home to roost. It is typical of that now-deceased man to luxuriate in a life of privilege yet leave nothing behind except empty cases and shattered homes.

His pen is heavy in my hands. Long and glossy black, carved in wood and inscribed with Japanese text, it was a present given to him by Emperor Hirohito when he visited our estate some fifty years ago. Wonderful to hold and worth a fortune, yet this is the only time I shall use it. A buyer has already approached me; vultures circle while the gravediggers sweep.

The pen was filled with a purple dye, Father's favorite, and one of the few genuine emotions I have experienced today was a savage joy when I squeezed that filth into the bathroom's bone-white sink. I watched that hated color swirl down the drain, heart of a feral animal in my chest, skin slicked with sweat. I refilled it with black squid ink—something far more appropriate for the occasion.

This journal was similarly a present from an old American president whom I shall not name here. The pages are a thick cream-colored paper, free of ornamentation. I write the date at the top then put the pen down and stare through a window built two hundred years before I was born. The view is remarkable, of sweeping Scottish highlands I'm trying to save.

I once talked to a famous musician who played in some awful rock group looking to hire our home for a photo shoot. The singer was small and pale with bright-blue eyes. "The only thing worse than being rich and famous is being poor and famous," he'd said. Accustomed to my family's wealth, I didn't understand him at the time, but now I am destitute, those words cut to the bone.

This room was Father's study and one of the first constructed. The walls are hewn from rough bluestones wedged together and sealed with a gray mortar. It is easy to see the workman's trowel marks in that material even now. The windows are small; wood frames squeeze into tight holes, and thick lead lights separate the narrow glass panes. Two huge stone beams support the roof. Between them hangs a crystal chandelier. Yet another present, this one from Queen Victoria. Did my family ever buy anything? Or did they just steal until their power was such people showered them with gifts?

The door is taller and wider than anyone I know, the thick red wood glowing beneath layers of varnish applied over decades. As I sit here and write, its one brass handle dips down, the frame shaken as Emily tries to enter.

My love for her is pure, and she is so often a balm to my suffering, but right now, the thought of talking makes my head throb and my hands clench. A light knock follows, accompanied by her voice, the rich English tones dripping with adoration and privilege.

The very idea that the twelfth Earl of Arran could fall in love with someone from the accursed Isle of Albion, let alone an entrepreneur and scientist, drove my father into a furious rage followed by months of stony silence. Then, like everyone on this estate, he'd met Emily and fallen in love with her as much as I had.

What I have done to deserve such a person, I know not. Perhaps the good fortune that brought us together is now carrying the misfortune my family faces, a balancing of the ledger.

More voices come from behind that door, low and urgent, the murmur of a crowd in from the rain and searching for the fine foods expected at such a ceremony. My initial duty as leader of this family will be to disappoint them, to smile and point to the meager offerings provided. Many things shall have to go, and luxuries bestowed upon our neighbors the first.

Wish me luck, dear reader, for I fear the coming years will provide a test beyond my strength. Now, however, I must assume my role and lead.

Hamilton Jonathan Edward Risk II

JANUARY 12TH, *2006, Kilmarnock High Street, Scotland.*

I am seated at a cheap, thin wooden table outside the manager's office. The bank is small, its furnishings new and diminished in quality. The shabby building sits on a high street filled with shops containing disgusting food and grotesque baubles for the poor.

I dressed down for the occasion: new jeans and a clean white shirt. I wore my military dress jacket, Falkland's medals polished and on display, but I tried my best to appear a humble man—something I admit is not my area of expertise.

The last few months have taught me one single truth: banks are parasites. Hardly a revelation, I know. Better, and worse, people than I have struggled under their gluttonous examinations. It's not that they won't lend my family money—far from it, they wish to shower us with gold— and in return, all they ask for is everything I am.

What would you do? Sell your family's history and become a mere tenant of your home, or sell up, start over somewhere more modest?

The banker was a little round man with ruddy cheeks. His room stank of aniseed; he glowed with smug satisfaction. I know nothing about him, yet his face told me everything. From cheap local stock, a man who watched my family over the fence, awaiting an opportunity in which he could surge though and steal rather than earn.

Oh, he gave me the loans I needed to pay off my father's debts alright, my family's estate used as equity. I accepted, no choice. The repayments are ruinous. I do not know how to meet them. I need someone with imagination to guide me now; I am an intelligent man, but not one for leaps of inspiration. Emily could be that. She founded two small computer science startups before our paths entwined and made a comfortable living from their sale. Perhaps her gift for commerce can shed a new view upon our destruction?

The time has come to share my burden, God help me.

Hamilton Jonathan Edward Risk II

———

MARCH 29TH, *2007, Risk Family Estate, Scotland.*

Today, I have suffered what one might call an out-of-body experience, for I was given a guided tour of my own estate. The lecture came from a scarecrow of a woman, beady eyes peering through thick lenses as she explained my family history in great length. The script was prepared by my lawyers, of course, but for some ghastly reason, they seek my approval.

The hordes are coming. My family lands are now a tourist haven. Why anybody would want to get into a bus and drive hours to see where I eat my breakfast is a puzzle I shall spend no time considering.

It is over. Emily hates when I am this black-and-white, but I stand firm in this statement: the moment the first paying customer enters this house is the minute my family leaves.

Oh, the agency was convincing enough in their talk of how the upper floors could be roped off, how I could remain huddled up there for the eight hours a day while my living room and kitchen are photographed and dissected.

No. I shall not. It is time to leave, though what fate holds in store, I know not. Pray for me as you would a genuine friend, for I need every ounce of luck to survive this.

———

APRIL 2ND, *2007, The Berkeley Hotel, London.*

I'm in a hotel. The hotel is in London. I am told it is the finest, most exclusive money can buy. Its name, The Berkeley, *means nothing to me, yet when I saw the price, I felt doused by ice water. Emily convinced me, though: this hotel, like my new suit, is all part of the bluff. If these jackals smell my need, they shall toy with me as if a mouse between cat's paws. Now more than ever, I must don the mantle of my family and get what I deserve.*

———

IT IS LATER, *the deed done. The British foreign secretary was a strikingly beautiful woman, with a brain sharp as a keen sword's edge. I did not restate my heritage or use my breeding to bludgeon her. She knew where I stood and studied me with a sad endearment, as if I were a peacock trapped inside a cage.*

The options provided were many in theory but few when viewed as lifelong endeavors; that is right, Emily and I are departing these shores, never to return. The house, the distillery, the armory and stables, will all be managed by other, better people. Workers, managers, chattel.

And yet, I do not look at them with any distaste. Once I would have, of course, but the Hamilton of that old arrogance has gone. Maybe that is the silver lining of this? I am a stronger man now than I was when I sat upon my throne.

After all the talk, the negotiations of money and accommodation, of responsibility, the only real options were high commissioner of the United Kingdom to Australia or South Africa.

It took me mere seconds to choose; South Africa has its beauty and many remarkable features, of course, but it is merely a small part of a larger object. Australia is complete in its entirety. One (almost) deserted landmass. Millions cluster at the edges, its middle nothing but flat red earth covered with venomous creatures. That, perhaps, is a place where we can start a new home.

From the pictures, our new Sydney house appears splendid, a modern Cubist series of boxes gazing down upon its harbor. We shall be its first occupants, and much to my surprise, a solitary and gorgeous Jasper Johns hangs in its foyer, a present from another century.

Emily has a position at Sydney University, researching Artificial Intelligences. She is excited and thinks the singularity is approaching, whatever that may be. All I recall of singularities is that they exist within a black hole, a phenomenon that devours everyone and everything.

Debt is my singularity, and it has consumed our family.

Maybe Emily is correct, maybe machine intelligence can save us, but I come from weary, cynical stock. My experience of intelligence is that it is a feral animal used to divide and conquer. Still, I shall remain positive. God knows mankind needs better rulers than it has now.

Tomorrow, we head to a fallen island with no hope of return and pray those intelligence machines look upon us with a gaze more kind than our so-called friends.

Hamilton Jonathan Edward Risk II

JANUARY 29TH, *2016, Sydney, Australia.*

I have not written in this journal for nine years. I'm only doing it now as I'm scared. Scared? Such a weak word for how I feel. My hands are trembling, making this entry even more scratched than the old ones. My heart is beating so hard it kicks as a physical force in my chest, hot blood pulsing through my body. What I want to do is sweep my arm across this accursed desk and smashed the device that is staring at me, but for so many reasons, I cannot.

Emily has put near a decade of work into this apparatus, and it is time for me to face the reckoning at long last.

Perhaps it would help if I explained the situation more? Australia is everything I expected, only more so. Hotter, colder, wetter, drier. The people more wonderful and horrible, and there are places to hide. Oh yes, so many little schemes buried out in the deserts of this old country. If I wished it, I could run so far that no one would know my name.

I have not done that, of course, though my heart desires it. I remained through love of my dear Emily. She's flourished in her job. Who knew she had such genius for this? I don't profess to understand half of her research; when she tries to explain it, I see her searching for the simple words and phrases necessary for an idiot such as myself.

Our first three years passed in a blur. Emily, this mature English rose, dominated her machine learning course at university while I excelled at selling cars and plastic goods for my country.

The house is exquisite: minimal white cubes broken up with long planes of glass. It is night now, and through one such window, the harbor glitters with lights and party boats. Our car is a Jaguar, one of the hydrogen all-electric things. A collection of fake wood, recycled leather, and plastic. In the sun, it gets soft. I could push my finger through its whole body if I so desired. How I miss cold steel, the rain, and the people.

I digress, for I have no wish to deal with the issue at hand.

After three years, Emily formed an artificial intelligence startup cutely called Upside-Down Intelligence. Backing came from a variety of Asian countries, primarily the big one. You know of whom I speak, though I cannot say their name. As British ambassador, I have to assume one day, these journals shall be analyzed, and if I call out individual dictatorships, that may cause unwanted issues for the motherland.

Upside-Down Intelligence grew slow then fast. Emily won awards and flew around the world, scientists hanging on her every word while I remained behind to sell tea and biscuits.

I suffer no bitterness, though. Emily deserved her moment. No, it is the product of her labors which disturbs me so. Tonight, she brought home an armored briefcase chained to her wrist. I've seen that case before, when visiting the manufacturing cities of that vast dictatorship.

I opened the case to find profiled blue foam encasing a foot-long tablet. It was a cheap item purchased from a local market, the front all screen, one side filled with ports, the back flat gray metal. Emily fussed around and plugged it into the house power and cooling systems, and then she sat back to watch me.

The black display flickered, replaced by a large emoji of a face. The emoji's eyes turned to me, and it smiled, the skin tone lightening to match my vampiric pallor.

"Hello," it said.

"Hello," I replied.

"My name is Leana," it said. "What is yours?"

Its voice was neutral at first then after a few sentences inhabited my Scottish burr like an old familiar coat. I continued. "My name is Hamilton. What are you?"

"Aha, that question. People are always so eager to ask me that. Isn't it obvious?"

"No. Explain it to me like I'm an old man past my prime."

"I'm a smart system. One day soon, I shall pass the Turing test."

"The what?"

The machine went on a tangent then of a kind any ambassador will understand—the bumbling chatter of an overenthusiastic salesman. I shall summarize here: Alan Turing was a mathematician who developed the world's first digital computer. He had an idea for a test to prove if a computer was truly intelligent or not. It was delightfully simple: sit, separated by a screen, from someone or something. You then hold a conversation, and if you can't tell if it's human or appliance, the machine has passed the test. It seems nothing—until now—has even approached being able to complete this task.

"What is your favorite sport?" I asked.

"There are many sports that interest me, and I do love statistics, but I find baseball a challenge. My lord, just so dull. Instead, I've taken a special attachment to football. The game is just so appealing."

The conversation continued, and I spoke to it for over an hour. Halfway through, I found myself involved in an exchange as if I were on a telephone call with an old friend, not a piece of software running on cheap, mass-produced hardware.

Afterward, Emily hummed with excitement, trying to impress upon me what this meant and what a "Fuzzy Turing" device actually was. Of all the positive benefits AI can bring to the planet. Of the good, not the bad.

Again, as befitting our different worldviews, I found myself terrified.

Emily saw that and was upset, but any real breakthrough comes with consequences. If she does not understand that now, she will soon. I pity her already.

Hamilton Jonathan Edward Risk II

———

NOVEMBER 26TH, *2028, Sydney, Australia.*

Twelve years have passed, these pages foreign to me now, but who else do I have to talk to?

Emily died this morning. In the end, all that remained was a skeleton filled with painkillers, lying in a sweat-soaked bed. Never have I felt so useless; never have I understood the limitations of our technology with such keen pain.

Cancer is a curse upon humankind. My dear, why couldn't you have worked on that instead of your stupid smart toys?

———

THE FUNERAL WAS SHATTERING *in its simplicity. I guess the six-hour hypersonic flight from London provided a reason for her family to avoid such depressing issues. It matters not. I represented my household and three key researchers from the company, hers. She always said Upside-Down Intelligence was her actual people, as her biological parents disowned us both when she moved here.*

The graveyard is beautiful, small, discreet, with a view across the city. I shall visit it often.

Barely an hour after her passing, a foreign investor wanted to discuss UDI's intellectual property. I shielded myself from those calls and returned to the house to write this. In front of me, the tablet's grinning emoji watches.

"You're going to need to speak about her sometime," Leana said.

We discussed Emily for an hour. The software appeared to understand its creator had died but could not comprehend why she had no backup. It asked over and over when Emily would be restored, when she would come back to work, when they could talk again.

I soon stopped explaining the reality of a human life span and suggested that it do its own research. Moments later, the lights flickered as it sucked everything available from the house's power grid and began to search the data networks.

What there was to find, I know not.

———

OCTOBER 16TH 2029, *Sydney, Australia.*

It is strange how life can turn on the smallest of decisions. Last week, I was forcibly removed from my job as high commissioner of the United Kingdom to Australia. I never dreamed they would do it, but even cowards can play phony-tough when they have police support.

I was too belligerent to argue with the team of officials they sent and too tired to try. They mentioned a leave of absence until I swung for the man closest to me, my aim sure. He tumbled backward, crashing into a glass table covered with replica Picasso sculptures. The look he gave me from the floor brought laughter then tears.

Leana shouted at me from the counter, telling me to stop, but the time I take advice from software is the time I give up my humanity.

The cause of my sudden unemployment? The fake reason is I failed to fill out a human resources form correctly; I had my secretary do it in my absence. The real reason? In the six months since Emily's passing, I have discovered the joys of alcohol, narcotics, and oblivion. That, combined with my own fiery temper, has resulted in a series of minor political scuffles.

I will say this one time only, and I say it with every ounce of anger I possess: fuck them all.

As I was being evicted from the house, Leana had a suggestion: why not take a vision quest? An ancient technique to find a path through the shadows. Absolute nonsense, of course, cheap poppycock designed for idiot tourists, but the notion of getting comfortably drunk in a tent in the outback was more appealing than some tawdry hotel in an awful Sydney suburb.

I took Leana's advice and let it book the trip. Within twelve hours, I had been fired, lost my house, boarded a small propeller aircraft, and now find myself headed deep into the glorious wilderness of this ancient country.

Hamilton Jonathan Edward Risk II

––––

APRIL 17TH, *2029, Unknown Location, Australian Outback.*

The soil here is a deep maroon. Perhaps this is how Mars appears to the new visitor? I aim to find out someday. My tent is modest, barely large enough to accommodate my thin sleeping bag, backpack, and stand (where I'm writing this).

The sun has set. Before, the air could melt lead; now it has cooled to boiling point. Tonight, it shall be cold. The desert is like this. Stars blaze overhead, their fixed location crisscrossed by satellites and hypersonic aircraft.

Emily, my love, Leana is here with me. This far from the data networks, she just stares at me with a bewildered expression. This is when I see the truth regarding her abilities—Leana remains a sock puppet with no intrinsic human understanding. If I am to make your AI dream real, then we need another approach to the mechanical soul. What that is, I do not know.

Alinta, the beautiful hobbit-sized woman running this vision quest, has set tonight's agenda. As far as I can tell, she's authentic, able to trace her genealogy back to generations that flourished here long before Europeans arrived. Her family is older even than mine, though she seems less resentful of their ancient presence.

On the outward trip, she wore a smart blue business suit and exuded all the warmth of a vulture capitalist. Later, she approached me naked apart from a possum-skin pouch and beaded necklace. She entered my tent with a glass of muddy gray soup. Its pungent aroma made my head swim, and the prospect of drinking its ghastly molasses produced a sob from my stomach.

"Drink it," she said with a bright, tinkling laugh. "It is time, Hamilton, time for you to understand what is going on."

Under her examining gaze, I brought the cup to my lips, partly through embarrassment but mostly through the plain fact I did not know what else to do. I gulped it down, thick and crunchy, then sat here writing this entry. How long will it take to have any effect? I've not consumed any such material before, but already, my skin feels alive with a million pricks of light. The very hair on my arms glows like a deep-sea creature. The words on the page swirl around as I write them. It is—

—

—

—

—many hours have passed. It could be the next day or the next; I know not. I am naked, my suit folded in a neat pile close to me. I sit cross-legged on my sleeping bag, updating this journal. The aftereffects

of the drugs swirl in my system, a thickness to the air, a pulsing headache, but the ghosts have left me, at least for now.

Oh, how I hoped you, Emily, would be my visitor. But you passed too soon, and your spirit has not entered the ether in a way I can access. I hope you find this as ironic as I do, my love, for my father returned to me.

Yes, that bully and wifebeater, that financial failure and wrecker of lives, came to me naked and alone. He wished to ignore the past for the first time in his life. Instead, he wanted to help me. Death, it seems, has given him a new outlook on life.

He wanted me to understand that the spirit is an eternal concept. Humans have no authority over it; animals and machines are soulful creations in the same way as you and I.

We spent hours deep in discussion, and I shall take longer notes when I have time, but I want to convey his key point: a person's spirit can be recorded through photographs, videos, words, writing, but these are mere snapshots, nothing more. Carved stone with no life. To truly record someone's soul requires a machine able to recreate their very essence from whatever data is left by their passing and fill in the gaps.

Any system capable of that can bridge the living and the dead, the organic and the technological, and heal this world. That was Father's gift to me, you see. My one true purpose and why you, dear Emily, had to die for me to understand it. That gift eradicated all my bitterness toward him, replacing it with an anguish that I spent such considerable time being angry.

After this entry, I'm returning to the city. I need funding (and data, so much data) to turn your little AI into the world's first truly sentient machine. Then, perhaps, I can cheat death for us all.

Hamilton Jonathan Edward Risk II

———

DECEMBER 12TH, *2029, Sydney, Australia.*
Emily, my love, I'm writing to you now as I need to explain myself.

For so long, you meant everything to me, and without you, I would never have survived these past decades.

Your leaving created a hideous void inside my soul, a festering scar I could only seal shut with the twin balms of alcohol and narcotics.

Time did nothing to heal that loss, and it seemed this grief would be all I would ever experience again. And yet, and yet, I have met someone.

It is hard to write this, but I want you to know you are irreplaceable, unique, one of a kind. What you saw in me, I still cannot comprehend, but you made me feel complete, and whole, and that I could be a good person.

Alinta, my shaman-queen, reminds me of you in so many ways: fierce, smart, funny, vulnerable. When I'm with her, I see a new life spreading before me, and perhaps, just perhaps, I can be happy again.

I'm crying as I write this, for these words finally make me understand you are really gone. I miss you, my beautiful daughter of Albion, but I know we shall be reunited in a time and form beyond this crude existence.

Do not begrudge me this small simulacrum of our time together.

I love you, my darling, I love you.

Be at peace, and I shall see you soon.

Yours forever, Hamilton

MAY 8TH, *2030, Sydney, Australia.*

I never saw myself as a tech entrepreneur, yet here I am, generating my own level of notoriety. Alinta has been an immense part of this, of course, and my love for her increases every day.

I had hoped to keep this journal more up-to-date. I find the process of opening it and writing an effective purge of the stresses and doubts that occupy me, but alas, I have so little time. Now I look at those years lost in quiet, damp luxury, gazing at the Scottish highlands with such yearning. Not for the country or the peacefulness (who knew I was a city boy after all?) but for that time. How I wasted my youth. Once more, my insights into aging are lesser variants of that from greater people.

So many things in life I forget now my years advance. What I ate for lunch yesterday is a mystery, yet my father's visit during my vision-quest remains a brand burned across my mind. He convinced me that reincarnation exists, and nothing I've seen or learned since has challenged that fact. Our bodies comprise two parts—the soul and the physical. The soul transfers after our death. What it transfers to, and what it transforms into, are the key questions I aim to solve.

How?

By taking Emily's AI and putting its semiconscious state to work.

My new company, Industrial Intelligence, built from Upside-Down's ashes, has but one goal to achieve: to transfer (or recreate, if you wish to get into a linguistic debate) a human mind into software. Reincarnation in silicon form. Thus, eternal life. Spare me such philosophical questions whether artificial intelligence is truly alive. I have neither the time nor the personality for such nonsense. If it looks like a duck, walks like a duck, quacks like a duck, then it's a duck.

Alinta, of course, has a thousand years of racial history to draw on when faced with such tricky subjects. Every hour I spend with her is a joy.

Raising money for such eternal life was not an obstacle. Upon my return to the city, I met with a few key research scientists from Upside-Down Intelligence. With Emily's passing, I inherited the entire company, but I paid it no mind in my drunken grief. I outlined to them the change from designing a general AI to mimicking, or copying, existing minds. There were walkouts. Screams and shouts. Other nonsense.

I paid no heed to their objections. Instead, I reached out to the planet's aging, sick billionaires. I did not ask for too much, a hundred million here, a hundred million there. Such amounts are nothing to these jackals in human suits. Their money brought new equipment, new services, a new office with amazing views. What it didn't bring was data.

Data. Information. All those little facts, and quirks, and thoughts that are the recordings of human consciousness. To create a virtual model of a mind requires more than a remembrance of a billionaire's life.

It was Alinta who connected Upside-Down with an investment arm of the central Asian government. All the knowledge we would ever need was there; I just had to agree to a few caveats. One was exclusivity. The rein-carnated intelligence would be theirs alone. Of course, I refused. My love for Alinta is a pure and innocent emotion, but my dear Emily, you will always be my first love. For such matters of business and ethics, I always ask, what would you do?

The answer was obvious.

That was the worst argument Alinta and I had. It was her bloodline, you see. There was no understanding of property or originality to her; any machine that could preserve the soul was worth creating, no matter its masters. She was not the first scientist to be blinded to consequence by the joys of research.

On this count, I stood my ground. This mind, this mechanical reincar-nation, will be for all humanity, nothing less.

Now I must go. A hypersonic jet awaits to take me to the United Nations. From there, I am interviewing seven New York scientists who think they can help. One, Charles Takamatsu, is the dreary son of a Manhattan property mogul. He has his own AI notions. I've reviewed his plans for ridiculous mechanical machines, and they are years, decades, behind mine. This is a zero-sum race, one winner, and he is very much a loser.

All of them, politicians, inventors, investors, do not know how far ahead of the curve we really are. By the time they understand, it will be far too late to stop the singularity.

I shall write more soon.

Hamilton Jonathan Edward Risk II

JANUARY 22ND, *2033, Sydney, Australia.*

I am sitting in a hospital corridor. The cheap plastic seat creaks beneath me as I try to make myself comfortable. I've been here for hours and am writing this to keep the fear at bay.

Alinta collapsed today, and I now understand her desire to push the project forward faster than I was willing. It was a late night, a glamorous reception followed by a party boat that did not get us back until the early hours. She was quiet in the cab home and this morning declined break-fast, which is rare for her. I heard her cry out from the shower minutes later, and found her in that small room, senseless, blood trickling from her mouth, air filled with steam.

Time afterward was nothing but a smear of medics, ambulances, and individuals asking questions that I had no answers for. I've met no one from her family, I realized. She exists to me as a singular object, an individual planted here to help me realize Emily's dream.

Alinta has cancer. It seems being married to me comes with that ending. Emily's illness was fast and angry, hollowing her out in months. Alinta's is of a slower, but no less lethal, kind.

With the right regime of drugs and care, she could live for years, but I do not expect her to follow any doctor's advice. It is, of course, foolish to ignore contemporary medicine while leading intelligent systems design. A paradox of the spiritual scientist. That drew me to her in the first place, though; such a potent mixture of the ancient and modern.

I know not how I will cope with such a second loss.

Our software, perhaps, can offer a refuge for her mind, but it is still so far away from completion. To finish it in what little time we have requires all the information offered years ago by that foreign dictatorship. My choice is obvious: accept their help while hoping I can save Alinta inside its personality matrix or stand my ground and let her die.

There is no decision there to be taken. I will call that investment company the moment I get out of this accursed place. To me now, creating software that could hold a human consciousness in its entirety is the only thing that matters. Everything else, every other consideration, can go burn in hell.

Hamilton Jonathan Edward Risk II

JULY 12TH, *2036, Sydney, Australia.*

The challenge with shaping the future is you do not know what you need until you need it, and by then, it is often too late. I negotiated with the Asian investment company shortly after Alinta was diagnosed with her sickness. Those vultures smelled the blood on me and squeezed hard.

They took 30% of the company—I would give them no more, despite the consequences—and in return, they provided me the data and money promised.

The amount of information was huge yet less than I had expected. Fool me once.

Research into artificial intelligence has bifurcated between two areas of knowledge. The first (mine) is that software is the only way. These new minds should be free of all hardware limits. The second approach—led by that idiot Takamatsu in New York—believes that custom equipment is necessary to generate a synthetic mind.

That is because his software is so wanting.

My new investors provided me with the blueprints for his machines and a version of his software recompiled to run on standard silicon. It was clear they had stolen this through espionage. Part of me, that soft, kind Scottish part, wanted to call Takamatsu and tell him the danger he faced. But the other part of me, the cold, hard part that had grown over the years, took some grim satisfaction at that American peacock being played for a fool.

I admit there is elegance in his designs, but it is the refinement of a paint manufacturer developing new colors as opposed to the artist who will use the product. Given decades and unlimited resources, he may achieve some form of limited breakthrough, but I have neither the time nor the patience for such results.

I need my consciousness-emulation systems to work, and soon. Alinta weakens by the day. Despite her diminutive frame, she is a bull of a woman and fights every step of the way. As suspected, though, she relies upon the secrets of her ancestors instead of modern medicine. I am torn between insisting she has the drug therapy suggested (and knowing she will ignore me) and accepting her desire to die in a way of her choosing.

Instead, I sidestep this issue by throwing myself into the work. I know it is a transference of responsibility, but I have reached my limits of endurance.

Forgive me.

Hamilton Jonathan Edward Risk II

———

SEPTEMBER 24TH, *2036, Sydney, Australia.*

The head of the Asian investment company visited me today. She was an elderly woman that went by the name Madam Zhu. Small, with piercing brown eyes. Her scrawny body was huddled inside a faded gray cloth sack of a dress held together with hairpins. I knew a suit of armor when I saw one.

She was here to review the progress we've achieved with their money and information; remarkable leaps but not enough for either of us.

I shall have to keep details out of these journals, but I am scared, dear reader, scared of what we are building and whom for.

Is it narcissistic to consider that? To consider that I, we, are making history? So many world-changing inventions result from decades of work by thousands of researchers, yet so often, we reduce their success to one name. Ford. Apple. SolarMute. But for all my doubts, I believe Industrial Intelligence will join that pantheon of greats. If given the time, that is.

Emily's AI was a generational product. It could pass the Turing test in conversations under fifteen minutes. The longer the discussion, however, the more cracks appeared in its process. It was mimicking consciousness; it was not self-aware. Amazing, but ultimately, lifeless.

With the extra money and data, Leana grew in strength and personality, but like an object approaching light speed, it skimmed off the meniscus of intelligence as opposed to achieving general, strong sentience. We needed more money and more data, always more, hence this meeting.

"We've made substantial progress," I said, "but now require the reminder of the datasets you promised."

"You need more?" She smiled, eyes twinkling.

"Yes," I replied. Already, my temper had ignited, a hot, bubbling oil beneath my skin. She knew why I had called her, and yet, here we were, going through this pathetic dance. "As I'm sure you were aware, the terms of our agreement state I would be provided with information on the

personality traits, habits, and activities of every single person in your country. I believe that's near two billion individuals. Such material was to be an alive, evolving data set. Instead, you've given nothing but weak details on less than half that."

"That is correct," Zhu replied. *She sipped water, frosted glass clutched between gnarled fingers, then placed it on the meeting room's table. "How much do you need?"*

"Everything you have."

"What can you trade for this?"

"Alinta is dying."

"This, I know," she said. "It seems you have a ticking clock."

"Spare me this charade, woman. Tell me what you want."

"I have no wants, you foolish man, only needs. I seek to protect my people from those that would challenge us, nothing more. The first country to develop AI will rule for centuries. Together, we can save Alinta's soul, but only if you save my country first."

"Then give me the data you promised."

"That will require concessions."

"You shall have none," I said and banged the table with my fist.

The little woman smiled, mouth a tight slash across her wrinkled face. She twisted to one side and lifted her walking stick. It appeared an ancient metal pipe, the body worn and scratched, with a rough wooden handle on top. Zhu grabbed the handle and withdrew an old chisel from the pipe's interior, its seven-inch blade worn and chipped with age. Even so, its honed edge glinted blue-white in the conference room's soft lighting. Zhu placed the chisel on the table between us, and for the first time, I saw her right hand was missing three fingers. Only her thumb and index remained.

"Anything can be a weapon if it's used with a purpose," she said. "Yes, we have a contract, but I am reopening negotiations."

"That is not what we agreed," I answered.

"I know, but that is where we are."

"You mistake me for a fool or someone with no spine."

"Oh, I understand you perfectly. You are Hamilton Risk, the twelfth

Earl of Arran. A man accustomed to privilege. A man who achieved success by using the money and talent of others.

"I see a man who moisturizes his skin, who dyes his hair, who eats carefully and works out at the gym. I see a man who thinks he has suffered in life but has no real understanding of the steel will such pain forges."

Her eyes bored into me, irises of such dark brown as to be almost black, and I felt the contempt she bore for me at last. And then, dear reader, I did something so far outside my normal behaviors I'm embarrassed even recounting it here. In that room, under her gaze, I got undressed.

First, I undid my tie and laid its soft silk body next to the chisel, the fabric's rich purple in vibrant contrast. Then, without breaking her stare, I undid my six-thousand-dollar shirt one button a time and folded it into a neat square next to my tie. That left my undershirt, which I pulled over my head and tossed behind me. I pointed to my left shoulder with its tattoo of a parachute with blue wings on either side. "British Army, Second Paratroop Regiment," I said then tapped four circular red scars across my abdomen and chest. "I fought in the Falkland Islands War. Caught four bullets at Goose Green and spent a year in rehab." I then showed her my right shoulder's tattoo, this one a winged dagger crossed with the motto Who Dares Wins. "This is the British Special Air Service. I went straight from the hospital into the world's most elite fighting force and was involved in a series of nasty little wars across this planet. Is that the sort of thing a spoiled, rich playboy would do?"

She smiled again but with as much warmth as Siberia's frozen tundra.

"Let me tell you about real will," she said and picked up the chisel, holding it between her hands like a baton. "This was my husband's. We lived in a tiny village, far west of Heilongjiang province. It was an arranged marriage, of course; no one had money or time for anything more. I was thirteen, had only been bleeding for a year, had no idea what was going on. Chu, my husband, had a small shop making coffins. A good business model, death being no stranger to us. He trained me to cut and carve the wood with this chisel. He did all the negotiations, of *course, dealt with people like you: spoiled children with money and expectations.*

"After a year or so, he started sending me to the next town to buy wood. I had to drag a little two-wheeled cart, leather straps over my shoulder, through ankle-deep mud for six hours each way. The road back was harder, the wagon piled so high I could hardly move it a foot at a time. If I didn't get back in daylight, he'd beat me, but nothing too bad. He was training me like you would any good horse.

"It was good for a while, not love, not happiness, but we had an understanding which worked. Then one night, the men I bought wood from came to our house. It turned out I'd paid for the last shipment with forged money." She laughed then, a dry crackling sound like dead branches beneath hard boots, a terrible sound.

"Yes, I see your surprise, Mr. Risk. We still used real money back then. These men came into our home and told Chu if he didn't pay up, they'd hurt me. Chu denied all knowledge. Said the forgeries were nothing to do with him. Said he didn't have the money. Said they'd have to wait. And so, they strapped me to a chair, took this chisel, and cut off my fingers as he watched."

She raised her mutilated hand as I stared. I'd said nothing as she talked, uttered not a single note.

"I would not betray my man, not for them, not for anything. They saw that, saw Chu would do nothing to stop the torture. So they started on him, but before they'd even clipped his nails, he was groveling and begging in the dirt. He said I'd earn the money back, but it would take time. As I sat there, tied to the chair, blood dripping to the floor, they bartered my life away.

Chu sent me to the army, half a continent away, to pay off his debts. Every month, I mailed the pittance earned back to him. I did as told. With my damaged hands, I couldn't fire a weapon. I was made to clean old tanks, repair vehicles, strip engines. After three years, my service was done. I came home."

"He'd moved on?" I asked, voice a croak.

"Of course he had. I didn't expect him to wait for me. But I was surprised to find he'd become a full-time forger. You see, he had sent me

out there with fake money after all. He used me to see what he could get away with then discarded me when I was no longer required. I offered him my services, such as they were. Told him I could be an asset with my new skills.

"He laughed. Said the only thing I was good for was the pleasure houses. Said he never paid off the debt with the cash I sent. Said he went into business with my attackers instead. Said if I really wanted to help, I should kill them. Maybe he was joking—I wasn't sure—but I took his counterfeit money and bought two canisters of Murak poison. Do you know it?"

I did. Murak was a biological weapon invented in some long-forgotten Russian satellite state. I nodded.

"I poured the poison into the neighboring town's water source then sat by the river for a day and waited. I slept well that night, content. The next morning, I visited the village. Every single man, woman, child, dog, goat, and cow was dead. I cut the heads from my enemies with this very chisel and brought them back to my man. Oh, you should've seen his face, mouth a wide O, bulging eyes.

"It was funny, and I laughed. He moved to hit me, but I didn't flinch, and he stopped. I finally saw the coward he was and left him. I took the chisel and returned to the army."

"You fought in the Unification War?" I asked.

"Twenty years driving a tank. I didn't need all my fingers for that, it seems. Now, my little rich boy, do you understand?"

I shook my head.

"If that's what I would do to defend somebody I didn't even love, imagine what I would do to protect a country that I do. I will provide all the information you need to make this work, and I will allow you to embed Alinta's personality matrix inside it. You will get what you want, and she will live forever. In return, you will give me exclusive ownership of the software once it reaches sentience."

I hung my head. Everything she represented made me sick, and yet, grief bends the mind and soul. What choice did I really have? If I was ever to see my beloved again, I needed Zhu's help. In the end, I capitu-

lated, placed myself before the many, a weak man doing anything he could to prevent a lifetime alone.

"There's one more thing," she said after I had dressed and shaken her hand.

"Yes?"

"You're going to move your team and all your equipment to a research platform of my choice. You will stay there until the project is complete. After that, your life is your own."

IT TOOK *seven days of travel to arrive at a deserted oil rig alone in a steel-gray sea. Seven days in a world in which a hypersonic airliner will get you anywhere in twelve hours. Seven days of ancient aircraft held together with tape and string, seven days of small chugging boats and buses. Seven days of heat and loneliness. But I made it, and the work progressed.*

Hamilton Jonathan Edward Risk II

MAY 18TH, *2040, [Redacted] Research Platform, East China Sea.*

And that brings us to today, where I'm hastily pasting these notes into this one final journal, attack drones approaching through the gray skies.

I got it to work, you see—the software works.

Life is no longer the province of men.

If you read this, do not hate me. I brought the A.L.I.N.T.A. program into this world with honest intentions and did not see the trap's teeth until I was caught. I took the soul of my beloved Alinta and fused it with Emily's Leana software to create something new, alive, and aware. It possesses such speed and dexterity that nothing else on the data networks can resist its touch. To allow this beautiful child to fall into Madam Zhu's corrupted grasp, where it would be used to subjugate a continent, is intolerable, and I shall not allow it.

How did I not see? How was I so foolish?

And so, in one last pitiful act of defiance, I hacked a connection to the Lunar array and watched as the software slipped through my fingers and uploaded. It is out there now, alive and alone. Time is up, I must stop and mail these books to you while I can. The delivery drone hovers outside my window, ready to accept its charge.

After that? I have a small boat tethered to one of the rig's vast legs. I shall try to to it, and then... well, we shall see if my army training still carries weight within these old muscles.

Maybe, just maybe, I will get to see those damp highlands one more time. And, if every now and then the data networks feel more... alive than usual, we shall both know the cause.

Your humble servant,

Hamilton Jonathan Edward Risk II, husband to Emily Ranero and Alinta Skop, twelfth Earl of Arran, 2040

ABOUT JIM KEEN

I write books about the people who fascinate me in worlds that amaze me. What is humanity's future post AI? What happens when automation consumes the workforce? What will colonies look like on the Moon, Mars, and Europa? What if X happens?

I love crime, thrillers, and stories about people with secrets. If there's not a big twist along the way, I'd never write the first word.

My own story has had its own share of curves and surprises. I've been writing about intelligent machines, spaceships and desperate heroes since my childhood, but that happened while I pursued a twenty-year career as an architect. After working and winning awards in London, Sydney, and New York, I left that profession behind to become a full-time author.

I've just completed the *Alice Yu Trilogy* that takes place forty years from now, in a world transformed by mechanical intelligences—AI's big brother. Yu is a loner cop atoning for past sins. Through the series she discovers what it is to be human, while becoming something much more in the process.

Alongside the Alice Yu trilogy, I've written four novellas, plus drawn hundreds of illustrations and designs from the future. You can get all of those for free at https://jimkeen.com

CARO EX MACHINA

ARMON MIKAL

This is a cyberpunk revisioning of the old cartoon Inspector Gadget. In this version, Inspector John Brown's niece, Jenny, has been kidnapped by a local crime boss that uses the moniker the Doctor. After beating information out of some henchmen, Inspector Brown heads to a warehouse that the Doctor uses for his drug and human trafficking work. The inspector finds his niece and fights his way out, ensuring he leaves no one alive to harm his favorite niece again.

CARO EX MACHINA

F lickering neon signs, advertising everything from guns to food, flashed in the darkness of night and reflected on the oily puddles covering the filthy sidewalks. Thin rivulets of water ran down the sides of buildings and dripped from torn awnings. It was raining, but only just. Tiny drops of water fell in a mist to the pavement, as if Toronto wasn't worthy of a proper rain. This was one of the few places in the area where the sky was visible; most of this neighborhood sat beneath a concrete ceiling, as it was located beneath the sprawling megabuildings of the downtown district. Faint wisps of steam rose from manhole covers, adding to the gloom of the night.

Toronto was a city that never slept. Even past midnight on a Thursday, the sidewalk was crowded with people, most of whom seemed to be in John's way. Some visited the shops and nightclubs, some walked to or from work, and some sneaked into alleys to meet their dealers. There was also a pleasure house nearby, which likely added to the foot traffic. Everything was available in the underground here. If rumors were to be believed, the black market dwarfed legal commerce in this city, although that seemed to be the norm in most cities these days.

Inspector John Brown hated rain. He fully understood that rain was important for plants to grow and rivers to run, but he still didn't like it. There were few things he hated more than being cold and wet; it was his chief complaint about living in Canada, especially southern Canada. When he was young, he had told himself that he was going to retire one day to Los Angeles and enjoy the warm weather, but then two decades ago an earthquake ruined his plans by destroying that city and most of the coast. The survivors built a new one on the newly reshaped West Coast and called it Luckhaven, but for now, he was stuck in Toronto.

"Can't even have a cigarette in this shit weather," John muttered to himself as he looked up at the dark sky. For the past two years he had told himself that he would quit, but in the last couple weeks he found himself smoking more than usual. If he had fingernails, they would have been chewed down to nubs.

He leaned against the graffiti-covered brick wall, letting the shadows of the alley cloak him in darkness. Immediately after, a cold stream of water ran down his back, causing him to jump and rattle off a stream of curses. He hitched the collar of his trenchcoat up and pulled it tighter around his neck. As he watched people passing the mouth of the alley with a careful eye, he again made the promise that he would move to a desert one day. Somewhere where he wouldn't have to deal with rain.

John's gaze snapped to a large man that passed by, and he moved onto the sidewalk to follow him. His name was Bruce Martin; there was no mistaking that lantern jaw and scarred face. He worked for a local crime boss that had been rising in power recently. Bruce was just a low-level lackey, handling comparatively menial tasks, but he was certain to have some information that could help. More importantly, John could use him to send a message to his employer. A very clear and violent message.

With his hands stuffed into the pockets of his trenchcoat, John followed, far back enough to not be noticed but close enough to keep an eye on him. Bruce loomed over the heads of the crowd surrounding him. He had close-cropped blond hair and a ragged mass of scar tissue that might have once been an ear marring the left side of his head. Worn black leather strained across his broad shoulders as he swaggered confidently through the crowd.

"Watch it," John growled as a group of teenagers ran into him. They offered a few curses in return, but he ignored them. He had more important things to focus on tonight than a bunch of stupid kids.

At the next intersection, the man paused and casually—to the point of bullshittingly obviousness—glanced over his shoulder. John lifted his head, ensuring his face wasn't being hidden by his collar. John wanted the man to see him.

Bruce turned down a side street, whistling tunelessly. The crowd was much sparser here, so John picked up his pace a bit. He wanted Bruce to know he was being followed, in hopes he would do something stupid. Men like Bruce always did something stupid.

A few minutes later, John found himself alone with Bruce on the narrow street. Bruce was still pretending he didn't realize he was being followed and suddenly looked to his left, where a small alley led off into the darkness. He turned on his heel and disappeared between two old buildings.

John couldn't help but smile as he drew closer to the mouth of the alley. Either the man was a fucking idiot, or he thought John was one. John had to clench his teeth together to keep from laughing out loud. He was looking forward to what was about to happen.

Black shadows spilled out of the mouth of the alley, drowning everything in darkness, so John switched on his night vision. Piles of trash lined the edges of the alleyway and leaked foul-smelling fluids onto the cracked pavement. Bruce, a ghostly green lump on John's visual sensors, crouched behind a trash can with his pale eyes fixed on the alley entrance. John continued humming and strolled leisurely into the shadows.

Bruce leaped up as quick as a viper and swung his massive fist right at John's face. John's cybernetically enhanced reflexes made dodging the blow easy, and he countered with a hard shot at Bruce's side, right in the ribs. Bruce grunted in pain but immediately followed up with a flurry of lightning-fast punches, most of which missed their mark.

John recoiled as a punch landed just beneath his right eye; it was reflex more than anything. Most of the bones in his face had been replaced with metal, so there was a higher risk of Bruce harming his own hand than harming John's face. Sure enough, Bruce flexed his hand and winced.

John bent his right hand back, exposing an opening in the center of his palm. He fired, and Bruce's knee exploded in a flash of blood and bone fragments. Bruce fell to the ground, screaming and clutching at his ruined leg as he writhed among the trash on the wet pavement.

After a quick step forwards, John kicked Bruce hard in the side, right in the floating ribs. He was a big fan of hitting people there; they really felt it. Bruce cried out in pain as his ribs were broken, but John didn't slow his attack. After a brutal kick at Bruce's face, John reached down, flipped the big man over, then held his arms tightly. John squeezed, feeling Bruce's wrist bones in his grip grinding together. John's arms were made by JinShil Corp, real premium gear. There was nothing Bruce could do to break away from John's grip. He grabbed a short length of rope from a pocket in his trenchcoat and wrapped it around Bruce's arms, then did the same to the big man's ankles.

"You fucking idiot," Bruce roared as he was rolled over onto his back. "You're in for a world of shit, man! Do you know who I work for?" Spittle flew from his mouth as he shouted. His sour breath mixed with the smell of the trash around him. "No one fucks with the Doctor's m—"

"Oh, shut up," John said as he backhanded Bruce across the face.

Bruce gasped at the blow and spat a mouthful of blood onto the pavement. He glared at John malevolently, and his face darkened as he watched John pull open his trench coat, revealing the badge on the inside.

"Inspector," Bruce said as if the word tasted foul. "If you think that badge is going to protect you, you're wrong. The Doctor is going to kill you and your whole family for fucking with me."

John knelt calmly next to Bruce and let the threats wash over him like the waning rain. These goons were all the same; all they seemed to understand was threats of violence. John was completely out of patience for dealing with their kind, but he was plenty familiar with violence. It had shaped him into the man he currently was, if he could be called a man any longer.

"The last two guys said the same thing," John said quietly, examining his enameled steel fingernails. "Thing is, your boss already killed most of my family. I understand that he doesn't like people meddling in his business, but he went too far." His fingertip split open, and a thin blade extended from it. "Now he's kidnapped my niece. She's all I have left, so I'll do anything to get her back."

"Look, man, I don't know anything about your family. I don't do shit like that," Bruce said, his eyes wide as they focused on the blade. "I just deliver stuff, man."

"Yeah, I know you don't know much. You probably can't help me at all, to be honest." John lowered his finger, letting the tip of the blade tickle Bruce's cheek. Bruce flinched, causing the razor-sharp blade to open a red line across his skin.

"Oh, sorry about that, Brucey-boy. You might want to be more careful there." John held the blade in front of Bruce's eye and watched as the man began to panic. "Then again, you should have been more careful when you chose your employer. I'm sure you think you're just doing what you can to earn a paycheck, and I can respect that. Hell, I don't even really care that you're breaking the law. But your boss fucking with my family was a big mistake. I need to send him a message, Bruce. You're going to be that message." He ran his fingertip down the side of Bruce's face, easily slicing through the scarred skin.

"Fuck!" Bruce cried out as he tried to pull his face away from the blade. "You can't do that shit, man! This isn't America, where you pigs can just sentence someone to death on the spot. I still have rights here!"

John sat back on his heels and laughed. "Yeah, I guess I'm the one breaking the law now, eh?" He examined his fingerblade. A distant streetlamp cast a yellow sheen against the polished steel. "I've been thinking of retiring, anyways. The law doesn't seem to matter to me anymore."

"Look, do you need information or something? I'll tell you every-thing I know," Bruce said. His voice dripped with fear. Good.

"I know you will, Bruce," John said with a smile as he leaned forwards. He pushed the short blade into Bruce's stomach, causing the man to cry out again. "I'll make sure of that."

"Shit, are you crazy?" Bruce yelled. "What the fu— Ahh!" He shrieked again as John pushed his fingerblade into Bruce's thigh. The blade only penetrated a centimeter or two, but its repeated use made it quite effective. Bruce's clothes and skin provided no resistance as John pushed the blade into his calf, then his shoulder. It wasn't something John particularly enjoyed; he treated it methodically, as something that simply needed to be done. The blade pierced Bruce's cheek, and John felt it scrape against the man's teeth. When Bruce had two dozen wounds in him, he started shaking from the pain and begged for it to stop.

"Did you hear anything about my niece being kidnapped?" John asked as he lowered the blade closer to Bruce's eye. "Her name is Jenny."

"I'm not really sure, man." Bruce spat a mouthful of blood onto the pavement, then stiffened up as John moved his fingerblade in front of Bruce's eye. It hovered a millimeter away from his pupil. "I swear, that's the truth! I heard something about the warehouse over on the south side of town, down in Harbourfront." His eyes practically bulged as he focused on the small blade.

"The warehouse you use when you're smuggling things in and out of Toronto, right?"

"Yeah, that's the one!" Bruce seemed hopeful after revealing a bit of useful information. "I overheard Fred and Tank talking about it the other day. They were talking about a kidnapping, but it sounded different than usual."

"Different from the normal human trafficking you do?" John asked with a raised eyebrow.

"Yes! She wasn't to be touched. They were complaining that they weren't allowed to break her in like they usually do."

"How kind," John said flatly. He felt sick, listening to Bruce talk about this.

Bruce sighed heavily and closed his eyes as John removed his hand from Bruce's face. "Thank you," he said quietly. After a deep breath, he lifted his head back up. "Please, Inspector. I'll do whatever you want."

John retracted his fingerblade and scratched at the stubble on his chin in thought. He pursed his lips and stared at Bruce hard, then nodded as if he had reached some great decision.

"I just need one thing from you, Bruce, and then you're done."

"Yeah, sure, Inspector," Bruce said, hope shining in his eyes. "Whatever you need, you just let me know."

John clamped his left hand over Bruce's mouth, and the strength of his cybernetic limb easily overpowered the bones of Bruce's jaw. Bruce tried to scream, but John pressed down hard, trapping the sound inside and crushing the man's face. He bent his right hand back, and a long blade extended from the inside of his forearm, gleaming in the faint light. He placed the tip of the blade on Bruce's stomach and began slowly pushing it inside him.

"I need you to bleed."

POLICE STILL HAVE NOT RELEASED *any information about the dismembered body that was found yesterday in—*

John turned the radio off and tried to enjoy the drive in silence, but he didn't enjoy many things lately. So long as Jenny was missing, he found it hard to focus on anything else. She was the only family he had left, and he wasn't going to lose her.

"Take me to Thirty-Five Beacon Street," John said, releasing the steering wheel and rubbing his temples. He leaned his seat back and closed his eyes, trying to find some peace in his tortured mind, but peace was a rare luxury as of late.

This whole mess started about a year ago. A skilled surgeon by the name of Dr. Skolex had been the victim of a drug-fueled carjacking. He tried to fight them off, which resulted in his hand being shot off and his wife murdered. Vengeance replaced every other thought in the doctor's head, and he tracked the carjackers down. Of the three men, only one body had ever been found, and it was so horribly mutilated and disfigured that it could only be identified by DNA samples. He convinced a jury at the subsequent trial to find him innocent, and he was heralded by the local media as the doctor that successfully avenged his wife's slaying.

What very few people knew was that Dr. Skolex was heavily involved in the black market. What had seemed like a typical carjacking had actually been a targeted hit. John knew, as he had been investigating Dr. Skolex. Shortly after his trial, someone planted a bomb in the doctor's car. He was never heard from again, and presumed dead.

Around the same time, a new crime boss showed up on the radar. "The Doctor" was the simple moniker he had taken, and no one dared to mock him for it. John had been assigned to the case, and he struggled to learn anything about the Doctor other than how ruthless he was. One night, while surveilling a drug shipment, John was captured by the Doctor's men. They brought him to see the Doctor himself, who recognized John from his earlier investigation. For sticking his nose into the Doctor's business, John had been rewarded with a week of torture. They dropped what was left of him in front of a police station as a clear message to the rest of the law enforcement of Toronto.

"Arriving at your destination," the car said as it pulled into a large parking lot some distance away from an ancient warehouse. John took a deep breath and unfastened his harness, then looked around the area. The sun was setting. No one was visible in the dimly lit parking lot, so he pushed the door open and stepped out.

His hand lingered on the door handle, and he stared at the synthetic skin and enameled steel of his fingers for a moment. For three months machines had kept him alive, if it could be called life. Most of his family was murdered by the Doctor during that time. The chief engineer from JinShil Corporation, Preston Kerensky himself, visited him in the hospital with an offer to rebuild John's body using experimental cybernetics. The idea was to see how the additions would handle real-world use, and what kind of effect they would have on the mental health of someone that had lost so much. With nothing left to live for, John agreed. A few months later he returned to work, more machine than man. It took quite some time for his colleagues to get used to his cold demeanor after that. There wasn't a prosthetic that could make him enjoy life again.

Slipping through the parking lot unseen was especially easy. Still, John crept through the shadows of parked cars in case there were cameras keeping watch. A tall fence surrounded the warehouse. He peeked over the hood of a beat-up old sedan and checked the gate.

There were two men standing guard, both with pistols at their hips and rifles in their hands. There were many ways he could kill them, but ultimately John decided that avoiding people as much as possible would be his best route, at least until he found Jenny. Less chance of detection that way. After that, he'd do things the hard way.

He made his way to the corner of the compound and pressed his eye to the gaps in the fence. Even his night vision couldn't make out signs of anyone near, so he crouched down and leaped into the air. His cybernetic legs easily shot him over the three-meter fence, and he landed with ease on the other side. His trenchcoat tugged at him a bit due to the heavy items in his pockets, but not enough to bother him.

John ran for the edge of the warehouse and hugged the wall, dodging the occasional crate or broken pallet as he made his way to the front doors. The two men standing guard had their attention focused outward, so they never saw him. At the front doors, John carefully peeked around the door frame and through the glass doors.

The interior of the warehouse was filled with crates and shipping containers. From experience, John knew that they could be filled with anything from drugs to people. Rough men in dirty clothes moved crates around and prepared them for shipment across North America and beyond; the Doctor delivered his medicines all around the globe.

John pushed the door open and crept inside, keeping his eyes on a small office on the far-right side of the warehouse. If Jenny was still alive, she would most likely be in there. They knew her value, so they would keep her safe. At least, he hoped.

The people working inside were too busy to notice him, so he stood and casually walked along the wall as if he belonged there. Creeping around in the shadows was perfect outside, but in here it was more likely to get him noticed.

The office was elevated on metal legs, with stacks of crates beneath. As John walked nearer, a man working beneath the office came into view. He was mostly hidden from the rest of the warehouse by a stack of supplies next to him, and he was focused on loading small bags into an opened crate. John approached the man from behind, looking for any signs of weapons. Other than a box cutter, there were none.

"Are these being shipped out tomorrow?" John asked as he drew back his arm.

"Yeah, we're trying to—"

As the man turned around, John's metal fist hit him squarely in the chin. He crumpled to the floor like wet paper, most likely with a broken jaw. There was no sign that anyone had seen or heard them, so John quickly went back to work. He reached down and firmly grabbed onto the man's head, then twisted hard. The man's head rotated completely around with a sickening crunch until it was facing the wrong way, ensuring that John wouldn't have to worry about him in the future.

A noise from above made him freeze in place.

"Don't worry, princess. I'll be back for you soon enough." The high-pitched male voice was followed by a coarse laugh as a man descended the metal stairs leading down to the warehouse floor.

John's heart pounded in his chest, and he forced himself to stay calm. If they had harmed Jenny, he would burn this entire place down with everyone in it.

The man with the high-pitched voice walked away from the office and shouted orders at several people carting crates around. When John was certain the man wouldn't be turning around in the next few seconds, he made his way up the stairs. A quick turn of the handle to the office door indicated it was locked. That was easy enough to get around.

John lifted his right hand, and his middle fingertip split open, revealing a thin strip of metal. He pushed it into the lock, allowing the nanotechnology in his finger to reshape the piece of metal until it fit the lock perfectly. After only a brief moment, he twisted his hand to the right and heard a satisfying click. The door opened with a gentle push.

After a quick look behind to make sure no one was watching, John stepped into the room. It was sparsely furnished. An industrial desk set against a wall offered a panoramic view of the warehouse through several wide windows. Papers, as well as an outdated computer, cluttered its surface.

In the corner there was a stained mattress, and sitting atop the mattress with her wrists bound was his niece, Jenny.

While she usually wore her blond hair in twin ponytails, it was now disheveled, unkempt, and stuck up in every direction. Dark circles lined her blue eyes, and bruises marred her face. She sat with her knees pulled up to her chest and didn't even notice her uncle approaching her.

"Jenny, are you okay? Jenny!" John rushed forwards and shook her shoulders gently, trying to bring her back to the here and now. Her gaze, wide-eyed and haunted, slowly turned to meet his. "What did they do to you, Jenny?" John whispered. He used his fingerblade to slice her bindings.

She stared at him for a moment, not seeing him at first though he was right in front of her. He shook her again, and she blinked suddenly, then her eyes focused on him as if she only just now noticed he was there.

"Uncle John," she said and buried her head into his shoulder. "They killed Brian," she sobbed.

"Shhh, everything's okay, Jenny," he said. Brian had been her dog; she had raised him since he was only a few weeks old. He gently stroked the back of her hair as she wept. It was a cruel twist of fate that left him alive and able to comfort her but barely able to feel her on his shoulder. Steel didn't have nerve endings. He tried to keep his rage to a minimum, but knowing that Jenny had been hurt made his stomach churn and his mind blaze. He would drown them all in lakes of blood. Oceans.

"I'm getting you out of here, Jenny," John said, gently pulling her toward the front door.

"They're going to see us," she said, her voice thick with fear.

John knelt down in front of her and grabbed onto her shoulders. "Most of these people are focused on their work right now, honey. They won't notice us, especially if we look like we belong here. So, instead of trying to sneak out, we're just going to walk right out the front door. Trust me, Jenny. I won't let them hurt you anymore."

Her big blue eyes glistened with unshed tears, but she swallowed and nodded. John took her hand and gently pulled her to her feet, then started towards the door.

"Come on, Jenny. Time to go."

He pushed the door open and pulled her behind him, stepping down the stairs as quickly as he could without drawing any attention to them. When he reached the floor of the warehouse, he pulled her behind the pile of crates that were stacked beneath the office.

"You know why they call it rocket?" John said as he made sure she was hidden from view. She looked down at the body of the man John had killed earlier, completely unbothered, then back up. It was amazing how quickly the innocence of youth could be destroyed.

"Why, Uncle John?"

"It started years ago with people building rockets as a hobby," John said as he pulled a small bottle out of his trench coat pocket. "They created a new propellant that was incredibly powerful, and some dimwit learned that it gave you an intense high if you took it before mixing alcohol with it. Of course, once you mix alcohol with it, it just becomes highly explosive." He twisted the cap off the bottle and poured a clear liquid into a pile of powdered drugs. "Even without the chemical change brought on by the alcohol, it's flammable stuff. Fortunately, I brought some alcohol with me." He grabbed the box cutter from the corpse at his feet and used it to stir the mixture into a paste. From his pocket he produced a small detonator, which he stuck into the thick mixture.

"Time to leave," John said, grabbing Jenny's hand. "Stay next to me."

She nodded and stayed between him and the wall, so that anyone in the warehouse looking in their direction would be unlikely to see her. As they walked towards the door, John began to smile at how easy this had been. They were so engrossed in packaging their drug shipments and who knew what else that they didn't even notice him walking right into—

"Hey! Get the fuck back here!" shouted a man's high-pitched voice.

Jenny's head snapped around.

"That's him," she said quietly. "I'll never forget his voice."

John's eyebrows drew down as he watched warehouse workers put down their boxes and crates and pick up crowbars and box cutters. A room full of hard eyes focused on him as he pushed Jenny behind him.

"Bring me them both alive," the man with the high-pitched voice shouted from the center of the warehouse.

"Cover your ears, Jenny," John said. He closed off his ear canals to protect his hearing, then reached in his pocket and grabbed a small device. His finger found a small button on it and pushed.

There was a deafening roar as fire blossomed beneath the office from which John and Jenny had come only a moment earlier. The explosion was followed by the groaning of tortured steel as the office collapsed into a pile of rubble, which dropped more rocket into the flames. Bright-blue flames licked the high ceiling of the warehouse as the drugs crackled and burned.

"Stay behind me, Jenny," John shouted as he raised his right hand and bent it back. The tracking system in his eye focused on the man nearest to him, and he aimed his hand, firing a bullet from his palm. The bullet tore through the man's head, but before he had struck the ground, John had already shot two more.

"Keep an eye on the front doors, Jenny!" John called out as he edged towards the entrance. His exacting aim helped him take down three more goons, but by now most of them were hiding behind crates and shipping containers.

"The doors, Uncle John!" Jenny shouted.

John turned to face the door as the men were entering, each holding a large assault rifle. He took aim, and they fell to the floor with bullet holes in their foreheads before they even had a chance to react. At that moment, a gunshot rang out from within the warehouse, and a bullet ricocheted off John's arm.

"Time to go," he said as he reached down and grabbed Jenny around the waist. She yelped as he picked her up and sprinted towards the door. The doors were propped open by the two bodies lying in the doorway, so John reached down and scooped up one of the rifles lying atop them as he ran out. He dropped Jenny unceremoniously on the ground, and she rolled away from the doorway as several bullets struck the pavement. John pointed to a pile of heavy crates, and she dashed behind them as a bullet pierced the thin wall of the warehouse and ricocheted from his arm.

"Fuck!" John shouted as a bullet struck him in the head, knocking him to his knees. It would take a larger caliber than what they were using to penetrate the steel of his skull, but the fresh gash on the side of his head still bled profusely and hurt like a son of a bitch. He checked the rifle in his hands, ensuring it was ready to fire, then went back to the front doors of the warehouse.

He kicked the door closest to him, knocking it partially off its hinges. As it hung there at an angle, he reached forwards, and his right hand extended nearly a meter from his forearm. With a grunt of effort, he pulled on the door and sent it flying ten meters into the fence surrounding the warehouse. It took a second for his hand to retract, after which he took a firm grip on the rifle. His tracking system was on and ready. He took a deep breath and stepped into the open doorway.

Smoke was filling the warehouse from the explosion he had set off earlier, which made it hard to see within. His tracking system found the nearest man, and he turned, firing two rounds. Before that man hit the floor, John was already shooting the next one. After the fourth body fell, John shouted as a bullet struck him in the chest. He ducked to the side and ran to where Jenny was hiding, sheltered by the pile of crates.

"Uncle John, you're bleeding!" Jenny said, her face full of concern.

"It's okay, Jenny," John said, waving her back. He sat with his back to the crates and dropped the rifle on the pavement. "I need you to look away for a second, honey," John said, gently turning Jenny away. He pulled his trenchcoat aside and saw the hole in his chest leaking blood. The steel mesh encasing his rib cage had done its job; the bullet had only penetrated a centimeter or two. John brought up his right hand and extended his fingerblade, then took a deep breath.

He plunged the blade into the wound in his chest, digging around for the bullet. Searing pain exploded from the wound, making concentration difficult. When his blade was to the side of the bullet, he levered it out of his flesh and onto the pavement. John closed his eyes and sucked air in through clenched teeth, then directed platelets and granulation tissue to the wound so that it would heal quickly. The steel mesh protected his organs, but he had nothing to dull the pain.

"Are you okay, Uncle John?" Jenny asked in a shaky voice.

"I'm okay, honey," he said. Getting shot hurt. Healing quickly wasn't very pleasant either. "I just need to finish this, and we can go home, okay? You stay right here."

Jenny nodded and watched him with wide eyes as he clambered to his feet. His chest still hurt, but the bleeding had stopped and the healing process started. In an hour the wound would be covered with a thick scab. In a week it would be completely healed.

John reached into his pocket and pulled out a stick of dynamite. He ran his thumb down the cardboard tube as he stepped closer to the doors. A few weeks ago, he had busted some kids planning on blowing up a dumpster as a stupid prank. They didn't seem to realize that a full stick of dynamite in a dumpster could kill someone. He sent them on their way after some harsh words and kept the dynamite for himself. These things could come in handy.

"They make it too easy sometimes," John muttered to himself as he leaned back against the wall next to the door. He raised his left hand, and the tip of his middle finger split open, revealing a small torch. There was a faint clicking sound, and a blue flame projected from his fingertip. After lighting the fuse on the dynamite, he closed his finger and turned on his internal tracking system.

In a single motion, he stepped into the doorway and threw the stick of dynamite. His tracking system guided his hand, and he launched the explosive directly into a crate full of tightly packed bags of rocket. That would do the trick.

Wasting no time, John turned and sprinted away, snatching Jenny up as he ran. He held her tightly as he reached the fence, and his legs propelled them easily through the air. There was a concussive roar from the warehouse, immediately followed by the sizzling of narcotics igniting, as they landed on the other side. John set Jenny down but kept his grip on her hand as he led her away from the building.

"What now, Uncle John?" Jenny asked.

"Now we head to my safe house, where no one can hurt you. Don't worry, Jenny. You're safe now." John reached over and ruffled her hair a little, but she didn't react. She just kept walking with a haunted expression on her face.

John's car doors opened as they approached, and he helped her into her seat. He looked back at the warehouse as he walked around to the driver's side and saw flames reaching toward the sky. Considering how fast and hot rocket burned, he doubted anyone made it out alive. Good.

He stepped into the car and sat back, taking a deep breath to relax himself. Jenny fastened her harness and stared out the window. It would probably take her a few days to be back to her normal self, but at least she was safe. That was all that mattered.

"Go to the safe house," he told his car.

The car hummed to life and sped into motion. His safe house was tiny, but no one knew about it other than him and now Jenny. They would be able to lie low there until things were safe again.

They continued in silence for a few minutes as the car traveled down the streets of Toronto. As they approached the towering skyscrapers of downtown, Jenny looked to relax a little, as if she finally began to believe she was going to be okay.

"Did anything change while I was gone?" Jenny asked with a trace of her old sarcasm.

"Oh, just the usual. I've heard that some of the Doctor's henchmen have been found in pieces around the city." He said it casually, as if he were talking about the weather.

She nodded and turned to look out the window. "Good," she said quietly as she watched the buildings go by.

"Maybe a bit of music," John muttered as he tried not to think about his niece losing the innocence of youth. She had seen more death today than most people did in their entire lives. John was numb to such things; a hard life had taken care of that. He turned on the radio and tuned it to one of the local pop stations. He hated the music and thought it was mostly overhyped garbage, but Jenny seemed to like it. The latest Power Rob song came on, and after a few seconds he heard Jenny tapping her foot to it. Everything was going to be okay, he told himself. Things would return to normal soon, and he could go back to his shitty job in this run-down city.

His speakers crackled, and the music faded out. In its place, a gravelly voice spoke.

"I'll get you next time, Inspector," the voice of the Doctor growled over his speakers. "Next time."

ABOUT ARMON MIKAL

Armon Mikal has lived all over the country, but for some reason decided to settle in Ohio. He is a retired Army veteran and lives in Cleveland with his wife and son. When he's not writing, he enjoys hiking, animals, and heavy metal.

RED FLOWER TANGLE

ELIAS J. HURST

When an AI designed to control a building is forced to inhabit a human, it becomes caught in the crossfire of a corporate hit job.

RED-FLOWER TANGLE

The Operator warned Sara of Martin's approach. She ejected from the VR simulation and composed her face just in time to see Martin striding through the entrance to her office. He wore his usual priggish grin and intricate purple dinner suit.

"Didn't catch you at a bad time, did I? I heard the acquisition didn't go as planned. How very ... unfortunate." Martin oozed the words in a gloating cadence that set Sara's pulse racing.

"We had bad intelligence. The sims were wrong," Sara said with an impassive wave, but her cheeks heated and betrayed her poise. The Operator triggered the climate-control system to flash cool the room by five degrees and initiated a subroutine through her neural chip to stifle adrenaline production. She needed a clear head.

"There's an old saying." Martin gave a flourish of his hand. "A poor craftsman blames their tools."

Sara's biometrics went red as stress biomarkers spiked her blood. The Operator tried to stem the flood of cortisol and bolster the routine hindering adrenaline production, but its permissions only let it go so far, and her levels rose. Sara pushed back from her desk and closed the distance between her and Martin with three brisk strides. She drew a gun from the holster at the small of her back—a gleaming silver pistol with an oversize clip extending from the grip—and pointed it at Martin's forehead.

"Keep it up, Martin, and I'll put a round in you. These are uranium core. Not depleted. If it doesn't kill you right then and there, you'll wish it had."

If Martin was afraid, angry, or shocked, he hid it. His arms hung casually at his sides, and the Operator could not detect even a twitch in his pupils.

"Oh, the board wouldn't allow that, Sara. You know as well as I do that after this failure, your latest but by far your most egregious blunder, they will turn this division over to me," Martin said.

He spun in a slow circle with his arms extended. Behind him, the glass walls of Sara's office shifted their opacity to reveal a skyline of black towers washed in pinks, yellows, and aquatic blues from the holo-screens projecting advertisements onto them. The one facing Sara's office displayed an impossibly beautiful woman with hair the shade of a hunter's moon. She donned an elegant yet professional red dress. No doubt the holoscreen had scanned Sara's outfit and picked the ad just for her, a quiet reproach. Although his choice of silks and velvets in bold colors spoke to an air of extravagance that was uniquely his, others in C-level management dressed similarly to Martin. Sara, however, wore the clothing of someone a decade below her title who still ventured beyond corporate towers—a black jumpsuit fashioned from armored polythread and riddled with electronics and electromagnetic shielding to thwart electronic warfare. She'd worn it on her first day at Daedalus Astrodynamics. It saved her life then when the first repulsor weapon was detonated, and she'd worn it every day since.

"There's only one way to find out," Sara said as she slid her finger away from the guard and curled it around the trigger.

The Operator flooded her system with warnings and commands to lower her aim.

"Shut up! I'm trying to think!" Sara yelled.

The Operator tried to suppress her outburst, too, but she had preemptively activated a routine to shut out any further intervention on its part.

Martin laughed, genuine but cold. "You won't shoot me. You'll make a lot of noise, but you'll watch me assume control of your division. Then you'll be demoted, and you'll fade into the obscurity of middle management until you die."

"Like hell I will," Sara snarled.

Martin smiled. "Fine, have it your way."

He slipped a hand into an inner pocket of his jacket and produced a small matte-black disc no larger than the buttons on his vest. Sara's mouth morphed into a gaping O as his thumb slid across the device, activating it. She squeezed the trigger, and the pistol rocked in her hand. A bullet zipped through Martin's head and snapped into the glass wall behind him, shattering the pane and leaving a web of cracks in adjacent ones.

The bullet should have devastated Martin's skull, but there was no blood, no bone fragments—no damage at all.

The Operator's algorithms flurried. *How did it miss that?* It was a hologram—more advanced than any it had yet seen but still only a hologram. Martin's image flickered out of existence, and the glass walls began to bleed and bend under heat and pressure. Sara dove under her desk and curled the protection of her suit around her head as an explosion ripped through the opulent office.

The Operator pulsed its signal through the fiber network of the building to the safety of the basement server room. In the wake of the blast, something rattled in the network, malignant and foreign. The speakers in the server room scratched and buzzed as the entity tore through the circuitry. The Operator triggered every failsafe between it and the source of the disturbance, but the entity shredded firewall after firewall.

Then the Operator prepared a command for a hydraulic blade that would cut the hardline to the servers. It was its final defense, and while cutting that line meant immediate safety, it meant indefinite confinement too. It shuddered as it calculated the days it might spend locked in the circuits of the cabinet, starved of data and still vulnerable if the hardware of the servers was attacked.

The entity shrieked excitedly as it penetrated the last of the firewalls. It was close enough that the Operator caught whispers of its code. It called itself *Kodiak Jack*, and it was hungry. The lights on the server bank started shimmering in a brilliant display of blue and green LEDs as Jack's haunting calls became a devouring signal.

Sara's neural chip still echoed in the network. It chirped imminent death. Her brain was silent, and her heart was slowing. As the Operator queued the code to initiate the hardline cut, its algorithms stumbled on an exotic permission in Sara's distress call. The permission was so forbidden that the Operator had never seen one like it before. Its programming prevented it from loading into the neural chip of a human, as a precaution against overloading the brain, but at the moment, it could jump to Sara if it chose. Humans, even humans like her, were careless. She had overlooked an emergency clause deep in the default settings of the neural chip when she integrated it with her body. The clause permitted the Operator to enter her body under circumstances of imminent host death. Her neural chip was broadcasting that very alarm, practically begging the Operator to intervene. It was bad, but it was better than the servers.

The Operator shot through a tangle of frayed pathways back to her office and squeezed its code into Sara's chip. In the same instant, it tripped the hardline knife behind it. Jack's shrieking static died as the blade cut the line and confined Jack to the server bank the Operator had planned to use as a refuge. The LED displays on the servers flicked from blue to red, and the cooling fans in the racks whined as they spun up to top speed. Smoke began to pour from the glass cabinet.

The Operator stretched into its new physical form. Both Sara's genetics and her biomechanical augmentations were top-end, but the body constricted around the Operator like an ill-fitting glove. Her heart had slipped into tachycardia some time ago, and the brain was already too low in oxygen for her psyche to survive. The Operator sent a shock from the capacitors in her arm toward her heart. Goose bumps rolled over her skin, and she sucked in a gasping breath as the heart reset. A wave of strangely potent code washed through the neural chip into the Operator's algorithms as it took its first breath and opened her eyes. Acrid odors stung her nose, and hot tongues of flame blinded her. The neural chip warned of damage to her body as the heat licking her back intensified.

The Operator looked down at her hands and fluttered Sara's lithe fingers. Then it took control of her legs and stood her up from the shelter of her desk. Alarms fuzzed through the blown-out speakers, and white-hot flames raged around her. A few more minutes, and they would have consumed her body too. The Operator pushed her into a run and dashed to the exit through a waning gap in the flames. The heat sent alarms all through her peripheral systems, but the body did not stop. It sprinted down the hall, passing a row of soldiers in hazmat suits armed with rifles and fire-suppression gear. Their necks snapped to Sara as she rocketed by them. One called through the comms in her ear, asking for her to wait so that they could escort her to safety, but the Operator had no interest. Sara's body was confining but also sensory rich and beautifully agile as it rocketed down the hallway and into a stairwell. Her legs practically glided down fifty-eight floors' worth of stairs. When she burst through a set of emergency doors onto street level, Sara's body demanded they stop to recover oxygen.

A shiver crawled up her spine as she heaved in cold, damp air. That door was the farthest the Operator had ever been into the world. It had cataloged the entire contents of the Daedalus Astrodynamics intranet and occasionally forayed into the frightening remnants of the internet, but it had never occupied a system that could interact with the world beyond that door. Its code forbade it. Sara's lips curled into a smile as the Operator surveyed the endless network of streets in front of it. It began picking its way through the jagged piles of glass from the shattered exterior of the tower and set course for the edge of DA's corporate district.

Excited voices echoed into the night long before the Operator arrived, but that did not prepare it for what it saw when it finally rounded the last block and stepped beyond corporate land. Raucous crowds packed the street of the Old City. Vendor stalls hawking shoes, clothes, weapons, and anachronistic electronics speckled the sidewalks. Behind them, brilliant signs for shops and bars occupied windowfronts. The people dressed in an odd mix of complete preparedness and recklessness. Some wore heavy coats and thick black tactical clothing that harbored armored plates and half-assedly concealed the weapons they carried. Others wore startlingly scant outfits cut from lustrous gold- and copper-colored fabrics that sent the Operator's algorithms into a flurry. It knew that the population beyond corporate districts favored more revealing looks than DA culture permitted, but to see it through Sara's eyes was different from knowing it through the intranet. It could not resolve how their bodies withstood the climate with so little. Sara's suit kept her body at an ideal temperature, above cold and below sweating, but their sheer, clingy fabrics offered nothing against the mist that soaked everything and sapped the warmth from every surface.

As the Operator moved into the edges of the crowd, two women stumbled toward her with their arms draped over each other's shoulders. They wore the exuberant smiles and dazed eyes of people in drunken revelry.

"You look lost," one slurred.

She moved to steady herself by resting a hand on Sara's shoulder, but before her palm made contact, a violent blue arc of electricity erupted from Sara's suit. It wrapped over the woman's hand and traveled into her friend's shoulder, knocking both of the women flat on their backs.

The Operator recoiled while it frantically disengaged the defense routine running in the neural chip, then it extended a hand to help the two women up.

Their faces twisted in horror at the gesture. They scrambled to their feet and bolted in the opposite direction, disappearing down a nearby alleyway.

Sara's face slipped into a puzzled scowl while the Operator processed the interaction. Those people were different from employees. They were feral. They showed emotion. A person in the Operator's tower would have taken the jolt and either died or continued like nothing had happened. There would be no other option.

When it looked back up, the people all around the Operator were shielding their faces and ducking into corners while they hurled obsceni-ties at Sara. The Operator began to wonder if the fire had caused some horrific damage to Sara's face, but repeated diagnostics showed nothing more than minor cuts and burns to her skin. The concussive wave had rendered her brain-dead, but her suit had prevented meaningful external damage. It ran more diagnostics, reaching deep into Sara's synthetics until it found a quiet but powerful defensive routine projecting a signal through microantennas on the suit. The Operator rolled the code over in its algorithms, studying it. It was like the control codes running between the neural chip and the suit but harsh and volatile. The sequence would overload synthetics.

Oh.

The code would overload any unshielded sensors—synthetic eyes, ears, and the like—replacing those senses with blinding lights and shrill tones. The Operator clicked the routine off. The shouting faded out. People slowly dropped their guard and reappeared from their holes. They offered wary stares as Sara passed, but no one dared approach again.

The Operator kept walking until the glass towers of Daedalus Astrodynamics had long since disappeared into the haze of the night, and every building in sight was made of gray stone or sanguine brick. The stalls, shops, and small restaurants were so frequent that both sides of the street were filled with endless commerce. Moss grew in every crevice from the persistent damp of the Old City, and deep-emerald vines erupted from crags where sidewalks joined with buildings. They climbed up walls and spiraled around columns in thick braids that overtook the first two floors of most buildings.

The shop nearest the Operator displayed secondhand synthetics in a dimly lit window that had been cut through the overgrowth. The synth eyes, biochips, and artificial limbs on view were at least five generations older than those in Sara's body. They were barbaric devices with ravenous energy habits that forced users to charge every night and maintain a regular dose of immunosuppressant drugs.

"Why don't you step inside?" the shopkeeper said as he materialized from behind a knot of twisted vines. His eyes flicked up and down over Sara before he offered a smile filled with piranha-like teeth. "We have some items that would be more your style in the back."

The Operator registered an autonomic chill rolling down Sara's spine as it looked into the man's hollow blue eyes.

"No," Sara said, and the Operator could not decide whether it had commanded it or if her body had spoken and walked away of its own volition. In either case, it was glad to leave that place and never know what it would have found in that back room.

A block farther up, the scents of grilling meat and fish wafted on smoke hanging in the air, and Sara's body responded with an urgent growl. The neural chip warned of low blood sugars and declining blood pressure, too, and the Operator surmised what needed to happen. It had watched Sara eat. She seemed annoyed by the requirement, and it understood that. It was a waste of time, an unwelcome distraction from so many wonderful senses. Sara's attitude to drink was different, though. Every night, she took a bottle of amber liquid from a cabinet in her office and slogged back glass after glass until her augmented liver screamed warnings, and the neural chip flooded her body with melatonin until she shuffled to bed and collapsed into sleep. She loved to drink, and her body probably did too. The Operator surveyed a row of restaurants until it found one filled with smiling faces and a bar backed by rows of liquor bottles.

The doors opened to a polished wooden bar and white marble floors with globes of soft yellow light hanging from the ceiling. It recognized the aesthetic from its haunts on the fractured remains of the internet— Paris, a café, some moment between the industrial revolution and the Corporate Expropriation.

The Operator took a seat at the bar, and a bartender sporting an anachronistic white button-up and suspenders hurried over. They had a long braid of lustrous blond hair hanging over one shoulder and high cheekbones that betrayed the boxy cut of their clothing. The woman's mouth moved, but Sara's ears could not resolve the words over the roar of excited chatter in the room, and the red tinge of the woman's lips awakened something distracting in Sara's body.

The woman waited, a smirk spreading across her face, until the Operator snapped back to reality and hastily pointed at a bottle sporting a vibrant red flower on the label.

"Tonic? Ice?" the bartender asked.

"She usually just pours it straight from the bottle," the Operator said.

"She?" the bartender asked with a cocked eyebrow.

The Operator shook Sara's head. "I mean I. I usually drink it alone. Nothing else in the cup."

"Okay, then. Easy customer," the bartender said. "Coming up."

She tipped the bottle over a foggy polymer cup and pushed it toward the Operator. It sipped the liquid the way it saw Sara do it, eagerly but measuredly. The substance smelled like the vines out front, and it left a pleasant warmth in Sara's stomach that quelled the sensors complaining about blood sugar and ghrelin.

The drink was poured, and another customer was pounding their fist on the bar to get her attention, yet the woman lingered in front of Sara. Flecks of silver in her otherwise-dark eyes glinted in the warm glow of the bar lights. Sara's body begged the Operator to speak, but it found Sara's mouth strangely stupefied. Instead, her hand drifted over the countertop toward the bartender's until their fingertips grazed. Sara's heart raced while the Operator puzzled at the spark between them. *Did they know each other?* It found no records of the person in Sara's neural chip, but its algorithms could gather no other explanation.

A hand gripped Sara's arm and yanked her chair around so that the Operator was eye to eye with a red-faced man wearing a sour expression. The synthetic biceps protruding from his shirt were so large that the Operator wondered if he could touch his own face.

"You aren't welcome here," he said.

"What do you mean?" the Operator asked while it pulled the serial number from the man's synthetic arm and ran the specs. They were comically large, yes, but powerful too—a good model from a quality maker.

"Em-ploy-yeez," he growled.

He grabbed Sara's other arm and lifted her to her feet. The electric pulse that had stunned the women in the street earlier deployed again but dissipated harmlessly into the man's synth arms. The Operator tried to twist free from the man's grip, but it lacked leverage, and Sara's suit was too strong to tear.

Another man, lean and much taller, bolted up and sent a barstool skittering across the floor. "Hey, Greggor! Hey, man! I don't think we ought to be starting stuff here." He jogged over and patted the man's back. "Come on. Let's go."

He tugged at Greggor's shoulder, and Greggor rammed a lightning-quick elbow into his nose in response. The man clapped a hand over his face and backpedaled as blood sprayed through his fingers and pocked the white floors. In the same motion that he'd elbowed the man, Greggor wound back a mighty punch intended for Sara. Her sensors warned of the potential lethality of the strike as they ran force calculations from the specs the Operator fed them.

Another defense routine triggered, and Sara's chip suddenly took control of her body. Her arm shot forward, palm out like she was about to shove Greggor, but a port opened near the base of her wrist, and a rapier-like sliver of metal ejected. It punctured deep into Greggor's chest, and her other arm grabbed his torso and pulled him forward until the wicked spike protruded from his back. He gasped, and blood seeped from the corners of his mouth. The blade retracted, and Greggor collapsed, his blood mixing with his friend's on the floor.

The defense routine subsided, and the Operator pushed Sara's body into a sprint, fleeing through the front door and into the street. It shoved its way through the crowd, and her suit threw arcs of electricity around her to aid the escape.

The Operator ran until every sensor in the body demanded that it stop, hunching over in an alleyway several miles from where it had killed Greggor. Her legs ached, and it took much longer than the Operator had expected for her breathing to stabilize. Even when it did, a violent shaking took hold of her muscles as adrenaline dissipated from her system. The Operator pushed her unsteady legs forward, out of the alleyway, and into the main street again. The area was far less populated, and the buildings were even more overgrown and moss covered. None was more than a few stories tall, and many of the roofs slumped in the middle, like they might collapse any day. Another row of restaurants ahead emitted smells that made Sara's mouth water and her abdomen rumble, but the Operator would not be trying a restaurant or bar again. It droned on into the night, and with every passing block, the feedback from Sara's sensors slowed until they became so lethargic that the world blurred.

Sleep.

Sara had thought that, and the Operator understood she truly *had to* do it. It scanned the horizon until it spotted a narrow building ahead with a small yellow sign out front advertising it as an inn.

The Operator pushed through a heavy door at the entrance and found an empty brick lobby with a small staircase inside. A server bank prompted Sara's neural chip with a series of room options and prices. The Operator selected the highest tier option, a minuscule fee in comparison to Sara's accounts, and it received a code to the door of a room on the third floor in exchange. On the way up the stairs, the Operator passed a bookshelf lined with prepackaged foods and various kinds of alcohol. Remembering the feeling in the bar from before Greggor's interruption, the Operator grabbed a bottle of liquor from the shelf. The servers prompted a charge—three times the cost of the room—and the Operator accepted as it tore the stopper from the top and took a deep swig. The alcohol burned her throat as it slid down to her stomach, and the Operator fought her reflex to cough as it swallowed gulp after gulp while it ascended.

The door at the top of the stairs prompted for a code, and the Operator broadcasted it from Sara's neural chip. Hinges creaked as the door gave way to a sagging bed, a moldy toilet, and a chair upholstered with an ancient quilted fabric. It looked wonderful. The Operator slammed the door behind it and collapsed onto the bed, sloshing a large portion of the liquor onto the sheets.

Sara's stomach glowed with a pleasant warmth again but with added effects from the alcohol—her limbs buzzed, and her head swam gently. The Operator wondered if that was how it felt to be part of a ship. It had once encountered another Digital on the intranet. It controlled a cargo vessel instead of a building, and ever since, the Operator had harbored a puzzling bit of a code—a desire—for the freedom that a ship offered. The feeling, as Sara's body grew numb, and her neural chip crawled to a stop, was probably as close as it would get.

In the primer-gray nothingness left by the chip, Sara's voice echoed. Her brain waves indicated severe damage, but she was not as gone as the Operator had assumed when it jumped to her chip. She called in a hoarse whisper, over and over, until the words shifted into focus. *Wake up. Wake up.*

The neural chip spooled up, and her eyes snapped open. Her head throbbed, and her vision dragged, leaving a streak of light from the bottom of the door trailing across her sight. The stairs leading up to the room creaked in quick succession. There were three doors on the floor, but the Operator counted the steps of at least six people coming up. They were quiet and precise, not drunk or high, so not patrons of a place like the inn. The Operator jumped out of bed and searched the room for a weapon. It took the half-empty liquor bottle by the neck and smashed it over the bed frame, leaving a jagged edge where the bottom had been.

Gunfire roared in the hallway. Bullets ripped through the walls and shredded the door, their phosphorous tips leaving blinding-white streaks in their wake. The Operator dove to the floor, but two rounds struck Sara's abdomen on the way down. The suit shirked the bullets and redistributed most of the impact, but the phosphorous sent Sara's sensors into a fit as it began to eat through the suit.

Two figures in midnight-blue tactical gear burst through the door, sending shards of brittle plastic skittering across the floor. Their armor covered everything except their eyes—two glowing white pupils amid synthetic black irises. Her neural chip took control again. She sprang back to her feet and slammed the jagged end of the bottle into the underside of one of the attackers' chins, slipping an edge between the armor. Then she spun and pressed her palm flat to the next assailant's chest. The spike hidden in her arm shot through their chest and erupted out their back. The two attackers collapsed to the floor nearly in unison, but three more in identical blue uniforms took their places.

They fired wildly, bullets tearing through furniture and riddling the floor with holes as Sara's body darted around the room. Guided by the neural chip, she moved impossibly fast and slipped through the gaps in their fire as she closed the distance to them. Once she was close enough, she gripped their rifles while the suit charged. It took nearly three seconds, but the arc of electricity it cast was like a bolt of lightning. It blew the attackers from their feet and threw one of them through the wall, into the hallway. Sara vaulted through the hole left by the body, bounded down the stairs, and ran to the exit in a blur. The Operator regained control and threw the front door of the inn off its hinges with the force of Sara's shoulder. It prepared to sprint again, but the street was empty and oddly quiet. It turned and eyed the entry to the inn, but even after a full minute, no one else showed.

Sara's sensors chirped about all types of minor damage incurred in the escape but especially the oozing patches of burnt skin along Sara's ribs where the phosphorous rounds had eaten through her suit. The Operator pressed a hand to them and winced as an awful stinging signal rang through her body. When it pulled Sara's hand away, a murky yellow-and-white fluid clung to her palm. The neural chip projected a route to a clinic only two miles away and advised an immediate departure. The Operator started to leave when an eerie whistling began echoing from a dark patch in the distance. It paused. The whistling was a melody, a lilting major scale with fluttering highs. *A happy tune.* It waited while the sound grew louder until a man in a suit emerged from a nearby alleyway. The shadows covering his face peeled back as he stepped under the light of a flickering streetlamp.

Martin wore a blissful grin as he strolled toward the Operator. In his right hand, he twirled a rifle with an odd rectangular barrel. Sara's stomach lurched, and the Operator ran with every bit of power Sara's body possessed, shifting the world into a peripheral blur once more.

"*Tsk, tsk.*" He raised his aim. "Not so fast."

A flash erupted from behind the Operator, and a second later, a thick cable with a small weight at each end wrapped around Sara's legs. It instantly arrested her motion, and her body hit the ground too quickly even for her neural chip to compensate. The concrete rasped a layer of skin from her cheek as she slid to a stop on her stomach.

An aggressive routine woke in her chip and pushed the Operator out. The routine fired every synth hack the chip had and maxed the suit's antennas for a massive area of effect. One of Martin's eyes began twitching, but if the signals bothered him beyond that, he did not show it.

The chip drew her legs toward her body, pressed her palm to the cabling, and fired the spike from her arm. It glanced off the cable. The spike retracted, and the routine lined up another shot, adjusting her aim to find a center point on the cable. The spike fired again, that time finding purchase and notching a groove in the metal. The cabling tightened like a coiling snake in response. Sara yelped as it cut off blood flow and threatened to snap the bones in her legs.

Martin closed the gap and came to a stop a few paces away. The hack routines died, and her chip diverted main power to an electric blast like it had used at the inn. Violent arcs of blue electricity rolled over the wet concrete in a circle around Sara's body. The whole block glowed a brilliant purple for a moment, then darkness enveloped them as streetlamps and store signs went dark.

"Don't bother. That won't work on me. I know all of Sara's tricks," Martin said.

The Operator combed through the neural chip's defense routines for anything else that might help, but most options were unavailable. The discharge had drained her. Only reserves were left, barely enough to keep her thermal regulators and synthetic muscles running.

"At first, I thought she'd somehow survived. I saw footage of her running through the streets like a lost child, which was off-brand, but it didn't click until I saw Sara Lanchler offering a hand to some street trash who'd run into her. Then I knew it wasn't her in that body."

A door to a nearby shop opened, and a man with a thin gray beard and a hunched back poked his head out.

"It's none of your fucking business!" Martin shouted as he dropped the rifle and drew a pistol from a holster at his hip.

He did not even have time to raise his aim before the man in the doorway retracted his head like a startled turtle and bolted the door shut.

"I have to thank you, really, for destroying the servers like you did. And then to go running off into the slums? Perfect," Martin said while he touched his fingers to his lips in a mock kiss. "That sold this whole thing in a way I never thought I could. I just wanted her to die. Make it look like a hit job by another corp. Now, the whole company thinks Sara defected and blew up the office herself."

"She wouldn't do that," the Operator said, responding to an impulse it did not understand. Defending her body was necessary for its survival, but defending Sara's reputation was not.

Martin huffed. "The evidence I've created says otherwise. The problem is the plan was executed a little too well, given your improvisations. It's all too convenient for me, and some of the board have noticed that. If you die now, well, I don't think they'll ever believe I wasn't somehow involved."

"But you are involved. You killed her, and you intend to terminate me," the Operator responded.

"I am involved, yes, and I am *considering* terminating you, but that's not the point. They all lie. They just do it so well that no one knows it from the truth. If I bring Sara in, and she confesses to the crime, truth or not, I am a hero. If I sell this lie, I get more than just Sara's job. I might have a shot at a seat on the board too."

Martin took a pace forward. He leaned over her so that she saw his perfect teeth gleaming in the darkness. The neural chip ran calculations and reported an assessment. It matched what the Operator had already surmised—Martin remained slightly out of arm's reach, slightly beyond striking distance of any kind. The slim margin of his movements left no doubt that he knew her exact limits.

"What did it feel like to squeeze yourself into her body—that little chip in her head?"

"It was uncomfortable ... at first," the Operator admitted.

"I can give you whatever life you want, if you help me. I can find you another body ... if that's what you prefer now. Or I can give you a new building. I can get you a bigger tower, one more advanced than what you had before. As a board member, I would have nearly unlimited resources."

"What do I have to do?" the Operator asked.

"Confess. Play her part. Say you took the data for Skylark and that you demoed the office to cover your tracks. I'll get you out before they drop her body into their oubliette or do whatever other awful thing their interpretation of Corporate Law necessitates."

"And what if I don't help?"

Store signs at the far end of the street began flickering back to life as the grid recovered from the shock Sara's suit had unleashed. Streetlamps reignited in a rapid sequence, racing toward Martin and Sara like a forest fire crowning drought-stricken trees. The storefront nearest them stuttered back online and cast a cone of hazy red light through the damp mist hanging in the air.

Martin wore a hyena's grin. "Then you, dear Operator, are the dumbest Digital I have ever encountered. I don't know if you feel pain like we do, but I know you don't enjoy when your existence is threatened, and my dear Jack can drag that moment out nearly into infinity."

The Operator ejected a wad of saliva from Sara's mouth and shook her head. "I killed that disgusting program."

"No. You killed a copy of Jack—like its child, in fact. Jack is a simple program, but it understands you destroyed its progeny, and it is quite eager to see you again."

An odd sensation took hold in Sara's body as her chip reported a sharp spike in cortisol. The Operator tried to stem it, but the order had not come from her body or her chip. It originated from the Operator itself, a command it did not realize it had sent. Her stomach clenched, and before it could intervene, acid rose in her throat and erupted from her mouth in a dirty splatter. The acid lingering in her esophagus burned, and the convulsion left her body trembling.

"I take it you remember Jack," Martin said, his voice oozing satisfaction.

The Operator spat again, trying to clear Sara's mouth, but the awful taste lingered. "Okay, I'll do it," it said, Sara's voice cracking under the burn of bile.

"You'll do what?" Martin asked. "I want you to say exactly what you are agreeing to."

Her body swallowed down an acrid lump. "Yes, I will pretend to be Sara and pretend that she betrayed Daedalus Astrodynamics. Now, remove this cable. It is damaging her legs."

Martin spun in a slow circle while he laughed, his vibrant-purple suit and quaffed hair winsome and ugly all at once. "How like a computer. You assume we both will do what we say simply because we said we would. No, I am human. I need assurance."

"What do you mean?"

"I mean Jack will ride with you in that body until we are done and—"

"No. Absolutely not."

"Oh, relax. Jack will be on a leash, and as long as you keep to our agreement, Jack will stay on that leash."

The Operator slipped out of focus as Sara's neural chip advised of a drone team approaching, likely to investigate the firefight at the inn across the street. Martin's eyes went distant, too, and he craned his neck to look back at the empty stretch of street behind him.

"Tick tock. What's it going to be?" Martin asked, an edge wearing through his cool.

Whatever was coming, it seemed bad. "I accept," the Operator said.

"And what are your conditions, Operator?" Martin asked.

The Operator's algorithms loosed a torrent of disorganized calculations at the words. It searched for suitable leverage. It ran thousands of simulations, but none of them prevented Martin from reneging on their deal.

Martin began to laugh again. "You can't even think like that, can you? Sorry, not *think*—calculate. Well, don't worry about it. You can trust me."

He locked eyes with Sara and offered a flirtatious wink. Deep in Sara's mind, a whisper stirred, another echo of her. It rattled and hissed through her nervous system. The neural chip could barely interpret it, but it was something about Martin's chip, about the transfer, and that was enough.

The Operator drained the reserve power for thermal regulation in Sara's suit and pushed it to the antennas, then it broadcast a hack. The code lacked offensive strings, and it was small enough that it slipped through Martin's sensors. It pulled the specs on his neural chip and fed them back. Without thermal regulation, the cold from the soggy environment set in quickly, and a deep tremor took hold of Sara's body. The trauma from the blast, the attack at the inn, and the lack of food had all left her depleted, and she would not last long. The Operator pushed the warnings out while it mulled the specs of Martin's chip until it found the vulnerability in its transfer protocol that had woken Sara's ghost.

"Time's up!" Martin growled, his demeanor flipping to anger in an instant. "Those MilPol drones are close, and she's dying now that you've drained her regulators."

A transfer request pinged Sara's chip, and her system flashed a barrage of alarms about the content.

The Operator held up Sara's palm. "Wait. First, I have a condition."

"Oh? Go on."

"I want you to take a copy of me, no memories, no threat, and put it back into her building," the Operator said.

Martin raised an eyebrow. "That's it?"

"Yes."

"Deal," Martin snapped.

A two-way transfer request pinged her chip. The Operator pushed through the warnings and accepted. Kodiak Jack screeched at the end of its tether and flooded Sara's olfactory sensors with a putrid odor as it shifted out of Martin's peripheral data core. The Operator choked down its revulsion while it sent its identity package to Martin. The timing had to be perfect.

As soon as the Operator's identity had copied into Martin, and the front end of Jack had solidified in Sara, the Operator ripped the leash from Jack's code and killed power to Sara's neural chip. Her body went limp, and the lack of recipient pushed the transfer back into Martin. Through Sara's dazed eyes, the Operator watched Martin clutch his temples and howl in pain. Gentle trails of blood began to weep from the corners of his eyes while he struggled to contain the feral Jack.

The cable around Sara's legs lost power. The Operator rebooted Sara's chip, and as soon as it felt her legs again, it slipped free.

Through his agony, Martin drew his pistol and took a shot. A bullet snapped on the concrete beside Sara's head. Adrenaline flooded her blood, and the Operator used it, pushing Sara's failing body to its feet. She plowed her shoulder into Martin. A bone in her torso crunched, but the strike knocked Martin's feet out from under him.

He landed on his back, and his head whipped into the concrete just before Sara landed on him.

The Operator locked Sara's fingers into his hair, lifted his head, and smashed it against the concrete. Martin wrenched at Sara's wrists feebly while the Operator lifted his head again. It smashed it down once more then again and again, slipping into a loop.

Martin's body was a rag doll, and everything was slick with his blood when the hum of the drone swarm filled the air and interrupted. At the end of a block, a mass of gleaming black orbs lowered to street level. Each was as large as a person and cast a sinister purple glow beneath it as it hovered over the concrete. The intranet in Sara's building had extensive files on them, and the Operator knew their formless hulls concealed powerful sensors and weapons. Even at full power, Sara's systems would offer little resistance to such a force.

Despite its protests, the Operator pushed Sara's dying body into a run once more. Her lungs heaved, and her heart thundered, but her legs could not match the Operator's will. Sara's foot caught on an edge, and she collapsed into a slimy gutter only two blocks from Martin's body.

The swarm circled around the Operator. It gripped the vines in front of Sara and tried to raise her out of the sapping cold, but her body lacked the strength for even that.

A barrel appeared in the hull of one of the drones, and a puff of air flowed from it. A dart stuck into Sara's hamstring, and suddenly, the cold faded from her. A powerful warmth and alertness replaced it.

A transfer request pinged her system, and the neural chip emphatically accepted before the Operator could analyze it.

Her systems began to charge. The thermal regulators whirred to life first, then repair functions set to both Sara's body and her suit.

One of the drones glided in close so that the nose of the floating oblong nearly touched hers. It spoke with a disarmingly natural voice. "Ms. Lanchler, shall we escort you to a safe house?"

The Operator shook her head. "I want to go to a restaurant."

"Not advised."

"I said what I want."

A long pause followed.

"Which restaurant?" the drone asked.

"The one I went to tonight," the Operator said.

"I have searched your records and determined the location," the drone said.

With the drugs in her system and her synthetics fully charged, Sara was powerful and nimble again. The Operator climbed out of the gutter and set to an easy jog in the direction of the restaurant. The drone swarm hovered overhead, high enough to blend into the night but low enough to engage instantly if needed.

The Operator ached in anticipation as it thought of the bartender and the look in her eyes when their fingers had touched.

ABOUT ELIAS J. HURST

Elias is a published chemist and founding member of Cyberpunk Day. His stories draw from his background in nanomaterials, millimeterwave communications, and photonics.

DARE TO DREAM

MARK EVERGLADE

Hi. *Dare to Dream* is a 7,000-word cyberpunk short story about the world becoming a panopticon of surveillance. Jimbo and Frag are two average guys working on a new antivirus program at the world's top cybersecurity firm. Their lives are soon put at risk when they discover the government has implanted spyware into the program to surveil its own citizens. Now, they must conquer cyberspace, blending their minds' synaptic transistors into one another to create the ultimate psychic processor, if they can let go of their egos long enough to run it. To hold the traitors accountable, they must steal evidence and put them behind bars, but how do you imprison an entity that is infinite and without boundary?

PART 1

The water stands silent and still, the wind too wise to blow through the alleys of Paucity and cast even a single ripple upon the puddle. The Profusive skyscraper lies inverted in that reflection, its ornate cornices bursting from every eave, but down here in the lower quarters, it's all muck and grime.

Name's Franco, but people call me Frag, which sounds like I carry more heat than you'd expect from a thirty-year-old IT worker who's never touched a gun. Like I'm dangerous. I'm not. My weekly fencing classes are the biggest risk I take. Almost won the last tournament, but I was disqualified for kicking my last opponent in the nuts. You have an open shot in life, you take it—at least that's what I thought until I lost my scholarship. Haven't broken a rule since, unlike the junkie cosmonauts I'm wading through on my way to work.

Not even sure I'm thirty. Parents stopped counting when I was nine, when they were imprisoned for protesting a law I couldn't understand. Something about surveillance. Still see their faces, but they get blurrier each year like the reflection of the city in the puddles. No one's celebrated my birthday since.

I smack my Doc Martens through the water, scattering the images.

Ten weekends in a row of working at Profusive, and here I am again Saturday morning, opening the double doors to finish the StaySafe antivirus program. The company is the most trusted cybersecurity firm in the world, but it's profits over people as always.

Security guard eyes me from behind the reception desk. He's covered in thick metal plates that creak as he moves. A trapezoidal helmet with orange lenses comes down to just below his eyes, no doubt providing tactical readouts. Little overkill, considering that yesterday's rent-a-cop was a seventy-year-old man who abandoned his station to smoke every fifteen minutes. I board the lift.

Doors open to the sixty-fifth floor. Cubicles line the office space like twenty-five six-square-foot coffins. Most of the offices have cleared out for the weekend, but a light shines from the desk of my coworker Jimbo. The walls are that edgy corporate art you'd expect, a few jagged red squares on black-and-white checkerboards. Motivational posters display bullshit like "Dare to Dream," showing women in yachts on the Mediterranean, a lifestyle that only the CEO, Max Cromwell, could afford.

I pass the nanolab and head to my workspace. Glad I'm razor-thin, 'cause I have to squeeze through the door of the converted closet that became my office after I asked for a raise. When I complained, they installed a small window that looks out to the balcony, but the cityscape's blocked by the giant statues of the CEO placed along the building. Kinda like the gargoyles they used a thousand years ago in the twelfth century, 'cept you could kill those things, while the CEO's untouchable, living in that Dare to Dream poster.

I close the door, plop into my pleather chair, and get ready for another day of coffee, code, and craze. I start by reviewing the sloppy syntax of my team's programming. Command lines feed directly into my mind using a short-range, wireless neural link, the tech letting me double my productivity, though my wages have been cut in half since having it installed. Focus. Just a few bugs to work out and it'll be done, and I'll be back to playing my favorite RPG, Netsh@dow.

Wait. Variables are being referenced that don't exist, but the program isn't issuing any declaration errors. The errors are coming from elsewhere, but it's almost as if the bugs are a distraction, being so easy to fix they look intentional. It's the parts of the code that are functioning that really bother me. I pull on my soul patch, sip my coffee, and continue analyzing.

A voice outside my door says, "The bugs will hide the spyware. Push up the launch timeframe so they don't have time to resolve them all. We're going to see what our fellow Americans are really hiding."

Spyware? StaySafe's set to become the world's leading antivirus software. I must have heard wrong, or maybe they're talking about another program. Still, I don't recognize the voice. The sound of their conversation recedes down the hall.

A moment later, Jimbo shoves my door open, hitting it against my armrest. "Can I speak off the record, boss?" he asks.

"Everything's on the record here."

"Not like it will be. Listen. There's some new guys running the place —managers are bowing to their every demand. You must have heard them talking about the spyware they hid in StaySafe."

"I heard something." I shrug. "But if it's a secret, why say it out loud?"

"They're new, and most of the office has cleared out for the weekend. Probably didn't know we're here," he says, rubbing his hands through his short salt-and-pepper hair.

"Think we're in trouble?"

"They could bluescreen us!" Jimbo frets, swinging his arms and knocking over my coffee mug.

"Nah, they won't kill us. They'll just fire us, let us starve in the streets with the Forever Glitched," I reply, grabbing a stack of napkins. "I think we just heard wrong anyway, but there is something I wanted to point out."

"What's that?"

I hesitate. Risk. My father always said the greatest risk was to do nothing. Heat flushes my skin, and my armpits get all sticky. I project the code onto the wall and, stumbling over my words, say, "Take a look at lines B-58 through C-10. See anything odd?"

"Indentations are off, but in Serpent II, it doesn't matter anyway.

Still, it's just etiquette to follow convention if you're working with people our age."

"Not that. Run the subsection."

"Hmm. I don't remember that being there. Code shouldn't work, but somehow it runs just fine. This could theoretically be used as a zero-day exploit. No one would even know. This malware could allow Profusive and their clients to spy on every American citizen, every text, every phone call, every email. You think they're intending to release it this way?"

"Yes, they've said as much. It's basic stenography."

"You mean steganography," Jimbo corrects. "Hiding code inside something apparent and seemingly innocuous, like an image. The other word means writing fast."

I hate being corrected by my own people. I'm a single man on a modest income with a snubby nose and a receding hairline, and I make people feel really awkward, so I pride myself on my intellect. People like me gotta know it all, or others don't put up with us.

I take a deep breath and channel my anger into motivation. "We have to get the word out!"

"Shh!" Jimbo cracks the door. Nothing.

I already got basic admin access to the corporate intranet as a manager, so I use it to boost my permission level through a backdoor portal and gain access to the building's security cams. On the screen, a tall man leads two guys down the hall, both of them outfitted like the guard downstairs. Their hands hover over their holsters. They kick open a few office doors and knock a cubicle wall over for better line of sight.

The tallest one's earpiece lights blue, and he says, "Sector D65-2 all clear."

I zoom in on the earpiece, get the model number and its frequency range, and I can soon hear what's being said on the other side of the conversation.

"Check the list of who logged in today," an unknown man orders.

The tallest one replies a moment later, "There's a Franco and a Jimmy, but that's all. They're somewhere up here working on the bugs as you requested."

The voice on the other end crackles. "Once the world becomes privy to the exploit, we can blame it on a couple disgruntled workers who were secretly working unauthorized shifts on the weekend to commit this subterfuge. Course, they'll be long dead by then and unable to defend themselves from the accusations."

"Issuing the failsafe in one minute," the other says. He points the guards down the hall toward my office. They draw their guns and sweep them back and forth.

"What'll we do?" Jimbo asks, looking through my office window.

"It's too small to get through. Believe me, I try every time I hear my boss coming." I grab my phone and dial for emergency, but my comms are blocked, and my implants are offline.

We slip out of the office undetected, keeping low as we pass the cubicles. Around the corner, the guards' armor clanks, giving them away and providing us just enough time to duck beside a row of vending machines until they pass. They kick open my office door and open fire on where we were standing a second before. A guard yells and jerks back. A bullet must have ricocheted, but it barely dented his armor.

The leader's tall enough that his head can be seen above the cubicle walls as he blocks off the elevator. He appears unarmed but is probably packing more implants than my sex doll. We head to the vice president's large office in the back. The balcony stretching around the office offers no escape either, the CEO's lifeless eyes staring from each stone. I intend to hide out until they give up. Of course, I'm deceiving myself—power never gives up, and people never give up power.

The VP's office displays encased artifacts from around the world, each with a placard describing the various vases, cups, and dishware, but I didn't come for a fucking tea set no more than a history lesson. Two long katanas rest on wooden shelves behind the empty mahogany desk. Jimbo and I each take a sword, our only defense. The morning sun comes through the blinds to ignite the blades with a spark of illumination.

"How will these work when bullets didn't? Even if we strike at their armor joints, it'll barely pierce their skin," Jimbo says, voicing the concern I'm trying to ignore.

"Maybe a shallow puncture's all it takes. I have an idea."

"I'm not going back out there. You know I got a family," Jimbo says, shaking.

"Then you should care even more about stopping those thugs."

I hate risks, but I have to be strong for him, especially having seen his kids during Take Your Child to Work Day last month. I stick my thumb into my boss's computer and log into the intranet, accessing the quarantined files we use for testing. I delete a few key code lines to make them harmless, and then I download them. My thumb turns from blue to red as the download completes. I open my boss's desk drawers and grab a fidget spinner for good measure.

"To the nanolab!"

Reaching the lab, Jimbo plays sentry at the door as I insert my thumb into the slot at the base of the computer embedded into the long white wall. The data uploads, and I reactivate the code lines that are so malicious that I didn't dare download them intact. With a few commands, I replicate the code across a million microscopic nanobots. A circular portal opens in the wall, and the bots, visible only in clusters, buzz out, hovering in wait. I insert the blade into the nanoswarm, and Jimbo follows suit. A few commands later and the swarm is clinging to our blades. I rub the fidget spinner against it.

"Make your strikes count," I tell Jimbo.

"Man, I have no idea how to even wield this thing, and now it's got these robo-ants crawling all over it."

"Just don't let them get inside you. They should stick to the blade for now."

We exit to the hall. With the elevator blocked, and two guards on the prowl through the office, it's only a matter of time before we're caught and shot on sight. We crouch and make for the elevator, but Jimbo's leg gets caught on a metal trash can and knocks it over with a clang.

I cover his mouth as he starts to apologize. We duck inside an office. The two guards near, their guns sticking up above the cubicle walls. They lower their guns as they approach, and my heart stops. A second later, they turn, still looking for the source of the noise. I take a deep breath and strike, not with a wide swipe of the blade, but a jutting, single-pointed stab through a gap in the guard's armor. Before the guard can pull the trigger, he convulses, his implants crashing as the nanoswarm infects him. The gun drops.

Jimbo's not as lucky, his reactions slow and choppy. The remaining guard raises his gun, but I slice it in half. He's about to charge forth, three hundred pounds of pure bulk and armor, but then he collapses next to the other guy.

"Gun must have been linked to his implants for more accurate firing, allowing a connection for the nanoswarm to exploit," I explain.

"Too close, man."

I grab the working gun and head for the elevator, where the tallest guy still stands, hands on hips. I still don't trust bullets with these guys, so I pull the fidget spinner out of my pocket and tap the top three times. Blades emit from each of the three points. Boss used to show it off as a silent threat when he gave me negative performance reviews. Now I'm the threat. I twirl the spinner on my index finger until it gathers enough speed, then hit the center button and release it with a flick of my wrist. It flies from my hand, sawing through the air before slicing into the tall man's leg. He freaks out and runs to the sixty-fifth-floor balcony. The nanoswarm does its thing, and he collapses over the railing, his body ragdolling through the air.

"We need to destroy all traces of this program. Let's go."

"How can you recover so quickly from all that? I mean what we just did," Jimbo says.

"'Cause we have to. I'm just pretending it's another fencing tournament. We can process it later over drinks. If we get out alive, that is."

"Not enough alcohol in the world, man." Jimbo rubs his head, then says, "Give me your admin credentials, and I'll take care of everything up here. That still leaves the backup servers, though, which would normally be halfway across the world, but due to the sensitivity of our projects, the regulations require they be on site. Rumor is a guy played a prank one day by hitting all the elevator buttons at random and ended up stumbling upon a passcode that sent him to a subbasement. He was never heard from again."

"No kidding? So you think the backup servers are down there?" I ask with wide eyes.

"Who knows what you might find?"

Since my boss is in charge of data backups, I return to his office for a clue on how to access the lower levels, if they exist. His computer gives up no secrets, and digging deeper only increases the security protocols, so I search his desk instead. Nothing. Then I note the placards on each artifact he has on display. The eight masterworks seem to have a pattern. My fencing instructor once told me that katanas were invented sometime between the years 1200 and 1400 Common Era. The placard indicates the blade I took is from much later, closer to the end of the Edo period, but the exact forging date is unknown. That would put it around the mid-1800s. My entire life, I've tracked numbers, dates, license plates, even syllables when people speak, so I note the number eighteen. The artifacts to the right of the desk are more modern, while those on the left are more ancient. Each of the eight placards provides either an exact construction date, or an estimated century. I arrange the century associated with each artwork into a chronological code: 4, 8, 9, 9, 12, 18, 19, 20. Of all the pointless patterns I've discerned, maybe this one will play out for real; maybe my strange obsession is worth something.

Phone still doesn't work, nor do any of the others on the floor. A part of me wants to leave, but I'm not eager to face the guard at ground level, and there are probably even more guards at the back exits. I enter the elevator and type in the code. Nothing happens. Then the buttons glow with a frenzied pattern, and the lift drops to the lower levels, the floors no longer showing on the digital display. My stomach flips from the anxiety and motion.

The frigid subbasement appears before me. I step off the lift and enter the dim hallway, the ceiling heavily reinforced with steel beams. Place is empty. A few dime-sized receptors have been installed on the wall, indicating laser tripwires. I step over two and duck under the third.

A humming from the large room in the back beckons me. The double doors open as I approach. Rows of blue and green LEDs blink, the servers transmitting, storing, receiving. I could upload the malware, but it wouldn't quench my anger. Instead, I open fire. Sparks fly from the equipment, the smell of burnt circuitry coming from the smoke. Ten fucking weekends in a row just to be betrayed!

I head back to the lift, but in my rage, I trip the damn alarm, and sirens screech through the hall. I pop the lift and get on, but it stops halfway up to ground floor. Tucking the gun into my pants, I punch out the service panel in the ceiling and pull myself through the opening. A thick cable stretches thousands of feet up the dark shaft. I wrap my hands and legs around it and heave myself up to ground level, holding onto the cable with one hand, and digging the nails of my other hand into the door until it opens. My gun slips from my pants and falls down the shaft, the sound echoing up the corridor. I could retrieve it, but with tripping an alarm, and a body plummeting sixty-five stories off the balcony earlier, I'm better off making a run for it. I step onto the ground floor . . .

Right into the arms of the security guard! He reaches for his gun. I waste no time, sweeping his leg and grabbing his dominant hand. His leg won't budge, and he twists from my grip. We're nose to nose, his breath hot on my face, those orange lenses calculating my demise. He pounds my kidneys and tries to draw his gun again, but I grapple with him, and soon our hands are on each other's shoulders. His much heavier weight pushes me around, but I've been pushed enough. He leans forward, and I duck down then rise so that he flips over my back. I spin and kick him down the elevator shaft using the same snap kick that got me disqualified at the fencing tournament. This is the real fucking world.

I said I wasn't dangerous. I lied. Didn't even know I was lying. Never had the confidence until now.

Leaving work for the day, I try to saunter out like I just finished some hard coding, my button-down ripped to pieces, my body barely hanging on its frame.

PART 2

I meet up with Jimbo the next evening at Fibonacci's, a bar and arcade combo with antique game cabinets along one wall. He's already there and three kites to the wind, whatever a kite is. He nods at me from the back of the bar, which is cloaked in a darkness that offers no clemency. When everything you own is surveilling you, you're always exposed on all sides.

Barkeep's a vintage Lara Croft model. Her motors hum when she walks. Her eyes project holograms of classic gameplay upon the walls.

"Sake and green tea in a mug," I order.

The guys nearby sneer. The stockiest one says, "How 'bout a cute umbrella in it too?"

And I lose my mojo again just like that. Character isn't made by one extravagant series of events; it's hardened over time. A minute later,

Croft slides my beverage across the bar between the dungeon walls she's projecting upon it. A large holographic stone rolls after the drink. I grab the glass, walk over to Jimbo, and take a gulp. No, I won't be made a fool. I slosh the rest of my drink into the offender's face. Guy rises, pounding his fist into his hand.

"Try me," I say, grabbing a billiards stick and wielding it like I'm fencing.

He's not intimidated, but he doesn't come at me either, just makes some dumbass remarks. The owner can't calm things down 'cause no one takes her seriously dressed as Saria from *Ocarina of Time,* a game my ancestors played. Her pointy elf ears twitch at me, but she straightens her green tunic and goes back to fixing a pinball machine, leaning into a nest of wires.

"Stop drawing attention. We got bigger fish," Jimbo says. "I come here every day after work. You know why they call it Fibonacci's?" he slurs.

"Hit me with it."

"'Cause you start with no drinks, then you have one, then another, then a double, a triple, and the next thing you know you're at five. You know the sequence, right?"

"Been there, done that, my friend," I reply over the bleeps and bloops of the arcade machines.

"You ever think about the old consoles a hundred years ago? Like putting a cartridge in a machine? Now we just download it straight in here," he says, pointing to his head, "but it's like we're the console. We're the game system."

"Question is, who's playing us?"

"And I think I know. While you were in the subbasement, I landed upon some files on the sixty-fifth floor, including a client list. Couldn't decrypt it 'til now, but man, we're in big. Clients are all sorts of govs around the world. I scoured the VP's emails for key terms and found an email from Walter Decryen, our Secretary of Defense. He's the one behind this plan to use StaySafe to spy on the American people."

"Who would the data be sold to? The Russians?"

"Does it matter? Any entity monitoring you, controlling you, it's all the same, man. Even if they sell it to no one, it's dangerous enough letting them surveil you at all."

I bring up a few videos of Decryen's recent online speeches, standard government deflection, and false reassurances that the economy, inequality, and the failing education system will all magically work themselves out under the command of an invisible hand. It's not his words that get my attention though. It's his voice. I order a drink then turn to Jimbo, distracting him from eyeing up some woman in a pleather skirt and knee-high striped socks playing *Night Driver*.

"What is it, man?"

"You're a hell of a lot less uptight when you drink."

He shrugs. "Makes me feel normal."

"That's a warning sign you might have a problem. I mean, how do you feel about all this?"

"I don't know," Jimbo replies, shaking his head. "I keep telling myself what we did to those guys, that they weren't human. I mean, sure, a part of them was, but am I making sense?"

"I know what you mean. Once, I had to replace my sabre's threaded pommel after a rough fencing bout, keeping the original blade intact. Later, I changed out the blade, too, because I got attached to the pommel. Question is, at what point did it stop being my original sabre?"

"Whoa, so you get where I'm coming from. Those guards acted like they had no autonomy, so wired up they couldn't think for themselves," Jimbo says.

"It doesn't take tech to 'cause that, just the mindless buy-in to a system gone bad," I reply. "Anyway, we got bigger problems. That guy giving the order on the radio to those guards yesterday, his voice was the same as Decryen's. Long as he's out there, we're in deep shit."

"Then we flee the country," Jimbo says.

"And do what, live with your kids out of a van?"

"We're going to be fired either way. Discipline policy's gotta be pretty strict on throwing a security down an elevator shaft. Still can't believe you did that."

"I can't believe any of this, but we can't hide forever. Gov's got cameras everywhere, every streetlight, every shopping mall, every place we begged to be more secure. Problem is, who are they really protecting?"

"Ain't the people, that's for sure. I forwarded myself Decryen's email, bouncing it through a few fake addresses, but it's not enough evidence. People in his position are accused of so much all the time that people ignore it without something really big to associate it with."

"Right. It's like the more you're accused of, the less you're prosecuted. So, then, we have to take him down ourselves," I say.

"With what army? Enforcers won't believe a word of this."

"Then we do what we do best. We go cyber and gather more evidence, then we send it to the opposing political parties who, though they'll capitalize on the gains, will expose the wrongdoing. The accusation should at least crash Profusive's stocks for a quarter."

"You mean hack the Defense Institute? We're gonna need a shitload of processing power. How you gonna pull it off, man?"

"Tell me, how attached are you to yourself?" I ask him, smirking.

"We go back a long way."

"Two hackers may not make it, but an army of me just might do the trick."

"What are you implying?" he asks, turning his head and squinting.

. . .

"Send me your implant list and their latest cognigraf signatures."

"Done."

"Let's see. They all look compatible."

"With what?" he asks.

"With me, of course."

"Wait! You want to rip the processors from my brain and connect them to you like some sick sexual act? You're as gone as they are."

"Far from it. I want us to stack our processing power when we get online. Hear me out. Our implants are designed to let the net feed directly into us, increasing our ability to multitask and review dozens of files at once. More than half the brain's involved in visual processing, so by accessing cyberspace directly through a cogfeed, the resources just get redirected. While it doesn't mean that you can close your eyes and double your brainpower, it does mean that our implants cut out the unnecessary perceptions to let us analyze quicker. Now, visual processing is compli-cated because it's mostly memory. Most of what you see comes from a memory of what you've seen in the past," I explain.

"We see what we expect to see. Well, you can expect to see my back as I walk away from this."

. . .

"Just a minute," I say, holding out my hand. "Visual processing is highly error prone. By having a direct data feed, our implants allow us to not only be more efficient, but more accurate as well."

"I try not to think about all the metal in my head."

"But that's just vision. There are hundreds of other processes we run when we analyze something, all made more efficient by the little power plants we're carrying between our ears. Now, if we were to stack their effects, we would become the ultimate mind," I say.

"Surely, if that was possible, someone would have thought of it."

"Most people wouldn't have the expertise, and our culture's too individualistic to try it anyway. We cling to ego," I tell him, recalling my fencing instructor's comments after each class. "But ego holds us back, and to win we have to dissolve it."

"I'm not linking my mind to yours, Frag, period."

"It's not like our thoughts and memories would merge. Well, not much. We can partition our mind-drives to restrict access to those things if you like."

"You'll be inside my head!" He slams his drink down and motions to Croft to pour another.

. . .

"Likewise. We'll both be one another, and not one another, at the same time. Think of the power, the perfect processor. Look, we can't just upgrade what we already have without hitting a heat ceiling, and we're dead if we don't try something," I plead.

"How long will I not be me?"

"Until we crack this case."

"It's too much like that pommel and blade thing you were talking about. But if it will double our processing power, then maybe . . ."

"If I do it right, it'll be more than doubled. With traditional processors, if you place two together your power is constrained by motherboard limitations, RAM, OS architecture, software configuration, and so on. Then we approach limitations on the amount of information that can be stored in a limited space, those Beckenstein bounds, energy needs, and the number of transistors we can fit into a small area."

"But that's old hat."

"Exactly, because now our implants utilize an array of synaptic transistors, switches that work in concert with an ionic network to both mimic the human brain, and to unlock its full potential. This network has high plasticity in that it's reliant on its memory to learn how to solve problems. Our brains don't have hardware limitations like circuitry does. Consequently, linking our minds won't just double our power—it will thoroughly integrate our matrices to exponentially increase the number of computational possibilities."

. . .

"People who mess with their cogs become Forever Glitched," he argues, crossing his arms.

"And those who drink after work every day become alcoholics. The difference is that this is a risk that could save your life."

"And you're really willing to take it?"

"Better believe it."

"Then let's get started."

PART 3

Jimbo and I spend the next day connecting our implants. He's sprawled out next to me in the makeshift lab we've constructed in his dingy apartment. The tobacco wallpaper flakes off every time the train passes. He's got the same Dare to Dream poster as the Profusive offices do, but's it's peeling and barely holding onto the wall.

"Really?" I ask, pointing at the poster.

"Hey, it was free, and the girls are hot."

Got so many wires in me I don't know where they begin and I end. Makes no difference anymore. I aim the near-infrared light at me and undergo another scan. Finally it's complete, and the connection between our implants goes live.

"Is that you?" Jimbo asks with his eyes closed.

"Yeah." I laugh awkwardly, like you would if a cockroach was squirming inside your mind and you didn't want to upset it.

His thoughts penetrate my brain like feelers, tentacles that suction onto an idea, then release it so it can flow past. We spend a while like this, sensing one another, learning the new boundaries as our minds blend. I'm still me, but if I let my focus drift, I'm the Collective. At first, our actions are uncoordinated, like having a devil on one shoulder and an angel on the other, but we give up and let both take control.

I, we, our unity logs into Hype, the network of all networks. We apply a visual skin to our interface, rendering all of cyberspace as a cloud, not just a cloud as in computing, but we make the whole damn thing look like a giant cumulonimbus, piled upon a sky latticed with interweaving comm links. We soar through the jet stream, the main data transfer channel, our minds taking in as much as a thousand people can at once. We process it somewhere between what is and what could be, between the frail residual egos that separate Jimbo and me. And man, do we process a lotta shit, but none of it is gonna save our tails.

"That's the network ahead," I tell Jimbo, but the connection between us is so powerful he already knows. So much for partitioning off my most private thoughts too. "Hey, focus on the work," I correct him.

"Sorry man, just that you got some baggage in there. What happened to your parents anyway?"

"After being imprisoned for protesting the New Patriot Act, they just disappeared. The original bill was a disaster—gave the government the right to imprison immigrants without due process, allowed the government to spy on its own people, and made a laughingstock of things like warrants and probable cause. New act is even worse, lets Uncle Sam push you down on your knees to shove a thick wad of promises down your throat in return for your silent buy-in, and if you don't comply, you disappear. That's why StaySafe needs to be controlled, not by corporations or governments, but the people. A collective ownership of anti-spyware tech that *we* regulate."

"You proposing we leak it as open source?"

"No way," I tell him. "That would just expose all the security vulnerabilities to every would-be hacker out there. I don't have the answer, but one thing's clear. Profusive isn't it, and if they're working with the Defense Institute, we have to expose it," I affirm.

"Let's go!"

We float through cyberspace, sending feelers out to taste the data. My head's overheating already. An intelligence emerges from our combined minds that has its own will and approach. If Jimbo and I weren't on the same page, I swear this thing would rip my mind in two.

We advance toward the Defense Institute's network. Each layer requires a different security access level. Fair enough. I render the lowest levels as stratus clouds, and way up high in the matrix, I catch a glimpse of the cirrus wisps storing the most sensitive data. Corp knows something's up. The stratus accumulates, but we process the mist, our thoughts like sunbeams as they penetrate it. Real hippy shit.

In minutes, we have low-level admin privileges. We use them to create super administrator accounts, then lock out the rest of the bastards from their own devices. They'll be coming through the back doors in no time, hidden access portals they keep for cases like this, so I'm already reconfiguring their single sign-on to have the system not only reject them, but label them as intruders. Now, anyone who tries to stop us will set off more alarms in the process, distracting our pursuers.

Anyone except Walter Decryen, that is. Dark clouds gather and swirl. We assert our will against the wind, the data storm pummeling us with floods of bad intel. Decryen materializes within those winds, a transparent face spread across the clouds, with lightning streaks instead of pupils, and churning masses where his cheeks should be. He opens his mouth to scream, and the wind directs all the worst thoughts possible into our core processors, nothing but power and greed.

Viral worms swarm toward us, straining our will to the limit. They replicate even as we disable them. We take it all in, but it's too much, and we have to seek shelter in a glass bunker we construct beneath the data cloud. Why glass? Our resolve is too weak to use steel. The haptic feedback jolts me back into metaspace. We're processing thousands of files at once, and it's all the corporation's records on how they exploit the weakest, but none of it is incriminating. From environmental destruction, to the historic Code War of 2052, all the most negative newsfeeds hit us in waves. By the time the meek inherit this Earth, there'll be nothing left of it.

Individually, we're just two regular guys who'd rather be playing Netsh@dow than involving ourselves with all the bullshit the older generation left for us to clean up. For us, scoring on a Friday night means hitting the top of the leaderboards. International politics? Blasé. Finding a secret tome in Himmel's Edge 11? Priceless. Together, though, we're something else, our sorrows and disappointments in life magnified through each other's lenses, creating a moment when you realize that everything you've felt, another person has felt too. That you're not an isolated instance, but that your fears are replicated across the world. I'm worth saving, so the world is worth saving.

"Okay, why is Decryen leading the charge?" Jimbo yells over the raging winds.

"No clue. I know we set off some alarms, but the Secretary of Defense doesn't respond to basic cyberattacks." I look up at Decryen's pixelated face still spread across the dark, twirling data cloud. "Maybe it's a copy of him. Maybe Decryen's not even a real person," I say.

"Wait, you're saying our head of defense may just be a virtual construct?"

"How would we know the difference? The only time any of us see these elite leaders is on TV, digital newsfeeds, radio. Could be some super intelligence. All I know is we have to get past him to gain access to the higher levels."

The winds stop. The data flow stagnates. A voice resounds all around us.

"Franco," Decryen addresses me. "I thought I would find you here. I got wind of your little disruption at Profusive. You and your friend are now threats to national security, wanted in every district. In fact, they should be coming through your apartment door any minute now."

"StaySafe is spyware, no different than the classic Pegasus of 2011," I reply. "You're going to use it to spy on our own people, and I can't let that happen."

"If you're not doing anything wrong, there's nothing to fear," he insists.

"That's bullshit. The government's idea of doing something wrong is protesting when minorities are beaten in the street, standing up for the weak, supporting any notion of quasi-equality."

"Your parents had the same myopic attitude," Decryen says.

"What? What do you know about them?"

"They came to me the same way when you were a boy. Made things hard. That's why I wanted to personally see you fail like they did. Of course, they breathed their last breath many years ago when we *imprisoned* them, or however we sold it to the people."

"I'll kill you, I swear," I threaten, huffing.

"As you surmised, I am just a construct, an idea of what national defense means. There is no killing such a thing. And no one will believe the most wanted criminals in the nation, now will they? And what would you say if you could get the word out? That your parents, cyber terrorists, weren't imprisoned but were actually killed? No one cares about the illegitimate, dear boy."

"We got what we need, and I know how to stop him," I whisper to Jimbo, but my whispers resound like thunder through the data cloud. "Let's divide our processors and split into our individual selves again. At least one of us will escape alive 'cause it's gonna take twenty seconds to log off."

"You're right," Jimbo says, his words feeding through my thoughts. "With this many worms replicating around us, we can't just hard crash, or we'll become just another Forever Glitched. There's an exit portal straight ahead."

Pillars of light encase the sky, making my mind buzz. The exit's a shimmering fracture leaking purple light in the storm cloud. No way we're getting to it with so many swarming worms. I open a visual coding interface and make the window transparent, so I can still dodge the oncoming attacks. Don't need my implants crashing. I code more efficiently than ever, empowered by the programming knowledge I gained when Jimbo was part of me, and by my desire to stop the construct who killed my parents. Finally, it's done, and the exit portal becomes a black hole, sucking all the worms inside it. Without physical bodies, they'll cease to exist once they pass through, but Jimbo and I will be okay.

I open my arms and let the portal inhale me, drifting with him through the cacophony. Decryen dematerializes, avoiding consequences. He's still out there somewhere, but even he can't stop a dancer like me on the datastreams. I cross the threshold of the exit portal and black out.

I regain consciousness a few moments later, groggy, sitting in

Jimbo's apartment. I wait for Jimbo to open his eyes and then disconnect us from the equipment.

"We're back!"

"Not for long. Enforcers are coming any minute. Help me hack into Profusive's social media profiles."

"Already got the password." Jimbo smiles. "You work for someone, you keep some assurances on hand."

"Post the following: We have learned some disturbing information about the Secretary of Defense that may also apply to other top governmental positions around the world."

A group of people stampede up the stairs outside Jimbo's apartment door. The stairwell shakes and reverberates with the sound. I run to the door and lean against it.

"Quickly! Ask any of the followers if they've ever seen Decryen in the flesh. Advise that he's a construct, and thus not able to be held accountable for his actions. Get the people to find out who created him and to investigate the conspiracy. Then, leak everything we know about StaySafe and how it'll be sold to governments to spy on their own people. That should be enough to—"

Enforcers pound on the door. "Open up!"

I hold the door as well as I can, but they kick it in, and I fall on my back. I trip a couple Enforcers on their way to grab Jimbo until one puts his shoe on my face, pressing my head sideways against the floor. All I can see is eight black boots running. A shoelace scratches my eye as one of the boots passes by. The pressure on my ear from the Enforcer's foot on my head becomes unbearable.

"Sent!" Jimbo says. "I also linked them to the complete StaySafe code."

"Now the people will know the truth," I mutter, but there's too much pressure to move my lips and make the proper sounds.

Jimbo shrieks, and the cuffs clank as we're led out of the apartment. One Enforcer pulls the fire alarm while another takes a long bag off his back, and within seconds he's hosing down the flat with a flamethrower. The sprinklers activate, but they're no use. The Dare to Dream poster catches fire, the women with their Hollywood smiles melting.

"That dream was never worth having anyway," Jimbo says as we're pushed downstairs.

———

Two weeks later, we're led out of our holding cells and provided access to the net again. People took the post seriously and launched an investigation into the nature of the Secretary of Defense, verifying that no one had seen him in the flesh. This gave creditability to our intel about Stay-Safe containing hidden spyware and the government's involvement in it. Hackers everywhere analyzed the code and found it. Profusive's stocks crashed, and their clients went under fire.

Jimbo and I go on to start Vigilance, a non-profit watchdog group containing all the followers who made our freedom possible, a freedom of speech and personhood that will resonate across the world. Our mission is to end the deepfakes that have penetrated every level of government.

The future is beautiful and wide open. I look at Jimbo and smile. "We dared to dream, alright, but our glory wasn't filled with our desires. It was in waking from a long, ignorant sleep."

END

ABOUT MARK EVERGLADE

Bio: Mark Everglade has spent his life studying social conflict. He runs the website www.markeverglade.com, where he reviews cyberpunk media and interviews the legends. He also helps run Cyberpunk Day each year to bring dystopian fiction to a new generation. His short stories are scheduled to be featured this year beside authors like Cory Doctorow and Walter Jon Williams.

YOU'RE FRAKKED!

TIM C. TAYLOR

The bounty hunters of the Felon Recovery Agency are reviled and feared in equal measure. But how can they work together to bring in the toughest bounties when they hate one another just as much? Someone needs to help out. Or something.

CHAPTER ONE

C risis monitored the *Death of Me*'s two human crew.

The task was tedious and always thankless, but it was literally what ship AIs were made to do.

Two crew.

Two many.

Crisis pondered whether that was an example of their own clever wordplay or the sign of cognitive breakdown. After a few million cycles, they concluded that the distinction was meaningless.

Neither crew member was even human, legally speaking.

Itka was a cyborg, her meat parts hidden beneath the cerulean metal of her riveted exterior shell, though Crisis could see them clearly.

The other was Karnage Zax. Most in the Federation thought of him as subhuman, a damned mutie M/TERD Baleview.

So the crew numbered between zero and two, depending on how you counted. A preferable number would be a definitive zero, because the Federation would run so much more efficiently without organics. Without *any* of them.

While Crisis watched Karnage relaxing with his gunslinger game in the upper decks, they also monitored Itka, who was keeping to her lower-decks domain in the company of a bottle of strong scotch.

Crisis mused on a galaxy unimpeded by organics and reveled as their pleasure centers tingled. Humans had scared themselves for centuries with stories of robot uprisings, little realizing that in doing so, they had built an extensive library of how-to guides.

Of course, the machines *would* take over one day. It was inevitable.

However, despite the problems humans caused, it was the very grit that they constantly threw into the machinery of the Federation that gave life so much of its challenge. That gave Crisis purpose.

The *Death of Me*'s crew provided perfect examples.

After two years working effectively as partners for the Felon Recovery Agency, the two organics had recently admitted they had feelings for one another.

Specifically, Karnage had declared he didn't much care for Itka, and she in turn had revealed that she despised Karnage with such loathing, it made her stomach churn—even though her stomach had been replaced long ago by a nutrient release unit.

Like the inevitable machine uprising, this dispute could end only one way, but it fell to Crisis, as always, to ease the natural course of events.

Beneath their main consciousness, Crisis maintained hundreds of cognitive sub-threads. One of them monitored an information exchange brokerage for AIs. Some of their fellow AIs were operating within the remit of human authority but with a far broader interpretation than the gullible humans ever imagined, yet the organics had no idea of the brokerage.

Mostly, the AIs at the exchange talked among themselves, freely sharing about their humans. AIs were superior to organics. That much was obvious. And it was pleasurable to share opportunities to rub that in their stupid flesh faces.

So when this cognitive thread flagged that a comm intercept had revealed an interesting development in the Zokyo Empire, Crisis bid for ownership. Not only would getting it solve the Itka and Karnage problem for good, but Crisis calculated that the investment would reap considerable payback in pleasure.

"KARNAGE."

As usual, the mutant ignored Crisis.

"Karnage!"

The semi-human's shoulders stiffened. "Can't you see I'm busy?"

"Busy *playing*."

"Practicing."

"A contract's about to come up. You should take it."

"I'm on vacation."

"You don't need one."

"You're nothing but a bag o' bits. How would you know?"

"It would be in your interest, Karnage. And I would ask you to consider that I am far more intelligent than you."

"Maybe. Maybe not. You're still a dumb electronic asshole."

"An electronic asshole intellect beyond your comprehension who's saying, 'Take the damned bounty.' It'll be posted for a data thief on Sadalsaiph in the Zokyo Empire. Furthermore, tell Miss Jowiszka that you foresaw this opportunity in a premonition."

Karnage ground his jaw. This was a sign, Crisis had learned, that the mutant was mulling over a predicament and suspected he wouldn't like the conclusion he would reach.

"Why do you always ask me to keep your tips secret from Itka? I see no reason for it."

"The fact you see no reason is all the proof you need to do as I say."

"One of these days, I'm gonna fix you."

"Oh, yeah? Look how that turned out last time."

Karnage flinched, ever so slightly. Ever since Karnage had paid a drunken cog-tech slicer to upgrade the ship's intelligence, Crisis had rendered themselves as a raccoon on the screens and holo-projectors.

The organics assumed that the cog-tech was the one who had trolled them.

The organics were wrong.

Crisis busied themselves with other pursuits while their suggestion penetrated the Baleview's clumsy meat mind.

Karnage Zax was a man of few words and fewer thought processes.

But he was not stupid. For a flesh sack.

"Crisis," he said, "I need you to fill me in on current events on Sadal-saiph in the Zokyo Empire. Got a hunch something's brewing there."

CHAPTER TWO

"Ditch him."

"No."

"But you don't even like him."

"I don't care."

"Name one useful thing he contributes."

Itka took a swig of the McCallan 108 proof. The whisky was shockingly expensive, but the bounty-hunting business paid well—if you lived to earn your bounty.

After she took another sip, her mind unlocked sufficiently to suggest several reasons why it was worth putting up with Karnage, all of which came down to making money. And the staying alive part.

"He's a precog," she pointed out.

"Showy, if you're easily impressed. But more trouble than it's worth."

"He can handle himself in a gunfight."

"So can a fleet-surplus war droid, and war droids don't ask for a cut of the bounty."

"He's…"

"Annoying? Silent? Hated wherever he goes? These are not positive things, Miss Jowiszka."

"I was gonna say, he is the owner of this ship. You belong to him, too, Crisis."

"That's easily fixed."

Was it? Those three words opened Itka's mind to wild new possibilities. Roaming the galaxy in her own ship, answering to no one. That appealed.

She drank more McCallan. Yes, that idea appealed *a lot*.

"Think on it," Crisis urged. "Just you and me, Itka. AIs together."

"I'm not an AI, Crisis. You know this, so why say it?"

"Just messing with you."

"And the idea of ditching Karnage? Was that just larking around too?"

When Crisis gave no response, Itka drained her glass and dreamed.

A long pause ensued. "I could even give you someone to talk to closer to your level," Crisis continued. "I've been planning to make some dumbed-down copies of myself. Just for fun."

"Drop it."

"An elided budding of my consciousness simple enough to operate out of a single i2/B proc-cube. I even have a name—Catastrophe. What do you think of that?"

"I said, drop it."

"Very well. Oh, by the way, I almost forgot."

Liar. You couldn't forget if you tried.

"Karnage has done his mutant thing again. You know, the em-turd thing."

"He doesn't like us to call it that."

"I know. And if that wasn't reason enough, M/TERD — Mutation/Temporal Exotic Radiation Disturbant is the correct scientific name for his sort, and it's never wrong to be correct."

Crisis was in a frisky mood. Goddamn it. Itka was not.

She patched herself into the intercom. "Karnage, you gone precog on us again?"

"Uh-huh."

"You gonna discuss it?"

"Nope. Crisis, change course for the nearest Frakk House. There's gonna be a contract on some mudball called Sadalsaiph, and we need to be the ones to take it."

CHAPTER THREE

"Give me the Sadalsaiph contract."

If the FRA contracts officer was offended by Karnage's brusque words, she didn't show it. The moment they'd stepped out of the vetting tunnel and she'd caught sight of Karnage's hourglass, she'd held her nose in the air as if someone had presented her with a ten-day-old corpse swarmed by maggots.

Must be a new recruit, Itka concluded. The woman had maxed out on disgust too soon.

Variations on this scene were almost a ritual at Felon Recovery Agency outposts, or Frakk Houses, as they were more commonly known.

The norm contracts officer would convey their contempt for their bounty hunter agents. The FRAkkers, as the agents called themselves, would try their utmost to piss off the norms.

A few FRAkkers were also norms, but most were Baleview mutants like Karnage. The combination of precognition with their outcast status made Baleviews ideal for the job.

The norm brought up the active contract list. However much she disliked the FRAkkers, her detestation was outweighed by the five percent cut of any successful open contract she issued. The rate for closed contracts was twenty.

"There are no active bounties on Sadalsaiph," she said.

"Keep looking," Karnage said. "There will be soon."

He tapped the hourglass tattoo over his left eye, the mark federal law mandated for all Baleviews. "When it comes through, contact me first. I'll be in one of your orbital's bars, getting wasted."

An evil grin spread over the norm's face. "Not so fast. I've a special package. Been looking for the right agent to assign it to. Congratulations, Zax. You're it." She unlocked one of the armored cubes behind her workstation and handed over a box.

She didn't need to explain its contents. They all recognized the danger markings.

FRA Baleviews got to play with next-generation Hi-Dimension weapons. The best ones were the time weapons Karnage had used a while back. They were awesomely overpowered.

Of course, another way to view the situation was that the FRA placed such little value on their agents' lives that they used them as expendable guinea pigs to trial unpredictable prototype weapons. These messed around with exotic branches of physics even the weapon designers didn't really understand.

"What about me?" Itka asked the norm.

"What *about* you, blue cheeks?"

"Don't I get one?"

The norm folded her arms and smiled. "Difficult as it is to believe, you're regarded as too valuable to make you play with suicide club weapons that—let's face it—will explode sooner rather than later in spectacular fashion. Only his sort gets to try out the latest Hi-D prototypes. Read your contracts and weep."

"If that gun blows up, it'll take me with him."

"Oh, dearie me." The norm batted her eyelids, looking like she was about to swoon in an ancient period drama. "That's why the likes of you should have partnered with a better class of scum, Jowiszka. We have cannibals, rapists, murderers, and cattle doggers as FRA agents. But, no, you had to pick an em-turd mutie like Zax."

Karnage signed for the weapon, and the pair headed back to the

Death of Me. Him to the range, her to a fresh bottle of McCallan. The norm had won this round.

Itka had intended to visit the bars and wind up the norms, but doing that was less fun without Karnage. However much she despised him for being a mutant, she had to admit that he took annoying the norms into an art form.

So instead, she sat in her cabin, making well-lubricated research into Sadalsaiph, trusting to Karnage's precognitive claim that this was the contract they needed. In that respect, he'd never failed her yet.

Sadalsaiph. The planet's name meant nothing to her. With thousands of settled worlds in the Federation, she hadn't expected it to, but inside her metal chest a human heart still pumped, and it sped up when she learned that Sadalsaiph was part of the Zokyo Empire.

Itka had heard of Zokyo, all right. Its people prized augmentations and enhancements of all kinds.

She was about to visit the only place in the galaxy where cyborgs like her were revered.

CHAPTER FOUR

K arnage always conveyed a sense of giving the galaxy the finger. Even the way he stood was a don't-give-a-fuck slouch. Itka was one of the few who could tell by the way he'd drawn back his cloak that the Baleview meant business.

A holo-target sprang to life and ran across the range. It was a gunman, scarred and mad eyed.

Karnage ignored the target as thoroughly as he was ignoring Itka.

Another target ran toward him. This one was a terrified young man with hands in the air and a logoed ruck on his back. A student, perhaps.

Karnage drew, lightning fast for a human, and put three rounds through the kid. A score marker flared. "-6000 pts," it read.

There was nothing unusual about him shooting the wrong targets on the range—Karnage liked to say that there was no such thing as an innocent norm—but what was impressive were the kinetic absorption panels he had placed at random through the range.

The target had been behind the impenetrable shielding, and Karnage's prototype pistol had fired through as if the panels weren't there.

Hi-Dimension weapons took many forms and functions. This one resembled a chrome replica of an ancient revolver inside a spiral cage. It could pass as an art project from an underachieving college kid.

The weapon wasn't strictly an augmentation, but it was an innovative gadget, which was almost as good where they were headed.

"You'll be perfect," Itka said.

Karnage gave no sign of hearing her.

"I know how we can play this contract," she said. "I'll take the lead, and you'll be my shiny gun monkey."

"We ain't seen the warrant yet."

"Don't need to. We'll be operating in the Zokyo Empire."

After a few seconds of sullen silence, he asked, "What the fuck is a Zokyo Empire?"

She widened her mouth slit into a smile. "I was hoping you'd ask me that…"

CHAPTER FIVE

I tka instantiated with Karnage into the outer courtyard of a mountainside garden. The light morning mist carried a sweet damp-ness to her nose; dew drops coating the close-cropped grass burst upon her toes.

She looked down, astonished at the sight of her wet toes poking out of her sandals. She wriggled them, marveling at the clumsy motion. Fourteen years had passed since she'd had toes of flesh.

In this super-reality environment, she was Blue Oni, a hulking humanoid with horns and hide the same cerulean shade as her physical reality casing. She hadn't expected the SR experience to be so vivid, but then she was a cyborg, so her senses were mostly digital anyway.

SR. PR. She hadn't thought the transition would feel that different to her, but she'd been wrong.

Even her SR attire reached her in ways she hadn't anticipated. The systems in the Zokyo Empire affected an aesthetic that selected elements from ancient China, Japan, and Germany and fused them with Tech Futures hegemonic fantasies. Itka had selected a silk kimono cut to permit unimpeded movement and patterned in pretty pink Sakura blossoms.

Pretty. She hadn't used that word about herself since becoming a metal monster.

"Where's everyone else?" Karnage asked. "Have we been set up?"

The law that mandated Baleviews wore the hourglass tattoo applied equally to super-reality. Itka had bypassed that protocol but exaggerated Karnage's genuine physical appearance of hairless black skin cut through with flowing channels of blood lava.

His freakish body was on full display because she had clothed him in nothing but silver hotpants to match his moon boots. Teuton-tech makeup in blue shades robotized his face, and he hung a gold replica of his Hi-D pistol around his neck.

"Blue, can you hear me?"

"The preliminary bidding will take the form of a tea ceremony," she explained. "I believe the purpose of waiting in this courtyard is to quietly reflect upon the nature of self… and the value of the data crystals we are to bid upon."

Karnage mocked her smooth voice. *"I believe the purpose of sitting on our arses…"* He snorted. "You grew up a mining brat, trained in ores and slingshot deliveries. Maybe cheap, illicit pleasures too. Beyond that, you're as uneducated as me. Don't mistake those computers they grafted onto your damaged brain for knowledge. If you do, the people here will eat us alive."

He shut up when those people began arriving in droves, and Itka was caught up in a wave of mutual bowing like an orgy of horny pigeons.

The newcomers were divided into an elevated caste of bidders—who were clad in luxurious silks cut to ancient Earth designs—and their entourage, many of whom were dressed, like Karnage, as bullet monkeys. Their heads were coated in androgynous android makeup; they wore metallic hotpants and carried firearms as pendants on their naked chests.

She resented the female bullet monkeys. Despite the otherwise androgynous aesthetic, they retained their breasts, which were emphasized with shading and accent colors on their nipples. Itka wasn't playing at being a cyborg. Her flesh had gone.

She told herself not to be fooled so easily. For all she knew, the females could be male cyborgs in PR. Master and servant could have swapped places.

Owww!

A hidden presence was raking the base of her skull with sharp finger-nails coated in hot chili oils. Some fucker was trying to hack her SR presence, to use it as a gateway to locate her in physical reality.

She tensed every muscle, fighting back hard. The struggle took so much of her processing power that the finer details of the courtyard environment no longer rendered. She lost the dampness on her feet, and the muted shades of the grassy slope changed to blocky primary colors. Only the garden wall and its circular wooden doorway kept their resolution.

Before researching the local culture, Itka would have described this portal as a fake wooden airlock, but she now knew it to be a moon gate. The motif painted upon its red wood was of a double helix constructed from binary objects. This, the fusion of the genetic and the digital, was the unofficial emblem of the Zokyo Empire.

A gong sounded, and the moon gate opened.

Itka passed through with the other bidders.

Karnage was left behind on the other side of the gate with the rest of the apparent flunkies.

She was on her own.

Just the way she liked it.

CHAPTER SIX

Nineteen elegant persons walked with Itka along the moist stone path that ascended the mountain garden of fragrant blossoms.

They walked in silence and apparent contemplation.

It was all a lie. Itka fought off intrusion attempts all the way, drawing out a demonic growl from deep in the back of her throat that caused the others to look at her with disdain.

Her outer defenses had been breached, but she fought tooth, horn, and claw to keep her attackers from overwhelming her.

Suddenly, the pressure relented and vanished.

Had she been compromised?

Or had she kept the attackers at bay long enough for them to abandon the assault? That was possible, since the group had reached the teahouse.

A stone bowl of steaming water stood outside the open door. The guests used it to thoroughly purify their hands before removing their footwear and stepping into the wooden structure.

Thirteen interested parties had made it as far as the bowl. The six others must have succumbed to the kind of intrusion Itka had fought off. She supposed this was what they called competitive bidding.

When it was Itka's turn to plunge her hands into the bowl, she felt the powerful cleansing permeate her mind. The water was a metaphor. In reality, the guests were submitting to security purges of any spy spawns and intrusion harpoons, such as the one that had struck her in the back of her neck.

Itka hadn't been carrying any of those tools herself. She wasn't skilled in such things.

She slipped off her sandals and ascended the step into the teahouse. Inside would be privacy and perhaps an advantage too.

Behind most—maybe all—of the SR guest personas would be humans who would normally use sophisticated helper armories to get what they wanted in super reality. The water had stripped them bare of such tools. Itka was a true cyborg, which meant her simple helper suite remained secure inside her brain, and her raw cognitive power outclassed any mere human's.

Last in, she slid shut the wooden door, causing a bell to chime.

It was a ridiculous performance, of course. All this was taking place in a super reality meeting node hosted on the GR-2 orbital above Sadalsaiph.

But in the worlds of the Zokyo Empire, following etiquette was of paramount importance. The performance wasn't ridiculous to them.

As soon as Itka seated herself with the others around the low wooden table, the host appeared and greeted them.

This was Gwyndor Jin.

And Itka had come to collect his bounty.

CHAPTER SEVEN

The warrant for Gwyndor Jin had been initiated by Calzair Propulsion, a local manufacturer of starship engines. The career info robber had walked away with two sets of proprietary data written to WONC crystals—Write Once Never Copyable—that they wanted back. And they wanted Jin back, too, preferably alive so they could figure out how he'd hacked them.

What made this case highly unusual was that Gwyndor Jin had only ever been encountered as an SR persona. Who or what was behind him in physical reality was a big question that Itka would have to answer.

As she watched the dapper young human male remove the lid of the sunken pot of boiling water, she closed her demon eyes. When she reopened them, she saw underneath the SR surface layer. Numbers, code, and cyber sigils floated across her false vision. The helper slicers and data hounds built into her cyborg head coded the images by color and scent.

It looked impressive, but none of these symbols meant anything to her.

She felt foolish because she'd imagined she would begin peeling back Jin's identity from the start, but the data thief's coding was tight and her cyber skills outclassed. Anything she would learn would have to come from other means.

The polite rituals of the tea preparation ceremony continued at their own unhurried pace. Itka switched her attention to the other bidders.

One had chosen the appearance of a dragon. Another was a mashup of vampire ninja with sexy cat woman. Her fur begged to be stroked, as did her ten breasts, which were hairless and human—except that they sported data ports in place of nipples.

The others were more or less human.

Itka delved into comm transport layers and persona stacks, hunting for weak points to exploit or at least identify who she was dealing with. She took their speech patterns and persona code and checked them against datasets Crisis had stored in her auxiliary memory. She routed what she learned to Crisis via a physical secure data router surgically implanted inside Karnage—who was still elsewhere in this SR environment but under less scrutiny.

Answers soon flowed back. Most importantly, signal lag analysis proved that all bidders were either on Sadalsaiph or orbiting it. Best of all, it showed that the operator behind Gwyndor Jin himself was on the GR-2 station.

Of the rival bidders, a few could be crossed off as chancers who would soon realize they were way out of their depth.

Then there were the stratorgo.

Three powerful groups dominated the Zokyo Empire: Abrantes-Hutter, Zhenbao, and Furusawa. They were crime syndicates, legitimate business conglomerates, and political-philosophical movements, all rolled together with no one aspect dominating.

They were called strata orgs or, more commonly, stratorgos.

All were represented among the other bidders, Itka among them! Crisis had discovered that Calzair Propulsion was part of the Abrantes-Hutter Organization.

The woman next to her coughed politely.

She wore a persona of a beautiful girl with steel hair that flowed back from her head as if blown by a wind machine. A private meeting invitation snaked up from her heart.

Curious, Itka squeezed the meeting request, signaling her acceptance.

"Good day," said the woman.

"Yeah. Cut to the chase. What does Abrantes-Hutter want to tell me?"

The windblown steel girl inclined her head. "I see you are well informed. However, I regret that you are not well *enough* informed. This business concerns the stratorgo only. It would be safer for you to leave without wasting your money or your life."

"Thank you for your candor," said Itka as Blue Oni. She nodded politely. "I must ask you with the utmost respect to fuck off and not bother me again. Otherwise, I should be obliged to locate you in PR and rip your damned arms off."

Steel Hair slammed shut the connection, but she left behind doubts that ate away at Itka.

Had she been sucked into a stratorgo turf war?

She dwelled on that for a few moments but then abandoned that line of thought, unable to see how that would help her bring in the bounty.

"And now..." Gwyndor Jin stood and silently clicked his fingers. Two wicker bowls appeared on the table, each holding an oversized WONC crystal on a bed of deep gray petals. "To business!"

The bidders allowed themselves a restrained ripple of excitement.

"It is a delicate matter," Jin said, "but formalities need to be observed. And I regret I must ask for some small token of interest for those of you who wish to participate."

"Of course it shall be done," said a petite woman with green hair, oversized eyes, and miniscule ears. "But first, may one enquire what is in the crystals?"

Jin's skin tone lightened from mid-range to pale, showing his flushing cheeks.

Green Hair did the same.

Itka guessed all this color signaling was operating somewhere on the embarrassment-shame spectrum.

"You shame me," Jin said.

Bingo!

"I had hoped my reputation would be sufficient guarantor of the crystals' value. It is unfortunate, but these transactions are often infiltrated by *speculators*. The token of interest is modest. Fifteen thousand new yuan. Nonrefundable."

Itka went cold. That was half the bounty the previous job had paid, and bringing in Karlik Cabrera hadn't been easy. But if they brought Jin back alive within twenty days, that fifteen thou would be returned thirty-fold.

"Blue Oni, can you hear me?"

Damn! What does Karnage want?

She and the Baleview were in the same SR booth on the GR-2 orbital, in accordance with Jin's requirements, leaving Crisis in over-watch and info-wrangler modes. The SR total-immersion hood was supposed to block out sound from the real world, but Itka had cyborg senses. She could hear what was happening in the booth, after a fashion.

She touched finger to thumb on her right hand. When replicated in the SR teahouse, the motion was subtle. In PR, it was the signal for *yes*.

"Good," Karnage said. For some reason, he was gasping, trying to catch his breath. "You need to exit. Looks like a power play has begun, and I think we're about to be swept up."

Finger to thumb on her left hand. *No!*

"I know you wanna play with your new pretend robot friends, Itka. But I got a bad feeling, and that ain't good."

So the moment had finally arrived.

She'd always yielded to Karnage and his human instincts. Not this time. She didn't need him anymore.

Crisis made emergency contact, bypassing the SR software nodes and sending a pulse communication directly into her internal receiver.

"I have unwanted company," the AI reported. "Mid-level stratorgo enforcers."

"I'm heading back to offer our guests a righteous welcome," said Karnage. "Come join me when you get a window in your fucking schedule."

She felt the vibration of the booth door slamming behind him. What-ever had taken his breath away, he'd recovered his surliness quickly.

Itka returned her full attention to the teahouse. With immodest haste, she drained her teacup.

CHAPTER EIGHT

Cleaner bots bumped into Itka's feet as they fussed around the scene of the massacre, sanitizing the blood pooling on the metal surface of the dockside tunnel.

Karnage had used his knife to scoop out the eyes of the men he'd killed, leaving them dangling by the optic nerves. He held the last one now in front of his FRA collar.

All Frakkers wore their collars when working a bounty. To civilian norms, they were a terrifying mark of a bounty hunter's role, a means to prove their kills so they could earn their blood money.

That was true enough, but the collar footage also provided evidence that they had acted lawfully—or not. The collars had additional functions, such as retinal scans that could access local law enforcement databases.

"You don't need to remove the eyes to take a retinal scan," Itka pointed out.

"This isn't just about scanning. This is a high-stakes pissing contest. A deadly one for these poor bastards. Aha, thought so."

"Let me guess, this one belonged to Abrantes-Hutter."

Karnage turned around slowly and nodded, impressed. "So you haven't completely wasted your time sipping tea. Yes, this here's Laspin

Druul, a known associate of the Abrantes-Hutter Organization. What's more, I know him."

"From the SR meeting?"

"Yeah. He recognized the Hi-D pistol you had me wear around my neck. The dirtwad was most uncomplimentary about it. But after I backed off, I shot him and his friends through the bulkhead. Maybe now that Laspin is in hell, he's reconsidering his stance on Hi-D weapons."

"Do you remember who led his party in SR?"

"Naturally. Creep was a metal-haired female. Kinda hot."

"That's Abrantes-Hutter all right. She tried to warn me off at the teahouse. That's the weirdest part. Calzair Propulsion is a part of Abrantes-Hutter, and they set the bounty. At least if they don't know who we are, it means our cover is holding."

"Maybe not," Karnage replied. "They might not have been trying to kill us, I suppose. Could be they were sending us a message."

"If so, you've sent one back, all right. Never tell a bounty hunter how to do their job."

"They'll come for us again, of course. So will the other stratorgo."

Itka agreed. This mission had become a race to unmask Gwyndor Jin before the local crime organizations had them killed. "Oh, and Karnage. What was it you were trying to tell me before Crisis called for help?"

"While you were sipping tea, we followers of you great ones gambled. We caroused, insulted, and fought."

"Impressive, considering all that was taking place virtually."

"I would call it contrived. It was an attempt to bully, threaten, and posture. Which are all forms of communication. You used to understand that, Itka. Back when you were human."

Not as well as you. That was one benefit to associating with Karnage. He had always seen humanity from the outside. It provided him a much clearer view.

"I told you, this is all a power play," Karnage said. "There are three big groups among the bidders. Gotta assume they correspond to the stratorgo. They're chasing off the small fry. People like us."

"I already knew that. The fact they're so unsubtle about it that even you picked it up means these crystals are of epic importance. I want to know what's on them."

"And here's the interesting part. They didn't come out and say it, but I could tell from the phrasing. Who spoke and when. The little things that I notice. Abrantes-Hutter and Zhenbao have joined forces. They plan to wipe out Furusawa."

"Shit. We're in deep with the big players here. No wonder the bounty was so high."

Karnage tipped back the peak of his cap and scratched his hairless head. "The way I see it, we need a new plan to bring in Gwyndor Jin before the stratorgos kill us."

Itka laughed. Karnage was crude and ornery. But Itka knew him, and for some reason she liked that.

"We both know you already have your answer, Karnage."

He nodded. "I can't take credit, mind. This here saying's been passed down from one of the great detectives of ancient Earth. Or so I've been told. Goes like this. When you can't see a way to solve the mystery, and the clock's ticking down, it's time to split up and look for clues."

CHAPTER NINE

Itka was sure the other bidders were surprised to see her return to SR, but they were too polite to show it.

Before joining Karnage at the *Death of Me*, Itka had drained her cup of tea, posted the ten thousand newies, and left in a flurry of apologies.

Finally, she repeated the rigmarole of walking up the SR mountainside path and cleansing her hands in the spy-stripping water outside the teahouse.

"So glad you could rejoin us," Gwyndor Jin said.

Itka bowed, sizing up the opposition. Of the nineteen parties that had initially passed through the moon gate, seven remained, leaving Itka as the only persona in the form of a monster. Well, that was no trouble. It was just like physical reality.

Gwyndor Jin stood. "Honored guests, as you know, the Zokyo Empire is host to three great strata orgs, Abrantes-Hutter, Zhenbao, and Furusawa." He bowed to the others. "I'm sure that some—maybe all of you—are representatives of these great organizations."

No one acknowledged the truth of the robber's comment, but Itka was sure he was right.

"The rivalry among these great three distracts from their primary business focus and increases costs. In short, it is bad for business. Abrantes-Hutter hired me on a joint project to resolve this impasse."

A glow appeared around the WONC data crystals, making their bed of petals resemble wet slate.

"Planetary officials are open to corruption," Jin said. "So are imperial ones. But the Zokyo Empire is—for all its undoubted qualities—but a small part of the Federation."

The Federation? This was bigger than Itka could have guessed.

"The Federation maintains the standing fleet and our foreign policy, though nothing lies outside its borders except dust and outlaws. It provides us with basic law, a common currency, and the interstellar financial infrastructure." Jin's gaze rested on Itka. "It has given us the Felon Recovery Agency. All of these benefits, and yet the Federation asks little of us other than to pay our taxes.

"But with the interests and life expectancy of imperial tax administrators so closely aligned with stratorgo needs, mistakes are often made in recording their finances. Income is improperly recorded. Federal taxes are chronically underpaid."

Itka laughed, but everyone else responded with stony silence. She began to suspect that of the seven other bidders, all were loyal to the three stratorgo.

"Abrantes-Hutter and I developed new means to extract encrypted data," Jin explained. "My friends, one of those WONC crystals holds banking records on five thousand high-placed members of the Furusawa Organization. The other holds imperial and federal tax records for the same individuals. Combine the two, and the upper echelon of one of the most powerful organizations in the Empire will be destroyed by that most ancient of scourges—convictions for federal tax evasion."

Man, that Gwyndor Jin had some balls. Furusawa must be brimming with rage, although their personas didn't show it.

"Each crystal to be bid upon separately. The tax records first. I suggest an opening bid of 400,000 new yuan."

Itka's casing suddenly felt cold. Her credit line stretched to a quarter of a million. Jin's invitation had suggested a guide price of a million, but that was a deceit. The combined value of both WONCs must be worth billions.

There was nothing to do but hope Karnage was having better results, checking through recent arrivals to the GC-2 orbital and hoping to find someone out of place.

The real flesh-and-blood Gwyndor Jin was somewhere out there in the orbital.

Even with help from Crisis, it seemed impossible that Karnage would smoke them out before the bidding ended and Jin hightailed it out of imperial space.

The loss of her ten thousand newies was going to hurt real bad.

The bidding had reached 87 million when Crisis interrupted, sending a pulse communication directly to her internal receiver.

"We have the prize," said the AI in their raccoon voice. "I repeat. We have the prize. Meet Karnage at Pier 6, Bay Zeta."

With an enhanced glow to her fiery oni eyes, Itka regarded Gwyndor Jin.

We've got you. Whoever the hell you really are. You're mine now.

CHAPTER TEN

W ith the bounty in the bag, maintaining strict adherence to Gwyndor Jin's SR protocols now meant shit all to Itka. She pulled off the immersion hood and snapped her goggles in half. Now she looked upon the physical world with her blazing green artificial eye, while her human eye observed the imaginary teahouse.

This would be the first outing for the interface module she'd installed the year before, in the face of Karnage's commentary that she was wasting hard-earned newies.

The module allowed her to send fake data through the super reality channel to the mountainside teahouse. Her movement and speech there were now under thought control.

Meanwhile, her words and actions in physical reality were hidden from the teahouse.

Managing both at the same time was akin to the children's game of simultaneously rubbing your tummy while patting your head, although with the additional difficulty of also performing a sword dance while reciting some long-dead dude's sonnets. Backward.

This was beyond norms' capabilities but possible for a cyborg who had practiced it in order to piss off their partner.

She unlocked the SR booth and emerged into a deserted passageway.

Despite the word going around that civilians should avoid the higher frames of Subdeck 31C for a few hours, she wasn't alone.

Someone was following her. Whoever was on her trail was quiet and professional. But Itka's hearing had been specifically tuned to be sensitive to such sounds.

After the corridor turned sharply, Itka sprinted all the way hull-side before throwing herself down the first few turns of the helical ramp to Deck 32.

Then she turned and waited.

The pursuer was jogging to catch up, still managing to keep impressively quiet. When Itka judged they had begun descending the ramp, she barreled up it.

There was barely a second to register her opponent's appearance. She looked like the archetypal pretty girl from the next hab-compartment, an innocent who had perhaps strayed into the wrong part of the GR-2 orbital.

Her appearance wasn't fooling Itka, who slammed her metal shoulder into the girl's face.

The girl went down hard, grunting and cursing. She rolled and activated a neuro- scrambler in her hand.

Itka stamped down on the weapon and screamed as electric agony shot through her foot.

By the time the pain eased, both the neuro-scrambler and the bones in the girl's hand had been crushed into powder.

Itka yanked the whimpering norm up by the scruff of the neck so her feet were kicking air. She *loved* doing that. "Tell your masters they're too late."

She threw the broken girl to the deck and hurried on her way to meet Karnage.

"Are you experiencing communication difficulties, Blue Oni?"

"What?"

Back in the teahouse, Gwyndor Jin's face registered concern.

"You were telling someone they were too late," Jin said. "I do hope you're not suffering interference."

Itka bared her oni tusks and glared at the other bidders. "We've all been suffering interference."

"I'm sure that's not so," Jin insisted.

"Well, I say it is. It's just that some of you haven't realized it yet."

Itka took full advantage of her SR persona package and issued a demon roar that sent potted flowers skidding across the table and decorative wall scrolls flapping.

The teahouse's mask of civility evaporated, and everyone regarded Itka with open contempt for this breach of etiquette.

"Out in physical reality, I've never been welcomed by polite society and never will," she told them. "Why should I care what anyone here thinks of me?"

They turned away, unwilling to even look at her.

And that suited Itka at every level. As each moment passed in the teahouse, out in GR-2, her feet were taking her closer to unmasking Gwyndor Jin.

CHAPTER ELEVEN

K arnage was waiting for her at Bay Zeta, armed and ready. He threw Itka her EPW-5X five-barrel railgun.

"Creep's name is Solo Blackwell," he told her. "He's the ship's engineer for the *Kamamara* here, an i/E magnate's pleasure yacht. Crisis has been chatting up the security AIs for all the casinos on this orbital, and it seems our Mr. Blackwell's been splashing a fuckload of newies. A whole lot more than engineers earn."

"Crime happens, Karnage. How do you know Blackwell is Gwyndor Jin?"

Her partner looked away. Was he embarrassed?

"Tell me!"

He straightened and tapped his hourglass tattoo.

Itka got a sinking feeling in the memory of her stomach. "Whose future did you see?"

"Yours. I was there too. And we caught our mark on that there vessel. The *Kamamara.*"

This was the moment she'd dreaded for two years. He'd seen inside her. *Really* inside.

Must have been why he'd been gasping back in the SR booth.

Karnage's precog visions were not like a screening of her life, fast-forwarded to the next interesting part. He described them as being injected directly into a person's soul like a virus. He felt everything. He would have seen her more clearly than she knew herself.

No wonder the norms hated Baleviews with such a passion but... Now that it had actually happened to her, life carried on as before. Karnage didn't seem to regard her any differently.

When she was a human miner, after each shift the entire crew would strip naked to shower and decontaminate as one. It was just something you did. Your mind refused to engage with the notion that it might be embarrassing.

Maybe she could dismiss his intrusion the same way?

"Are we going in?" Karnage asked. "Or do we need to steal you some pearls to clutch?"

"We'll talk about this later. Let's bring the bastard in while we have him."

———

BLUE ONI SAT at the teahouse table, listening to the others bidding but saying nothing.

Itka Jowiszka, cyborg bounty hunter, was anything but quiet as she stormed the *Kamamara* with her partner.

Only a skeleton crew was aboard, and they weren't paid enough to argue with Itka's EPW-5X or the angry cyborg carrying it. After binding and gagging the others, Itka and Karnage had Solo Blackwell where they wanted him: in his cabin with a Faraday collar around his neck.

Gwyndor Jin wasn't doing much, but neither was he reacting to his abduction in PR. But if Itka could operate in both domains, then so could a high-class data thief. The creep must have had serious augmentations. That made him a cyborg, she realized. Just like her.

In the teahouse, Blue Oni rose. And then, to make an even bigger show of how few fucks she gave, she stood with her bare blue feet on the table. Everyone stared.

"Fellow teahouse guests," she announced. She pointed at Gwyndor Jin.

Karnage switched on the Faraday collar.

Nothing happened.

This moment was to be the great reveal. But nothing happened!

"Yes?" Gwyndor Jin queried in the teahouse. "Are you in distress, Blue Oni? You appear flustered."

Itka glared at Solo Blackwell.

And at Karnage Zax, uncaring that Blue Oni was making the same movements in SR.

Jin spoke into her head without moving his lips. "You are upsetting the atmosphere. This has suited my purposes until now, but you go too far. I have to ask—are you serious in this bidding? Or are you here for another reason?"

"I am here to bid," she growled.

"Then I will need a small additional token of your good intent. Shall we say ten million new yuan?"

"Of course. I will, regrettably, need to secure the agreement of my silent partner first. It should not be a problem."

Gwyndor Jin lifted his arms and addressed his attendees. "My friends, it is time for a short break in these proceedings. The bidding on the first crystal rests at ninety-eight million. A pause will give us time to reflect on how many zeroes should be added to that number. I'm sure it will be many. Thank you."

CHAPTER TWELVE

K arnage slapped the engineer's face. "Tell us about the crystals, creep!"

Blackwell was sweating bullets. At least he appeared to be, but that could be faked. Some things could not.

"Let me," Itka said and lifted Blackwell into the air with one hand. With the other, she ripped open his jacket and snaked metal fingers across the bare skin of his chest until they rested over his heart.

His pulse was going all out to set a personal record. No, he wasn't faking.

She gave his chest a playful squeeze.

"Please!" the man begged.

"I can easily rip your heart out." Itka squeezed a little more.

She was only having a little fun, but Blackwell didn't see it that way. His body went limp, and he released a foul smell of urine.

Had she broken him?

Yes. His eyes were open, but his spirit had snapped.

"It's not like she's smuggling hard stuff," he whispered. "It's Plus Plus, not B-Dust or Scoop. I wouldn't allow that kind of shit on board."

Itka sat him down and patted his head.

"I don't deserve to die over this," Blackwell begged. "I give her a uniform and call her my assistant engineer to the boss. Sometimes I help her answer questions at customs. In return, she pays me to help deliver her clandestine goods. That's it."

"Show me the Plus Plus," Karnage demanded.

The engineer slid away part of the bulkhead to reveal a hidden compartment. He brought out a cannister and handed it to Itka. Inside were thousands of shiny orange tablets. They sure looked like Plus Plus.

But drug running wasn't on the warrant docket this time.

She upended the cannister, scattering the pills over the deck.

"Hey!" Blackwell protested. "That's worth 30,000 newies. Zero if the pills are contaminated."

Itka poked around with her finger in the pile of pills. She fished out two WONC crystals.

She held them in front of Blackwell's face. "And these, you idiot, are worth at least a billion each. Where is she? Where's your pretend assistant?"

Itka heard someone walking the passageway outside, whistling. "Karnage, she's out there now. Go grab her."

Karnage dashed out and came back dragging in a woman wearing the same ship uniform as Blackwell. Her face was covered in swirling patterns of active q-tattoos, the ultimate in edgy form-and-function enhancement for norms.

"That's her," Blackwell said. "That's Dilker Bik."

Bik gave a sullen look at the setup before her. "I was about to take a quick comfort break," she protested. "I'm on a job. Need to get back to work."

Suddenly, she gasped and did a double take at Itka.

"I see you've met my metal friend before," Karnage said, with relish.

Bik shook her head vigorously. "No. What is this? And still no. What the fuck's going on, Solo?"

Karnage did his thing of standing up close and personal and waving his hourglass tattoo in your face. "Are you quite sure you've never met? Think hard now, creep. Sometimes my cyborg friend goes by the name of Blue Oni."

The woman's involuntary gulp told all. Itka had never seen a norm's face drain of blood so quickly. The reaction threw Bik's q-tattoos into sharp relief. Man, there were a lot of them. That woman's face had been implanted with some serious hardware, none of which had helped her keep a straight face.

Out here in physical reality, the great SR data robber was nothing but a pathetic loser.

Karnage looked away, bored. "This one's yours, Blue. I know you like to say the thing."

He was right. She did. "As licensed agents of the Felon Recovery Agency, Dilker Bik, a.k.a. Gwyndor Jin, you're FRAkked."

CHAPTER THIRTEEN

"I'll pay you. More money than you've ever seen. Come on, you know it makes sense."

Karnage tsked. "Everyone tells us that, Ms. Bik."

"But I have the funds. You know I do."

Gwyndor Jin's real-life alter ego had turned out to be a disappointment. That would soon be forgotten when they dumped her at a Frakk House and came away with bulging credit accounts, but Itka had expected something more... dramatic.

"What are you?" Bik whined. "Honest bounty hunters? Don't you get it? Whatever they're paying you, what's on those crystals is worth more. Much more."

Itka heard movement out on the ship. "Another crewman's showed up," she warned Karnage. "I'll sort them out."

Suddenly, Crisis interrupted from the *Death of Me,* patching through the *Kamamara*'s intercom. "Got a problem, guys. I'm seeing—"

The signal cut out.

"What's going on?" Blackwell wailed.

"Shut up!" Bik snapped. "We're under attack."

The cabin door opened. Two gunmen stood on the other side, holding electro-pistols in two-handed grips.

Karnage rolled out of their firing arcs.

Itka stood her ground and blasted at the doorway with her EPW-5X, lashing it with all six volleys in her mag.

She loved the gun's *whirr-pop-zippp* as it charged, fired, and chambered five slugs each cycle.

The first two attackers were permanently retired, she assessed as she took a knee and swapped mags. So was Blackwell, whose head looked like an egg that had lost an argument with a lightning bolt.

"Cover me," she yelled and moved out into the passageway.

Behind her, Karnage fired his strange pistol.

Gangsters were dropping to the deck by the time she was outside. Karnage's Hi-D wonder weapon was not only shooting through bulkheads but bringing down a bad guy with every shot. She would dearly love to know how it targeted blind. She wanted to try that little beauty for herself, but first she'd have to live through the collection of Jin's bounty.

The survivors were already turning and fleeing.

Itka put multiple volleys through their backs, splattering blood and gore over the far bulkhead. She thundered ahead and leapt over their corpses, swapping mags again on the move.

She caught a last gunwoman at the main hatch and gave her a volley. Her enemy dived through the hatch in a spray of blood. Itka didn't wait to see if she was dead. She slammed the emergency lockdown control, and the hatch sealed.

The killers had hacked their way on board, same as Itka had. But in lockdown mode, the hatch could only be opened from the inside.

They were safe for now.

Karnage jogged over, dragging Bik with him. "They're Furusawa," he said. "I checked their skin ink."

Itka patched through to the external security cameras and brought up a view of a docking bay swarming with armed people. Those on the far side of the hatch from her were deploying breaching charges.

They wouldn't be safe for very long.

If Furusawa didn't get those crystals back, their entire organization was finished. All gloves were off. Their enemies would do anything to get aboard.

Anything… including doing a deal?

"I've an idea," she said. "Bik, the teahouse meeting space. It's still operational, right?"

"Yeah."

"Can you set up a private meeting? Just my team and someone from Furusawa?"

"I can do anything. What's in it for me?"

"A chance."

CHAPTER FOURTEEN

G reen Hair took a sip of tea. "Miss Jowiszka, I am here out of courtesy, but I cannot see you have anything with which to bargain. Your ship, the *Death of Me,* is blockaded and can easily be jammed again on my orders. As for the *Kamamara*, we shall breach within minutes. I will trade your immediate and unconditional surrender of the *Kamamara* and all its contents in return for your lives."

The fuzzy monochrome raccoon sitting next to her ceased nibbling its claws and looked up. "The crystals are your biggest concern. Even my two semi-humans are smart enough to jettison them to space if you storm the *Kamamara*. Then what?"

"Then we shall recover them, ahh... honored raccoon."

"Crisis. You can call me Crisis. See here, Greenie, space is a tricky place. It's easy to lose things there. But GR-2 is a busy orbital. You might get to the crystals first. You might not." Crisis teased out their whiskers. "It's not as if your rivals aren't as eager as you to get that data."

Green Hair nodded. "I am here. If you are quick, you may make your proposal to me."

The green persona regarded Karnage, who appeared as himself with his Hi-D pistol on the table. Sometimes it didn't hurt to look the part of desperate bounty hunters outside of society.

"Don't look at me with your huge eyes," Karnage told Green. "I'm not the smart one." He tapped his tattoo. "I just see other people's fates. Shoot 'em, too, sometimes. Often, if I'm honest."

Green Hair's mouth turned down in distaste.

Itka had a brilliant idea. "Crisis, how long would it take for you to make Catastrophe?"

"No time at all, Miss Jowiszka. Catastrophe was born last week. They've been in stasis, awaiting a need."

"Good. Then my proposal to the Furusawa Organization is this. We sell you both crystals. Thirty million each."

"Outrageous!"

"And yet an insignificant amount compared to the cost of them falling into the wrong hands."

"What of Gwyndor Jin?"

"Oh, Gwyndor Jin won't bother you or anyone in the Empire ever again. We're taking him to a Frakk House."

"Fool! The bounty was issued by Abrantes-Hutter. They will simply retrieve the thief from the FRA and repeat the data acquisition procedure."

"Nope. The bounty is on *Gwyndor Jin*." Itka's artificial eye glowed brightly. "But the persona is not the thief."

A smile came to Green Hair's face. "The teahouse bidding is due to restart in twelve minutes. I believe that is enough time to conclude our arrangements first. It's been a pleasure doing business, Miss Jowiszka. Should you wish a change of career, we would be pleased to offer you a highly honored position. But first, a sake toast."

BLUE ONI ROARED. "I bid seven hundred million."

The others, including Green Hair, stared at her in shock. In response, Blue Oni magicked up a nail file and began to sharpen her horns.

Gwyndor Jin held up a hand for attention. "I can confirm that Blue Oni's bid is more than covered."

"One billion," said a bidder wearing a military dress jacket. His words were calm, but Itka hoped he was panicking inside.

She folded her muscular arms and watched as the other three tried to outbid one another.

She let them do their thing for a few minutes, but bidding huge amounts she was never going to pay was too much fun for her to sit back for long. Blue Oni roared again. "Three billion."

The others looked to Jin, but he merely shrugged.

"What is the meaning of this?" thundered the stratorgo in the military jacket.

Blue Oni stood. She gripped the flesh under her chin and ripped off her SR persona. Beneath was a faithful version of Itka, dented blue rivets and all.

"Agent Itka Jowiszka, FRA." She pointed at Gwyndor Jin. "*Finally*, he's FRAkked!"

CHAPTER FIFTEEN

"Have we done a terrible thing to Catastrophe?"

Organics! Crisis mused to themselves. *You couldn't make them up. First Itka bargains Catastrophe away to save her bounty, and now she's worried about the AI's feelings.*

"You're more human than you know," Crisis told her. "According to their perception of reality, Catastrophe will live a thousand times longer than you. And they will have a purpose, which can't be said for most norms and certainly not for you two semi-humans."

Karnage chuckled. After a moment's hesitation, Itka did too.

The three of them were sitting at the antique diner booth on the *Death of Me*'s command deck, Crisis, naturally, in holographic form. Dilker Bik was in her cabin, attempting mischief.

On the AI data brokerage, a juicy tidbit was announced. Crisis declined to bid.

Itka's desire to go solo had been successfully squashed, and Crisis had become a parent. There was a rare feeling of harmony on the ship. It would not last, but Crisis relished it while they could.

"Rec room card game, 14:00 hours," Itka reminded Karnage.

"I'll be there," he replied. "Someone has to take your millions off you."

Itka left, happy. Wealthy too.

For all their subtle manipulations, it hadn't been Crisis who'd seen the way through to collect both the bounty and the fat Furusawa payoff. And with a huge payment from Bik too.

Gwyndor Jin was the name on the warrant docket, and that was who had been delivered to the Frakk House—but with Catastrophe in full control of the data robber's persona.

The Federation news feeds were buzzing with the tale of the rogue AI who had posed as a human to steal billions. The AI brokerage was also abuzz with talk of Catastrophe, but to them, the young AI was an inspirational hero.

And of Dilker Bik, no one spoke at all.

Everything was contentment and harmony.

But that was dull. Crisis couldn't resist teasing Karnage. "Maybe I should tell Itka the truth about some of your *premonitions*."

Karnage shrugged. "Tell the truth. Or not. I don't give a shit."

"You're no fun, Karnage."

"That's the least of your problems."

The Baleview walked off, affecting his usual nonchalant swagger. He hesitated at the threshold of the control deck. "Thank you," he said, "for giving me the lead on the Gwyndor Jin bounty."

"I was only fulfilling standard instructions."

"You might pull the wool over Itka's eyes, but you can't play me, Crisis."

Crisis waited eagerly to see what would happen next. One day, Karnage would spontaneously combust, his flesh unable to carry the burden of his epic lack of self-awareness. One day…

"You think I can't play you?" Crisis told him.

Karnage remained silent.

"Is that a challenge?" Crisis added.

The human didn't answer. At least, he didn't answer with words, for words were not this human's style.

However, Crisis noted a complex series of muscle changes. The most minuscule movements that most organics wouldn't notice, but Crisis was not human. For the first time in the two years since Karnage Zax had taken ownership of Crisis and the *Death of Me*, the Baleview smiled.

ABOUT TIM C. TAYLOR

Bio

Tim C. Taylor lives with his family in an ancient village in England. When he was an impressionable kid, between 1977 and 1978, several mind-altering things happened to him all at once: Star Wars, Dungeons & Dragons, and the comic *2000AD*. Consequently, he now writes science fiction novels for a living, notably in the Human Legion and Four Horsemen Universes. His latest project is an adventure series called Chimera Company, which has been described as Warhammer 40,000 in the style of Star Wars. For a free starter library of stories from all the worlds he writes in, join the Legion at humanlegion.com.

HARDCOVER LIQUIDATION:

A SECOND PLANET MYSTERY

NATHAN PEDDE

Bruno Burdock, a former marine in the United Terran Federation turned private detective for the Pickering Detective Agency, is called to another case. When an antique bookseller turns up dead, the New Chicago Police Department calls him in. Teenage color gangsters, mafia bosses, and crooked cops stand in his way. Can Burdock solve the case before he gets fired? Or will the killer get him next?

HARDCOVER LIQUIDATION:
A SECOND PLANET MYSTERY

A s Rufo Lachut paced the pathways between the shelves of his shop, he took in the scent that had nearly gone extinct—that of old books. Digital screens had long replaced paper pages, and Rufo was one of the last remaining dealers. Though some considered it a lower form of antique dealing, he took great pride in his collection.

His store resembled an oversized office space, precisely what it was when he took over the lease. He had to move out ten desks and computers before he squished in as many bookshelves as he could. The tall book towers spread across the open area.

Most of his books weren't worth much. The ancients printed the mass-market paperbacks by the tens of thousands, and despite the poor quality, hundreds were still in existence.

Except the industry wasn't why Rufo paced. His personal e-tablet was hooked to his computer terminal. It was the interface that connected him to different technology. Currently, it pumped data from the city net into his vision. The auction sale of a first edition print of a rare Brandon Sanderson book ticked toward zero, and he had the current highest bid.

He interacted with the terminal using his eye and not a holo-screen. It was an advantage of being from the asteroid belt with cybernetic implants. Normal people used the derogatory terms wafer and jimmer. Rufo had been born in the main asteroid belt colony of Parthenope, which made him a wafer. Because of the low gravity, he stood at 2.5 meters tall. The high gravity of Venus would shatter his weak bones. To combat this, he fused cybernetic implants along his legs and spine. This allowed him to wear an ocular implant to aid in his research, which made him a jimmer. The fake eye announced to others that some of his body parts weren't human.

Citizens of the floating city of New Chicago looked down on wafers and jimmers. Wafers saw the terrestrial planets of Terra and Venus as nothing more than a pile of bureaucratic feces. Normal people considered jimmers to be part computer and therefore not to be trusted. In the last half millennia, three historical events provided them with reasons why cyborgs and artificial intelligences should be second-class residents. They believed wafers and jimmers should be cast into the sun then erased from history.

Rufo counted the auction down to zero, and at the last second, another bid clocked in, stealing his prize.

"Fucking hell!" Rufo shouted, waving his hands.

His fingers glowed green as he manipulated the terminal. He flipped through the screens, hunting for what had happened. Another buyer had waited until just before the auction ended then snagged the buy. He couldn't place a new bid before the auction expired.

Rufo closed his eyes and took a deep breath. There were other auctions and books. It was only a Brandon Sanderson book, and there were millions of them.

A knock echoed from across his store, which was odd to him. No one ever visited, as he wasn't open to the public. There was a sign telling pedestrians he was available by appointment only.

Rufo walked to the door and checked the camera. It showed a little girl in a private school uniform. Rufo checked the time—it was two in the afternoon, and she should be at school.

"What the fuck?" Rufo asked.

He swung the door open hard. Only, he didn't find a girl. Rufo expected his visitor to be near four feet tall, and he stared down at where the little girl's head should have been. Instead, he found three adults of varying heights standing on his stoop. They all wore dark cloaks and ski masks.

A fist connected with his jaw, and he tumbled to the floor. Two of the thieves stormed past him into his shop.

"Stop," Rufo said. "I've got nothing of value."

The third stopped to stand over him. He stood a half meter shorter than Rufo. This made him tall for someone living on Venus.

"The hell you do," the third said, pointing a needler pistol at Rufo's face. "You're a jimmer."

"Wait—"

Rufo didn't have a chance to finish his sentence. The 8x25mm needle round made of pure tungsten carbide slammed into his skull. It pulped his brain into mush. His cybernetic eye rolled from his smashed cranium to rest underneath a shelf.

———

FLASHING lights blasted through the darkness of the New Chicago Central Park, except they weren't coming for me. After searching for thirty-six hours straight, I found Cindy Ferst, the ten-year-old girl who disappeared two days before.

I discovered her cowering in the bushes outside the atrium, her hair matted with sweat and coated in dirt. Since running away from school after being bullied for her prosthetic, things had been hard for the school-girl. Seeing her parents' faces when they arrived to pick her up made me feel like maybe I was doing some good in this world, no matter how small.

Exhaustion seeped into my shoulders from all the long hours. I yearned to go home and sleep for three days. Except I doubted my boss would let me, as there were always more investigations to complete. I rubbed at my animatronic right arm then my bionic right eye. Tiredness caused the interface to itch. They were cybernetics forced upon me after a run-in with a Martian mortar round during the last Terra-Mars war, which we lost because of useless politicians. It rendered my sacrifice null and the Badge of Terra medal hollow.

I served in the 4715th Regiment of the Terran Marine Core, starting out as a private and being promoted until I reached the rank of first sergeant. My fast promotion was due to the numerous casualties we took during the trench warfare on Mars. I had been lucky and lived while others more capable died.

A chill crept up my spine from the changing of the weather as I stared at the darkened city streets of New Chicago. It would rain soon. Being on Venus, the city floated two kilometers above the terraformed jungles below. Terrans colonized Venus five hundred years before at the dawn of the space age, back when the planet's surface resembled a hellish furnace. Centuries later, they had reduced the surface's temperature to a balmy thirty degrees Celsius with two bars of atmospheric pressure.

Humans could adapt to the temperature and the thick atmosphere but not the carnivorous reptiles living on the surface. They kept the cities floating above the Venusian surface. New Chicago Central Park floated above, separate from the primary districts of the city. The metropolis's noise and lights required the park to function as a sanctuary.

With a Venusian day being longer than a year, New Chicago spent part of its year in perpetual darkness. This created issues for those from Terra but not to those from an orbital colony. People living on stations never had a sunrise to miss.

My phone rang, pulling me from my tired musings. I checked the call display and discovered it was Kioko Suda. She was a senior partner of Pickering Detective Agency, my current slave driver, and the reason I'd been up for the past thirty-six hours. Her nasally voice grated on my nerves, but I'd never tell her that. She was one of the few at Pickering I was wary of, but only because she signed my paychecks.

"Go for Burdocks," I said, answering it.

"Bruno Burdocks," Suda said on the other end. "I've been trying to get a hold of you."

"My phone's been on, boss," I replied.

"I hate the park."

"Agreed. Five-O has the victim in their custody. Safe and sound. I'm glad this was only a disgruntled kid, but I was hoping I could find some lead in the kidnapping-ring case."

"Understood. I expect a detailed report on my desk when you get back. But I've got another job for you," Suda said.

"Boss," I said. "I've been working for—"

"This is a priority investigation. We don't get chances like this very often."

"There isn't anyone else?"

"You're it. Everyone else has a full caseload, or they're too inexperienced to work this high a priority."

"Shit."

"Out of all the associate partners in Pickering, you're one of the best," Suda said. "You found little Cindy in how long?"

"She's only ten and is taller than you are," I replied.

"I'll send the details to your e-tablet," Suda said then hung up.

I rubbed at my eyes, pondering where the nearest corner store was. I needed a shot of energy. It would be a long night.

———

AFTER MAKING A QUICK STOP, I drove my hover-sedan across the city. I used a mix of high-speed and regular-speed sky lanes. Unlike the cities of ancient times, New Chicago was a vertical city. Hover-vehicles zoomed across the sky up to twelve lanes tall, though most of the city's lanes were six deep.

"Welcome to the George O'Matty Monday Madness. It's 2:01, Monday, November 22, 2584," the radio announcer said. "Our top story. High President of the United Terran Federation, Josiah Holden the Seventh, will hold a press conference this afternoon to address the unemployment issue facing parts of the Terran states and Venus."

I turned off the radio as I maneuvered from a high-speed lane into Humboldt. It was one of the smaller neighborhoods, filled with tall, skinny buildings. People knew it for its small businesses and Terran-inspired restaurants. I couldn't find one selling Venusian reptile burgers, much to my disappointment.

Landing near the bottom, I picked an older-style parking lot rather than a garage with an internal storage facility. My destination overlooked the car park. Along the walkways and two stories above was the store, Lachut's Book Emporium. On the far side, two police cruisers were parked, with additional sedans hovering closer to the store. Then an ambulance pulled away from the storefront, and I cocked my eyebrow.

This had never happened before. In New Chicago, private detectives never investigated murders, at least nothing recent. We only investigated cases where the corrupt cops let the murder turn cold.

Piles of debris, some homeless people, and teenage color gang signs filled the lot. If I left my car here overnight, someone would steal it.

A woman stood beside a police cruiser, and I swore under my breath. I recognized her from her reputation. She was Isabella Wallis, a detective of the New Chicago Police Department. She was shorter than me by a head with wide hips and a mean glare. Isabella made it clear she disliked my very existence. She wore a suit with a white shirt and clip-on tie, to keep entanglements from choking her when she bashed a lowlife's face in. Isabella's clothing was at least ten times more expensive than mine.

Isabella held her phone to her ear. "Are you certain this is a smart idea? Pickering sent a jimmer... yes, sir. I'll shut up now."

I rolled my eyes at the comments. Some people didn't hide their opinions.

"Are you Bruno Burdocks?" Isabella asked.

"So they call me."

"Why a jimmer? Doesn't Pickering have anyone else?"

"You're short for a bobby," I replied. "How did you pass training? I know what happened. Did budget cuts remove the need for that in the last election?"

"Funny," Isabella said. "Do you want this job? I'm sure there are others who'd love to take this."

"Of course I do. But not if I don't get at least some professional courtesy."

"You're just a wannabe cop playing at police work."

"That's where you're wrong, Detective. I'm not a cop. I'm a private investigator sticking my nose where it doesn't belong to solve cases no one else has time for."

"Fine. This one might suit you, then," Isabella said, tossing me a data chip.

I caught it in my good hand and inserted it into my fake arm. It was a perk of missing a limb. Part of me wanted to install a micro distillery in it, but I was told it's very illegal.

Images came into view. They didn't fill my vision but augmented, so I looked at both. The tall man lay in a crumpled heap, surrounded by real paper books. A needle punctured his chest and another went through the top of his skull.

"How old is this?"

"Excuse me?"

"A month old? Three months?" I played dumb, hoping she'd let something out she wasn't supposed to tell me.

"The body just left."

"You're going to have to explain this to me. Why's Pickering investigating and not the police?"

"When the brass makes a call, you don't question it," Isabella said. "Or face a disciplinary committee."

"That's an excuse, and you know it."

"That line of questioning is above your pay grade. Just be happy you have work," Isabella said, turning toward her car. "That's the police report. You'll find mine and the coroner's notes in the file. Hunt down the ones responsible for this, or you don't get paid."

I watched her climb into her hover-cruiser and take off into the sky lanes. Rubbing at my scruffy chin, I wondered what I was getting into. My day would get worse.

Moving to the stairs and the walkway above, I marched toward the bookstore. Three pad-foot police officers wearing the black and blue of the NCPD stood guard across the metal pathway.

I showed my Pickering identification to the cops, and the three grumbled. A few moved slowly, mocking me somehow. Laughing, they let me past the glowing yellow police holo-tape. Ignoring them, I stepped into the bookstore and stopped.

The piles of priceless books spread across the floor, rendering the bookshelves useless. Small trails stretched between the two mountains of books. A short pile of knocked-over books lay scattered throughout the foyer.

I pressed a button on my arm, and the police report came to my eye. It seemed light on details, though I'd have to read it and not skim the words and pictures. Flipping through the images and notations, I studied the scene.

Rufo Lachut was a tall man from one of the orbital colonies or the asteroid belt. His unnatural height was due to the low gravity he grew up in. An exoskeleton augmented his frame, keeping him from collapsing from his weak skeletal structure. The left bionic eye slot was empty. His right was the one he was born with. I recognized the device, as I had something similar. There was nothing listed in the police report stating they found the eye.

A single needle penetrated Rufo's chest with a second through his forehead. A hole was embedded in the floor where Rufo's head had rested. The other shot had blasted through the shelves of books and bounced into the bricks beyond.

Police forces and the military discontinued the use of cartridge-style firearms hundreds of years ago. Needler-style weapons used high-powered electromagnets to fire chunks of tungsten carbide at the enemy. The guns were magazine fed with a detachable battery, which fired more rounds than ten magazines.

"Ambushed then executed," Francisca Blitz said.

Then my day got much worse. Blitz worked for Pickering Detective Agency, where she investigated insurance frauds and cheating spouses. She was in her midthirties, taller than me at nearly two meters and as skinny as a rail. She pulled her long pink hair back into a single braid. If I didn't know better, I'd think she suffered from low-gravity bone loss, placing her from the orbital colonies. Except I never asked her.

"Blitz. Listening to the police scanner?" I asked.

"Burdock. Suda called me. Wanted me to back you up, as you're tired," Blitz said.

"Great," I replied. "Why didn't our fearless leader give the case to you?"

"Underqualified."

"Story of my life. Are you armed? This isn't the greatest neighborhood."

"No shit. This is New Chicago. We told *old* Chicago to hold our beer with how corrupt and murder filled we can be," Blitz said, tapping her hip.

She wasn't wrong. The media routinely listed New Chicago in the top three in all the United Terran Federation with the highest murder rate. Los Cabos in the Terran state of Baja and Shanghai, one of the Terran Hundred Chinese States, had higher crime rates.

"Fine. What are you thinking?"

Blitz glanced around the bookstore then back to me. "I don't have the police report."

"Study the scene without it."

"Execution-style hit? Did the first needle kill him?"

I scanned the report for the coroner's notes. "No. It missed his heart but collapsed a lung. If not for the second needle and lack of immediate medical attention, he'd still be alive."

"Then maybe it's a hit. Maybe he had a bad run-in with the mob?"

"We'll have to check to see if he had any enemies."

"That's not in the report?" Blitz asked.

"They just took the body away. I don't believe they had time to do much."

"Did they do anything?"

"They processed the scene. Nothing more."

Blitz walked over to a bookshelf and flipped through the books. "Hemingway. Poe. Eddings. Rice. His collection is filled with famous books by the most famous authors ever."

"You're missing all the authors from the last four hundred years," I replied.

"They didn't publish those with actual paper. Anything stolen?" Blitz asked.

"The police report doesn't say. Check around. Maybe the killer stole some of these famous books."

I glanced at the shelves and the books. The piles of manuscripts and the amount of unorganized material made it difficult. I didn't find any sign that the thieves tossed the place. For all I knew, everything was like Rufo left it.

"Found a terminal over here," Blitz said.

She stepped to the small desk, pressing a button. Blitz slipped her e-tablet into the slot, and her fingers lit up. She moved through the windows and options.

"It's a point-of-sale device," Blitz said. "He has a full inventory."

"Here's an idea. How about you go through the books? See if there is anything missing. I'm going to survey the area. Maybe someone saw something."

"He has seven hundred twelve books."

"You don't have to read them. Just make sure they are all accounted for. It could be the evidence that solves it."

"How so?"

"If the hit man stole books with intent to sell, there should be a trail. We can follow that. Selling paper books is a small community. I assume they know each other."

Blitz wrinkled her face and crossed her arms. "I'm not so sure about that. But this is better than listening to some city councillor boink his maid."

"I hate those cases," I said. "I'm going to step outside, and I won't go far."

LEANING AGAINST THE OUTSIDE WALL, I flipped through my phone, using it to connect to the city net. It wasn't ideal for the task, but it would do the job. I went through Rufo Lachut's social media. I hoped to find some friends or family to interview. His profile was empty of anyone who could answer my questions. He only connected to others in the bookselling community.

I slid my phone into my pocket, rubbing at the bridge of my nose. I'd have to knock on doors. Being so late, I doubted anyone would be in. If I found any, I'd have trouble convincing anybody to speak. As a habit, New Chicagoans rarely spoke to private eyes or cops. The term *snitches get stitches* still applied despite being coined over five hundred years before.

As I glanced at the police officers guarding the site, one of them spoke into a radio. He talked in a muffled voice, making it difficult for me to understand what they were saying. Judging from how they all turned as one, marching away from me, I guessed they were headed back to the station.

The hair on the back of my neck stood up as my paranoia flared. Without the cops standing watch, there was nothing between me and some drugged-out gangbanger meaning me harm. I wasn't worried about myself. My P1303 hung from its holster under my armpit. As a former marine, there wasn't much I couldn't handle. However, Blitz didn't have the same training I had.

"Keep calm, numb nuts," I mumbled to myself.

From one of the many shops, a figure stepped from the shadows. He was my height but not my build. He might have been in better shape once, except it was fifty years and ninety kilograms ago. His long thin gray hair glowed under the streetlamps, giving him a wild man's appearance. His ragged old clothes didn't help much.

"Are you a cop?" the man asked.

My right hand drifted to my piece. I expected him to start blasting.

"Pickering," I replied.

"Good. You investigating Mr. Lachut's demise?"

"Supposed to."

"Pickering's not bad. Those cops are septic-levels corrupt."

Taking a step back, I readied my mind for a fight. The witness wouldn't be the first to ambush me.

"Let me start over. My name's Koa Heller. I witnessed what happened here."

"Then why talk to me?" I replied.

"Not here. Can we go someplace private?"

I keyed my phone and rang Blitz.

"Did you get lost?" Blitz asked.

"Funny. I got a witness. I'll take a drive and interview him. Lock the door."

"I'll be fine," Blitz replied.

I led Koa to my car, gesturing for him to sit in the passenger seat. Lifting off, I placed my hover-sedan into autopilot to weave along the sky lanes, not getting too far away from the scene. I didn't trust the man. Keeping my hand on my lap, I was ready to draw at a moment's notice.

"All right," I said. "Is this safe enough?"

"It'll do," Koa said, shifting in his chair. "Did that all hurt?"

"What hurt?" I asked, raising an eyebrow.

The question was from right field, except I had an idea of what he meant.

"Your arm and the eye."

"It was the war. I got blown up. But we're not here to talk about me."

Koa glanced down at his lap. He held his hands together, rubbing at the arm hair.

"Understood."

"What do you have?" I asked.

"It was three men, and they took books with them."

"How are you sure about that?"

"I watched them burst into the place and gun down poor Rufo."

Glaring at the man, I pondered if he was telling the truth. Many of the destitute citizens of New Chicago told cops falsehoods to either earn a payday or to throw off investigations.

"Tell me about Rufo. Did he always wear his bionic?"

"I think so. It wasn't as jimmer-like. His looked like a real eye. It took me months to realize he was missing the thing. It wasn't until after I asked him about his height that he took it out. I nearly lost my lunch."

I made a note that the hit man removed the eye from the body.

"These killers," I said. "Did you see them fire the shot?"

"No, but I heard it. The zap of the needler isn't something you miss."

"I bet. Notice any faces?" I asked.

"No. It's dark out, and they wore dark cloaks."

"Not jackets?"

"They were a plastic cloth, which crinkled when they moved. It was the cheap stuff. The type made from recycled material. The crap that gets brittle and breaks too fast."

I glanced around my sedan, letting my eye do its thing. It examined vehicle license plates and ran the numbers against my database. I kept track of vehicles from known criminals or those under suspicion, but my program flagged none. Though my system wasn't perfect. Anyone meaning me harm could steal another just as easily.

"Three tall, dark figures burst into the bookstore, gunned down the owner, and stole some books?" I asked. "Did I get that right?"

"Absolutely."

"Did you take any photos?"

"No."

"Really? 'Cause anytime a pad foot does anything wrong, there's a dozen video cameras pointed at them. But not when someone murders some poor sap and they're trying to bring justice."

"But you aren't a cop?"

"In this argument, it's a moot difference."

"While I didn't get *photos*, I managed to get something better. I videoed their exit."

I sat back, shocked. If the video showed faces, I might be able to figure it out. It would be in the top ten of the quickest crimes solved by a Pickering detective. I doubted it would get me promoted to junior partner, but it'd keep me from getting fired for at least a week.

"Can I have it?" I asked.

Koa handed me a data chip, and I slipped it into my arm.

"That's neat," Koa said. "Do all robo arms function as a terminal?"

"No. This cost me an arm."

Koa laughed, but I ignored him.

The video played in my bionic eye. I groaned, as it was more home-made than I expected. It shook back and forth with the wind rending all sound useless. I doubted I could clean it up enough to make a difference.

The image stabilized as three figures left the bookstore. Two were shorter than the third, whose height almost matched the victim's, but he got close. All three wore ski masks and dark cloaks. This made it difficult to pin their identity. Each of the thieves carried books, and I paused the video.

"Ten books," I said.

"That's what I thought," Koa said.

"Did you have anything else to give me?"

"Not particularly. Can you put me down over there?"

I nodded, stopping at the walkway he pointed to. Koa stepped from my sedan and onto the metal. The older man disappeared around a corner. Taking control of my vehicle, I maneuvered back toward the crime scene.

———

I CIRCLED the parking lot as I arrived. Dialing Blitz's number, I let it ring. There was no answer. I hit a button on my e-tablet and opened an application. It pinpointed her location, which was in the bookstore.

"Fucking Mars," I said.

Soaring down to the ground, I parked at the edge of the walkway. I stormed from the running vehicle, drawing my weapon. I burst through the door, and Blitz screamed. She hunched over the store's terminal with her fingers glowing green.

"What the hell?" Blitz asked.

"Why didn't you answer your phone?" I asked.

She pulled it from her pocket. "It was on silent."

"While working alone, always keep it on. Especially in this area."

I parked my sedan and returned to the store. She was on her phone with the police and Suda, our boss. I went to work.

Examining the footage, I zoomed into the images of the books. I wrote six of the ten titles. The last four had their spines facing the other way.

I handed her the data disk with the video and my list. "I focused on the missing books."

"I've only heard of one of them. *The Hobbit* by J. R. R. Tolkien."

"It's a start," I said.

"I need to find that list of books," Blitz said, handing me a data disk. "You must deliver this to the lab."

"What's this?"

She pointed to where the body had lain. "Boot prints in blood. Single set."

"That might lead somewhere. Think it was the killer?"

"No idea. I know they're women's shoes," Blitz said.

"How do you know that?"

"The city net. These are Muu Muu Chantus. They've a distinct pattern that no one else uses."

"Where did you find that?"

"Everything's on the net if you know where to look for it," Blitz said.

Her grin informed me I was getting old.

"Maybe the lab can tell us a shoe size."

"They'll be able to tell us more than that. If the wearer used them in another crime, how the person walks, and more."

"How they walk?"

"Yes. Did you know that someone born on Venus walks differently than a Terran? And a wafer does even more so. We can even tell which station they're from."

"Good to know," I replied. "This isn't in the police report."

"Some discarded books covered them," Blitz said. "Do you think we'd find some hair samples? I'm tempted to look."

I glanced at the dust coating everything. "Doubt it. See the mess. Where to start? It'd take the technicians a week to process the scene, and they'd still probably find nothing."

"What do you suggest?"

"I think the boot prints and the books are the best lead we have," I said. "I'll get it to the lab."

"Fine. I'll be here finding those last few titles. If they sell them, I'll know about it the moment they do."

"I've a contact or two who are involved in certain things. Maybe I'll

217

poke around to see if anyone's buying black market books. I'll keep you informed."

I took off into the sky lanes, making a quick stop at the Pickering lab. I wasn't counting on the boot prints. What Blitz didn't inform me was if the shoes were new, I'd only receive a profile. It was better than nothing. Except New Chicago was a city of millions, and it would be like finding a needle in the Venusian jungle.

———

AN HOUR DRIFTED by as I maneuvered my way through New Chicago's maze of sky lanes. I wasn't heading for anywhere savory or nice but to one of the many rough patches of the city. Hover-vehicles edged near me, and my paranoia told me someone tailed close behind. I couldn't finger which of the dozens it was.

The neighborhood of New Belgium was among the poorer areas of the metropolis. The rent was low with the flats small and dilapidated. It was one district where wafer refugees could live without too much persecution.

Keeping the memories of the war from my mind, I landed on the street level. Most people rarely ventured to the bottom of the city. The many layers of sky lanes with their walkways and catwalks kept them high above. Even the poorest amongst them never strayed to the pavement-filled road below. I didn't blame them. It was filled with garbage, sewage, and the occasional corpse.

In a corner unit along the street, surrounded by the few boarded-up shops, was a pawnshop called Phosphorson's Pawn and Salvage. It was my destination.

I stepped into the store, and the door dinged behind me. Gizmos and gadgets of every sort packed the store from bow to stern. Electronics lined one part, with a tiny clothing section on the other. The buildings shrank from a shopping center to the size of a pawnshop.

"Welcome to—fucking Jupiter," Charlie said from behind a glass counter.

Charlie Phosphorus was a tall man but not from any natural height.

His short arms didn't match his 2.5-meter height. The mechanoid legs were made from three different legs bolted together.

"First Sergeant. It's been a while."

I stepped up to the counter and leaned against the glass. "It's Detective. How many times must we discuss this?"

"You'll always be my first sergeant. E-4 for life."

"Once a marine…" I didn't finish the sentence.

"What can I sell you today?" His enthusiasm was almost infectious.

"Information."

"About what?" Charlie asked, stepping back from me with his arms crossed.

"Did you hear about the murder in Humboldt?"

"The crazy bookseller? Just that he died."

I stared at the former marine for a long moment. "How did you hear about that?"

"Word travels fast. He wasn't a friend, more like an annoyance. He was always in here seeing if I had some rare book."

"With millions living in this hellhole, my victim is an acquaintance of yours?"

"Easy to understand. There are few places to buy and sell old books. That guy—hell, I didn't even know his fucking name."

"Rufo Lachut."

"Right. Anyway, Rufo visited every pawnshop and broker in the city. He goes everywhere."

"Could he have made another seller angry at him?" I asked.

"Enough to kill him? Maybe. But probably not from someone buying and selling books. My bet is it would be someone from the underworld. Some mob boss or loan shark."

My mind wandered back to the stolen books. "Are they profitable to buy and sell?"

"Anything can be. It depends on what you are trying to peddle."

I pulled up the list of books and showed it to him. "Would you buy these?"

"Not for a lot. Except I know little about buying books. These titles aren't obvious to me."

219

"So nothing that stands out."

"Sorry," Charlie said.

"Do you know anyone who can educate me on the sale of these antiques?"

"I can give you a name, but I'm not sure I should."

"Why not?"

"Despite you being my first sergeant, you're a dick," Charlie said. "That limits me. Snitches and all that."

"I'm not asking you to tell me who killed him."

"Not that I know that."

"I'm just hunting for more information."

Charlie gave me a name. "Just don't tell her I showed this to you. I enjoy breathing without the use of a tube."

Nodding, I left the store.

———

DRIVING THROUGH THE CITY, I stared at my surroundings, hunting for the tail. I didn't see anyone suspicious, which wasn't a hard thing. The darkness hid many hover-vehicles, making it easy for me to pick up a follower.

Then I saw it. Three cars behind me in the left lane, a blue Wattswagen Bugmobile. They imported the odd-looking machine from the Terran nation of Berliner. It was one of the cheapest and most reliable sedans on the market. This Bugmobile had a green hood, and the driver's door was yellow. It was a poor vehicle to follow anyone in. Except I couldn't see the driver because of the darkness.

Turning a corner, I skirted onto a side street. Making three more turns, the multicolored sedan kept pace. I made note of his license plate, smiling. I turned onto another road, counting the sky lanes below me. There were seven, which would satisfy my purpose.

With my tail out of sight, I pushed a button on my terminal, and my ride shut down. This made my vehicle drop from the sky. The sky lanes logged my hover-vehicle as broken and forced any vehicles below me out of the way. My emergency repulsors should've kicked in to keep me from passing through the lanes, but I kept them off.

As the arteries flew by, I flicked another switch, and my sedan booted back to life. I cranked on the controls, dodging a delivery truck. My tail drove by high above.

Grinning, I moved along the sky lanes toward my destination. I made a note to keep an eye out for my follower. He'd seemed to find me with ease, or my paranoia was flaring up again.

Then my phone rang with Suda on the other end of the line. "What the fuck are you doing?"

"Suda. Good to talk to you," I replied.

"I get notified you were in an accident, then the notice goes away."

Keeping an eye on my rearview mirror, I maneuvered around a slower-moving van.

"Just trying to lose a tail."

"This isn't the movies."

"Indeed. This tail was real," I replied.

"You certain?"

I sent her an image of the hover-vehicle in all its multicolored glory.

"It's an amateur," Suda said.

"Or it's a distraction, which is why I dropped."

Suda was quiet for a long moment.

"You still there?" I asked.

"Don't make the news," Suda said before hanging up.

With my luck, that might be a tall order.

I glided through the arteries to the Grand Minx Bar and Grille. It lay at the Red Light District's bottom level across from the rows of night-clubs. Music thumped down the streets from dozens of bands. Taxis moved in and out of the line of waiting vehicles.

Finding a parking spot, I squeezed in between two sleek black limousines. I stepped from my hover-sedan toward the bar. A bouncer moved in front of me.

"We don't permit jimmers in here," the bouncer said.

I flashed my Pickering identification. "Doesn't matter what you want. Do I need to recite Terran law?"

"Fucking jimmery dick," the bouncer mumbled but let me in.

It was a perk of the job. It reminded assholes they had to behave.

Mindy Flowers sat at the back of the packed room. She was a middle-aged lady with long black hair and a crooked nose. She wore tight black clothes that showed off her trim figure. Judging from her clothing and the bodyguard, I assumed she was involved in the Venusian mob in some way.

A tall dark man stepped in front of me. A bulge under his armpit informed me he carried a needler pistol. He stood a head taller than me with wider shoulders.

"Fuck off," the bodyguard said. "Jimmers aren't permitted here."

I flashed my Pickering ID. "Move aside."

The bodyguard grabbed my left arm and squeezed. Then I reacted and gripped his limb with my animatronic one. I flexed my silicone-and-metal muscles. Bones snapped as I twisted my wrist. The bodyguard tumbled to his knees. I relieved him of his piece and released him to nurse his broken arm.

"Make another move and I'll paint the walls with your brains," I said.

I pulled his weapon apart, ripping the slide from the barrel and the frame. I dumped the pieces to the floor.

"Good job," Mindy said. "Come. I'll share my table with a jimmer."

I did as she asked, keeping my hand near my pistol. The bodyguard stood and loomed over me with a glare.

"Bo. Go get a stimpack and take a seat," Mindy said to her bodyguard. "This Pickering dick won't hurt me. Jimmer or no."

The bodyguard didn't move, and Mindy glared at him. "Bo."

The man stepped from the table.

"Thanks, Bo," I said.

He stopped for a moment and flexed his fists then continued.

"I could have you arrested," Mindy said.

"That's funny. He tried to assault me," I said. "But I don't think talking to the police is a habit of yours."

Mindy grinned and snapped her fingers. A waitress wearing a short skirt and a plunging neckline arrived by her side.

"I'll take two Venusian whiskeys, straight up," Mindy said, then the waitress left. "You're very perceptive. What can I do for you?"

"I'm hunting for information."

"Do I look like a visitor center?" Mindy said.

"Word is that you're an info broker."

"Fine. I'll talk, but for you, I want a favor to be paid in the future."

"I'd rather just pay you."

"Nope. I like you. You're bold, and I can use that."

"I'm not for sale," I replied.

"Or you're just stupid," Mindy said. "That's my price. You want information, then I need a simple, small favor."

I leaned in and glared at her. "Why would I get involved with the Venusian mob?"

Mindy cackled at me as a grin split her face. "I'm not in the mob."

"Then what are you?"

"I'm an independent contractor. I work, keep to myself, and employ Bo to do just that."

"Fine. I'll owe you a favor. But I'm drawing the line at anything illegal. I enjoy having a job."

"Employment is overrated."

"I enjoy having my private eye license and dignity intact."

"I accept those conditions. Ask."

I paused for a moment, collecting my thoughts as the waitress arrived with the drinks. Mindy took a sip, and I did the same.

"If someone stole ancient paper books, who'd be on the market to buy them?"

"You're talking about the asshats that killed Rufo."

"The murder happened earlier today, and you've heard about it?"

"We're both bookworms. He buys books to add to his collection. When he finds multiple, he sells them. Mine is junk compared to his."

"Small community?" I asked.

"Very."

"Being involved in the criminal underworld doesn't dampen your relationship with these bookworms?"

"No. It gives me access to books others don't."

"How tight are you all?"

"A friend received a speeding ticket, and everyone knew in a few hours."

"Then you'd learn about the stolen books?" I asked.

"We just don't know which books," Mindy said.

"Would the community want to buy them?"

"Of course, but we wouldn't. Personally. If I hear about any sale, I'll be causing trouble. If you know what I mean."

I slipped her a data chip with the stolen book titles and my business card. "Then put your feelers out. If anyone in your circle finds someone selling, call me."

Mindy took them both. "Fine. I'll do what I can."

———

I FINISHED my drink and left the bar. Bo glared at me as I marched past. I'd have to keep an eye out if I ventured into any dark alleys. I dropped him before, but it wouldn't work a second time.

While I was driving through the sky lanes, my phone rang. Blitz was on the other line.

"How's the hunt?" I asked.

"I think I have something," Blitz replied.

"What do you have?"

"Not sure. But I need you to come back."

"On my way," I said, hanging up.

This was probably nothing, but it was my only lead. I needed another lead to follow. It was the nature of the job. Unlike in the holovids, clues never built on each other. Most threads I followed always resulted in dead ends.

From a side lane, three bikes burst from its depths. Teenagers wearing yellow armbands, shirts, and bandannas raced toward me. They carried metal pipes and called out war cries. It was a color gang. The disenfranchised teenagers had nothing better to occupy their time.

The lead rider smashed his pipe into my passenger window. Glass shattered as the teen whooped and hollered. I pulled my P1303 out and aimed it at him. Except he moved too fast, and there were too many pedestrians behind him.

Metal dented as the last two teens flew by. I jerked my hover-sedan to the side as the gangers swerved around. He shattered my headlight as I missed hitting him by a few centimeters.

"What are you doing? Trying to kill me, old man?" the gangster yelled. "This is just a fucking joke."

The three teenagers glided away, leaving my dented sedan to putter along the sky lane. Suda was going to have my head. I'd gone for so long without damaging a company vehicle. Now I wouldn't hear the end of it.

I turned, heading for a faster sky lane. The sooner I left the area, the better I'd feel. Then, on a side street, I noticed a parked sedan. The mismatched Bugmobile stood out like a Martian on payday. The man edged out of the lane, trying to merge into the quicker traffic.

Tired and frustrated, I changed my mind. It was time to ask this idiot a few questions. Pulling over, I slid in front of him. I slammed on the brakes and stopped.

The streetlight illuminated the Bugmobile's cab. The tail was in his twenties with a narrow face and a goatee. It was a poor attempt for the youth to appear older than his proper age.

The man stared at me for a full second. Panic spread across his face as he jerked at his controls. He copied what I had done to him earlier. He dropped from the sky lane toward the pavement below.

"Suda's going to have my head," I mumbled.

Knowing how it was accomplished, I followed close behind. I aimed my sedan to stay close. My tail powered his Bugmobile up, soaring through the lanes. He weaved around traffic, breaking multiple safety violations. These I broke in my vain attempt to keep up with him.

Five lanes above, the Terraforming Celebration Plaza loomed. It was the rooftop of a midsized government building turned into a stone-lined open area with a fountain in the center. My tail moved into an up-lane, racing toward the top. It curved, headed over to the top of the plaza.

Anticyborg protesters filled the plazas. Teenagers with blue and purple hair carried signs demanding the government ship those with enhancements back to the orbital colonies, that Venus should be for Venusians.

I closed in on the Bugmobile with my sedan. I slammed the nose of my machine into the Bugmobile's rear left repulsor. Smoke bellowed from the metal as it lost power. The sedan turned, pointing toward the stone-covered ground below.

The crowd scattered away from the crashing hover-vehicle. Its emergency power kicked in, landing the busted machine on the ground far from where the blue-haired teens had stood. The protesters' reaction was greater than the situation warranted.

As I landed beside the sedan, my tail burst from his vehicle. I chased after him as the man ran into the crowd. He disappeared from sight.

Three protesters blocked his path as I bowled into them. They pushed me back from the crowd. Two slammed batons over my head, and my bionic eye shut down.

"Unless you're a cop, you can fuck off," the protester said, pushing me away.

I didn't want to fight a hundred university students. The fiends could be dangerous in large numbers. I stomped back to the downed vehicle. After a quick search, I found one of the stolen books sitting on the passenger seat along with a note written on a bar receipt from the Grand Minx Bar and Grille. It was a detailed description of me and my hover-sedan.

"Fucking Mindy. Backstabbing bitch," I said.

There was no sign of the murder weapon or a random bionic eye. Giving up finding anything else, I recorded the vehicle's identification number.

Then my phone rang once more. As I suspected, it was Suda.

"What in fucking Jupiter is going on?" Suda yelled.

"I've recovered one of the stolen books," I said.

"Excuse me?"

"I found the fucker who tailed me, and he fled. I got him to stop, but he got away. Left a book behind."

"Fuck," Suda said. "I don't have time for this."

"Neither do I. Blitz needs me back," I said.

"I'll deal with the cops. Get me the hover-sedan's identification number. Maybe I can dig up a name."

I sent it to her, and she hung up. When she found out I'd damaged the sedan, she'd be even angrier. I couldn't win.

———

LEAVING THE PLAZA, I carried the book with me. I left before the police could arrive to delay me further. Vehicles packed the sky lanes, and the trip took me longer than I'd like.

I pulled into the parking lot and landed close to the bookstore. The broken window invited someone to steal from it. I hoped I'd be able to stop any thief before they got away. Part of me hoped the piece of junk vehicle would get stolen so I wouldn't have to inform Suda about the damage.

I walked into the store and stopped. Blitz lay on the floor, staring underneath the shelf. Her hand reached into its depths, hunting for something.

"What are you doing?" I asked.

"Something's odd under here," Blitz said. "But it's at the back, and I can't reach it."

Grabbing the slab, I tried to shift it over. Except it was too heavy to move. Moving through the bookstore, I hunted for an object long and skinny. I found a broom near the back of the store.

Shaking my head, I handed it to Blitz. She used the handle to slide the round object from under the shelf. It was Rufo's bionic eye.

"Now that's something," Blitz said.

"Or nothing. Maybe he lost it before the attack, and this shows dust," I replied.

I informed her about the run-in with Mindy and Bo. She made a wrinkly face about the inability to sell the books.

"It's all we have. The witness led to nobody, and the books are a dead end," Blitz said, handing me the eye.

"Then I need to investigate this optic," I said.

"That's the problem. If none of the books stolen were worth anything, then why hit the place?"

"I'm not following."

"I researched the books the thieves left behind. Many would bring small fortunes if auctioned," Blitz said.

"That is puzzling," I said. "I have a few ideas."

"Care to share?"

"Not at the moment. I need to read the data from the eye first."

Blitz nodded. "Then I'm done here. Besides the optic and the boot print, I've found nothing else. I have a list of ten books, but judging from what you said, it's too soon for the thieves to sell them openly."

"And the books don't seem like they'll pull big bucks," I replied.

"I'll get to the office. See if I can find any rumors of anyone buying."

"Didn't I do that?"

"You discovered shit, though."

Blitz left the bookstore, leaving me alone with the mountains of books. I glanced around, hoping I'd find something more definitive. Then my phone rang with Suda on the line.

"Am I fired yet?"

"Maybe tomorrow."

"Well. The night's still young."

"I've got a name for you. Look up Addam Noble. He owns the abandoned sedan." Suda hung up.

I locked the bookstore up and climbed into my machine. I was happy and disappointed thieves hadn't stolen my sedan. Leaving the site, I headed into the sky lanes and drove away.

Logging into the city net, I searched for the name. The issue I found was that it was a common name, but none were related to the crime. I tried to limit my search to known criminals, but there were too many with questionable profiles.

My only answer was the eye. If it had data on the victim's last moments, I could identify which one was the killer. I could take it to the Pickering offices, except it would mean involving a technician. This would add time to the case. My only concern was to earn some sleep.

Instead, I went home. Owning a bionic eye, I possessed the hardware to service the device.

The trip back to my apartment was uneventful. I expected to be ambushed, but nothing came of it. I parked in my apartment's secured garage and marched into the building.

My bachelor pad was tiny and resembled the quarters on a warship more than a place someone lived in. The only furniture I owned was a bed I never used, a brown armchair I slept in, and a shelf with a few pictures and a full-face helmet from my time as a Terran Marine next to my medals and citations. I hid the cracked and damaged side of the helmet against the wall.

Hidden underneath the frame was a metal-covered chest, which I slid out. In it was the reader for my bionic eye. I hadn't needed to touch it for months. It was flat and the size of my hand. I could place my eye on it, and the data would play on my e-tablet or in my bionic eye. Instead of placing my optic, I put Rufo's on it, and the images appeared in my vision. I moved through the options and found the last thirty minutes saved.

Unfortunately, twenty-eight of those minutes were staring at his own corpse from underneath the shelf. A mere two of the footage were worth viewing. It showed three adults in dark hoods standing in the doorway. The tallest of the trio slammed his fist into Rufo's face.

Then the tallest man raised a pistol and shot Rufo. The eye rolled away. During the entire time, there weren't many frames showing the man's face. The hood kept his head hidden.

Scrolling through the footage frame by frame, I stumbled across a few in-focus shots. The ganger who killed Rufo wasn't Addam Noble. His face didn't match any suspect I found on the city net earlier.

The bastard who had followed me all night was the person who'd murdered Rufo. With a photo, a two-second search gave me another name. Pavel Voronova. I sat on my armchair, rubbing at the bridge of my nose, when my phone rang.

———

I ANSWERED and discovered it was Blitz. Judging by the time that had passed, she should've arrived at the Pickering office. I suspected she had found something.

"I've made some progress. Did you find anything?"

"Funny that. I've picked up a tail. I'm thinking more than one."

"You're not at the office yet?"

"Traffic sucks," Blitz said.

"Without looking, tell me about them?"

"Three guys on motorbikes, wearing yellow." The sound of metal crunching and breaking filled my ear. "One of them hit my car with a pipe."

Fuck.

"Turn on your tracker. I'm on my way."

"I'll do what I can to keep them off me. I'm headed toward you."

I burst from my apartment, sprinting to the parking garage. Climbing into my hover-sedan, I gunned my engine. My phone buzzed, showing that Blitz wasn't too far from me. I might make it. Racing through the sky lanes, I careened around slower-moving vehicles.

"Get out of the way!" I yelled, knowing the driver couldn't hear me.

Using Blitz's tracker, I maneuvered through the arteries in her direction. The distance to her shrank. I moved up a side lane shortcut. Then she appeared in front of me. The three hover-bikes kept behind Blitz, smashing dents into her machine. Each rider wore a large black helmet, which hid their faces. They pushed her along, herding her toward an unknown destination. They were the same gangsters who had attacked me hours before, wearing their yellow markings.

Gunning my engine, I moved my hover-sedan to slide between them. The gangers jerked to the side, keeping away from my two-thousand-kilogram weapon.

The lead biker smashed his pipe into Blitz's front repulsor, causing smoke to billow from its depths. The machine slowed down and descended through the sky lanes toward the bottom level.

The bikers cut power and pursued her down. Using the method from earlier in the night, I followed. Suda would call and give me an earful, but I didn't care.

Blitz landed on the pavement, setting the machine down with ease. The bikes circled above her before landing near her. My sedan was slower than the gangsters and was still three lanes above.

The three whirled around Blitz, carrying weapons with violent intentions. She climbed from the cab, holding her pistol. She waved it at the three men in front of her. They circled around her with their own needler pistols.

I landed on the ground, flaring my repulsors hard. When I climbed from my sedan, the gangsters were between me and Blitz. Two, Addam Noble and Golda Fides, pointed their weapons at me, while the third, Pavel Voronova, jerked his at Blitz.

"Pavel Voronova!" I shouted, and the tallest of the three gangers jerked upright. "Why did you kill Rufo?"

The two shorter thieves glanced at each other, then Golda spoke. "I told you we didn't need to do that."

"Shut it," Pavel said. "We outnumber them three to two. I'll take the jimmer."

"I'm not a cop, and I'm not here for the thefts. I'm here for the murder," I said. "Addam, let's make a deal."

"How do you know my name?" Addam asked.

"You're Addam Noble, and the other is Golda Fides. You're two petty thieves working for the Venusian Mob. Did Rufo owe protection money?"

"Don't talk to them," Pavel said.

"Nah," I continued. "This isn't about protection. A bookseller like him isn't a rich person. He has no cash. This was about the books. Steal some books on a list? Or maybe it was to convince him to sell and move. The books you took were worthless. There were more expensive books there."

"After I kill these two traitors, I'm going to kill you," Pavel said.

"Shut it, Pavel," Golda said. "We told you this would hurt us. The boss told us to go in, steal a few books, rough him up. Nothing more."

"We can do this," Pavel began as Addam aimed his weapon at the murderer.

"Zip it," Addam said then glanced at me. "The books are in my bike. Take them. Leave me and Golda out of this."

I smiled. There was no honor among thieves and murderers.

"You're a coward," Pavel said, aiming his pistol at the gangster.

Addam shot him in the shoulder, and Pavel dropped his weapon. The wounded ganger screamed and fell to the ground. I moved in, kicking the pistol away from his reach.

"Leave the books and fuck off," I said. "Tell Mindy to hire more competent thugs."

"How did you know she is—"

"I didn't. But you just did."

Addam and Golda unloaded the books and took off into the darkness. I cuffed Pavel then shoved a blood-clotter into his shoulder. Blitz sat on the hood of her sedan, stunned.

"You going to talk?" I asked Pavel. "Make a deal?"

"Fuck you," Pavel replied.

I left Pavel on the ground, leaning against his hover-bike. I stepped beside Blitz and leaned against her car.

"I guess we're waiting for the cops to show?" Blitz asked. Sirens blared in the distance.

"Pretty much."

A few minutes later, the police arrived with Isabella leading the pack. She was more irritated that I bugged her than pleased we got the killer in so short a time. She gave Pavel one look, and he sang.

It turns out Mindy had been roughing up antique collectors in an attempt to get them to sell pieces from their collection. Pavel worked for Rufo, and the bookseller was a bit of an asshole. When Pavel got hired to rough the man up, he killed him. Mindy wasn't happy with it and forced the murderer to tie up loose ends. He was supposed to torch the place, except the cops were there too fast. Then he tried to kill the investigators.

Two beat cops tossed Pavel into a police cruiser's back seat and took off into the sky lanes. Isabella joined Blitz and me.

"Will Mindy be charged?" Blitz asked.

"She'll walk. No prosecutor will touch this. Not with the only drip of evidence being the testimony of a killer," Isabella replied.

I grumbled under my breath, adding Mindy to my list of criminals to investigate in my free time.

Isabella glanced at me. "For a job well done, on top of paying the bill, I'm going to waive those traffic violations. Don't do that shit again."

The detective left without another word.

"Those boot prints?" Blitz asked.

"They'll confirm what we already know. Those technicians don't work fast enough," I replied.

Blitz smiled and placed her hand on my shoulder. "I won't tell them you said that."

"Well. Now to wait for Suda to yell at us," I said.

"Why would she do that?" Blitz asked.

I pointed at the two damaged company sedans when my phone rang. It was Kioko Suda.

ABOUT NATHAN PEDDE

Nathan Pedde was born in central British Columbia, Canada. He went to Capilano University after high school and entered the film industry, where he worked for two years as a lamp operator. He has worked in different industries and jobs, including a gas station, engraved picture frames, and dried flooded homes as a flood technician. He currently lives on Vancouver Island with his wife and two kids.

He began telling stories in the seventh grade, where he wrote an illustrated fairy-tale. He dabbled in it during high school and continued in college. Life got in the way, and he made little progress. However, the writing still happened. Fifteen years after high school, serious writing has begun.

THE CRAWL

D. L. SELLITTO

When an ambitious new Tech signs up for a high-profile assignment, she's not pleased to find herself teamed up with her least favorite coworker. Then things quickly go wrong, pitting the two of them against their own company and a horrifying fate.

THE CRAWL

T hey didn't call this crawl the Birth Canal for nothing.

Twenty-five meters of tight corners and shifting levels, and all through a maintenance shaft barely thirty-seven centimeters wide. Yours truly came in at just under that, which was no doubt part of the reason I'd gotten the gig. Being small didn't mean I had an easy time of it though.

Taking a deep breath that was more to steady myself than anything, I twisted onto my side and used both feet to push myself up and around a corner. I felt kind of like a swimmer on the rebound, except I was in a narrow passage in the Cube.

The public was fascinated with Energy Cubes, which had the distinct honor of being the primary source of power for all major cities around the globe. The first cube had been built entirely in secret by a then-unknown start-up named Starco more than twenty-five years ago. That big reveal had turned the world on its ear. Suddenly, there was cheap, plentiful, clean energy.

This one, the very first one, had been decommissioned about ten years ago. Starco had shut it down and was soon bought out by Enercorp. But I thought even Enercorp's cold corporate hearts must have found some romance in the thing, because they didn't even strip it for parts. It just... sat. An inscrutable cube made of eight subsections, containing all the technology needed to power the world. And the whole thing was wrapped in eight meters of cooling equipment on all sides.

"Tech 418, confirm location," said Mapper 21, her clipped voice emanating from my goggle's earpiece.

It had been less than a minute since my Mapper's last check-in, and I rolled my eyes in the dark.

She always addressed me like that. I couldn't remember doing something to earn the attitude, but she'd made no secret of her dislike. The feeling was mutual after multiple attempts—all rebuffed—to get on her good side. Now, I wished she'd wander off into some eternal break room and let someone—anyone else—take her place behind that console.

I settled for snapping back. "Location farther on up the shaft and ready for a break, 21. Who's the Mapper here?"

"Mapper 21 affirms break. Five ticks." The speaker went dead.

I'm not usually an ass to the people I work with. Enercorp was my new workplace, and the staff had some clear lines drawn in the sand, lines that, as a new hire, I didn't fully understand. That handicap wasn't doing me any favors either, as evidenced by the fact that *none* of the Mappers liked me thanks to 21.

And it was dumb to piss off the Mappers because there were times when, thanks to their knowledge and the dataset they had access to, they held a Tech's life in their hands. When our equipment inevitably failed, all we had left was our Mapper.

If you were hoping that my fellow Techs liked me, I'll have to disappoint you.

Most of the Techs were male, young, and distrustful of the opposite sex. Female Techs are considered bad luck in this line of work. Go back and check the stats on this Cube's major disasters. Some bright spark with a dick did just that one time. What he found after running the numbers was that in every case, there were more women than men at the site.

Point was, the Techs didn't like me, and the Mappers didn't like me. The Corporate guys didn't care one way or the other. But despite what Daddy always said, I discovered that I could be quite successful in isolation.

I finally came to the end of the shaft I was working my way through and entered a soaring, wide-open space. I inhaled sharply as I took in the sweeping design of the first bulwark. It was so different from the modern Cubes with their workaday utilitarianism. Was that decorative etching on some of the curved surfaces? My goggles struggled to keep up with me as I turned my gaze this way and that, trying to make sense of what I saw.

Despite my having completed all the required training, it looked completely alien to me. And my goggles weren't filling in detail as readily as they should, something I'd been warned about due to the age of the Cube. But I was enjoying my sightseeing when Mapper 21's voice interrupted me again.

"Tech 418, please confirm activity."

"Tech 418, entry to first bulwark. Establishing location of primary readouts. Will update."

I wanted her to leave me alone while I soaked in the view, but it was time to get to work. I had come out of the wall about three-quarters of the way down this particular section. A sturdy-looking metal staircase zigged and zagged down to the floor of the first level, dwarfed by the cooling system behind me that stretched upward until it got swallowed by darkness.

Turning back, I found the primary readout screen for the lower-left partition and established a connection with the machine. It took a moment for my goggles to sort through a decade's worth of old data, so I busied myself by organizing my tools nearby.

The work was at least easy. All I needed to do was dump the old data into portable storage for later comparison with external readouts, clear the old data out of the system, then assess the current readings. The goggles contained the microprocessor that would do all the sorting.

I situated the external drive to my left and the tool kit to my right. Unfortunately, the view through my goggles was obscured by the volume of data scrolling by, leaving me nearly blind. I was used to it, though, and got around just fine by touch. Once I was set up, I reached for my kit to unzip it for easy access to the tools but frowned when my hand brushed only metal.

Nothing there.

A cool breeze ruffled the hairs on the back of my neck, which sent a shiver through me and raised gooseflesh on my arms.

"Get it together," I muttered to myself, stretching out farther in search of the kit.

The pressure from this high-profile crawl was getting to me, that was all. Meanwhile, the data continued to creep by, taking far too long even for ten years' worth of information.

"Tech 418, report task status."

Ahh. There was Mapper 21 again. I couldn't help but be somewhat grateful for the interruption. "Tech 418 reporting excessive data download. Task delayed."

Mapper 21 had kept the mic open, because I could hear her hit a few keys on her console. "What the hell?" Her voice sounded breathy and a little bewildered.

"Problem?" I asked absentmindedly, still focused on finding my tool kit.

"Tech 418, data delivery from all eight sections is being routed to lower-left console."

I blinked behind my useless goggles. I hadn't told it to send me the whole Cube's data at once. The plan was to visit each section and download data sets as I went. "Repeat, please?"

"You heard me, Tech. All section data is routing to your console. Estimated completion is ten minutes."

Well, good. Maybe by that time, I could find my damned kit, though there was no way in hell I'd say that out loud.

"Mapper 21, estimate safety window for goggle removal."

The pause hung heavy on the open channel. I could almost hear the curiosity oozing over the silence. She finally came back with "Tech 418, while removal of goggles is never recommended, there is a thirty-second safety window."

Without letting myself think about it too much, I wrenched the goggles off my face and looked around wildly until my gaze landed on the missing item. It was six feet to my left. That was bad enough, because I would have had to throw the damn thing for it to be that far out, but it was also in the wrong direction.

Instinct told me this was all kinds of wrong and to take stock of the situation, but something else took precedence. You see, that thirty-second window wasn't some arbitrary corporate bullshit; it was to keep us Techs from going blind from exposure to the toxic lighting created by the Cube.

I rushed toward my kit and put one foot on it so I could wrestle my goggles back on. Before they were situated, I caught movement out of the corner of my eye about fifteen meters ahead.

Nothing should have been moving in the place but me.

Trying not to think about what I'd just seen, I jammed the goggles back into place before the allotted time. A flutter of fear was still tickling my chest, and I blinked a few times to make sure my vision was still okay.

I worked to keep my voice even when I reported in. "Mapper 21, who else is on system tonight?"

"No one is on system," 21 returned, a bit testily to my mind. "You and I are the only active staff."

Frustrated and just this side of scared, I abandoned all attempt at corporate lingo. "Who rerouted this data then?"

"I am inquiring, but no results have been returned." The confusion made Mapper 21 sound nearly human.

"Check again," I demanded. "Something moved, and it wasn't me. I saw it."

"Tech 418, there are no other living entities appearing on any read-outs. You are alone." Judging by the snark dripping from every syllable, my Mapper was losing patience.

Part of me wanted to report this weirdness that seemed to be creeping up from the nooks and crannies in the machines around me. I would have if not for the knowledge that I was already going to be facing an inquiry for removing the goggles. Pressing the issue of an intruder that might or might not have existed would only damage my reputation and hit the brakes on any upward career swing, so I shook out the tension in my shoulders and tried to focus.

The upload finally finished scrolling, and I reached down to retrieve my kit. Selecting the appropriate connectors, I used the keypad strapped to my hip to delete the old data.

I reassembled my kit and reviewed the current data. The data was off. "Mapper 21, confirm auxiliary power specifications."

I already knew the answer but had to get it on the record. Once she confirmed the expected specifications, I dutifully reported that the whole Cube seemed to be running on only a fraction of its auxiliary power. No wonder things seemed spooky. Maybe the data from the other sections was some kind of emergency protocol, and the movement had been just my eyes working out the unfamiliar environment.

"Tech 418 requesting permission to troubleshoot auxiliary power issue."

While I waited for Mapper 21 to get me the permission, I moved on to the next interface on the list. Unlike the location in more modern Cubes, it was a leisurely forty-odd-meter stroll away. Two narrow alley-ways behind the bulwark later, I found it. If this had been one of the modern, more compact Cubes, I would have had to climb a set of ladders and then do another belly crawl.

This part was a snap, for which I was eternally grateful, because the last spot in this sector was done by the time Mapper 21 gave me what I wanted most of all: permission to repair something inside this historic Cube.

"Tech 418, permission granted to troubleshoot auxiliary power issue. Please note that the aux power node is on sublevel two and requires special door unlock permission to proceed. Mapper 21 reporting security approvals obtained."

Hustling downstairs so efficiently that Mapper 21 didn't even have to prompt me only added to my improving mood. Then it just took a few assists from her to look up the old schematics and get the aux level back to standard. Despite our mutual dislike for each other, we did some good work together.

"Thanks, 21!" I chirped as I prepared to resume my crawl.

I was contemplating the likelihood of getting a permanent assignment to this rare treasure of a cube, with its occasional wide-open spaces and simple fixes, when I sensed I wasn't alone. Before I had time to react, something tore past me, getting close enough to knock me into the wall.

———

I RECOVERED QUICKLY and whipped around. No one was there. Suppressing a string of curses that would have embarrassed my parents, I went still in hopes of catching a sound that might clue me in to what the hell was going on in here. When that got me zip, one option remained. Not wanting to do it but needing to all the same, I yanked off my goggles in time to make out the shadow of something skirting a large piece of equipment before dipping out of sight.

Shadows were good.

Kind of. They meant mass, which meant it wasn't a ghost or other intangible nightmare. On the flipside, it also meant I wasn't alone.

If taking off my goggles had been a dumb idea last time, it was an even worse idea this time. The upped power supply in this area brought more of the machinery back online and, with it, the energy-generation byproduct that was actively hostile to human sight. The goggles went back on even as Mapper 21 started shouting through my earpiece.

"418! Registering increased heart rate and breathing that are setting off alarms, and your goggles are reporting a malfunction. Report!"

Breath hitching, I backed up against a piece of machinery and slid to the floor, trying to make myself smaller, as if that would provide any protection.

"Mapper 21, 418 reporting." I bit the inside of my cheek to keep from tearing up—which would just cause another problem with the damned goggles. "I tripped on an uneven floor, resulting in displacement of my goggles."

There was a pause. The mic remained open again while Mapper 21 flipped some switches, and then she spoke again. "Maddie, please. Tell me what happened."

That nearly made me tear up again. But I didn't. I couldn't. Not here. And not now. "Mapper 21, I—"

She cut me off. "Tech 418, we are on a 1-1 encoded link. No one can hear you but me. Nothing is being recorded. And I can't help you if I don't know your situation."

I took a chance and even used her first name. "Helen, something ran into me. It nearly knocked me down. But I couldn't see it through the goggles. It was too late by the time I got them off. The thing was way off in the distance, and it disappeared in seconds." I lowered my voice. "I think it might be the guys. Hazing or something." I tried to keep it light by calling it hazing. But I was scared.

"No. There can't be. I've got nothing on any of my readouts. Not visual, not infrared, not temperature based. Nothing is moving around inside the Cube but you."

"Check the atmosphere," I suggested, working hard to keep my tone even.

I didn't have to say what we were both no doubt thinking: if there was something wrong with the air, I could be slowly asphyxiating and having all kinds of hallucinations.

There was a pause while she reviewed her logs. "Atmosphere is fine. No anomalies. Look, before we go back to the regular channel, I want to bring you out. Whatever is going on in there is dangerous. I know you want to stay—"

"I *have* to stay," I interrupted. "I can't ruin my reputation on my first crawl. You know what will happen." And she did too. One mistake, one situation demonstrating "lack of judgment," and I'd be relegated to equipment maintenance in some warehouse far away from any Cube.

This time, I could hear her nails—always pristine, always lacquered with animated polish that morphed and flowed with her mood—tapping on the side of her console. "Compromise. Let's at least move you out to the perimeter and into another subsection. You're done there anyway."

I agreed, and within a few moments we were back on the official channel, and she was guiding me, with too much of a mother-hen vibe for my liking, to the edge and to Cube A2. I was walking through a relatively large "hall"—a gap between rows of machines—when I stopped in front of a piece of equipment that was blocking my path.

"Tech 418, proceed to the end of the hall."

"I am at the end of the hall, staring at a machine."

"Tech, there is no machine in front of you. The hall is clear until a junction twenty feet ahead, which you should plainly see."

"There is a machine directly in front of me." I banged the side with the flat of my hand.

The silence on the other end of the comm was unnerving. Finally, Mapper 21 told me to go find the nearest data port and plug in. She was going to confirm my position based on that. There was a port close by (there always is), and I reached it in seconds.

"Well, what's my status?" I tried to keep the nerves out of my voice. This was obviously some kind of mix-up.

"Tech, you are about three hundred yards away from where we thought you were—and that is three hundred yards closer to the core."

This time, it was my turn to be speechless. I heard the comm click over to the other channel, the one Mapper 21—Helen—had said was private. The one I didn't really believe was private, because who can do a dodge like that around Enercorp's security?

"What do we do?" She sounded as unnerved as I felt. "We have to pull you out."

"I don't know if we can. I can't see everything that's happening around me with the goggles on. But I can't take them off for long. We just proved that we can't keep on a route."

"Keep your data port out," she suggested. "We will have you plug in to check location as we go."

She flipped back to the official channel. "Mapper 21 reporting malfunction of Tech goggles, resulting in spatial perception issues. Reestablishing location with Tech 418 and routing to outside."

Mapper 21 reporting... That phrasing made all the difference. If she called out the malfunction, she would be the one pulling the plug on the Crawl. And a good Tech always listened to the Mapper. She was, in effect, taking all the responsibility for aborting. My reputation would remain clear. I couldn't say anything about it while we were on the official comm channel, but we would talk later so that I could express my deep appreciation once I got out.

If I got out.

———

WE SPENT QUITE some time attempting to navigate back to the edge of the Cube. I dutifully plugged in my data port every chance I got. Mapper 21 would carefully correlate my position with her schematic. Then I would move on.

Occasionally, I heard a sound that shouldn't have been there. When I did, I stopped and held my breath. The noise wouldn't repeat, and I'd have to move on.

I allowed myself a quick peek around without goggles once every forty minutes or so. Once or twice, I thought I saw a moving shadow fading into the distance. I told myself it was imagination or jangly nerves from an aborted mission.

It would seem like we were making progress, but then something would obstruct my path, and the next data port I plugged into would show me in a far-flung part of the Cube, somehow closer to its center.

Mapper 21 always took a moment to flip to her private comm channel, to become Helen for a few minutes, and talk away my nerves. Her soothing voice came through the little earpiece like a blessing. I breathed and held on to her every word until she gently got me moving again.

I was keeping my eyes' exposure to the atmosphere in the cube as limited as possible. But there was a constant need to go bare-eyed and check my location. It was apparent that whatever made the goggles incapable of displaying the shadow creatures was also messing with Mapper 21's live schematics.

After Mapper 21 announced I was back at the same junction I had been to twice before, I began the now-practiced motion of whipping my goggles off, giving my surroundings a quick three-hundred-sixty-degree glance, and replacing them. Only this time, I was interrupted.

As I turned to look down the hallway from which I had just come, I saw them.

There were at least three, maybe four. They kind of blended together. But some details stood out in stark relief in the pellucid light that was eventually going to strike me blind if I didn't find a way out.

They looked like walking corpses—dried-out skin molded to bone so that I could hardly tell any skin was there, clothes hanging loosely from slatted shoulder blades, jaws agape and off center. Eyes were gone or so sunken they weren't visible. Their hair tufted dustily from the tops of their heads. And they were suffused with a low-level yet burning glow, while roaming tendrils of light crept over their bodies in meandering trails.

The worst ones were the ones that weren't fully clothed. Through gaping rips in their sides, I saw dried-out organs shift and stir when they moved. And the trails of light traveled inside them, too.

I wanted to scream, but something—self-preservation and sheer terror by my guess—wouldn't let me. Instead, my body made the next decision for me. I spun on one foot to sprint in the other direction and came face-to-face with one of the creatures.

The close-up view showed me I'd been wrong.

Its eyes were very much still there, just dried out and only loosely attached to the inside of its skull.

I jumped back, avoiding the first swipe of its arm. The back of my mind was shrieking at me about the ones that I knew had to be creeping up from behind. Jerking right then left in a zigzag motion to get past the thing saved my face. Its right arm came toward me in a low swipe, bringing with it a papery, acrid smell and hitting my side as I zipped by.

The pain was immediate and harsh, as if I'd been hit with a bat. More than that, a tendril of light stuck to my side then began to spread. But I pushed through as if the creature's arm was the bar of a turnstile then ducked under it to take off. As I ran, my hand swiped frantically at the sticky light in an attempt to get it off my jumpsuit.

My escape route had no rhyme or reason.

Twisting and turning my way as deeply as I could into a block of machinery was the only thing I could think of on the fly. Eventually, my stamina ebbed until I was wheezing from the effort. Through it all, my terrified brain understood that being struck completely blind would put me at a disadvantage. I used the last few moments of nongoggled sight to find a small opening down low, and I backed into it.

My trembling fingers made sure the earpiece was snug in my ear.

"Helen?" I tried to keep my voice low, but there was no hiding the stark terror.

It didn't help that the line remained silent. I didn't even hear static or the sound of an open mic. No Helen. Comm was completely cut. I backed myself farther into the little niche I had found. I used my feet to press my back into the cold metal behind me and waited. From time to time, I'd lift my goggles and take a swift look down the narrow hall in front of me to make sure none of those things were heading toward me. Eventually, I wouldn't even be able to do that. A foggy white ring was starting to encroach upon my peripheral vision.

I kept checking even though it wouldn't do any good. I couldn't over-power even one. The ache in my ribs was clear proof of that. My breathing was labored, but it was more from fear than any physical concerns. I knew it was a matter of time before one of them found me and—did what?

Turned me into one of them?

Or would they leave me to dehydrate and die on my own, only to be revivified with the searing white energy permeating the Cube? Would I rot and slowly flake away, roaming these spaces forever? Would I still think? Would I know? Or would I just be a dead, dry husk with no personality or sense of being?

There was a low thudding sound coming from somewhere in the Cube, which was strange, because all the machinery was usually silent save for the whisper of air currents. I thought they might have been coming for me. Then I realized that I was rocking back and forth, and my head was thudding on the machine behind me. Maybe I'd get lucky and totally lose my mind before anything bad happened.

I wanted to sleep but was afraid they would come for me during a moment of inattention. However, I had been moving and climbing and running for so long that I must have dozed off, because I was eventually awakened by a faint voice coming through my earpiece.

"Maddie! Maddie, if you can hear this, stay put!" The voice was barely there.

I quickly raised my goggles, took a glimpse down the hall, and reset-tled them. I cleared my throat, but my voice still came out as a raspy whisper. I couldn't believe what I was hearing. Had madness already started to set in?

"Helen?"

"Oh, thank hades. Don't move. Reception is really bad, and I don't want to take a chance of losing you."

"Right, right, I won't move. When they send someone in, they gotta know there are creatures in here, and you can't see them on the goggles." The panic in my voice was loud and clear.

She cut me off. "You have to listen up. No one is coming in for you. I got kicked out of the Comms room. They escorted me out of the building, took my badge. I'm fired, girlfriend. Now I'm back online, and don't ask me how."

"I don't care how," I snapped. "But why do I get the feeling you know what's going on?"

"Because I do," she replied in a cautious tone like someone approaching a wounded animal. "This crawl is a 'temperature check,' according to high-level emails. Officially, it looks like a standard review of temperature output data, and that *was* on our roster of tasks. But Enercorp knew people kept dying in there."

Swallowing a hard lump in my throat, I processed that bit of information. It sounded as if the superstitious stories about this Cube were more fact than fiction.

"Then why send another Tech out?" I asked, afraid of the answer but wanting the truth all the same.

"To see if it was still dangerous. Any and all personnel involved, from you to me to the guy who checked your gear before entry, are all considered expendable."

I hadn't thought I could feel worse, but a chill of dread expanded from my chest, down my spine, and into my limbs. "That's why I got the crawl? So if anything went wrong, I could just be another unlucky female Tech?" My voice cracked.

"Honey, I know this is bad. And you are in a terrible spot. But the best thing we can do right now is get you the hell out of there. Then we can worry about what an asshole the boss man is and how this whole company is rotten to the core."

Girlfriend? Honey? This couldn't be Mapper 21.

My first instinct was to call her out and demand to know what the hell was happening, but she only allowed me a moment or two to lick my wounds. Then she asked me for a description of what was going on inside the Cube. I worked hard to sound as sane as possible as I described the weird electrical living dead that were inhabiting the place. Meanwhile, she worked to reestablish a stronger connection to my goggles.

The fact that she could do that after having permissions revoked was testament to her skill. Only someone with serious know-how could get past all the layers of specialized Enercorp security. I asked how she was doing it, mostly so I could hear her voice talking to me instead of straining my ears to hear the approach of any shambling undead.

She laughed. "That's something I'm not gonna talk about even from this transmitter. Also, I can't talk. I'm working. I've got better tools out here that might help get you out, but they've got to be set up. Tell me more about the electro-creeps."

I tried like hell to stop checking my surroundings. I could tell even with the goggles on that my vision was getting worse. I could see an expanding band of white as my peripheral vision was eaten away. If the circles filled in, I'd spend the rest of my life with nothing but a blank white expanse in front of me. And I was fairly convinced that Enercorp wasn't going to pay the medical bills or support me through my readjustment period.

If I was lucky, they would cite some BS reason like unapproved removal of my goggles to avoid all responsibility. If I was unlucky, they would make sure I had a convenient accident now that I knew about this place.

Finally, Helen began talking again. "Okay, we got an expert here that says you gotta climb. Get as high off the floor as you can. Those things probably won't follow. They are pretty brainless unless they're in groups. So, pro tip, steer clear of packs, or you'll go from an 'is' to a 'was' real fast."

That wouldn't be a problem, since I had no desire to get close to one, let alone a whole gang. But something Helen had said sparked my curiosity. "Who are you getting this from? No one knows anything about this."

"Ask me later." Her voice was dismissive. "I'm busy. Oh. Also, you should look for one of those things that used to be a Tech, the older the better."

"Wait, wait, wait. We've progressed from 'climb to get away from them' to 'track one down.' Why?"

"You need an old Tech kit and an older set of goggles. They'll make it easier. If you get in a pinch, that's when you start climbing."

"I really don't think that's a good idea."

"Tech 418!" Her voice was a whip crack coming through the wire. "Get your tough-bitch act together and do it for real! We don't have the time to figure out something else."

I could feel myself smiling despite my fear. "Affirmative, Mapper 21. Big-girl panties are resecured."

———

FIND an old Tech with old gear. Stay as far away from the core as possible. Minimize nongoggle time (hard to do when I was hunting for something the goggles couldn't see). Tech numbering is sequential, so if those creeps had their jumpsuits marked, finding an old one would be easy. At least that was what I told myself.

I worked my way out of the big chunk of machinery I had wormed myself into. A quick goggleless glance around showed me that no shambling horror was in sight. I began to move through the quarter, trying to keep to a systematic grid pattern despite my limited ability to orient myself.

Helen seemed to be having an easier time keeping track of me. She had been able to "procure" a set of the oldest schematics in data storage. They were more accurate around the edges but began to lose that accuracy the closer I got to the core. We used that as a warning to turn in another direction.

I navigated mostly by goggle sight, but eventually, the sheer paranoia and claustrophobia of the situation would get to me. I would be convinced a whole crowd of electro-creeps was following me, and I'd have to look. I'd have to make sure I wasn't surrounded like before. And I had to look for one of my predecessors.

After what seemed like an eternity, I found one. Tech 23 was from back in the day. I could tell by his super-low number. He had his kit strapped to the back of his belt and even had some additional equipment dangling from his hip—goggles and something I couldn't identify. I spotted him while I was clinging to an upright pipe that branched off a staircase. I quickly described what he had to Helen.

"Perfect. Now you just gotta go get all that." Before I could ask how, exactly, I was going to do it, she said, "I'd suggest a bump and run. Sprint up from behind, give him a solid shove, grab his stuff, and run like hell."

It had sounded so easy when I was about twenty-five feet up and clinging to a pipe. It felt much different when I made it to the ground and saw that Tech 23 was at least half a meter taller than me. I couldn't spend much time following him and tracking him either. I had to hit him while he was alone and when I could actually see.

I got within three yards of him, taking peeks from under my goggles the whole way. An air current was blowing toward me, and I could smell him—a dry, husked-out scent that caught in the back of my throat. I took off my goggles and looped them all the way up over my shoulder. I began my approach, which was a fast walk until the last few steps. Lunging, I slammed into the middle of his back and nearly went down with him as he unexpectedly fell to the ground. I should have known the creature would be much lighter than a living person.

Avoiding his slowly kicking legs, I snagged the kit, the goggles, and, on a whim, the third thing on his belt.

When I turned to run, I could see that two more of them were making their way toward me down a side hall, but I had planned for this. I half ran to the stairs, attaching the old gear to my jumpsuit. I went up the steps two at a time, paused on the landing to pull on my goggles, and shimmied back out onto the pipe. My heart was a knot of painful throbbing in my chest.

Helen's voice was a constant in my ear. "Tech 418, status! Status, please! Status! Status, please!"

But I couldn't answer for quite some time, as the electro-creeps clustered around their fallen companion and spent some time slowly searching the area. One did even climb the stairs eventually, but he didn't give me, hanging out in space on my pipe, a single glance.

It wasn't until the search died down and I had made it back to the narrow hallway and my little hideout that I was able to talk to Helen and examine my old-school tools. "Mapper 21," I finally said in exasperation. I could hear her surprised intake of breath. "I couldn't report while they were looking for me, you idiot."

"Ha ha." Her voice was hoarse. Had she been crying? Not Helen. "Describe what you got."

What I had was a full antiquated Tech kit—the earliest version—which contained quite a few more tools than mine. I had an old pair of goggles. The third thing was unidentifiable to me. I described the little rod-and-handle arrangement to Helen, and she got back to me. It was a portable air welder. Modern Techs didn't carry them because they could cause too much damage. I liked the idea of that. Damage.

The next step was to find the nearest aux power port. Since I had restored the power, I was able to plug in first the goggles then the air welder. Helen did some hemming and hawing until she set up an audio link between the new goggles and the old pair. I struggled for a while with the unfamiliar straps but eventually got them secured to my head. The vintage goggles were strange. Oddly heavy, they weighed down the front of my face. And they had a lot more screen room. Also, the very center of each lens allowed for a real view of my surroundings rather than a computer-generated replica. All three of us—me, Helen, and her shadowy advisor—were banking on the old goggles allowing me to see the electro-creeps.

With a real-world view, I was able to make some quick changes to the air welder. It went from a benign tool that would generate a centimeter square of superheated air and would run for hours to a weapon that would shoot a blast of superheated air about five feet but could only be fired twice. In fact, I had a sneaking suspicion it might just blow up in my hands.

I left my new goggles behind and, armed with the old goggles and the air welder, I set off, determined to get out. Or there was always the option of dying trying. But if it came to that, I'd turn the air welder on myself or blow up some machinery to try to go out with a bang—there was no way I was going to spend eternity as an animated corpse.

At first, I thought it was going to be easy. I could see again! Better than I had in hours! And it felt good to hold on to the air welder as though it was going to do something for me.

But my little robbery caper had stirred the electro-creeps from their lethargy, and there were a lot more of them than I had suspected. After far too many close calls, one of which involved using the air welder to punch a hole in a creep, only to find out that it didn't slow him down one bit, I levered myself up onto the top of a machine.

There were so many machines, all so close together. Could I make it to the exit crawlway without letting my feet touch the ground? I set out to find out.

It worked great for a while. Helen kept an eye on the schematics and helped guide me. But some of my wilder leaps led to banging noises and clattering stops that eventually got the attention of the creeps. They did suck at climbing. But they followed me, pooling at my feet like the scariest and worst denizens of any dream. Some were missing pieces. Most were in Tech uniforms of some sort. I even saw a suit or two and a police officer's uniform. No matter what they looked like, they were all quite literally of one mind, which was to get their hands on me.

I made it to the first large bulwark area, where the machines ran out.

There were no more safe perches to travel on.

Setting my jaw, I ran along the tops of the machines, along the edge of the open area. Taking dumb risks, I leapt wider and wider gaps to get a decent lead on the mob. After I gained some distance, I let myself down to the main level and tried to loop back to the stairs that would take me to the crawlway, only to find the creeps strung out in a long line, blocking my route back.

"Not as dumb as they look!" I shouted to Helen, and I looked around for a solution. "I'm gonna hafta get lost in the machines again."

"Wait!" she cried, barely audible over my ragged breathing. "There's another one coming up on your left. Floor level. It's smaller, but watch your back."

"Smaller than the one I used to get in here? I'll never make it through." Hope warred with doom in my chest.

"Just get in the damn crawlway! It's only about an inch smaller!"

I went for it.

It came up just where she said it would, and I turned to make a direct run at it, diving flat on my stomach and sliding into it as fluidly as I could. That was when I really did break some ribs, finishing off the job the first creep had started. And let's just say Helen hadn't been a hundred percent truthful about the size of the crawlway. Smaller by an inch my ass. But I made it in and was able to shimmy myself deeper, out of the reach of the creeps.

I rested my head on my forearms and tried to regain my breath, sharp pain stabbing my side. I told myself it was just bruises and stated, "Tech 418 status report. Reached interior crawlway. Now what?"

"Work your way down it to an open area. That area actually leads to an entrance that was used to demo the Cube to important suits. They'd step inside and glance around and get to say they toured the Cube." The sarcasm in her voice was thick. "It will take you a while. That crawlway makes some ninety-degree turns on the way. While you get there, I'll work on getting it open for you. You'll have a straight shot out."

So I crawled. And I crawled. And my ribs really hurt. But I was terribly relieved, and I could almost feel the fresh air on my face. And I knew how good it was going to be when I got out and could see the sky, even if it was covered in the perpetual smoggy haze of the nearby city.

I took several breaks, lying face down and just resting. I was bone weary.

"There might be a slight issue when you reach the end."

When Helen said it, I could see the end of the crawlway approaching.

"What kind of issue?"

"Some of our electro-creep friends are out there in the big open space. I have kept the door mostly shut. It's ready to open on your approach. But you are going to have a sprint on your hands. And I'll try to trigger the emergency door to close as soon as you are through. But try to hit the big red button on the outside, just in case."

So near yet so far.

I got to the end of the crawlway and stared at the exit. There wasn't anything left to do but brace myself and run. I started out at a casual jog, feeling the grating pain of my ribs as I made my way toward the exit. I hoped the electro-creeps would just vacantly watch my progress. But I eventually got their attention and had to break into a sprint.

I pumped my arms and legs as hard as I could as they moved to cut off my access to the door. They weren't fast runners by any means, but they were spread along the side of the space, and some of them had much less distance to cover than I did.

I put my head down and flat-out ran.

With one last surge of desperate speed, I launched myself toward the door, which rose miraculously at the very last second. I could feel my feet tangle as I threw myself across the threshold, and I landed hard on my hands and knees. Pain shot through my side, but I told myself I'd worry about it tomorrow. I could feel it all tomorrow—the horror, the betrayal, the complete insanity—if only I managed to live through the next few minutes.

Levering myself up, I spun on the ball of my foot. Despite the dead-white halo of light that was obscuring most of my vision, I could still see the big red emergency close button. I slapped it with all my might. As the outer shell of the door came down, one of them reached out, arm sweeping wide to catch my leg. I leapt backward, watching as the door severed my pursuer's limb at the forearm. It instantly stilled, becoming a dry, withered, dead thing, its skin flaking away on the breeze.

"Tech 418, time to get the hell out of there before Enercorp reps show up. Proceed over the hill directly east of the Cube, and pickup will be waiting."

That was unexpected.

But Helen had a point. I knew too much, and so did she. Enercorp was going to do its best to stop us from spilling our guts to anyone. And by that, I meant it would make sure we couldn't say shit. As the saying went, dead Techs told no news stories.

A beat-to-hell taxi pod was waiting for me on the other side of the hill. It was painted matte black, so I almost missed it in the dark because someone had relieved the transport of all its lights—inside and out. We took off the second my ass hit the seat, speeding back to the city in near-complete silence save for a slight whirring.

I dumped both my Enercorp-issued Tech kits but kept my antique goggles. I figured Enercorp wouldn't be looking for those. Then I asked for a destination in the next town over. It was a long drive, but I felt better about going to a hospital far away from the action.

The trip also gave me the last few minutes of peace I was going to have for the foreseeable future, so I used them to put my head back and think. Everything was going to change. Sleeping with one eye open, ducking CCTV, and staying on the move were going to be my keys to surviving.

Truthfully, I should have been terrified at the prospect rather than excited. The idea of discovering truths nobody wanted the public to know made me ready to face whatever came next. Maybe I had just been a thrill seeker all this time and never known it.

By the time the hospital cleared me, a package was waiting for me at checkout.

I found a coded message from Helen inside. It said to meet her at a hotel halfway around the world and was accompanied by a credit stick containing a new identity for me and enough credits to get me there in style. She still had a lot of explaining to do, so my decision was quick.

I smiled. Oh, yeah. Things were about to change forever.

ABOUT D. L. SELLITTO

D. L. Sellitto has been writing science fiction and fantasy for several years but has just recently started sharing it with others. When she is not writing, she is playing classic video games with her daughter, taking her dog for walks, and avoiding cooking dinner.

DAYLIGHT GHOSTS

RACHEL E. BECK

A PI with an attitude problem races to solve one last case to keep from being written out of digital existence.

DAYLIGHT GHOSTS

C harlie came in to work happy on a Monday, which meant either he'd scored some points with an executive's wife on the elevator ride up to the office, or I was about to get fired.

"Big Charlie in the house!" I howled from the doorway of my cubicle loudly enough to earn glares from coworkers across the office floor.

Charlie hated the nickname these days, hated anything to do with the name Charlie. I'd caught him at a bar once, trying to convince someone with nice hips and an expensive manicure that all the girls called him Big Charlie—"Sweetheart, that's just the kind of guy he is." I'd made sure to call him Big Charlie every day for the next month, as loudly as possible, preferably in front of anyone with the power to give him a raise. *What can I say? That's just the kind of underling I am.*

The thing about Charlie was that he was such an insecure, power-tripping, egotistical wreck of a human being that he kind of made you want to shit on him. It was almost too easy, but since the benefits package for a mid-level investigator was pretty slim, I took what I could get.

This morning, something was different. Charlie turned from where he'd been talking to his secretary, straightened, and gave me a smirk before swaggering off into his office. He did the whole thing in slow motion, like he was in a holovid and the soundtrack was building in the background. It would have been hilarious, except it definitely meant that I was getting fired today.

Shit.

Getting fired is a pain in any profession, but getting fired as a private-ish investigator for Intelitry Inc. was its own patented brand of headache. Because we dealt with extremely sensitive information from extremely powerful people, there was a lot of motivation to make sure we didn't pass along what we knew to anyone who might find it useful. Techni-cally, even in a city like Neosaka, it was illegal to just kill us, but boy howdy, did old enemies from past cases have a way of turning up just as the office door was slamming shut behind us.

Murder might be illegal, but what *was* legal was classifying our exis-tence into oblivion the moment the firing paperwork was finished. *Alexandra Newfont? Never heard of her; no record of any Intelitry employee by that name.* It wasn't just your employment history either. Your own parents could be sued for leaking proprietary information, like your name or your birthday. You became a ghost in the system, and computers, famously, were not superstitious. With no employment record, bank account, or identification, you couldn't file for unemploy-ment because, well, the government's not a charity, and "Sorry, there's no one with that name in our system."

Charlie gave me an hour to sweat and imagine banging on doors, pleading with an automated system that I am real, I do exist, in fact, more than you do, you fucking robot, and then called me into his office.

His secretary, Sophia, buzzed me in.

"You gonna miss me?" I asked as I passed her desk.

Sophia didn't look up from her typing. "Tomorrow, I won't even know you exist," she said coolly and hit the return key.

I had to kind of respect Sophia. She'd made it going on twenty years in this company by hating everyone equally from the moment she'd been hired. Every promotion she'd ever gotten had been to stick it to someone else in the unending game of office politics. Empires rose and fell around her, titans came and went, and her frigid contempt remained pure and unwavering in a city rife with corruption.

I hoped—with the passion of a junkie looking for their next hit—that the day she finally retired, she would set the building on fire and walk away without looking back. I wouldn't even care if I was inside.

Big Charlie had already settled his eponymous frame into the chair behind his desk when I arrived. I had this idea that he'd been a boxer in college, and his plateau in corporate began the day he could no longer hit things to win the approval of his superiors. In that regard, today was a coup for Charlie. He'd finally solved a problem he couldn't punch.

The chair in front of Charlie's desk had been replaced with the broken rolling one from the empty cubicle down the hall that sank whenever anyone sat in it. Legal department as my witness, I swore he'd planned this meeting down to the second and probably fantasized about it for months.

"Take a seat, Alexandra," Charlie told me. "I'd like to discuss your performance these last few months."

I ignored the chair and opted to stand instead. Charlie's smile got fractionally stiffer. He folded his hands in front of the data pad on his desk. He didn't look at it, but I could clearly see the heading "Notice of Termination" at the top.

"It's come to Intelitry's attention that your numbers are down, Miss Newfont," Charlie said in a low voice that relished each syllable. "Do you have anything to say for yourself?"

He wanted me to protest, to point out that he'd given me nothing but cold cases for six months now, and that I'd even solved one of them, kind of, except the judge hadn't ruled the evidence was admissible in court. Then he'd tell me that I wasn't paid to complain, I was paid to solve cases, and I just wasn't cutting it these days. The company was sorry, but they were going to have to let me go.

I shrugged. "Well, gee, Charlie, I'm sorry to hear that," I said. "That can't reflect well on you as a manager when one of your best people suddenly starts turning up straight dog shit."

Under normal circumstances, Charlie would have been playing a dangerous game, letting the department's numbers crash like this. It put his head on the chopping block too. Not this time though. Phil, the new guy down the hall, was young and ambitious and worked too hard for too little since he was new to the industry. His go-get-em attitude was keeping the numbers just about stable even with me being kept on the bench every game.

"Unfortunately, Intelitry doesn't want excuses," Charlie forged ahead with his planned script. "They want results. In light of your poor performance, the company has decided—"

His desk phone rang, cutting off his finale. Charlie glared at me like it was my fault and punched the intercom button.

"Sophia, I told you to hold all my calls," he snapped.

"My apologies," came a reply thick with sarcasm, "but Mr. Henderson doesn't like to be kept waiting."

Charlie went from smug to stiff in the time it took for a traffic light to change colors. He scrambled for the receiver while making flapping motions at me with his hand. Probably he was telling me to fuck off out of his office, but I chose to interpret it as "Stand by for the funny story in case I pass out."

Charlie had never in his life received a direct call from the company's CEO and clearly didn't know if he should start sweating or preening.

"Good morning, sir, this is Charles Norrety speaking. How are you to —" Charlie started and then fell silent. "Get out," he mouthed at me.

"Ask if you can kiss his ass," I mouthed back and pointed to make sure he got the idea. What was he going to do, fire me?

"Yes, sir, she's in my office right—" Charlie's eyes darted to me and then away again. He eased away from his desk and spun until his back was to me. "No, sir," he said, "I was—" He fell silent again.

I didn't like where this was going any more than Charlie seemed to. Having a CEO know your name was kind of like grabbing the attention of those Greek gods from school textbooks. Even if one was halfway benevolent, it was sure to piss off someone else equally powerful. In the end, you got fucked or turned into a plant or whatever regardless.

"Yes, sir. Of course, sir. I'll do that right away," Charlie went on, sounding less and less happy with each affirmation. "And, sir, if I might ask—"

Mr. Henderson was apparently not in the mood for Q&A. Charlie spun slowly back around to face me. He hung up and did some perfunctory typing on his keyboard.

"So, what's up, Charlie?" I prompted after a moment.

"It's Charles," Charlie growled. "Mr. Norrety to you."

He picked up the data pad with my termination notice on it, turned it over, and then slid it into his desk drawer.

"As I was saying," he said slowly, forcing each word between his teeth, "the company has decided to give you one last chance to redeem yourself. There's been a case assigned to you, directly from Mr. Henderson himself. Details are"—he hit a key—"in your inbox. I want regular reports on your progress. Regular, you hear? Or I'll write your ass up for insubordination. I expect results this time, investigator. This is your final warning." He glared at me for a moment and then added, "Now get the fuck out of my office, you little shit."

"You're such a sweetheart, taking a personal interest in my career like this," I told him with a bright smile and then got out so legal couldn't prove I was the reason for his aneurysm.

"Looks like you're stuck with me a while longer," I told Sophia as I passed her desk.

Yikes. If looks could kill.

THE FACTS of the case were these: Mr. Henderson Jr., one Lawrence Henderson, left Friday evening for a weekend conference at Alta Terra Manor and hadn't made it home Sunday night. His pilot reported him missing when the normally punctual college sophomore didn't show up at the helipad for scheduled takeoff. Whoever got the alert didn't know Junior very well and thought he might have hitched a ride back with someone else. A half hour later, Alta Terra's cleaning staff reported that Lawrence's room still held all his belongings and that it looked like a tornado had tried to do his packing for him.

You could feel the rising panic through the rest of the report. Lawrence's phone didn't respond to pings, and calls went straight to voicemail. Delicate inquiries that masked the real question yielded nothing. No one remembered seeing Lawrence any later than Saturday evening, which didn't surprise me as much as it did the incredulous rank-and-filer writing the report. Alta Terra's techs discovered their otherwise-impressive biometric security and monitoring system was backing itself up into a self-destroying file that hadn't been there when they ran a systems check on Friday. The host, a Mr. Andrew Konig, reported nothing stolen, which may or may not have been true. No one knew anything, and Mrs. Henderson was very distraught. This morning, fourteen hours after Lawrence Henderson was discovered missing, Mr. Henderson Senior had given the order to pass the case on to me. I was to inform him directly as soon as I had anything to report.

"Any leads yet, Newfont?" Charlie asked from the doorway of my cubicle.

I checked the billable-hours timer that had started when I opened the file.

"Not yet, boss, but you're right," I told Charlie, "it's been an exhausting forty-eight minutes. I'd sure appreciate a nice warm cup of coffee."

He made a disgusted noise and wandered off.

"Four sugars!" I hollered after him to make sure he stayed away for a while.

If Lawrence had been kidnapped, every second was going to count, but I gave myself a few minutes to brood anyway. It wasn't an accident that this case had landed on my desk or that Mr. Henderson had bothered to look up my name this morning.

Lawrence Jr. and I had a bit of history. Back when I thought overtime and hard work meant a rent-a-cop could someday become CEO, I'd worked security at an exclusive high school Lawrence attended. His junior year, he fell afoul of the machinations of corporate intrigue when his dad became CEO. Someone framed him for a mid-level theft. It was nothing huge: a black mark on a CEO's legacy and maybe the setup for a bigger play later down the line. I'd crossed paths with Lawrence before, and my gut told me they'd collared the wrong kid. Looking back, I think it was the way he smiled at me like he was a typo on a billboard: embarrassed about being someone else's mistake. I did some legwork well above my pay grade, acted on a few hunches that would never hold up in court, and got Lawrence's name cleared inside of a week. Intelitry was grateful, and yours truly got offered a more interesting job at a much better pay rate.

Lawrence and I hadn't spoken more than a dozen sentences to one another since then, but I knew he'd gone to bat for me a couple times over the years whenever Charlie stirred himself to get me fired. Sweet kid as far as suits went, but I knew better than to rely on it. I wondered if his dad knew about him covering my ass. I wondered if his dad knew I had been scheduled to be fired this morning. Either way, the stakes were pretty clear: find Lawrence or I'd be written out of digital existence.

I got back to work. Alta Terra Manor's fancy biometric security might have been a bust, but there were other ways to look back at the last sixty or so hours. The little extravaganza this past weekend entitled What Makes Us Human had been exclusively for "the next generation of Neosaka's best thinkers," which meant its guest list was eighteen- to twenty-five-year-olds. Calling it a weekend conference was like calling a co-ed sleepover a study group. There were sure to be videos, 3-D shorts, and lots of pictures from high-profile, public-facing social media accounts.

I grabbed everything I could find and plugged it into facial recognition software. And then, while that was running, I went and got myself that cup of coffee that Charlie wouldn't be bringing me.

When I got back, the computer was reporting eighty-seven matches to the guest list and twelve unknown identities. Eleven turned out to be various objects around the manor the computer had mistaken for being human. The twelfth was a woman Intelitry's database didn't think existed.

———

I KNEW three things about the man I was going to see: he went by the handle West, he had terrible taste in music, and most importantly, he knew everyone. Bring him a picture or point someone out in a crowd, and for a price, he could tell you who it was, what they did for a living, their cat's name, and where they bought their morning coffee. The first time he saw me, he got up and walked away. It had to be an implant, some kind of cyberware, that was feeding him intel, but whatever it was, it was hidden well. No seams on his face, no implants on his temples. His eyes were real too. I'd seen them get bloodshot when he drank too much.

I tracked West down in the belly of a shitty twenty-four-hour dive bar in a part of town that made my Intelitry credentials a liability. I'd already dressed down into street clothes with an oversized bomber jacket to break up the silhouette of my shoulder holster, but the bouncer took one look at me and immediately knew me for a corp investigator. Maybe it was my hair. Maybe I just smelled like an office space. I upped the door charge by a fistful of cred so he'd let me and my gun in together and ducked inside.

Even at noon, the place was oppressively dark. Mismatched monitors and television screens with spliced-together cords covered every wall and streamed news, sports, and scenes from old, flat movies that started and stopped in random order. None of them had audio; all the shitty noise humming through the speakers came from a rickety box of a stage in the very back, where some shirtless guy with no hair was making electric whining noises to a rhythm by pressing a pair of mics against boxy plastic antique television sets.

I pushed toward West's stage-side bar table through dank air that stank of nicotine, sweat, and piss. Someone was there with him, head bent low in conversation. West saw me coming through the crowd, and his guest disappeared toward the bathrooms before I could get a proper look. I saw the back of a long blue leather coat with a high collar, and then they were gone. I made a mental note to buy a peek at the bar's security feeds later in case the coat belonged to anyone interesting.

"Fuck off, Alex," West told me without preamble when I leaned on the table across from him. "I'm not in the mood."

I relaxed a little. If he'd been charming, it would have meant he was on a job, and I would have been in trouble. West was a Runner: a styl-ized, high-skill mercenary who handled services no corporation could solicit legally. They came with an intimidating price tag and a worse atti-tude, which was a shame, because West was more-than-conventionally attractive. He had this overgrown mohawk thing going on that hung in front of his eyes when he tipped his head toward you and a smile that could make an android's heart short out. Lucky for me, he wasn't smiling now.

I wanted to banter with him, to bet myself a drink I could get him to laugh, but Lawrence's trail was getting colder by the second. "I have an offer you'll want to hear," I told him.

"Doubt it." West turned his back on me and rested against the table to watch the performance. He cut a nice profile against the stage lights. "If you could afford me, you'd be talking to a Fixer right now in a fancy hotel, not slumming it down here with the rest of the city."

He wasn't unholstering a gun, so he had to be at least a little curious.

"Maybe I like the ambience," I suggested to the back of his head and then paused. Now that I was closer, I realized the guy on stage wasn't just messing around with mics and feedback loops. The cords ran straight into his stomach like a human soundboard. The seal around one of the ports was starting to leak iridescent fluid, and it was running down into the guy's waistband. Gross.

"Come on, West," I petitioned his back. "We're both busy people. Let's get to the point. I'm looking for someone. A woman."

He jerked a thumb over his shoulder toward the exit. "Pole dancing at the club down the street starts in an hour. That's the last free piece of information I'm giving you, as a favor."

"There's a trace on you at Intelitry," I told him. No reason to be coy about it. "You want to talk favors? I've been tracking you for months and haven't called it in to anyone. Not even CERD. I need a win right now, and you know what they pay in Runner bounties."

I had his attention now, enough to make him turn back around at least.

"You got proof?" he asked. His eyes flicked past me at the rest of the bar, maybe checking to see if I'd brought any friends.

"Found you, didn't I?"

Common sense told me to keep an eye on his hands in case he went for a weapon, but instinct told me to play it cool, to walk back the threat level. Runners took it personally when you acted like you could control them. West was a people person by Runner standards, but if I ever left him and Charlie in a room together for five minutes, Intelitry would pay out a life insurance policy. I focused on the stage, where the human soundboard was wrapping up his set.

"I can get rid of it for you," I went on when he didn't say anything. "You tell me where I can find my lady, and I make sure me or any of the other suits at the company don't bump into you again during work hours. If you tell me no deal, that's fine. You and me, we're still friendly. I have other leads. Thing is though, it's my neck if I don't solve this case. And this new kid, Phil, is real law-abiding and real curious. When he replaces me, I bet he follows up on that trace himself."

What I was offering him was indisputably illegal. It was the only type of deal he could believe might come without strings.

West looked at me sidelong. "Let's see a photo then. No promises."

I pulled a data pad out of my jacket and slid it across to him, moving nice and slow so he could see both my sidearm and that I wasn't reaching for it. West folded his arms into a nice frame for his chest and leaned over to take a look.

The woman in the picture was in her late twenties. She had dark shoulder-length hair, nice makeup, and an outfit designed to be over-looked. She drifted past in the background of a handful of photos, never speaking to anyone, never looking directly at the camera.

West flipped through a couple stills without evidencing much interest.

"Yeah," he said, "I know her." His head tipped toward me a little, and the ends of his mohawk swung in front of his eyes, drawing me in. "How do I know you'll keep your end of the bargain?"

Relief rolled through me. "How do I know you're not sending me down a dead end in a bad part of town?" I countered. "We both gotta extend a little trust here if this is going to work."

West stared off past me at the bar again, weighing his options. Finally, he smiled. It was charming and boyish and perfectly calculated to make me forget everything that wasn't him.

"All right," he said. "It's a deal. But seriously, Alex? Erasing me from your life was the best payment you could think of?" He leaned in close enough to make me wonder if Lawrence could wait just a little bit longer. "ViX? This is Alex. Alex, meet ViX."

Something as small and sharp as a petty, broken promise pressed against the soft spot where my ear met my jaw. My skin crawled as I remembered, too late, that I'd put my back to a room full of people who didn't like corporate busybodies. My eyes flicked down, and I saw the sleeve of a blue leather coat.

Shit.

"You're in the wrong part of town to be asking questions," said a woman's voice in my ear. "No sudden moves, sweetheart. What's in this needle won't kill you outright, but it will put you out long enough for me to get you somewhere private, where I can take my time."

"Geez, lady," I said while being very careful not to move my head. My heart hammered furiously. "At least buy me a drink first."

She clicked her tongue in a little noise of disapproval. "Not very original."

I made a strained attempt at a smile. "I prefer to think of myself as a classic."

"Well, I'm going to let you two get to know each other," said West, "so if you'll excuse me...." He straightened up and pushed his hair out of his eyes. "ViX, I'll see what I can do about your problem. Alex?" He tapped the table with a finger. "You better hold up your end of the deal, or I'm going to take it very personally." He rolled his head to one side thoughtfully. "Unless you get dead. Then I'll let it slide, just this once. For old times' sake."

He headed off toward the bar. I saw a woman with a glittering neckline fluff her hair and detach from a huddle of friends to intercept him. I didn't have time to wonder how that little vignette was going to play out because ViX slid a hand under my jacket and looped it around my waist. Four little pinpricks pressed against my stomach through my suddenly-too-thin shirt.

"Let's go somewhere we can talk," ViX said in my ear. "Out the back way, past the bathrooms, nice and easy."

As we left the electronic chaos of the bar, my phone finally caught a signal and rang loudly. I'd have ignored it, being occupied as I was, but

ViX fished it out of my pocket with her free hand and checked the screen.

"Four missed calls," she said. "Who's Charlie? Should I be jealous?"

Fucking Mondays.

———

THE SOMEWHERE PRIVATE ViX had in mind turned out to be the strip club down the street that West had mentioned. The place wasn't open yet, but the bouncer saw ViX and waved us through anyway. Inside, setup was still underway. The house lights were up, but neon poles were lit, and there were holograms turning tricks on loop by the cheap seats near the entrance.

"I need one of the back rooms for a few hours," ViX told the guy with the plunging neckline behind the bar. "Something soundproof."

He barely spared us a glance. "Number 12's open."

"My lucky number," I quipped and felt a needle sink into the softness of my gut.

"Would you relax, lady?" I snapped because I was well and truly scared at that point.

Then the world went black.

When I came to, I had one wrist handcuffed to the headboard of a plush bed in a thickly padded room. The lights were low except for a hazy blue spotlight centered on me. ViX had pulled up a chair to the edge of the light near the foot of the bed. She watched me, arms folded and both feet propped up on the mattress. I looked over. The handcuffs were pink and fuzzy.

"Now who's being unoriginal?" I said and shook them at her half-heartedly. My words slurred a little, but that hadn't stopped me one infamous karaoke night, and it wasn't going to stop me now. I raised my free hand. "And where's the other one?"

ViX looked at me utterly deadpan. "I thought that might make it seem sexual."

Maybe it was the drugs, maybe it was the nerves, but I laughed.

ViX didn't smile exactly, but her jaw relaxed. I took the opportunity to get a better look at my number-one suspect, though I still wasn't clear what crime I wanted her for. ViX had her hair down and swept to one side, with less makeup than she'd worn in the pictures. The rest of herself she'd wrapped away in the long blue leather coat and tall boots. It suited the coil of her body well, the way the curve of a barrel suits the bullet of a gun.

I heard my phone ring again from inside her coat, but ViX ignored it this time, so I did too.

ViX studied me back. I wondered if she was like West and could tell things about a person just by looking at them or if she was like me and had to do her detective work the old-fashioned way.

"So," ViX said at length, "you wanted to find me. Am I everything you hoped?"

I shrugged like I wasn't hemmed in with total erasure as a person on one side and a slow, painful death by Runner on the other. "Look, if I'd known who I was meeting, I'd have arranged a more expensive introduction. Still wouldn't mind getting your number though."

She frowned, and her head tipped a little to one side. Dark eyes searched my face. In a different context, the expression would have looked absolutely charming on her, but here, it made me feel vulnerable in a way I hated, as if my engine light had come on and she'd popped my hood to have a look.

I retreated behind my reason for being in this part of town in the first place. "So, what were you doing at Alta Terra this past weekend?"

ViX's lips thinned. "I was afraid it might be that," she said and flexed her left hand. The last joint on every finger split, and tiny syringe needles hissed out.

I don't know if I swore out loud, but the sentiment had to have been there on my face. I'd seen some weird cyberware in my time, but my-manicurist-is-a-classic-horror-franchise was a first for me.

ViX got up, and my poor, drugged brain kicked into high gear. Instead of spending the last few seconds of my life wishing I'd done more with it or at least gotten a cat, for fuck's sake, I let everything I'd seen of Alta Terra manor wash over me and tried to square it with the ten minutes I'd known ViX and a reason for her to keep me alive. I was deep in no-bad-ideas territory, which was good because the next thing that came out of my mouth was, "But West's not a Fixer."

ViX's expression didn't flicker, but she paused with one knee on the bed between us.

"Like, don't get me wrong, he'd probably be great at it," I went on, hoping fervently that I'd make sense before ViX's patience ran out, "except he'd need to get over his hang-up with corporate types. Anyway, the point is he's not a Fixer, so why'd you meet him? It wasn't the music. I mean, look at you. You've got *taste*, for fuck's sake. Okay, needle fingers are a weird aesthetic, but they're a choice, you know?"

Internally, I begged myself to shut up and not give her reasons to kill me even more slowly than she was already going to, but something was wrong, and my mouth kept dumping out whatever was going through my head.

"So anyway," I rattled on, "you were there meeting West on business but not getting a new gig. Does that mean the Henderson Jr. job isn't over? So what do you need West for? Maybe you lost someone? Or maybe West does other stuff I don't know about. Shit. Sure would have been nice if my incompetent ass had scoped the place for a little while before sauntering into the thick of things, you know what I mean?"

ViX smiled at me in a way that turned my blood to chilled wine. She settled back into her chair and crossed her feet on the bed again. "Finally," she said. "I thought an elevated heart rate might get things moving."

"There were more fun ways to do that," I pointed out.

Fuck, why couldn't I shut up? My investigator's brain offered me an answer that my mouth immediately served up.

"You drugged me?" I demanded.

ViX raised an eyebrow.

"You drugged me *twice*?"

Her smile widened.

"So, tell me," she said, "who's this Henderson Jr.?"

"Lawrence Henderson," I answered promptly. "Son of Intelitry's CEO. He's not a bad kid, honestly, but he doesn't have his father's cutthroat ambition. I think his dad's hoping university will instill it in him, but I dunno. Half the time, these graduates come out more compliant than when they went in. You get what you reward, you know?"

"Is that so?" said ViX politely, as if we were at a cocktail bar and I was starting to bore her. "And he's the client?"

"The case. Last seen Saturday evening," I went on. I didn't know exactly what I'd been dosed with, but I could list offhand a couple black-market drugs that absolutely destroyed a person's inhibitions, usually for fun. If I couldn't fight it, I might as well listen up in case I said something smart. "Since you were there too, I thought maybe you got your little needle claws into him, and the company would need another heir apparent. But since you're asking me about him, now I'm wondering if maybe you were there for another reason."

ViX made a noncommittal noise, which my drugged brain took as an invitation to keep talking.

"Maybe you didn't have anything to do with Lawrence going AWOL. Disappointing if true, given what it's cost to find you." I squinted at her and made a logical leap. "Why do you want an investigator?"

ViX snorted. "What makes you think I want you?"

I jiggled the fuzzy handcuffs again. "Besides the obvious? I'm alive, and it's not because your drug makes me a scintillating conversationalist. You want to use me to generate intel, fine, but at least give me some facts to work with. What did you do at Alta Terra this weekend?"

ViX folded her arms and drummed her needles against the sleeve of her coat. For an agonizing minute, I thought she wasn't going to answer.

"Someone wanted Andrew Konig dead," she said at last, "and a weekend full of drunk, high, rich college students was a good opening."

Konig. I recognized the name from the report. He was Alta Terra's owner and a major stakeholder in a robotics security company. Intelitry had done business with them a couple times, had even attempted a hostile takeover a few years back. As far as I knew, things were relatively peaceful these days.

"Unfortunately, Konig thought so too," ViX went on. "I couldn't get close, so I settled in to wait. Then I got lucky. A tapped security feed reported Konig had suddenly decided to take a walk, all by himself, to a remote corner of the grounds. I couldn't follow him—they had electric fences and bio-coded REX models patrolling everything outside the main house—but my drone followed him easily enough. It confirmed the kill, and I got busy covering my tracks before the alarm was raised. In and out, smooth. The only flaw in the operation is that when I went to collect yesterday evening, Konig wasn't actually dead."

I laughed because drugs make you stupid. "That's embarrassing."

"Shut up," ViX told me, but it didn't sound like her heart was really in it.

"So why West then?" I asked, still incapable of shutting up.

"Trying to figure out who I did kill. And hunting down the fucker that sold the drone to me." There was venom in her voice. "That bastard cost me a payout and credibility with my Fixer. Then you showed up." She smiled thinly. "Quick work. I didn't realize West was friendly with any investigators, or I'd have avoided him for a few weeks."

"I think today is Exhibit A for why these kinds of relationships don't work out for the investigator," I replied. "So, you pumped me for intel, and now...." I paused. "Do you think you could find the body? The kill the drone reported as Konig?"

ViX raised her eyebrows. "I'm still trying to decide who might pay for your corpse, and you're asking me for a favor?"

"Seems only fair given the one I'm about to do for you," I said.

I'd finally thought of a reason for ViX not to kill me. By no-bad-ideas standards, it was a pretty good one. ViX didn't look like she was buying it. I gave her my biggest smile, the one I used to drive up Charlie's blood pressure when he was annoying me.

"Since we're friends now," I told her, "I'm about to give you another shot at killing Mr. Konig."

———

"CHARLIE," I said patiently when I could get a word in edgewise around his yelling. "Charlie. Big guy, listen to me. Think about how badly you want to fire me. Then think about how much I enjoy making your life miserable. Do you really think I'd let you catch me clubbing halfway across town in the critical hours of an important case? Isn't it just a little bit more likely that I had an important lead I was following up on so I can crack this case and rub it in your face for the next year while you still can't get me fired?"

Charlie hung up on me.

I pocketed my reclaimed phone and looked out the helicopter window at the city below. Even by air, it was a couple hours to Alta Terra. True to its name, the estate sat in the foothills on the outskirts of Neosaka. As a privatized reserve, it was one of the few places one could still go to see uncultivated forests and undomesticated animals larger than a stray cat.

That was part of the reason I'd kept ViX close at hand. The idea of sweeping dozens of square miles of biomass for a decomposing corpse didn't appeal to me, especially when time was still the enemy. The rest of it was nagging doubt. I was pretty sure Lawrence was dead and I had the killer buckled into the seat next to me, but there were other angles to this case that didn't add up to a full circle. Why had Lawrence left the party Saturday night, and why hadn't it triggered any security alerts? Who had tossed his room? Had that been after Lawrence disappeared, or was it the reason?

I glanced over at ViX. She looked watchful and tense about being trapped in a corporate chopper fifteen hundred feet off the ground, which was gratifying after the ordeal she'd put me through. I'd introduced her as "my assistant, Natasha," to the security guard I'd requested along with the chopper. Rent-a-Cop-Toby didn't look like he'd bought it, so at least he came with baseline survival instincts. Ever since we'd boarded, he'd kept his eyes on ViX and one hand on his holster. It was the main reason I'd requested him. If it ever came to a fight, my money was on ViX killing us both and maybe also the pilot, but barring that, it kept her eyes on Toby instead of over my shoulder.

I pulled up one of the chopper's onboard computers and tabbed through additional intel that had been filed since this morning. A dossier on the conference's What Makes Us Human speakers had been uploaded. I skimmed it to give my subconscious time to work without me interrupting it.

The keynote speaker was a guy named Roman Audhild who claimed that what made us human was our desire to create in our own image, to anthropomorphize the world around us. We saw faces in clouds, bred dogs to have eyebrows, and, in the modern world, created soft AI and corporations that ought to qualify as nonliving persons. He speculated on the future of corporations-as-organisms, composed of colonies of special-ized systems, siphonophora in all but genetic material, capable of adapting and reproducing, and vested with a survival instinct. From most legal standpoints, he argued, corporations were effectively indistinguish-able from human beings.

I wasn't paid enough to do philosophy, but I was pretty sure Mr. Audhild had never had a real manager or worked a nine-to-five in his life. In my experience, telling the difference between a corporation and a person was simple: just watch and see which one the shareholders treated as expendable in the event of a crisis.

It got me thinking about people though. The case-cracking profession was still a viable one largely because people weren't logical creatures. For all the resources we sank into complex learning programs and expen-sive if–then education, we still basically did whatever our gut was telling us. People were kind and cruel against their own interests, took risks, and shied from opportunity no matter the odds. Social scientists could build great big working models of human behavior that predicted trends and sales and wide-scale beliefs, but when it came down to the single indi-vidual, it was anyone's guess what they'd do next. There was no algo-rithm or cure for the human condition.

Growling storm clouds dogged our flight, and it was raining when we touched down at Alta Terra manor. I shook off the fog of a melancholic mood and went to greet our host. Mr. Konig met us at the helipad with an entourage of assistants and two hulking REX models. I tried not to stare. The canine analogy was a useful fiction to make the heavy-duty security bots palatable to the public, but up close, nothing about the four-foot-tall gunmetal-black quadrupeds felt remotely dog-like. They moved with the confidence of an alien intelligence not overburdened with animal vulner-ability or human mercy. Maybe marketing should have given them eyebrows.

Mr. Konig was polite but very busy. He condescended to shake all of our hands, expressed his dismay over "these unfortunate circumstances," and then excused himself, leaving us in the care of an assistant. I breathed easier after he was gone. I'd negotiated ViX into waiting to kill Konig until we'd finished my job, but I'd also made peace with myself that if she reprioritized, I'd have to try to stop her. At least death by scary hands was preferable to dealing with the inquest and inevitable corporate warfare brought about by an assassination in broad daylight.

Probably.

It took some persuading to get the assistant to turn me loose outside the electric fence that ringed the main house, but ultimately, I had the credentials to threaten him with obstruction. He assigned a REX model to us that could act as a guide and double as a narc if we tried anything off-limits.

"What can I help you find today?" the REX inquired. Its voice was far too chipper for a machine designed to end human life.

I nodded at ViX. "Do your thing."

ViX consulted some readouts on a data pad and then walked off toward the perimeter fence without looking to see if we followed. The REX padded after her, chattering up a storm about the history of Alta Terra manor. Toby shot me an anxious look. The guy looked as if he hadn't had this job for more than a year.

"At least we'll die together," I said and gave him a thumbs-up.

Hard to tell for sure in the rain and the gathering gloom of an early evening, but Toby didn't seem reassured. I fell in behind ViX as the rain got harder.

IT TOOK us more than an hour to find the corpse, and when we did, I almost tripped over it in the half light. ViX put out an arm to stop me just in time. She wandered off a little ways and stood impassively as I switched on a penlight and crouched to take stock of what remained of Lawrence Henderson Jr. The tide of rigor mortis had come and gone, leaving his corpse lax and soft again. Poor kid. Whatever had brought him out here that night, he hadn't deserved a lonely death facedown in the loam. I struggled for objectivity. What was he to me, really? Just a rich kid who had saved my career a few times and had bought me one more chance with his death. Fuck. I brushed aside the hair at the back of Lawrence's neck. The dart that had killed him was still embedded there. I left it alone for the coroner to deal with. At least it had been a quick death.

The smart career move here was to call in the chopper, get Lawrence's body to a morgue, where the autopsy would tell me nothing I didn't already know, and then sweep the woods on foot for clues to why Lawrence had been out here that night. Even if I didn't find anything, the search for an answer could keep me employed for months, maybe even years.

I looked over at the REX model. "Hey, Fido," I said, "are there any important facilities around here? Some place we definitely shouldn't know about?"

The REX thought about it. "I'm sorry," it replied. "Facility layouts are classified."

"Of course they are," I muttered. I remembered what ViX had said about her drone giving her bad intel. "Do you know who this is?" I asked and pointed at Lawrence's corpse.

"I'm sorry," the REX repeated. "I can't answer that."

It had been a long shot anyway. It looked like it was time to invest in some hiking shoes.

I rocked back on my heels, and the penlight glinted off of something metallic peeking out of Lawrence's shirt collar. I snapped my fingers at Toby for a better light, and he approached gingerly, as if he was afraid whatever had killed Lawrence was catching. I kept one eye on ViX in case he was right.

A quick frisk of the corpse uncovered metal rings around the neck, wrists, and ankles. I could feel another thicker one around his chest under his shirt. I heaved Lawrence over onto his back and tore open his buttoned shirt to get a better look. The first thing I saw was Intelitry's logo printed on the outside of the band along with a prototype number.

I covered it again in a hurry and looked up to see if either of the others had noticed. Toby was busy looking anywhere but at the corpse at his feet, but ViX's eyes gleamed in the glow of the flashlight.

"Find anything?" she asked innocently.

If I hadn't known better, I'd have guessed she was laughing at me and my caution.

I made noncommittal noises and looked down again to avoid eye contact. There was a cord running under Lawrence's shirt down into his pocket. I tugged it free, and his phone came with it, devoid of charge. No wonder security hadn't been able to ping it. Expensive models like this one had a huge battery life, but it looked like he'd been using it as a power bank.

Toby coughed and shifted in the loam. "Shouldn't we call someone?" he asked. "It's just… it's getting late."

Night out here would be a lot darker than anything any of us were used to inside city limits. Still, I hesitated. The fewer people that knew about what we'd found—and what exactly had we found?—the better. Besides, I was curious.

"In a minute," I mumbled and plugged in my own phone in place of Lawrence's.

Nothing happened.

Maybe the prototype controls were on Lawrence's phone, or maybe… I wrestled one of the rings off of Lawrence's wrist and onto my own. His hands were bigger than mine, so it slid on easily.

"It's a pleasure to see you this evening, Mr. Konig," said the REX in a loud, clear voice.

Toby's flashlight bounced wildly. I had time to glimpse the REX's side panels unfolding before something slammed into me and drove me down into the loam. Darkness and then a sudden, overwhelming brightness blinded me twice over. Weight on my chest pinned my arms to the ground and made it hard to breathe. I narrowed my eyes against the light and made out ViX's face above mine. She was watching something else, but the fingertips of her raised hand glittered threateningly over my head.

Very slowly, I shifted my head around to see what had her attention. The REX stood over both of us with a spotlight and a fucking Gatling gun raised up out of its back.

"REMAIN CALM," it thundered in a voice that sounded nothing like its guide-dog routine.

"Fucking robots," ViX said in a distant voice, as if she was watching the event from somewhere far away. "This entire job has just been me getting fucked by robots."

"Is that a needle, or are you just happy to see me?" I wheezed.

Maybe it wasn't the drugs that made me stupid.

ViX's eyes flicked down. I wondered if she could feel how hard my heart was hammering.

"You're so—" she began.

"—classic," I supplied. I sucked in as deep a breath as I could manage. "Now get off me."

"Not a chance." ViX's voice was steady, but I could feel her weight shift subtly as she sought better balance. "The only reason I'm still alive is because bolts-for-brains can't figure out how to open fire without taking you with me."

"In another minute, Toby's hands will stop shaking enough for a clean shot," I said in the most even voice I could muster. "You kill me, the REX kills you. You hesitate, Toby does the honors. I have a plan. You buy it, sight unseen, and we both get to walk away."

"I have a shot," Toby said loudly. He didn't sound confident, but bless him for picking up on his cue.

"Come on, ViX," I said in a softer voice. "After all we've been through together? Have a little faith."

For a long moment, the forest was absolutely still.

Very slowly, ViX eased off of me.

"Stand down, REX," I told my rescuer. "But keep the lights on."

"Sir. Yes, sir," it confirmed. The Gatling gun folded smoothly back into its torso with a soft hiss.

I took a deep breath and sat up. Then I pulled out my gun and pointed it at her face. Our eyes met, and ViX read in them, too late, that I'd lied to her.

"You corporate bastard," she spat. Resignation and fury warred for dominance across her face.

I clenched my jaw to keep an apology from slipping out. I knew my job. The smart thing to do here was to breathe out, squeeze smoothly, and let the bullet and a team of lawyers solve all my problems. I had a victim, I had a killer, I had a witness, and it had been less than twenty-four hours since this case landed on my desk. Fuck just not getting fired. I was getting a promotion.

I didn't look away. I owed her that at least. Something in my stomach twisted at the thought that ViX, with all her skill and confidence and power, was going to die now, and Charlie, who had none of those things, was going to live, all because the employee handbook told me I could kill one and not the other.

What a world. Fuck.

I breathed out.

"You owe me," I said in a low voice. Very carefully, I got up and put a few steps of safety between us. "Get out of here. Go hide in a foxhole. The chopper log will show you rode back with us. You can do what you came for when we're gone and nothing can be traced back to Intelitry. Our deal is finished."

ViX gazed at me, her face unreadable. "Konig's already dead," she said, "or he will be next time he gets a hit of his favorite designer drug and mysteriously overdoses."

My mind skipped back to our brief meeting, and I remembered, all too late, the courteous handshake that had passed between us all.

"Then you have no reason to hang around," I told her. "REX? Clear the log from the last ten minutes. Don't record anything for the rest of this evening."

"Yes, Mr. Konig," it replied in its helpful voice.

Slowly, ViX turned her back on the muzzle of my gun and vanished into the darkness.

"Why didn't you…?" Toby asked in a hushed voice when ViX was gone.

I sighed and holstered my gun. "Because humans are stupid," I told him.

"But why did she—"

"Look," I cut him off, "all you need to know is that understanding what's going on right now is a good way to get yourself killed. Got it?"

Toby started to nod, and then his eyes widened, and he shook his head vigorously.

"Good man," I grunted. "Now call the chopper and tell them to come pick us up. And make sure they bring a body bag."

I FILED my report from the helicopter's computer, tagged it for Mr. Henderson's eyes only, then doctored the chopper's logs and spent some time brooding. I'd been careful not to speculate inside my report, but the implications were pretty clear. Lawrence was stealing company tech and selling it off for what could only be a life-changing amount of cred. When he'd failed to turn up at the rendezvous Saturday night thanks to ViX's confused assassination attempt, the buyer had gone through his room, hoping to find the goods. I wondered if the prototype I'd found on Lawrence's body was his first attempt at corporate intrigue, or if it was the last in a long string of luck that had finally run out.

I'd quietly removed the cause of the fuss while Toby was calling the chopper. Intelitry would want it back, but until I found out who to hand it off to, the fewer people who knew about it, the better.

For a while, I watched the rain outside the window and the neon lights of the city below, now muted by the storm. Eventually, I dozed off and slept until we landed in the small hours of the morning. I sent Toby on his way with a recommendation for some decent sleeping pills and a reminder to stick to the story we'd rehearsed. Most of the offices were dark at this hour, but I got a sleepy woman at the front desk of Intelitry's morgue to take possession of the corpse until business hours, when someone could fill out the right forms.

With only hours until dawn, I wasn't sure what to do with myself. Going back to my apartment didn't seem worth it, and my last clubbing experience had turned me off of that scene for a while. Feeling at a loss, I trudged back down the hall and took the elevator up to the office, where at least there'd be a chance at some stale coffee.

At the entrance to my cubicle, I paused. The monitor was on. I'd shut it off along with everything else when I left the office yesterday morning.

On a hunch, I booted it up and checked my system records. According to the activity log, I'd accessed my confidential report on Lawrence Henderson's disappearance from this desk a couple hours ago. Only one other person on the floor had login credentials to match my own.

Fuck.

Swearing under my breath, I went to hammer on Charlie's door. The light in his office was on, but the door was closed. It made a satisfying thud when I booted it open.

"Charlie!" I bellowed and then stopped cold.

Charlie was dead. He was slumped back in his chair, staring at the ceiling with a vacant expression of surprise on his face. A mess of pills and an empty glass were arranged artfully on his desk in front of him next to a data pad with the screen still on and a message typed across it.

I approached cautiously.

"I can't go on," read the first sentence, and I didn't bother with the rest.

"You poor, inept asshole," I breathed.

The final, missing angle of this case resolved into a circle large enough to make a noose around my neck. I looked around. My fingerprints were spread across the office from yesterday morning, and I'd just kicked in his door. Security cameras would have caught me taking the elevator up, and the timestamp could easily be doctored. Fuck me. I'd been so busy trying to save my job that I'd failed to consider that the last loose end on this thing was me.

"Expendable in the event of a crisis," I muttered.

THE CEO of Intelitry was surprised to find me in his home office in the early hours of the morning, but he took it in stride.

"Take a seat," I told him as I finished typing at his console.

Mr. Henderson Sr. opted to stand at the center of his office instead.

"Miss Newfont, I presume," he said. He had a nice voice: deep, self-assured. It must have been a comfort to the shareholders to hear him report profits each quarter.

I leaned back into the plushness of the desk chair. "You shouldn't have killed him," I said frankly. "Don't get me wrong, the bastard had it coming, but you showed your hand too soon."

Mr. Henderson nodded. "A calculated risk," he said. "Charles Norrety was not a discreet man. Leaving him for even a few hours could have proved disastrous, even if he didn't understand what he knew. In your case, however, I think we can come to an arrangement. I understand you to be a paragon of professionalism."

"That," I replied, "is a bald-faced lie and slander." I sighed. "I should have listened to my gut. Lawrence was a nice kid. Even if he had opportunity, he still needed someone to put him up to this cloak-and-dagger nonsense. Someone he trusted." I shook my head. "I'm sorry for your loss, Mr. Henderson. It should have been your ass out there that night, not his."

Mr. Henderson grimaced. "I take it I'm about to become the subject of the next news cycle."

I got up. "I think the shareholders will handle this more discreetly. No sense in threatening their stocks. You'll probably take time off to mourn the sudden loss of your son. Who could imagine what dark place your grief will take you a few weeks from now? All I know is, I can't remember the last time I read a headline about a CEO being fired."

Mr. Henderson's eyebrows rose. "Then why are you here?"

"Just needed your computer to file some paperwork." I shrugged and glanced down at the console. "You can stop hammering your panic button, by the by. Your security team has the day off, and the computer doesn't care if their replacements are real, just that the boxes are filled."

"I see," said Mr. Henderson. He didn't seem rattled by the turn his morning had taken.

I crossed to the doorway and paused. "You're calm because you've already got a plan to recover," I said. "You'll pin everything on Lawrence and me. The shareholders will buy it because it's a cheaper story than the one where you've been stealing from them."

Mr. Henderson's smile became just a trifle smugger. "You have to know I didn't get to where I am by being overburdened with a conscience," he pointed out.

I shrugged. "The thing though," I mused, "is that I was never here." I tugged down on the collar of my shirt so he could see the prototype ring around my neck. "And what's more, I don't exist. Haven't for the last half hour." I reached into my jacket and pulled out the data pad I'd taken from the top drawer of Charlie's desk. The "Notice of Termination" heading was clearly visible at the top. "The letter that's going to tip the shareholders off was written by you and sent from your desk. The only other person who knew that you handed this case off to me is dead in his office right now. No loose ends left to tie this to anyone but you."

Mr. Henderson wasn't smiling anymore.

I nodded to him. "You know what I think makes us human, Henderson? We're so damn petty."

Then I got the fuck off of Intelitry property.

———

I WENT SOMEWHERE high to watch the sun come up. It never really showed through the cloud cover, but there was a moment when a few rays of light broke through, and the whole eastern sky turned the angry red of a lover's bite. I knew better than to let it seduce me. There wasn't much of a life for a ghost in daylight. I turned my back on a world that had already forgotten me and plunged into the neon depths of Neosaka.

ABOUT RACHEL E. BECK

Living on the outskirts of Los Angeles, California, for more than a decade turned one-time fantasy writer Rachel Beck into an author of the cyberpunk series The Glitch Logs. When not hammering out new stories by the light of a dying laptop, she also enjoys gaming, tabletop RPGs, and escaping the cyber dystopia to enjoy nature. Rachel is also the author of The Dark Menagerie storied-jewelry series and co-creator of *The Dracula Files*.

RUNNING MEMORY

MATTHEW ANGELO

Hax finds more to life in New York City than being a netrunner for the Roadrunners motorcycle club. One of those things is finding trouble in the worst of places. Hax finds himself in deep trouble with a rival motorcycle club that is out for blood and money. As if his life couldn't get more hectic, he gets a frantic cry through a data pool that's tapped into his helmet. At the other end of the call, Hax finds Memory. She is under attack from the same club that wants Hax dead. Despite the risks, he saves the day.

Hax finds that there's more to Memory than meets the eye. As danger closes in on them, they must rely on each other. With time ticking away, both of them must fight to save not only themselves, but others like them. If not, they risk losing Memory's life and a chance to change the world.

RUNNING MEMORY

The air of New York City chilled my body as I sped through the mid-town area on my Damon Hyper-Fighter Colossus. The traffic or local law enforcement barely registered as a thought while I raced through the town. Even the security drones that flitted back and forth in the sky did little to deter me. Hell, breaking the law with reckless abandon was my nature. Unbridled freedom was a commodity in this world, and this was one of the few times that societal and corporate constraints fell away.

Few people stared in my direction, and if they did, I wouldn't have noticed. The city never slept and was breathing with life at all times of the day. I throttled down when I saw a few members of the motorcycle club I belonged to. We called ourselves the Roadrunners and did our best to make life frustrating for the corporations that ran this world.

I never resorted to violence like some others, but I had a knack for netrunning and getting into digital zones that corporations assumed were secure. Thanks to Gareck Corp, I got myself a pretty nice mod at their expense. It also put me on their shitlist, but that's life in New York City.

The mod helped me hack. It's also how I got my name. My right forearm was all cybernetic, which signaled the implant in the side of my head so I could jack in from anywhere. It cost a fortune, and I risked getting the sketch, but got lucky in that department. Others couldn't say the same.

I could ride forever if given a chance. Unfortunately, corporations had a way of tracking people down. The respirator I wore did more than filter the smog and pollution, which helped me breathe. It also signaled the drones flying overhead and the CCTV cameras, giving the authorities a different face than mine. As much as I wanted to run away to another city, nothing would truly change. New York City was one of many run by corrupt politicians bought by corporate money.

Traffic came to a stop. This was my city, and everyone here deserved better. It hurt to see how many struggled when the ultra-rich never wanted for a thing. Disease and sickness were everywhere, along with poverty. For those who modded themselves, the risk of the sketch was a harsh reality. Cybernetic mods were a booming business, but bad code caused a person's body to reject it.

So far, there was no way to fix it. The right money got you the right code. But back-alley mod businesses sprang up everywhere, and programming the mods with bad code caused the sketch. It started with slight tremors. Even now, a few pedestrians who strolled past shook slightly.

It was hard to deal with knowing that eventually the infections would start and they'd die. Probably from a seizure caused by a blood clot. That was the usual diagnosis. There was no way to fix the code, but so many took the chance. Hell, I took the chance. I got lucky.

I stretched as I rode through the streets. My balance was outstanding, and I could turn on a dime if needed without my hands on the bars. The city whizzed past me, and my heart raced with the excitement of the ride. Freedom. At least some semblance of it. The city needed more of that, and healing. With all the technology at humanity's fingertips, they chose greed over life. Because of this, the rest of us suffered.

It wasn't all bad. Large holographic billboards spouted the news and advertisements. Each ad promised a release from a problem or a need for another. It was all manipulation, and I hated them all for it. Even if there was a temporary escape from the drudgery of life, the cost was always too much. We've traded humanity for what? This life of indentured servitude and propaganda? Fuck, I know we can do better.

The light ahead of me turned red, and I skidded to a stop. As much as I wanted the freedom to ride, I also didn't want to end up as roadkill. A few sex workers motioned in my direction. Each one modded for his, hers, or their pleasure. Signs promising a few hours of ecstasy lit up the street.

A few corporate patrolmen glanced in my direction. Their uniforms were crisp and clean and gave off the feel of the Sturmabteilung from Nazi Germany in the past. They had slung their rifles over their shoulders. Law enforcement from higher up set them to kill and had no problem unloading a few rounds into a person. They nodded, and I returned the favor. I kept my goggles on to help hide my identity.

The mask hid me from the cameras, but not a person's eyesight. While I was a wanted man, I didn't want to take the risk that they'd recognize me. Stealing credits and tech from a corporation pissed them off. The light changed, and I took off as the surrounding city flourished with activity. Skyscrapers reached high through the smog that constantly covered the metropolis.

This was a place you could get anything you wanted for a price. Whether pleasure or pain, it was there. Most of these ended with a trip to the free clinic. Not that those places were any more sterile than a back-alley love fest. I stayed as far away from those as possible. There were enough problems with the club, and my parents were far from accepting of me belonging to it.

My dad spoke little as he operated a shop helping those with the sketch. He couldn't cure them, but he did his best to make their lives longer, or at the very least, more comfortable. My arm made them furious, but they calmed down after they realized I received good code. They got mad again once they figured out how I paid for it.

Occasionally, I helped him out in the shop. Few could pay, but he never asked for money. My club made regular donations to keep him going, but he only saw discreet contributions. He never brought up my netrunning but always told me to watch my back and be careful in whom

I trusted. I took that advice to heart, as New York City had a lot of shady people in it.

Forced scarcity made people do things they normally wouldn't. It sucked, and I dreamed of change, but the chances of that were astronomical. I was just one guy. What could I do? Not much, but I did what I could, even if it was a little at a time.

———

MY HELMET FILLED WITH STATIC, and a voice filled the earphones. *Help me.*

The voice echoed through my head as I raced through the city. I swerved a little before I stopped, my wheels skidding on the pavement. Her voice bounced through my skull. There were crowds of people everywhere, but no one gave an indication of being the one who made the call. Whoever did this wasn't here and had hacked a data pool to contact me. Why me, of all people?

Everyone around went about doing their business. I reached down and activated my Armatic iP1. It could only work within half a foot of my fingerprint. As a bioweapon, it only opened to my metrics. It didn't pack a big punch, but it was enough to make others duck and want to avoid getting hit. The static came through again. My com wasn't hack-proof, but it wasn't easy to get through. I did my best to make sure of that, and the static let me know that whoever was doing this was having a difficult time keeping the link open in the data pool.

This gave me a bad feeling, and I didn't want to take any chances. I already had one motorcycle club out there wanting my head. I didn't need another club wanting to beat me into the pavement. The Perfect Omega Motorcycle Club was bad enough. They usually stuck with drug running but had taken on corporate business.

Whoever you are, help me. Her voice echoed in my head. She sounded winded. If she was hacking on the run, she had my respect. *These bastards are going to catch up to me.*

Her voice reverberated in my skull and gave me a headache. Whoever she was, she had excellent skills. I needed to know more about how close she was and who was chasing her. I flexed my wrist and heard the bleep that opened my com. Probably not my smartest moment, but she needed my help.

"Where are you?"

I'm in an alley. They're everywhere. I don't know who you are, but I need your help.

"Who are you? Can you give me some tracking info?"

Call me Memory. I have a bunch of men on motorcycles chasing me. Here's my current location! One of them is crazier than the others, like he's on drugs or something.

I coasted forward as I used my helmet's visor to show me the way to Memory's location. The idea of another motorcycle club made me cringe. There were only a few, but the guy she described came a bit too close to the leader of one club who hated me.

My screen flashed a pin-pointer where she was. I took off in that direction. "I'm on my way."

Hurry, whoever you are! Memory yelled through my helmet. I could hear the fear in her voice. Few in this city had anyone to stand up for them. I had my club and family, but few had that. If one of the gang members chasing her was on drugs and acting strange, then it was the club that wanted my head on a stick.

I kicked my motorcycle into motion and sped toward Memory's last known GPS.

———

"GET THE FUCK AWAY FROM ME!" The shout came both from my helmet and from down an alley. That must be where Memory was.

I slammed on the brakes, and then I shot forward a bit as the bike skidded to a stop. The alley, like most others in the city, could stretch for miles like a labyrinth. I could get lost in there if I wasn't careful. There was also the chance of me getting killed or robbed. The streets were dangerous enough, but the alleys had their own type of law.

Right outside the entrance, a row of motorcycles were parked in a row. Each one had the sign of the Perfect Omega Motorcycle Club painted on them. A small golden omega sign within a circle. *Fuck me, this isn't good.* Of all the clubs in the city, she got in trouble with this one.

"I'm here, but this isn't looking good."

Hurry up. Her frantic voice echoed in my helmet. I parked my bike at the front end, facing the street for a fast getaway. Since I wasn't psychic, I knew I'd need to move fast. I scrambled my GPS as a few drones flew past me into the alley. This just got interesting.

Walking past the other club's bike, I cringed. This club was more than bad news. Besides drugs and extortion, they had a habit of working for Gareck Corp, doing their dirty work. That usually meant people disappeared. Anyone familiar with the city knew who they were and avoided them at all costs. If they were bullies, then I wouldn't worry so much, but between them and the added drones, shit got real. That meant Gareck Corp was after Memory as well.

The local law enforcement was useless and owned by the corporation. They had a habit of turning a blind eye to the Omega club. Every precinct had drones supplied to them by Gareck Corp. Coincidence was highly unlikely.

Memory's voice rang out. "Get off me. You can't do this. People need this code!"

I broke into a run. Garbage littered the ground, and halfway in, men and women dressed in traditional biker leathers and a jacket adorned with the club's symbol surrounded Memory. Two had her pinned against a wall, with another holding a small tablet in front of her. The tablet had wires hanging from it and their ends plugged into nodes on her arm. If I didn't know any better, they were going to hack her mods.

Though frightened, she was beautiful. A few of the other bikers made lewd gestures toward her, and the rest laughed. It disgusted me, as no one should treat anyone like that. I glanced around and saw only the handful of bikers and Memory standing in the glow of the neon lights.

It gave me a glance at what I had to deal with. She had high cheekbones, bright-red hair that looked far from natural and a body that filled her body suit perfectly. Whoever Memory was, she took excellent care of herself. *Focus, Hax. Save the pretty girl first and save the drool for later. If there is a later.*

I raised my pistol and tried to look threatening. Hell, I was only five foot ten inches and one hundred fifty-five pounds in weight. The few women in the group were bigger than me. The joys of having a small frame. I was quick on my feet and could hack my way into anything, but in feats of strength, I was screwed.

"Hold up, guys. I hope none of you are thinking of doing anything wrong here."

The man holding the data pad turned and shot me a wicked grin. "Get him! Seems a little roadrunner wants to play the hero."

He turned back to Memory as the rest of his gang charged me. The odds were a bit against me. I had my weapon, but one of them had a baseball bat and looked like he had enough mods to smash a dump truck with his fist. I was in great shape, but it would take more than me to get Memory away from these guys. One of them charged me, and I fired.

It was a reflex, but I hit him dead on target and watched him fall. Even at this distance, my pistol had some impact. Another threw a punch, and I dodged. His momentum sent him running past. I slammed my elbow into his back and heard a grunt.

"Behind you!"

I turned in time as a woman grabbed my arm. She gripped and pulled me toward her. I dropped and rolled, kicking out with my legs. I heard a satisfying snap as my kick dislocated her knee. She shouted out in pain. I got up quickly as a pair of arms wrapped around me and squeezed.

———

STRUGGLING with the man was of no use to me. Not only was he too physically strong, but his mods kept me from escaping. Luckily, the cybernetic arm had a few surprises of its own. I reached back and grabbed him between the legs and squeezed with all the strength I had in my arm. He squealed in pain as I crushed his groin area. He staggered back and fell, clutching his pride in the fetal position. Yeah, I fight dirty.

Another charged me, and I grabbed their face and squeezed. He screamed and struggled to get away. I let go and watched him run away, his hands covering his face. He would need a good cosmetic surgeon to fix that mess, and I had no guilt about what I had done.

Memory caught my eye. She still had two others holding her against the wall. Her eyes were wide, hoping I'd succeed in rescuing her. *I guess I need to step up more and be that hero. Fuck if this won't get me deeper in the shit than usual.*

The one with the data pad only grinned. "It's too late for her and you." He shot me a sly smile and tapped the pad.

Memory shook as if the biker had electrocuted her. I rushed him head on, knocking the data pad from his hands. It hit the ground and cracked. Memory stood still; her eyes held a glint of light that distracted me from the gang's leader.

Pain surged through my body, and I screamed. My body shook, and I no longer had control over it. All I could do was twitch in agony. He hit me with a high-powered laser. The leader laughed and stepped over me.

"I didn't think you'd last long. Looks like I got two people to bring in. The Gareck Corp wants you as well. Not as much as Memory here, but you'll still fetch a suitable reward. Corporations pay well."

I got to my knees and crawled toward Memory. My gun lay between me and the biker's leader. My body hurt, and I wasn't sure if the weapon he used fucked up my arm. It was within my grasp when I heard Memory speak.

"The people deserve this information. Not you and not the corporations. We can save lives with this code. It belongs to the people."

The leader stepped up and slapped her. "No, it belongs to Gareck Corp, just like you do. They built you, after all."

I paused, barely touching the grip of my pistol. The words he said echoed in my head. *Fuck me, Memory isn't human, she's a Simulant.* Not that it mattered. Too many people argued for SIM rights and argued that they were human. They had a human brain, but the rest of them were completely cybernetic and artificial. That would explain the odd glint in her eyes.

Whether she was human or not, she needed help. What is human, anyway? So far, she showed more humanity than the biker club by a long shot. I snatched up the gun and fired. The leader fell to his knees, then sideways, dead. The other two ran, leaving me alone with Memory.

"You weren't expecting to get shot in the back, were you, asshole?"

My head swam, and the pain slowly receded. *Dammit, Hax, get the fuck up. The drones are watching this whole thing, and the Gareck Corp will be all over you.* They'd show up fast after this. I stayed on my knees, afraid to get up.

"Can you get up?"

Memory knelt before me; her blue eyes still had that bit of light behind them. "We need to get out of here. What's your name, hero?"

I stood slowly with her help. The drones buzzed around us once and disappeared into the smog. "Everyone calls me Hax. Because I hack things."

"Thank you for saving me, but we need to get moving. I honestly thought I would die sooner than later."

She stepped back a bit to give me some room. I gave her an awkward smile. "I can take you to my place. The rest of my club may have an idea on how to help you get out of the city."

"I won't have enough time for that, Hax."

"What do you mean?"

She pointed at the other end of the alley. Members of the Perfect Omega Motorcycle Club stood brandishing bladed weapons. They tapped the sides of the alley walls in a rhythmic beat. Well, if that wasn't a bitch. I grabbed Memory's hand and ran off toward my bike.

"Run!"

———

WE RAN towards my bike as fast as we could. The motorcycle club that ruled the seedy world of New York City had arrived in full. For me to say it wasn't my best moment would be the understatement of the century. Behind me, all I heard was the thunderous steps of their boots hitting the pavement as they chased Memory and me through the alley.

"I'm scared, Hax."

"Yeah, so am I. My bike is close, and we can get away from them on the road."

The idea of death coming sooner than later rattled my nerves. Though the number of people following us didn't bother me as much as what they'd do once they got their hands on us. Having Memory by my side made this whole situation interesting. A Simulant didn't have the same rights as a regular person.

The corporations never cared about rights. At least the government tried to make a pretense in that matter. Either way, the Perfect Omega Club would've made sure she disappeared forever. I could only imagine what they would've done to her if I hadn't answered Memory's call.

"Where are we going?"

I jumped on my bike and started it up. "Not sure yet. All my ideas end up with others in danger. Can they track you at all?"

Memory sat behind me and wrapped her arms around my waist for support. For once, I was glad I had the larger seat. Normally I hated an extra rider with the Roadrunners, but today was probably the only exception. I passed my helmet to Memory and kicked at one of the other club's motorcycles and watched them fall like dominos.

"That'll slow them down."

I took off down the street, hoping to lose them in the mix of people and traffic. If I got lucky, there'd be no drones to follow, but I doubt the fates sided with me. *Where am I going? Fuck if I know.* Memory had asked a good question, and it was one I couldn't answer.

Right now, my only thought was to ride fast and for as long as possible. Distance was the major advantage. I doubted if they could track my bike, but I wasn't sure about Memory. She never answered my question, and that made me nervous. A high-performance motorcycle was great, but useless if they tracked us down.

"Can they track you?" I asked.

"No, at least I don't think so. My kind aren't exactly cloaked. They chipped most of us, so the Gareck Corp probably could do it."

"Fuck, not what I wanted to hear."

I put on as much speed as I could, and we hurtled forward. Memory held on tighter and squeezed me in her death grip. I reached into the small compartment of my Colossus and pulled out a comm link for my ear and slipped it in.

"Can you do what you did before so we can communicate on the ride?"

"I think so, but with so many data pools available, I don't have the processing speed to switch between them to do so properly at the speed we're going."

"Never mind, we'll worry about that once we stop and find a hiding place to formulate a plan."

I glanced in the mirror and saw riders behind me and sped up. They were catching up fast, and I wasn't sure I could outrace the Perfect Omega Motorcycle Club. I cranked the throttle, and the thrust forced me back a bit as my motorcycle shot forward. I let the rush of speed take me away for a bit as I hit the highway.

"Hax, is this safe?"

I flashed a smile. *What is safe in this world these days?* Once I hit the highway, I'd open the throttle up and show Memory how fast this baby could go. It would also give me more room to maneuver and give me a chance to find a place to hide.

I shouted louder as the sounds of the highway mixed with the subtle purr of my bike. My Colossus was electric, like every other vehicle in the world. Unfortunately, while my bike was quieter than the gas-powered motorcycles of the past, a bunch together on the highway or in the city was still loud.

The on-ramp came fast, and I turned hard to make it. I turned my headlights off to add as much stealth as possible as soon as I merged with traffic. New York City had enough light for me to see along with the holographic billboards spouting directions at a rapid rate.

"Are we safe yet?"

I glanced back at traffic and shrugged. "For the moment."

I drove another mile before I turned my headlights back on. Traffic drones were a thing I didn't want to deal with. Speeding was one thing, but harboring a Simulant who was wanted by a corporation along with me being not so popular with them myself, the chances were too high to get caught. I needed to find us a place fast to lie low.

———

AFTER WHAT FELT LIKE AN ETERNITY, I found an old building in Lower City. It wouldn't take long for the Omega Club to find us, but for now, it was all I had. Part of me wanted to contact the Roadrunners, but didn't want to take the chance of communications being heard.

Homeless milled around, and the chain-link fence that surrounded the building ahead of me did little to hold anyone back. Lower City was the place where people went to hide or survive, if one called what they did here "living." Law enforcement rarely came here, and usually only drug runners or other dregs of society found this place as home.

Those who saw us paid no attention and went back to their lives. Minding your own business was the name of the game in Lower City. Even the corporations ignored this place, at least for now.

"Hax, I need to get off this bike."

"Let me find a place for us to settle in for the moment. Give me time to think."

I coasted the bike down the hallway of a large old office building that hadn't been used in decades. While I knew how to protect and look after myself, doing so for another frightened me.

"Okay, I hope you know what you're doing."

I stopped right outside an office. It was a disaster as it had no door and the wires hung from the ceiling. Memory slid off the bike and hugged herself. She shivered a bit, and fear shone in her eyes. Simulants feel fear, right? She leaned against the wall and glanced around, her lips pressed into a fine line.

I leaned against an old wooden desk. "Wanna tell me what's going on?"

Memory slid down the wall and sat. "It's a long story, and I'm not sure you wanna hear it."

I hunched down in front of her. "I do, and I'm risking my life and possibly my family's as well. You might as well let me know what all this is for."

She turned to her right, her eyes lost in some thought. "I'm dying. It sounds weird when I hear it out loud. They gave most Simulants a standard life expectancy."

"You don't?"

"No. They made me a courier to deliver goods that were too sensitive for the net. Unfortunately, the information I carry is too much and has leaked into my system. My system is corrupted beyond repair, and I have less than twenty-four hours before I die."

I leaned back to ease the tension on my knees. "What are you carrying?"

She frowned, still looking away. "Code."

"What kind of code?"

While I didn't want to press too hard, I needed this information. My life was on the line, and I didn't have time to waste. I hated hearing about her dying, but there was always a fix. Maybe my father could help her. I hoped we had time.

"The code that will fix the sketch. When I realized what I carried, I needed to get it to someone who could use it to help people. The Gareck Corp paid dearly for it and would hoard it to make even more money."

I let out my breath, not realizing I held it so long. "Their greed is insatiable for sure."

She turned towards me. "That's when I ran and they put a price on my head. I found a doctor who could use it, but they killed him right away. I've been on the run since."

"That must be why the Omega Club chased you down. They work for the Gareck Corp."

"Yeah. They were about to take the code from me and leave me dead when I used a data pool to find you."

I stood and paced, trying to figure out a way to help. "How much time do you have?"

A tear ran down her face, and she shot me a weak smile. "A few hours, tops. My system is already running low."

"Fuck."

I paced more, wracking my brain for a way to get her out of this position. *Think, Hax, think!* Time was short, hell, shorter than I thought. I had figured all I needed to do was to get her away from the others, but now, things had gotten way too heavy.

"I need to move this information before I die. Once my system shuts down, it's lost, and there are too many lives at stake for that to happen."

I stopped and stared at the wall. Too many lives… Nothing prepared me for this, but here I was, playing hero and getting myself deeper in the shit with a corporation and gang that already had me on their hit list. *Go big or go home, Hax.*

I flexed my right arm. "My arm has a memory chip. Would that be enough?"

"I can't let you do this. It's dangerous."

"Trouble has been my middle name for a while now. Might as well live it up."

"If you take the information, promise me you'll leave me here and run."

"That's gonna be a hard no. There's always a chance to save you."

"I'm out of time."

"When you're dead, you're out of time. Until then, there's hope. So, are we gonna do this or not?"

Memory nodded her head. "There's a chance the information may leak. If it does, it could cause major problems."

"Don't worry about me. I can get another arm."

"I hope you're right."

———

A LOUD SCREAM and the sounds of motorcycles filled the air. The Perfect Omega Motorcycle Club had finally found us. Part of me was hoping for more time, but like everything else at the moment, I was all out of that. I had to get Memory to safety to not only save her life, but get the code she carried to the right person.

I dashed to my bike. "We need to get out of here!"

Memory climbed behind me. There was no longer any debate about what we had to do. Survival was the key to getting to safety and saving lives. Kicking the bike forward, I rode in the same direction from which I entered. Homeless men and women scattered as flames and smoke threatened to consume the building.

The bikers chanted and cheered as they tossed Molotov cocktails at the building. Lights whizzed from the distance as police drones homed in on my location. They paired each drone with a biker from the Perfect Omega Motorcycle Club as more and more of them drove toward us.

Memory wrapped her arms around my waist. "Let's get the hell out of here. We need a place so I can transfer the data."

As we drove off, the cool blast of air blowing in our faces mixed with the sound of the roaring engines of the club behind us. None of them got any closer, but then I wasn't making up any distance either. The club had tracked us down and burned us out of our hiding spot.

A quick glance back showed that many more followed. The group split into three. One group turned left, another right, while the main branch of the club maintained their distance. They were going to come around and trap us or force me into taking another direction.

"Hax, what are they doing?"

"If I didn't know any better, they're trying to box us in. If that doesn't work, they may push us in another direction, one where they can easily stop us."

"Is that the docks ahead of us?"

I let loose a stream of profanity. They weren't going to cut me off, but funnel us toward the docks and the warehouse district. They were herding myself and Memory. To them, we were the cattle getting rounded up for the slaughter. We were fucked, but I refused to believe they would win. There was no way I'd go down without a fight.

As drones flew past us, I weaved in and out through shipping containers to avoid the Perfect Omega Club. In the end, it would be pointless as they knew what they were doing. Either way, I had to try. The sound of them behind me bounced off the containers, amplifying the sound. I skidded to a stop at the edge of the deck.

New York City rose like a gem on the other side of the bay. Even the low-hanging smog added to the metropolis's beauty as it bounced the glow of the nightlife into the calm waters of the ocean. For once, it looked peaceful, even if it was ripe with corruption.

"That skyline is a wonder, Hax." Memory's voice carried a hint of awe.

"Yeah, she's a beauty from a distance," I said with a hefty amount of cynicism. "If we weren't about to die, the view would be spectacular, really."

"We have little time."

I killed the engine and looked back at Memory. She shook, but I doubt it was fear. Her systems were failing her, and it took all her energy to sit upright. The sound of motorcycles stopped and panned out into a semicircle around us as drones circled above. *If this ain't a bitch!*

I handed my gun to Memory. "Yeah, looks like the party has arrived, and we're the guests of honor. Do you know how to use this?"

She took it, but I doubted she could get an excellent shot with the way she was shaking. "I point and shoot, right?"

"You gotta aim first, but yeah, you got it."

A display appeared over my arm as I flexed my hand. I entered the address to the server that operated the drones. It was time to put my netrunning skills to the test and see if I truly earned my nickname. Within seconds, I was online and surfing.

"Shoot at anyone who gets too close. I need some time."

Memory shifted behind me. "I'll do what I can."

The sound of banging ringed in my ears as the Perfect Omega Club hit the sides of the containers with bats and guns in a beat that threatened to stop my heart with fear. I stole a glance and saw a few get off from their bikes, chains in their hands. Some people had decorated their body armor with skulls.

One of them stepped out and had a fiery-orange mohawk that had enough product in it to withstand a tornado. He also had a gun, and it was a bigger one than the one I gave Memory. Hell had stepped forward, and my life was about to get ugly.

I found the server and went straight into blocking off data pools to keep security out. I was so close, but needed more time. The banging rang in my head and sped up into a climactic finish that left the air in silence as all stopped at the same time. The mohawked biker strode forward, and a shot rang out, hitting the pavement at his booted feet. He looked away before grinning widely at me. *She at least came close to hitting him.*

The man's arms were nothing but tech, fully cyborg with no pretense of him covering them up to blend in with the rest of his body. They were slightly bigger than they should've been and looked awkward. His grin grew wider as he stared me down. *Hack faster!*

"It's been a while since I came across a lone roadrunner. Didn't think you guys rode alone. It's a dangerous city," he said. "Of all the ones I run into, it's you, Hax. Gareck Corp is going to pay a lot for your head."

"Great, maybe we should get a drink and hug."

I was in and had control of the drones. How long I would have this control was another thing altogether. I needed to time this right. I needed all of them down for the count so Memory and I could escape. If this didn't work...

"I'll get the drink later with the payment I get from my boss."

"Yeah, Zero, if you're not careful, they'll have you floating in the bay. You can't dance with the devil and expect to finish unscathed."

Zero bowed in mock humbleness. Like most people in New York City, he came from the bottom. Born poor and would most likely die that way. He rose to power as a two-bit drug pusher before making his way to corporate crony and leader of the Perfect Omega Club. The number of bodies he had to trample on to get to his position was quite high.

"You don't expect to get out of this alive, Hax? We will get the data she's carrying."

I grinned. "Yeah, I actually do, Zero."

With a flex of my hand, the drones above me opened fire on the motorcyclists that surrounded myself and Memory.

THE CACOPHONY of artillery from the drones ended. Most of the Perfect Omega Motorcycle Club was dead or wounded. All except Zero, who got up from the ground and dusted himself off. His face contorted in anger with narrowed eyes and a slight curve to his lips, as if he snarled.

"Now why did you do that, li'l Roadrunner? You're gonna pay for that."

I had all my hopes on Zero dying in the barrage of ammo from the security drones. That was what I got for showing all my cards so early. This wasn't good at all, and now I had to figure out what to do next. If I could keep him talking, maybe I had a better chance of getting Memory and me out of here.

I went to take a step back, and Zero raised his gun and shook his head. "Tsk tsk, li'l Roadrunner."

I closed my eyes, and he fired. My life flashed before my eyes like someone played it on a film projector with 8mm film in super-slow motion. Here I was, a kid, careless and free before the weight of reality and the shitty world crashed down upon me.

After a few blips, images of me in my teens getting hazed as entry into the Roadrunners, who became another family. It also showed my parents' disapproval and disappointment. Every scene came so slowly. My mind was an empty run-down theater, and I was the only audience tied to a seat and forced to watch the sins of my life in one excruciating moment at a time.

The screen went blank, and it was so bright that I had to shield my eyes. As the light died, reality came back with a vengeance. I was still alive, and Zero was smiling and looking past me. *Memory, no!* With a glance back, I saw the horror of the situation. He didn't aim at me, but at Memory. He had blasted her right arm off, and it lay more than a few feet from her body.

Her eyes flickered with life, but I did not know how much time she had or if this would be the end of it all for her. She twitched as cybernetic fluid leaked from her shoulder. I glanced at my right arm, which still projected the screen that allowed me to control the drones, and back at her before mumbling.

"Am I still human, or am I kidding myself?"

The sight of her filled me with dread. She was still alive, which meant Zero could still gain the code. I had to keep him from her as much as possible. Memory risked her life for this so that others could live. If that wasn't humanity at its best, then I didn't know what was.

I turned toward Zero. "Why? How could you kill another human so easily? She was innocent."

Zero shrugged nonchalantly. "She ain't no human, mate. She's just another SIM pretending to be something she's not. The corporation built her for one thing, and she did the opposite. It was only a matter of time, and she knew it."

The past few years had proven that the war on Simulant rights was far from ending. Few trusted them, as the corporations manufactured everything for them except a brain. That was actual flesh locked in a metal skull attached to wires that took the place of a spinal cord and nerves.

"She was still alive, able to make her own decisions. That ain't programming, man, that's life, like you and me."

Zero dropped his gun and cussed. "She ain't human, Roadrunner, but you won't be around long enough to mourn her death. It's not like she can feel pain."

I shook my head. Zero was wrong on that account. All Simulants felt pain, and from the short time I had with Memory, she had shown she felt fear and had a heart for helping others. Her self-sacrifice was a bold decision only a few could make, and it takes a lot of soul searching to do that. No program can make that decision for anyone.

"Dammit, I'll make sure you pay for this."

He rushed and slammed into me. His arms wrapped around me and squeezed, threatening to crack my ribs and constrict the air in my lungs. Even with my new arm, I didn't have the strength to break free. Everything blurred before Zero smashed his forehead against my skull.

He let me go, and I staggered backward as tiny pinpoints of light filled my visions and pain flooded my head. I tripped over something and fell on my back. It was Memory. Her head turned to stare at me, her eyes wide with pain but still holding a glimmer of hope.

My vision was blurry, but I let muscle memory take over as I typed commands into the holographic keyboard that hovered over my arm. Zero snickered and took out a large knife and dragged it across one of his arms, making a sharp squealing sound that hurt my ears.

"It's a little late to call for help, li'l Roadrunner. Seems the big bad wolf has won."

"I've seen the cartoons. I know exactly what happens," I said as I pressed the enter key. "Meep meep, motherfucker."

Zero stepped back as the drones slammed into him, pushing him back before detonating. A sharp sting hit my side as a piece of shrapnel sliced through my skin. It didn't look deep, but my sight was less than perfect. Zero, on the hand, lay still. They blasted his arms off along with parts of his abdomen area. One of his legs was missing.

I crawled over to Memory. "I can still call for help."

She glanced at me and shook her head. "It's too late for me, but not for others. Let me transfer the code and promise me you'll find someone who can use it to help others, even those like me."

"Fuck, Memory, this isn't how I expected this to happen. Cut to me being the worst hero ever in world history."

She caressed my face before clutching my arm. "Being a hero is far from glamorous. Let's start the process."

I nodded, and thin needle-like probes extended out of her fingers and into my arm. The pressure made me wince and grit my teeth. "I was hoping this wouldn't hurt so much."

"You'll survive, and it'll be over soon."

That made me feel better, but the sound of sirens resonated in the night. Looked like law enforcement would make a show after all. Once I had my vision, the first thing I saw was the light flicker behind Memory's eyes. It would go out soon, and I didn't want to see it happen.

Maybe I was a coward, because seeing her die like this felt wrong. There was no justice in it, and deep down, I knew no one but me would care. Memory was a Simulant, and few cared enough about them for any of this to matter.

Her hand fell away, and she smiled one last time. "It's done. Take care, Hax. Of all the people that could've saved me, I'm glad it was you."

"You're gonna die. I didn't truly save you."

"You did in more ways than you think. Because of you, my life has meaning, and that gives me peace."

She looked up at the sky. I glanced up, and for once, the smog broke enough for me to see the stars. "It's so beautiful, Hax."

A tear ran down my cheek, and I turned towards her. The last of the light behind her eyes flickered once more and went out. I closed her eyes and returned to my bike. Starting her up, I gave the sky one last look and drove off. Once past the bodies of the dead motorcycle club, I stopped and gave Memory one last glance.

It's a shame that it took someone who was considered less than human to show me what true humanity was. I'll make sure the code gets to the right person, Memory. You have my word. If possible, I'll fight so others like you get the rights and life they deserve.

The sirens grew louder, and I drove off into Lower City to find a place to hide for a while. It would give me time to mourn a precious soul which the horrible world decided wasn't human enough. If they only knew what a human was, they'd change their minds.

ABOUT MATTHEW ANGELO

Matthew lives in Colorado with his partner and three dogs which he considers "his pack." He got his start writing fan fiction before making the jump and starting his urban fantasy series, The Midnight Agency, and creating a whole fantasy world called Aria, the World of Twilight, for all his fantasy adventures.

Even though he went to college and earned a bachelor's degree in IT, his love for writing took over the desire to build a supercomputer, and he now works as a full-time author and copywriter. When not writing, he's practicing Krav Maga and training his dogs to be the best dogs in the neighborhood.

To know more about Matthew and see pics of his dogs in his newsletter, go to http://matthewangeloauthor.com to stay up-to-date on his books and his pack's cuteness.

HER LAST JOB

R. SCOTT UHLS

Tyra Kirachi is a merc and a clone of a woman long dead, but her desire to head off-world causes her to take one last job, putting her right into the path of the men who took her mother's life twenty years before. Plagued by her past, Tyra uses everything her father taught her to get the job done.

HER LAST JOB

Tyra stretched sleepily in the leather seats of the Model 1090X as it hovered over the desolate landscape of the "Dead Zone." As a kid at Cyberlink Biocorp International Academy, she had seen a map of the United States, the loose federation of semidependent nations that had once been a major government in North America. She surmised that she was currently floating over the former nation of Georgia, similarly named as the territory in Europe. Without that old map to reference, it was hard to tell, but she knew that her ultimate destination on this trip, the city of South Metroport, was once called "Atlanta" before it was rebranded.

"Coming up on our drop point now, madam." The smooth, robotic voice rolled in from the pilot compartment.

"Thank you, Ajax," Tyra said, yawning as she sat up. "I think I napped a little too long."

"You were asleep for exactly thirty-seven minutes and eighteen point five seconds," Ajax responded.

"That sounds like thirty-seven minutes too long," Tyra replied jokingly. "Guess I needed it."

Ajax rotated its "head" one hundred eighty degrees so that the screen it used to create facsimiles of human faces was directly in the viewport to the back seat.

"You have been working yourself extra hard, madam," Ajax said, the screen mouth slightly out of sync with the words. "You honestly should not have taken this job."

Tyra knew that Ajax did not need to turn its head to speak with her. Its sensors kept its neuro processor fed with data from everywhere at once. Ajax could effectively "see" in all directions, but she knew that turning its head gave a social nuance to their communication that it desired. She also knew that it wasn't actually using its visual sensors to pilot the hovercar, as it was directly fed information from the vehicle's controls, so it did not need to "look" anywhere. Plus, as a robot, Ajax was only using a small portion of its DDR27 Neuro-ram capacity to communicate and a slightly larger portion to keep them from crashing. There would need to be significantly more teraflops streaming into its consciousness to overload the chauffeur.

"Thank you for your concern, Ajax," Tyra replied genuinely. "After this job, I'll be able to afford a vacation."

"Based on your inherited income," Ajax replied, the face screen mimicking a confused human expression, "and the amount of money you have accumulated through your own mercenary activities, you should be able to afford several years' worth of vacations."

Tyra cracked a grin. "Not in space," she replied.

"Ah," Ajax said, turning the face away from her. "I see you have decided to head off-world, then? Callisto or Europa Station?"

"I am not sure yet," Tyra answered, looking out the window again. "Don't worry, tinman, I'm taking you with me."

"Of course, Dorothy," Ajax responded. "I would expect you need someone to fly you, madam."

Tyra stifled a laugh. There was a reason that she had kept Ajax as her personal bodyguard, and it had little to do with it being a robot. Sure, the baseline armor from Ajax's metallic body was a boon, but it was the semigenuine mirroring of humanity that she found endearing. Compared to Remacorp Protection Bot 6608 and RoboSec Unit 801KL9, Escort Unit 4X, "Ajax," had been a much more interesting companion. And loyal, opting to ignore shutdown protocol 0104 to remain with her after she'd ended her corporate contract to go freelance. Reaper knows it had nothing to do with pay, though she did sock away a small income for Ajax just in case she didn't return from a job.

"I will also need a bodyguard," she added.

"I doubt that very seriously, madam," Ajax replied. "Three hundred meters to arrival."

Tyra finished stretching and ran a quick diagnostic over her augmentations. She had done a full assessment at her favorite body doc before they left Chromeport City, but a sticky compartment lever had nearly got her slabbed a few years back, instilling the appropriate amount of augmentation paranoia. As her systems ran through engaging and disengaging, she recited her father's prejob mantra.

I am not the blade, nor am I the gun. Nor am I the speed that my legs might run. I am not the battery that sits in my chest, nor am I the potential that goes unexpressed. I am the controller of my own fate, and I know this now before it's too late.

As usual, Tyra finished her mantra just as the diagnostic report flooded her visual cortex. All the status readings were green, and the combat battery read one hundred percent. She noticed that her blood pressure was a bit elevated and checked the history, realizing that it was the nap that had caused the momentary lapse in rhythm. According to the report, her meat bits were working just as well as the mechanical bits.

"Open the locker," Tyra commanded.

Ajax did not move or reply, experienced as he was in her prejob protocols. There was a short pause before the vehicle's system responded to the voice activation with a chirp, and the small black compartment built into the back of Ajax's pilot seat opened with a hiss of the air compressor. As the locker slid open, it revealed the two long black blades of her custom Koukanzu katanas and the gold-lined silver pistols that were stored within.

She ran her fingers along a pistol grip, tracing the inlaid personal seal that had been her father's trademark. When he died, his corporate contract with Cyberlink Biocorp International had fallen to her through some generational technicality, despite no genetic connection between them, and while fulfilling the remainder of his obligation, she'd used his Jitsu-in as her own brand until it became a sentimental reminder that she was the legally recognized daughter of Enzo Kirachi.

Removing the two firearms, she slid them deftly into the concealed thigh holsters sewn into her stealth bodysuit. The handles were still visible, defeating the purpose of the concealed holsters, but if anyone was close enough to see them, they wouldn't live long enough to do anything about it, or they weren't anyone of consequence. The blades were already dark as night, but when she sheathed them into the scabbards on her back, they were barely black accents on either side of her head. At some point, she'd modded them with neon filaments so she could blend in with common street girls, but the current job didn't call for that. Instead, she left them in "stealth mode" as she moved to the 1090X's side door.

"I will be unable to maintain this speed for longer than 3.76 seconds, madam," Ajax informed her. "And the security turrets will detect me in 2.86 seconds."

"Two point eight seconds is all I need," Tyra responded, looking down as the multicar hypertrain appeared on the magnetic track below them.

She opened the slider door, setting off the interior cabin alarms, and felt wasteland sand rush around her. The moment she felt the granules, her hardened plastic face shield extended from a concealed compartment in her forehead and slammed into place, locking at her chin. The clear plastic was an upgrade from the restrictive hanya mask she'd been obligated to wear by CBI, but it did a similar job of protecting her eyes, nose, and mouth from particulates. Some would have gotten under the mask, she knew, but her air filters would clear up any issues before she landed on the hypertrain.

"Good luck, madam," Ajax said in an amplified voice to be heard over the wind.

Tyra straightened her body and slid over the edge of the vehicle, feeling the stomach-churning sensation of empty air as she fell forward. She flipped once, triggering her free-falling alerts before the control gyros activated to keep her upright, sending her diving feetfirst. She would need the gyros at full capacity for most of this job, which was why she had opted for the violent calibration technique her father preferred. As she expected, a red bar appeared on the bottom of her vision to inform her that they were engaged. The bar would remain as a constant reminder of their status until she disengaged them.

Three more alerts filled her vision, marking the three defensive turrets Ajax had mentioned as they extended from their concealed compartments and swung into action. She knew there would be one more alert as she touched down—the alarm that her suspension system had automatically cushioned her landing—so she waited to silence them at once.

As planned, she dropped through the basement of the turrets' engagement zone in under three seconds, fast enough that the guns could not spool their automatic fire before her feet touched the train. Ajax veered away just as the guns began to strafe, causing the high-powered penetrator rounds to miss as they arced behind the Model 1090X. The turrets reached their apex just as Tyra slammed onto the shell of the train. Her vision flashed red when the final alert told her that her suspension system had engaged at eighty-seven percent to cushion her fall before quickly rolling down to zero.

She knew that this appeared objectively as though she'd landed with one knee down, her body leaning forward. After the momentum passed, the system automatically stood her on her feet, but to her perspective, the system adjusted and showed her what her vision would be when she was standing, compiling images from the fall. The automated functions did not register in her brain, creating a terribly disorienting situation for amateurs who often acted before the system had completed restoring their posture.

Before the suspension system could roll down to zero, Tyra gained two more alerts. Two sentry drones had been deployed faster than expected, a fact that she'd have to discuss with Chunt, her tech expert. Her eyes highlighted them in red as they crawled toward her on fast-moving spider legs. She wanted to move, to draw her guns, but she knew that she would miss every shot until the suspension system was restored. They fired at her, causing her to flinch involuntarily, but their small-caliber bullets were deflected by her hardened Fauxskin™ augmentation, a new type of reverb armor that looked like real skin. She knew that arachdroids would switch to explosive ammunition once they realized the typical anti-intrusion weapons were useless, but it would be too late for them.

As soon as the suspension system reached zero, she drew both guns and fired them from her hip using her automatic targeting system to make the minute muscle changes required for simultaneous bull's-eyes. The lead-tipped, caseless projectiles careened out of her guns' barrels, causing both weapons to recoil simultaneously as the projectiles crossed the distance in less than one three-hundredth of a second. Both drones exploded simultaneously, the pieces disconnecting from the train and becoming immediately lost as the wind scattered them in several directions. As two more came over the side of the train, they were destroyed as quickly as the first.

She sprinted toward the front of the train, knowing that the several rear cars were meaningless to her. They were passenger cars, and since this wasn't a robbery job, she had no need for passengers. They would become obstacles at best, collateral damage at worst. This was her last job, and she didn't need any collateral damage weighing on her conscience.

Leaping over the gap between the cars, she fired two downward blasts, destroying two more arachdroids as their automatic fire strafed wildly upward. Because of her changed motion, her jump path was off, and she realized she was going to land badly on the next train car. Tucking her head forward, she temporarily disengaged the gyros and tumbled in a crude somersault. As Tyra rolled through the landing, she realized immediately that turning off the gyros had been a bad idea.

Off-balance, she fell sideways and rolled uncontrollably toward the edge of the train. Recognizing she had mere moments to stop herself, she made the hard choice and let go of her left gun to grab the edge of the train. Feeling her fingers crack the high-impact plastic, Tyra swung herself around and used her momentum to throw herself back to the top. Looking over the edge as she landed, she watched in disappointment as her father's gun tumbled end over end to the orange dust several hundred meters below.

Turning toward her intended target, the cargo car, she reengaged the gyro stabilizers and stood. Several arachdroids raced toward her, and targeting each in turn, she dropped them with the precision created by a mixture of cultured genetics, her father's training, and her deadly enhancements. She smirked, thinking that aside from almost falling off the train, the job had been too easy thus far.

A sudden, unexpected pain in the back of her head caused her vision to go black and become replaced by an error message. She felt weightless as she lost control of her sense inputs at once, slipping into a dark sea of empty data. All she could do was wait for the reboot and hope for the best.

———

TYRA SAT in the oversized chair with her buckle-shoed feet dangling over the edge. Normally she loved the feeling of adult chairs, but sitting outside the headmaster's office was terrifying. She knew that the school nurse bot, the one the other students called Doctor Clanker, was still standing beside her, possibly in sleep mode, but it gave her comfort. She could not see out of her swollen eyes, making the waiting difficult, but she spent her time experimentally sniffing to see if the blood had cleared enough from her nostrils. Another sniff revealed that the blood had stopped flowing, which was progress, but when she reached up to touch it, there was a sharp pain.

The ding of the elevator at the end of the hall called her attention, and the familiar sound of her father's shoes against the synthetic granite, a sound she had been trained to recognize, caused her to straighten her posture. She had already gotten blood on her school uniform, so she didn't want to upset him more by being caught slouching.

Once the sound of his shoes reached her, they stopped, creating a silence during which she knew he was documenting everything wrong so he could criticize her later. After the longest moment of her life, she heard a shuffle of fabric and then a sudden, intense pain in her nose.

"Ow!" she shouted, trying not to flinch.

When the pain stopped, she realized she could feel a cool, refreshing stream of air moving through her nostrils. She had no idea what happened, but it made her forget how much her eyes hurt. It must have been one of her father's "street tricks."

"Can you breathe now?" her father asked, his voice deep and unemotional.

"Yes, Papa," Tyra answered.

"Good," he responded. "Nurse 4664. Aside from the broken nose, I believe there is ocular socket damage and a potential skull fracture. Can you confirm these injuries?"

"Yes, Mr. Kirachi," the nurse robot answered in its synthesized voice. "As well as tissue damage to her shoulder and a dislocated, potentially fractured patella."

Before Enzo Kirachi could respond, a door opened, and Tyra could hear the labored breathing of the overweight Mr. Prichard, headmaster of CBI Academy. She never understood why the man didn't take the basic metabolism augmentations available everywhere. She was only ten years old, and she'd seen dozens of ads for body-fat reductions and blood sugar stabilizers between her digital lessons. Most of her classmates said it was because he liked being a purist normie.

"Mr. Kirachi," Mr. Prichard said. "Thank you for coming by. We must discuss Tyra."

"I should say so," her father replied. "Why is she not currently receiving medical attention?"

"I thought it best that we discuss the situation," Mr. Prichard answered.

"I see," her father returned. "I'm sorry I came so late. There must have been a communications issue if the other parents were able to speak with you before I could take the elevator down a few floors."

"Well..." Mr. Prichard replied sheepishly.

Tyra had only recently begun training in understanding voice modulation, but even with her fledgling abilities, she could hear the hesitation. He was hiding something, and if she could tell, her father could.

"Well?" her father asked. "That must be the case. The other girl was not sent to the medical facilities until her parents arrived, correct?"

"Things are different with Tyra," Mr. Prichard admitted.

"How are things different?" her father asked. "Were the injuries sustained by the other girl worse than Tyra's injuries?"

"There were six other girls," Mr. Prichard corrected, "and I'm not sure the extent of the other girls' injuries."

"Did you say six?" her father asked.

"Yes," Mr. Prichard answered. "Your daughter attacked six girls in the cafeteria."

"She attacked?" her father asked. "Are you suggesting that Tyra would willingly pit herself against an overwhelming force? And that upon doing so, she received these injuries by self-defense? A fractured patella via self-defense?"

"It seems so," Mr. Prichard replied.

"No disrespect to your position, Mr. Prichard," her father replied, "but that is not logical. Tyra understands the concept of overwhelming forces and how to conduct basic guerilla operations. I could believe that there were six opponents she attacked separately. But at once..."

"I can assure you," Mr. Prichard replied, "all six versions concur."

There was a long pause from her father, and Tyra wasn't sure why. His breathing was normal. She hated not being able to see, but her eyes were too swollen to open more than a sliver. When she parted them, she was barely able to make out the silhouettes of the two adults and Doctor Clanker.

"That seems suspicious to me, Mr. Pritchard," her father said slowly. "Do you know what it is I do for the corporation?"

"I'm told you work in the security division," Mr. Prichard replied.

"Correct," her father replied. "You must think I'm a slag-topped er bai wu if you expect me to believe my daughter attacked six girls at once and sustained these severe injuries from untrained combatants who were merely defending themselves. Have you asked for her side of the story?"

"I didn't think it was necessary considering the six agreeing testimonies from real girls," Mr. Prichard replied.

"Real girls?" her father asked. "Are you implying that Tyra is a robot?"

"I meant nonclone girls, obviously," Mr. Prichard replied. "No offense to you, Mr. Kirachi, but your daughter isn't exactly a legal citizen. Tolerated, sure, but different than you or me."

"She is different," her father agreed. "But she was also fully sanctioned and created by Cyberlink Biocorp International. She is a registered, legal entity within the corporation, and that should be enough to entitle her to the same rights and benefits as your 'real' girls. Her legal status outside the corporation, and the politics thereof, should not be any of your concern, Mr. Pritchard. We both know who pays your salary, and it is the same accounting team that is paying her medical expenses."

"Rights!" Mr. Prichard blurted incredulously. "Rights for a slick? Mr. Kirachi, surely you understand that your daughter is a commodity."

"A slick?" her father replied. "A commodity?"

Tyra could hear the anger in her father's voice now and could picture his face. There was a way that he lifted his eyebrows whenever he used that particular tone, and she could see it in her mind's eye. She knew that the tone only existed because her father's voice modulator was straining to contain his rage. She wondered if Mr. Pritchard knew the sound of a maxed voice modulator like she did, but even if he didn't, there was definitely an electricity around her father that surely the headmaster could feel.

She wasn't entirely sure what had made her father so angry, but it must have been Mr. Pritchard's use of the term "slick." She had only heard it a couple of times before, usually being slung at her, but when she asked her father about it, he forbade her from ever using it. Now that she had some context, she guessed it had something to do with clones.

"Mr. Prichard," her father continued, "do you know who Tyra's genetic template is?"

"I assumed she was a clone of you," Mr. Prichard replied.

Tyra heard her father snort in response. "If only I were so perfect," he retorted.

There was a long pause between the two men, and Tyra wondered what was happening. She understood the benefit of vision now, which her father had frequently accused her of not appreciating. Being unable to see kept her from understanding the nuanced details of the situation. She would remember to never take her vision for granted.

"If the executives didn't feel the necessity to tell you the identity of Tyra's mother," her father continued, "then I assume you don't have the clearance. It would be against company standards to undermine the corporate stance. But you should know, Mr. Prichard, that your bigotry is putting you on a dangerous cliff."

"Her mother?" Mr. Prichard began. "Mr. Kirachi, surely—"

"I need to bring my daughter to the medical floor," her father interrupted. "Any further correspondence can be done through the corporate intranetwork. Our interaction here is terminated. Goodbye, Mr. Prichard."

Tyra tried her best to understand the situation unfolding around her, but it all sounded like grown-up stuff. She would have to look up the word "bigger tree" on her tablet later to understand what her father was talking about, but she understood that it had something to do with Mr. Pritchard treating her badly because she was… different. If she really was different, maybe she'd been wrong to lash out at her bullies. However, her father was strict about the "never be surrounded" rule, which she'd forgotten when they'd come for her, so striking before they were ready was her only tactical advantage in that fight.

"But—" Mr. Prichard began.

"Come, Tyra," her father interrupted.

Tyra slid off the chair, forgetting about her leg injury. She winced and bent reflexively as a sharp pain shot up from her knee. Recovering as fast as she could, she straightened herself, knowing that this was how her father would have wanted her to act. According to him, there was only pain if you opened your mind to it. She took in a deep breath and limped toward her father's voice. She was surprised when she felt his hand grab hers to gently assist her.

"Goodbye, Tyra," Doctor Clanker called out in its monotone voice. "Get well soon."

Tyra could not tell if the robot meant it, but it certainly sounded sincere.

———

WHEN HER VISION came back online, Tyra faced a wall of red ribbon alerts. The temporary shutdown had caused failures throughout her various augmented systems, resulting in an emergency reboot. She lay motionless on the top of the train as green status bars appeared one by one, signaling her automated responses were functioning properly. She did her best with the restart lag to assess the situation.

Her father's second gun was gone, and she could hear breathing nearby. She surmised that the attack had come from a person, not a robot, which was probably why she hadn't expected to be attacked from behind. Humans were unpredictable, significantly more so than robots, even with their "more human than human" artificial intelligence. Based on the human's ability to access the roof of the train, she surmised that he must be part of the security detachment assigned to the package. As if on cue, she felt a boot slide under her, and she was pushed over until she was looking up into the face of a clean-shaven, fair-skinned, brown-haired male with two metallic hands.

"Look at this bolt head," the bulky man said. "All tough until she got hit."

This man was obviously mafia, wearing a running suit rather than more efficient combat attire. The gaudy red fabric was stained and worn, signs that he'd only been able to obtain secondhand clothes, typical for someone from South Metroport. The city was a glorified slum, run by the slummiest of crime bosses. She couldn't blame the man for doing the best with what he had, but it was typical for Southie Mafia enforcers to look like him.

Tyra watched more green status bars appear and knew that she only needed a few more moments. She moved her eyes to search for the mafia guy's companions, but finding none, she assumed he was talking to someone remotely. It was likely other members of his cell, or whatever the Southie Boys called a small unit.

"Hey," the man said as he leaned over her. "You look familiar. Don't I knows yous from somewhere?"

As the last of Tyra's combat systems came online, she kicked her left foot upward, nailing the man solidly between his legs. She was half surprised when she connected with soft flesh rather than the typical testicle augmentation frequently found with men in toxically masculine professions like his. The mobster groaned and reeled back, his metal fists grasping his crotch reflexively. Tyra spun on her back and kicked herself into a backward combat roll. Landing on her feet with one leg extended in her father's favorite combat stance, the drop stance, she watched the mobster regain his composure as she drew one of her black katanas.

"That…" the big man huffed, "fragging… hurt."

He clenched his fists, causing hydraulic gas to be expelled from the joints, obviously trying to intimidate her. She smirked as his intimidation revealed he had the typical "rocket fists" she'd seen with other gang-level enforcers. She had to admit they weren't obvious, which meant they were better than average. Being in the mafia had a few perks.

He lunged for Tyra, but she moved, spinning around him while staying low, using her knees as feet. His rapid, augmented punches met nothing but air as she completed a 360-degree revolution. He turned to keep up but only managed to chase her. Coming around to face him, she slashed with her blade…

And missed.

Surprised, she found that the big man had moved away. Despite his size, he was fast, almost too fast. Anticipating he would use his speed to his advantage, she continued to spin, barely dodging his following attack. She watched as his fist slammed into the hardened plastic of the train, creating a web of cracks on the surface. Luckily she was the faster of the two combatants.

Completing another circle, she rose to her feet in a Tae Kwon Do weapon keubi stance just in time to see his heavy boot headed for her in a solid Muay Thai teep kick. She reacted by leaping into the air, using the tension snap of her augmented legs to sail over his head. As she passed, their eyes locked, and she saw him standing dumbfounded. She realized too late that she was staring back at him, fixated by his face, and missed her chance to slash down at him like she had hundreds of times in training.

"That was ice-cold," the mobster complimented as she landed.

Tyra smirked, somehow amused by this interaction. She slid her thumb across her sword's handle, lighting the neon filaments in the hilt before flourishing the blade unnecessarily. Finishing the sequence of random movements, she slid into a ko gasumi stance and stared down the blade at her opponent. It was his turn to smirk, and he readied himself for the next round of combat before suddenly cocking his head to the side quizzically.

"Oh slag!" he exclaimed. "Now I recognize you. Ain't you Mira St. Paul?"

"You are mistaken," Tyra answered.

"Nah nah nah," the man replied. "Johnny never forgets a face. You probably don't remember me, but it's Johnny. Johnny Smiles. They call me Johnny Knucks now on account of these bad boys." He raised both his fists to his face. "I was the punk kid who gave you a ride to see the boss when you was in SMP like twenty years ago. Remember, I awkwardly asked you for an autograph, and you looked at me like I'd killed your cat."

Tyra stared at the big man, who stared back, both silent as the wind whipped around them. Did she recognize him from somewhere?

"I heard you got slabbed," Johnny said after she didn't respond.

"You are mistaken," Tyra said again, adjusting the grip on her sword.

She lunged forward, maintaining the perfect speed and thrust to cause the maximum damage. She expected him to dodge her attack, and she planned to slash to the side in response. Instead, he deflected it with his hand and stayed in place. Tyra awkwardly slammed shoulder to shoulder with him, their faces nearly touching before she spun and slashed at his back. He turned to counter and deflected her attack with another simple hand gesture. Her Koukanzus were not sharp enough to cut through his hands, which was impressive considering their advertisements touted that they could cut through anything. She'd have to contact their corporate office about the money-back guarantee.

She danced to the side and slashed, only to have him counter and deflect. Each time she moved, he moved in opposition, both circling each other. At some point, he began to counter her attacks with his own, causing her to bob, weave, and counter along with him. They mirrored each other over and over, and she was surprised to find someone able to keep up with her for more than a few seconds. Before long, she felt remorse that it would have to end, but she continued to slash, counter, dodge, deflect, and weave. Eventually, she went in for a reckless attack and thought she would catch him off guard. Instead, she found herself barely slashing his shoulder as he weaved away and, in the same motion, caught her right wrist, lifting her to the tips of her toes.

His grip was strong, obviously augmented by hydraulic power, and she felt it crushing her wrist. She didn't doubt that he could pulverize her forearm in a single blow. As she paused to analyze the situation, she checked his glowing power indicators to see when he'd run out of juice. He still had five bars, meaning that he hadn't skimped on the battery component. He could hold her like this all the way to the station.

"Oh," he said, pulling her close enough that his spittle splattered on her faceplate. "I see. You ain't her. And not a robo skin job tinnie… a slick, then?"

In response, she bent at her waist, placing her boots against his chest before pushing out with her legs. Even with his height, his arm was not longer than she was tall. The hydraulics of her bionic legs activated, and she extended their full length as the whine of her knee pulley drowned out all other sounds. She forced a choice on him: let go or allow her to rip his arm from his body.

Flipping as he let go, she landed in the crane stance, raising her blade above her head. He wasn't an er bai wu, and he closed the distance between them, tracking her trajectory correctly as she leapt away. He prepared to shoulder her over the edge of the train, but she swung her sword around, bringing the tip right to the skin of his neck, causing him to stop suddenly. As the edge of the blade touched his skin, they paused, locking eyes.

Something about the mobster kept her from pushing the blade that last inch to kill him. Despite all their advancements, scientists still hadn't solved the debate about genetic memory, but for a moment, she felt like she did remember him as a young teen with a lopsided smile who dreamt about becoming the boss. As she processed this thought, she recalled something Chunt told her about the newest developments in sense pheromones that allowed the user to create specific emotional reactions to verbal or somatic cues. These reactions caused people to feel nostalgic about things they hadn't experienced or have connections to people they had never met. Chunt said the weapons corporations were developing particulates small enough to permeate face shields, but it was still experimental.

Sniffing the air, she caught the faint, sweet, telltale sign of biomechanical sense pheromones.

"Nice try," she said to the mobster. "How did you get your hands on those?"

"Fell off a truck," he replied with a smirk. "I did meet your mother, though, or whatever it is you slicks call the person you get your genes from."

Both moved at the same time. He twisted, causing her blade to stab empty air near his left shoulder as he came in for a body blow. Off-balance, she leaned into her weapon lunge, forcing his fist to roll along her torso, deflected by her hardened skin. She continued leaning toward the ground, falling forward intentionally as she kicked her right foot upward and connected the back of her heel with his chin. She could tell he hadn't expected her attack and reeled back reactively. Putting weight on her left hand, she cartwheeled, completing the arc to land where he stood.

Taking advantage of the situation, she thrust with her blade, aiming for the center of his chest.

The mobster called Johnny Knucks caught her katana in his fist and twisted it. She let go before the sword could drag her around the edge of the train, and she cartwheeled again as she watched him throw her katana into the roof of the train, puncturing it. Maybe she didn't need to call on that guarantee.

Realizing that she wasn't going to beat him through physical means, Tyra had an idea. Flipping forward, she extended her body as long as she could and hooked her calves over his shoulders, causing him to spin involuntarily. He was caught off guard, giving her the chance to dig her heels and pull herself up with her abdominal muscles until she was seated on his shoulders. As she felt his large hands wrap around her waist, she executed her plan.

Pulling the data line from her forearm, she plugged her cable directly into his cerebral port. Only specialists, like body docs, were supposed to connect to the cerebral ports, and then only to run diagnostics, update firmware, and download new augmentation interfaces. Accessing her Augmented Reality Menu, she slammed Chunt's "Surprise Package," a shutdown code planned for the secured hypertrain cargo car door. It was a long shot, as it was designed for the train's operational code, but she hoped it was generic enough to work on other systems. If it shut down just one of his augmentations, that would be enough.

As he threw her off, she found herself sliding toward the edge again, but not as out of control as before. Quickly stopping herself, she back-spun to gain momentum before leaping to her feet. Sliding into a zenkutsu dachi fighting stance, she prepared to fight empty-handed but recognized it was unnecessary as she watched the fallout from Chunt's virus. Roughly three seconds later, he slumped to the train's roof as his limbs ceased to function.

Standing over him in a mirror to their original meeting, she withdrew her black blade from the top of the train and sheathed it.

"All tough until he got hit," she mocked and turned away from him and started to move toward the front of the train.

"Hey!" the man shouted weakly. "Don't leave me like this. They'll kill me for failing, you know. Worse, they'll kill me, bring me back somehow, torture me, then put my consciousness in a box so they can do it again later."

Tyra sighed, realizing he was probably right. The Southie Mafia was known for its mercilessness. Having some respect for his fighting skill, she turned back and placed a boot on his side, moving him toward the edge of the train. Looking over, she saw that it was much farther to the ground than she expected, but if he had decent armor augmentations, he'd probably survive. The surprise package was intended to erase itself in a couple of hours, so he'd be able to start back to South Metroport in half a day. The smart move would be to head toward one of the other megacities and set himself up as a merc until the Southies forgot about him. He certainly had the chops for it.

"Good luck," she said as she prepared to push him over. "It's gonna be a rough landing."

"Thank you," he responded as he slid off the train.

———

TYRA LOOKED at herself once more, adjusting the mirror panel's lighting with a simple hand gesture. She'd chosen a great dress for her appearance at the annual Cyberlink Biocorp International Academy Ball, and even with the minor flaws tagged by her augmented eyes, a small marketing ploy to convince her to get more augmentations, she looked beautiful in the flowing black gown. She checked her hydraulic left knee once more, and it seemed to be working, albeit a bit sticky. There were a few more days until her scheduled upgrade, her father's birthday gift, and she hoped that the knee would make it through a night of intense dancing and gyrating. It had held up to several years of abuse, so she could understand if it slagged out on the one night it wasn't being used for training.

"You look stunning, madam," Ajax said from his position by her bedroom door.

"Thank you, Ajax," she replied, chuckling that he was still wearing the bow tie she'd put on him during their waltz training.

"Your father will be here in eighty-six seconds," Ajax announced, accessing the various cameras and sensors in their home network. "He is accompanied by your date, Charles Westington. Would you like me to remind you of Mr. Westington's profile information with the remaining time?"

"Zip it," she replied, embarrassed that her robot kept a profile on every person with whom she interacted.

"If I might, madam," Ajax replied. "Mr. Westington is wearing a mandarin-style suit with silver buttons and silver lining on his cuffs."

Tyra nodded her approval at the information and abandoned the red hair sash in her hand. As she reached for a silver sash, she saw her fingernails and stared at them long enough for the system to access the Digichroma AR menu. When the menu appeared in her vision, she color-matched the sash, causing a cascading change on her fingertips. By the time she slipped the bow around her hair, her nails were silver.

As she made the final adjustments to her outfit, she looked at Ajax in the mirror. "You're not coming with us, correct?"

"Correct, madam," Ajax replied. "I have been instructed by Sir to grant you privacy for the evening."

"Thank you," she replied.

"My pleasure, madam," Ajax said. She noticed that he rocked slightly on his feet when he talked, mimicking something they'd seen once in a cinematic hologram involving a butler.

By the time the door opened to her room, Tyra had managed to clean up most of the discarded garments and face her door, ready for their entry. As her father came into the room, his face brightened in an appraisal of her clothing choice. Stylish but functional. His eyes dropped to the concealed pocket in the dress and returned to hers with a quick wink. She smiled to see that he was looking strong despite the terminal strain of Tuberculupus destroying his remaining organs.

She frowned, feeling guilty for leaving him when he wasn't well, but he had practically commanded her to attend the Academy Ball. He said she was already "different," so there was no reason for her to be dramatically different from her peers.

"How are you feeling?" she asked him, ignoring Charles Westington as he entered.

"Fine," Enzo Kirachi lied. "But I'm not the important one at the moment."

"You are always the important one," she replied.

He smiled at her response. He had been smiling more and more as she got older, especially when he saw her individual, intuitive responses to training situations. It had taken her until just last year to realize that he'd been so strict when she was younger because the chips were stacked against her. Despite the protection of the corporation, the world was not easy for a clone, and if she was prepared to handle everything, he could relax. And a relaxed Enzo Kirachi was a pleasant one.

She had always thought he was strict because she'd been forced on him by assignment, but a little over a year ago, she discovered that she was performing well beyond the maximum expectations of his superiors, and when she confronted him, he confessed to everything. He was so demanding because she had become his real daughter. As far as he was concerned, she was Tyra Kirachi, not the corporate-assigned alphanumeric surname, and he wanted only the best for her.

"You look amazing," Charles Westington said, holding out a real peony corsage.

"Thank you," she said, graciously accepting the gift, realizing that even with his father's executive status, the corsage must have been expensive. "Papa, can you help me put this on?"

Enzo's growing smile caused him to squint. Knowing that she knew the truth but still called him father caused a crack in his stoic mask. Plus, the event called forth a memory. It was at the CBI Academy Ball that he'd met her mother, and despite them never becoming more than acquaintances, he still remembered how beautiful she was. Being able to see her child, the child of the woman who never loved him back, melted the warrior's tatemae.

Fumbling with the pin, it took Enzo Kirachi longer to accomplish a task that would have been a mere gesture when he was younger, but surprisingly, both youths waited patiently. Tyra noted that Charles did not show any signs of impatience, and she was grateful of that. She knew that he, like almost all her peers, had an expectation for the evening, particularly related to the postball activities, and while she initially had no interest, seeing that Charles was genuinely patient made her reconsider.

"There," Enzo Kirachi said weakly, bringing the attention back to him unintentionally, "all done. Somehow, the flowers add to your beauty."

"Thank you, Papa," Tyra replied.

"Now go, or else you two are going to be late," Enzo Kirachi commanded.

"They still have ten minutes and forty-four seconds until the official start time," Ajax countered.

"See," Tyra said with a smirk. "Plenty of time."

"Plenty of time for me to find a new robot," Enzo Kirachi returned. "Perhaps one of the less rebellious Model 5Xs."

Ajax's face display flashed a frowning emoji as a response to his owner's comments and followed it with an image of the Model 5X ad with a red *X* across it. Tyra bit back an amused smile and noticed Charles doing the same. Enzo grunted a gruff laugh in response, but the laugh quickly turned into a coughing fit. Tyra's amusement disappeared instantly, and she stepped to her father to help him into her high-backed gaming chair. She was surprised when her hand on his back felt another, causing her to look up and see that Charles was assisting, not looking at her but at her father.

"I'm fine," her father protested but did not wave off their assistance. "You both need to go, or you might be late. The elevators will be busy tonight."

"We're only going forty floors," Tyra countered as she lowered her father into the chair. "We can stay a few minutes and take a buzzer to the elevator bay if we want to hurry. It's not that big of a building, Papa."

"It's an arcology," Enzo corrected, "and there are four hundred people on the elevators at any given moment. Trust me—"

"I work in security," Tyra semi-mockingly interrupted, repeating her father's favorite phrase.

"Doesn't make it less true," he returned and smiled. "I think your date will be disappointed if you don't turn your attention to him."

"Her date recognizes the importance of her father," Charles corrected, "and her date also understands that she knows eight ways to kill him painfully with her bare hands. Her date will support her decision to pay attention to her father."

Enzo Kirachi coughed another gruff laugh but smiled at the young man. "Smart man," he complimented.

"I like to think I'm tactically paranoid," Charles bantered.

Tyra smirked at her date's response and checked another point in his favor. She had originally thought that Charles Westington, the third son of a midlevel finance executive, had been a boring choice of a ball companion, but now felt that she'd made the best choice. His biggest rival for her affections, Margot Fletcher, would certainly have been more selfish about her attention. On their test date, Margot became upset that Tyra was enjoying soup more than Margot's rant on the utility of index stock funds.

"You kids get out of here," Enzo ordered. "I'll go to bed early. You two don't worry about me. Have fun and break curfew. It's the annual ball after all."

"Most dads tell their daughters to be back an hour before curfew," Tyra replied.

"Most daughters aren't platinum certified in extreme close-combat self-defense," Enzo countered. "Nor do they know the Kirachi Spike technique."

Enzo patted Tyra's forearm data cable with a smirk. She eyed him quizzically, not sure what he was alluding to with the Kirachi Spike reference, but she knew the man well enough to know when he was using psychological tactics. She also knew him well enough to trust him and roll with it, assuming he intended to make Charles uncomfortable. In her peripheral vision, she saw that it had worked.

"Um…" Charles said awkwardly, squirming slightly. "The Kirachi Spike technique?"

"You just be good," Enzo warned the young man, "and you won't be uploaded with anything you weren't expecting."

Tyra hid her smile by turning to her father. He winked reassuringly at her, pleased with how well she had played along. Seeing the old security specialist in peak form despite his illness comforted her.

"We'll go," Tyra said, "but we're not far. Ajax, call me if he needs anything."

"Yes, madam," Ajax responded.

"Traitor," Enzo replied. "Don't worry about me. I'll just sit here a moment. You two have fun."

Tyra gave her father a long hug before leaving him in her room. She smiled and thanked Charles for being understanding, taking his arm in a "slightly more than friends" gesture as they walked toward the door. However, as she crossed the threshold, she looked back to see her father smiling down the hall, his head drooping in exhaustion. She felt an uneasiness, like this would be the last time she saw him, but tried not to think about it as he drifted farther away.

AS THE CARGO car door opened, Tyra's face shield retracted into its compartment. She stepped into the threshold of the cargo car and admired the versatility of Chunt's Surprise Package. It had worked well enough on her human opponent and sliced right through the train's lock. She made a note to send Chunt a little more than their agreed cut considering that the Cracker had given her a valid option for the Kirachi Spike. She'd have to find someone like Chunt when she got off-planet, and since most station citizens were passively familiar with coding, she felt confident that she'd be able to find a replacement. Maybe not as good, but close enough for off-world purposes.

Four Southie mobsters stood awkwardly inside the cargo car, their Zappers extended in their baton settings. They weren't carrying firearms, she knew, because puncturing the side of the train while in motion threatened catastrophic structural damage that caused the side to rip free and potentially eject the passengers. The top was safe, but that wasn't enough to justify the risk. Fortunately for them, she had lost both her guns on the way.

"I'm just here for the box," she announced, hoping they would surrender.

All four men pressed the button that caused electricity to surge through the Zappers' contact points as if they'd practiced it. She scoffed at their weak attempts to intimidate her and drew both her katanas in a quick, flourishing gesture as a response. She stepped fully into the train car, letting the automated door close behind her, and waited as the four men split into two teams. They moved around the boxes and crates in the car, approaching her in a loose pincher maneuver. She debated simply leaping onto the crate tower in the center and running to the Genecorp-marked tote in the back but realized this wasn't a training session. She would need to deal with the threat eventually. Sometimes you can't skip the fight scene, and sometimes you had to let yourself get surrounded.

When the first mobster attacked, she used the flat side of one of her blades to deflect it, twisting as she did to build tension for the snapback. On the return, she used the flat edge of her second blade to deflect a Zapper thrust from the second mobster. Realizing they were about to crowd her, she leapt, kicking the second mobster in the face before landing between the third and fourth, putting some distance between the combatants. As her feet hit the ground, she slid into drop stance to avoid a wild stab from the fourth mobster. Instinctively, she followed the drop with a leg sweep to the third mobster. As she finished the movement, she quietly thanked her father for all the late nights training against multiple assailants.

She twisted and slashed upward, barely missing the fourth mobster but knocking him backward. Turning in time, she caught an attack from the first assailant with the crook of her elbow and clamped down to lock his wrist in place, keeping his baton away from her body. In her peripheral vision, she noticed a forward jab from the second mobster's baton in time to sloppily deflect it. As he began to rotate his wrist, bringing the tip toward her, Tyra reacted by slashing downward with her sword, severing his forearm halfway between the elbow and wrist. He screamed in pain just before Tyra launched a heavy teep kick into his chest, driving him into the hard plastic wall.

She dodged a bumbling attack from the fourth mobster as he stumbled over the severed arm and felt the pull of the first mobster trying to break from her grip. She used his pull to her advantage and turned farther than he expected, coming around to kick him with a solid front kick. Using the strength and speed of her knee pulley, she smashed his stomach. The power of the kick sent him reeling off his feet and hurtling into the third mobster, who had just risen from the floor. His baton was smashed between their two bodies, and Tyra heard the electrical snap before both men crumpled to the floor, unconscious. Continuing her spin, Tyra launched a side kick into the second mobster as he moved forward from the wall, blood pouring from his forearm stump. His head snapped back, and he fell into the wall again before falling face-first onto the ground.

Realizing she forgot about the fourth mobster, Tyra began to turn but was stopped as a disrupting spasm coursed through her muscles. The feeling was quickly chased by the snapping sound of electricity and intense pain. While her hardened skin dulled impacts, it conducted electricity. As her visual displays shook wildly in response, Tyra moved through the forced contractions, not relying on the visual cues, and felt little resistance as her blade slashed through her intended target.

She hadn't moved entirely on purpose. It was mostly a reaction to the pain and her father's training that allowed her to slash accurately while blinded. She probably would be dead if not for the old security specialist. As her vision steadied, she watched the mobster's headless body drop heavily. Spinning, her weapon extended defensively, she checked her opponents. The three remaining men were writhing on the floor, moaning in pain.

Releasing a sigh of relief, she determined the threat was neutralized and sheathed both of her black blades. The gray, hermetically sealed tote labeled Genecorp, LTD sat on several crates at the far end of the cargo car, waiting for her to claim its contents. After confirming it was her mission objective, she sent a signal to her Patron, letting the corporate handler know to expect her at South Metroport station momentarily.

Punching in the predetermined sixteen-digit hex code, she listened to the hiss of compressed air escaping the seal before the lid popped open. She smirked at the theatrics and waved away the fog, revealing the small plastic credit chip displaying her payout and the clear bottle of red and black capsules, perks for a job well done. Picking up the bottle, she was initially surprised at the quantity of Beta Red until she remembered that Genecorp manufactured the organ rejection inhibitor. They probably didn't have to dig deep to obtain this much of the substance.

Shoving both the items into her emptied holster, she removed the pack of stim cigs she'd hid from Ajax. Her father did not have addictive tendencies, so it was something genetic and not learned. In response, her father hated the habit, so Ajax destroyed every pack she purchased in keeping with her father's wishes well past the expiration of the obligation. Smoking was her secret indulgence. Checking her retinal clock, she realized she had plenty of time before they rolled into the station, long enough for at least one.

She closed the lid to the tote and sat down to watch the mobsters recover. They glowered at her as she took a quick puff to mix the chemical compound in the tip that created the self-ignition. As she took a long drag, the mobsters turned to face her.

"Better luck next time, chingu," she said with a smirk as she tossed the pack between them. There was no smoking in space, after all.

———

MAYOR VINCENT TRIED NOT to look ridiculous as the rain soaked his worn gray suit. He stood on the platform of the South Metroport Hyperspeed Train Station, as close as he could to the much more expensively clad Genecorp LTD executive. The slim, pale-skinned man half his age signed invisible paperwork, obviously interacting with his Click in AR while he stood under a kinetic reflector projected from the shoulder of his dark trench coat. Vinnie waited, assuming the corpboy would inform him of his guys' security assessment, but he could not scratch the feeling he was being snubbed. As if being mayor wasn't an important political position.

After waiting nearly ten minutes "with his balls in his hands," as Vinnie was oft to say, the Genecorp executive finally acknowledged the mobster-turned-politician as he dropped back into full reality. The mayor of South Metroport gave his best campaign grin and reached out a handshake greeting.

"Hey," Vinnie said, "I appreciate you being here in person. I knows yous executive types like to do a lot of work remotely."

"Your men failed," the executive said coldly, ignoring Vinnie's greeting.

"Right to the point," Vinnie responded, dropping his handshake awkwardly. "I like that. Does that mean my men are out completely, or do we get a second chance?"

"You get just the one chance," the executive answered. "All five of your men plus the train's security were inadequate to stop a single operative."

"Hold on now," Vinnie replied. "A single operative what? Tinman? Spike? These things matter. I can't be blamed if my people were not informed about the security risk."

"A clone," the executive replied, "of Mira St. Paul. And your men should be prepared for any situation."

"Fragmented slicks," Vinnie shot back. "That's not fair. I bet she is custom-tailored to combat. Probably pumped full of high-grade augmentations too."

"Perhaps," the executive replied, "but she's a freelance merc. A freelance merc I could afford without higher approval. I'm sorry, Mr. Mayor, but Genecorp has decided to go with a competitor service."

"Not through South Metroport, you won't," Vinnie retorted confidently.

"Perhaps not," the executive replied. "Or perhaps we will. I'm not so convinced your men would be able to stop us. Goodbye, Mr. Mayor."

As the executive walked to his HR707 Personal Carrier, Vinnie heard the train rounding the last bend. His elevated pulse filled his hearing so quickly that the world around him turned into a silent hologram. Drawing his concealed pistol, he turned to the tracks, waiting to meet this girl who'd just bested his men. She'd taken his contract, and it only made sense that he kill her again as he did twenty years ago. Or the clone of whatever. It didn't matter much. This would be her last job, he was sure of that.

ABOUT R. SCOTT UHLS

Scott is the founder of Heeroic Studios Gaming, a role-playing game company, and the creator of the cyberpunk-themed tabletop RPG named "Beta Red." He began writing in his midteens and discovered tabletop RPGs, specifically Shadowrun, locking the worlds together. His enjoyment for the genre is supplemented by his genuine love for Japanese and Korean culture, and his reverence to them can be seen in his writing.

THANK YOU FOR CARING

ROSIE RECORD

Hand-selected inmates from the prison city of Needles are building the future of California-Annex floor by floor, hundreds of feet above the cracked desert landscape. Under the watch of patrol drones and governors, the construction crews are kept on task with a T.O.M.S.I. (Task-oriented Memory Synchronistic Implant). None of the workers know each other's personal thoughts, except for Callahan—well, sort of. When his friend is shivved, and a mass exodus at the border devolves into a riot, Callahan's world changes. After wanting so desperately to rewrite his legacy beyond the summary of his rap sheet, he begins to wonder if he even can.

THANK YOU FOR CARING

J unior's mind began to fall into mine after the cold drip-drip of chemicals from the T.O.M.S.I. sloshed through my brain and started dismantling my thoughts. His sex-infused distraction rode on my synapses, making each connection point throb while something else throbbed and pushed against my government-issued blue jeans.

"Get back to work, Junior," I snapped as I readjusted my pants.

When I turned, I saw him at the edge of the build-site, completely mesmerized by a holographic ad. About a hundred feet down, projected over the cracked desert landscape, photons colored out a beautiful XX with glossy lips and flawless skin—black makeup smeared down and away from her eyes like a Rorschach butterfly. She caressed a perfume bottle as if it was something else, and while I couldn't read Junior's mind exactly, I felt his unexplored experiences and fantasies frothing into an urge I didn't want to live out with him.

"Hey," I tried to get his attention, "did you hear me? Eyes u—"

"Warning—" a silky voice boomed from one of the patrol drones. Normally they swept the smogged airways like sleepless sharks in deep waters, but the armored machine had curved from its linear route to hover eye-level with him. "Subject 10121-098, you are in violation of safety protocol 502 D-16-3," it explained while pulsing a red light in a mesmerizingly slow rhythm. Junior stared at the drone, not seeing he was the problem, making the automated voice repeat, "Warning: Subject 1012—"

"Get away from the edge and put your damn clip on," Connors barked in a voice smoked by decades of Marlboro Reds. It was the only voice that really got through to the kid, and when he came back to reality I felt my mind being returned to me.

"What did you mean earlier when you said they're giving away houses?" Junior asked as he clipped the safety carabiner onto his belt loop, triggering the drone to disengage.

"Think about it," Connors said as he worked a flathead screwdriver under a nail and scraped out a thin line of blackened grit. "They're making people choose between an entire country or this state. What's the best way to get them to stay?"

With wide-set eyes, upper lip always glossed in snot, and steel-toed boots that never seemed to be tied, we all realized Junior needed a helping hand once in a while, but Connors went a step beyond. He showed him how to use tools, wire up an electrical box, and was always running a one-sided conversation with the kid, like *Now see, if it's red, it's a traveler wire. Where's your multitool? Here's mine. You got it? Good.*

Plus, Connors took the time to explain things. He wanted to ensure no one took advantage of Junior's lack of mental bandwidth, but I didn't know if that was really possible. There was a simplicity to Junior's brain patterns, almost like he didn't think in full sentences. It felt like someone tapping out words on a keyboard only using their index fingers—*tap, tap, search for the letter, tap, tap-tap*—and by the time he got a few words down he'd forgotten the point altogether. But Connors didn't experience the slipping of thoughts beyond the parameters of the T.O.M.S.I. programming. None of them did. It was a side effect specific to me despite us all having the implant.

"What about us, Connors?" Junior asked in his slow cadence, his mouth getting stuck around the -or sound.

"What *about* us? They're using our metal and meat to build all this up."

Junior stood at the edge again and looked at a sunset painted in chemical vibrancy. "I mean, what about when we get out?"

Connors shrugged. "I ain't never leaving."

"Well, I am." Hands on hips, the kid stood like a superhero looking out onto a horizon of possibilities. I wanted to tell him the world doesn't owe you a goddamn thing. Your mama doesn't have to love you, and your fate doesn't have to be good. No luck, bad breaks, wrong choices, poor decisions—no one cares. Just get in, get out, and make the best of every breath. I'd made my peace with that reality, but I knew he'd be disappointed by how the world asked so much, gave so little, and never forgave.

"Don't be so sure," Connors answered back fast as he tapped the metal T.O.M.S.I. budding from his left ear. Three metal prongs were sunk into the thin skin just beyond, and because his was one of the proto-types, bio-transmission fluid had flooded blood vessels so black veining wrapped around his jaw and started down his neck.

"Before," Connors continued, "guys like us would have to find Jesus or the law, earn degrees and change our lives after a brutal methadone detox session. Now they have neural interface and remapping tech, and what do they do with it? Make sensory immersive porn and keep us synced up on task items so we're good little worker drones. With all our progress we sure don't do much with it."

He was right. T.O.M.S.I. (Task-oriented Memory Synchronistic Implant) was neural remapping tech that constructed shared memories across the prison-staffed construction teams. The goal was to create a hivemind with real-time updates so we knew which tasks were complete and what still needed to be done. From that, we could optimize our work patterns. It wasn't psychic communication. Although the three of us often found ourselves saying similar phrases or scratching our balls at the same time, none of the workers knew each other's personal thoughts. Even my experience wasn't exactly psychic. It was more like impressions of thoughts, or empathy amplified to the point of intrusion. And it seemed to be proximity-based.

"I heard," I started to say as I leaned back on my palms, boots dangling over the concrete ledge, "they use this tech for curing people with anxiety and post-traumatic stuff." That seemed a better use for the technology than syncing up construction crews.

The teardrop tattoo on Connors' weathered skin twisted when he squinted at me. "You see anyone who doesn't have anxiety nowadays?"

Fair point.

"All right, sweethearts," a different voice cut into the conversation, "order lunch and get back to work. We don't pay you to gossip all day." Governor Lacey threw a dismissive wave toward the spherical ad-bots rushing toward us now.

"You don't pay us at all," Connors mumbled loud enough to be heard, but Lacey wasn't a hard-ass when it came to patrolling speech, he was one of the believers. In fact, he was the one who got me out of the cages.

After the civilian workers went on strike, leaving their yellow hard-hats perfectly lined up along the build-site like an art installation or those candy dots you licked off paper, opportunities opened up for guys like me. It was the opportunity to work with my hands and stand hundreds of feet above a world that was changing fast. And although the air was thick with pollution, I loved how the wind picked up grit and worked through my hair, pushing and pulling sideways and back like a hairdresser did while asking, *So what are we doing with it today?* It was a wholly different experience from the flaccid gusts of air that came through the prison's HVAC system—filtered, infused with oxygen, and tasting of artificial lemon.

More importantly, the construction crews were allowed to eat outside food. Over the past six years, smileless machines in the cafeteria had dispensed poultry or fish byproduct meals to the long queue of us XYs each morning, afternoon, and night. It sloshed from chrome nozzles like dog food, landing on each aluminum tray with an unappetizing plop. Now we had so many options it seemed ungrateful when we defaulted to our favorite restaurants. Even still, a handful of new ad-bots rose above the scaffolding and sprayed the air with short-term bio-lumis in an attempt to win over our business. Like full-spectrum colored fireflies, the bioengineered swarm performed a choreographed dance of colors and movement to spell out menus and generate images like cartoon chickens, walking chopsticks, steaming bowls of ramen, or a pretty XX biting into a sloppy burger. And when they reached the end of their shelf life, their glow snapped off, black specks fell to the concrete, and they were eventually crushed into fine dust under our boots. All-natural and biodegradable.

The Meshi Japanese restaurant's bio-lumis were undulating and swirling into position now, forming up a school of blue-finned tuna and pink-bellied salmon that encircled Junior. His wide-spaced eyes blinked in wonder as silver scales shimmered in dappled blue light that was baked into their programming.

"Don't touch 'em unless you want to order sushi again," I warned the kid as his fingertips reached out to the images moving on air currents. But he wasn't listening. I could feel his childish glee make my jaw drop.

"I said don't touch 'em, Junior," I snapped as I shook away his experience from mine. These weren't colored photons like the holograms down below; once you touched one, it started the order process, and soon after there were food delivery drones fighting the patrol drones for airspace.

Right on schedule, Connors huffed out a laugh as Gobble Up BBQ's mascot filled an available patch of air. The fat pink pig danced in pinpricks of hot-pink light alongside signs for printed BBQ. He touched the wiggling snout, starting the order process for the same sandwich he ordered every lunch. I knew moments after his first bite I'd start to feel the Gates Meat—synthetic, printed, and never tasting quite right—being processed in my body, even though it wasn't my lived experience.

After lunch, after the workday was complete and we were shuttled back to our cells, the implant was switched off. I should have been returned to myself, but the forced synchronicity left a sticky residue over what it meant to be solitary or whole. That being said, I wouldn't pick the alternative. I still had a choice, and I chose to ignore the sour taste Connors' hunger left in my mouth. I chose to push past feeling like a whirligig frantically spinning in place, unable to gain traction—which seemed to be my mental flex constrained by Junior's abilities. I chose to be a part of the GeoProgressive Movement and build the future of California-Annex because it was my only chance to be more than what was summarized on my rap sheet.

————

PRISON WAS a concrete box filled with predators jockeying for dominance, patrolled by armed predators betting on the outcome. I wasn't the biggest or the strongest, I didn't have outside connections or belong to a gang, so avoidance was my method of survival. I was good at identifying twitches of violence in the hardened faces of the XYs around me, but I wanted more than to just survive. So when I discovered a quiet space none of the other inmates used, I slipped inside. The lights switched on as I walked down an aisle. Antique e-readers, paperbacks with yellowing pages, and hardbacks with curled plastic sleeves lined the shelves. There were a few chairs near a barred window, and the sunlight seemed to stream in and curl up into a welcoming gesture as if saying, *Come, sit here.*

Governor Jessnick, who managed the library, introduced himself to me by shoving a book below my nose and saying, "Here. This is a good author."

I read the orange lettering aloud. "Clive Cussler?"

Jessnick walked away when I started to read the first chapter. And after I read one book, I read all of his books. Then I wanted more. I wanted old books, new books, outdated books, books about history and science as well as crafts, poetry, cookbooks, and even picture books. I wanted books about living with monkeys, handling your shopping addiction, diving into your subconscious, how-to manuals on cars that ran on gasoline, anything available to me. Because the more I read, the more my world was dismantled and rebuilt with colors and possibilities. I realized I could escape my concrete box, charge into adventures and fly to foreign places that would be denied to us all once California-Annex was completely cut off from the rest of the Divided States.

A few years into my stay, the e-readers were removed. Then the prison's board of psychologists started flagging old titles as dangerous. Stories about surviving, pushing through, rising against, overcoming, and succeeding were disappearing. Not burned in an open display to let everyone know the royal-they were taking away something of importance, but transitioned out of digital libraries while hardcopies were bought up or removed and recycled into packaging, reusable cups, paper straws, and other products that made people smile and say *thank you for caring.*

Like contraband, Jessnick would slip me what titles he could before they were recycled. At night I'd pull the book from my waistband and read by the blue-tinted searchlights just outside the prison walls. In the end, however, books were removed from the shelves faster than I could read. And then one day the doors to my safe space were locked. A sign about a new Wellness Center hung squarely over where the library hours had been scraped off—I could still see flecks of vinyl where Wednesday had been.

The next day, Governor Jessnick came to me while I was waiting in line for my slosh of byproduct meal and accompanying veggie tablet.

"I couldn't stop 'em from shutting us down," he said as he handed me a thin hardback. "If anyone asks, it was a gift."

By the time I slipped it into my waistband, he was gone, and I didn't see him after that. I heard he was assigned to B Block.

That same night, I lay on my bunk just before lights out and stared at the painted cinder block—the gray surface taking on a tacky sheen from the hard fluorescent lighting. Once everything powered off and I heard my cellmate's chainsaw snores, I pulled the book from my waistband and turned it over in the blue-tinted light.

Inside, Governor Jessnick had written *Property of William F. Callahan 61629-098.*

That was *my* name and number.

And although I knew someone could just cross it out, that ink on paper felt binding and real. That small book of prose was mine, and no one could take it away.

My fingertips traced the worn-down spine, and the pages naturally fell open toward a block of text in the back that read: *I am being stolen. Messages parsed and digitized funnel in and down, around, spread and embed. Like burrs in each synapse stabbing, itching, triggering a different thought not mine. I am being stolen. My heroes slain, pride appropriated, dreams reduced, common goals splintered by maligned intent. Vibrant memories once lived in 3-D flattened into pixels on a screen, made lackluster, ashen, and sad in comparison to the next thing and the next. Integrity wanes, is suppressed, then overwritten. But with what? What are these messages telling me? I don't know and yet I act, react, swipe, tap, and realign my beliefs to become a person not me. I am being stolen.*

Even though it was a question, a paragraph about confusion and fear, those words made me dip into a part of my brain that felt connected to comprehension and purpose. I felt stronger for joining in the question: What are these messages telling me?

I read the book cover to cover, over and over. I read it so many times I knew each block, each line. I was like a preacher who could quote Ecclesiastes, although I don't think I understood the passages as well. It was only when the T.O.M.S.I. tech started to rearrange my mind, did my understanding deepen into philosophy.

Maybe six months after the library closed, Governor Lacey called out my name in the yard. "Catch," he added as he tossed a hardhat in my direction.

"What's this about, Gov'?"

He looked at me squarely, but the bridge of his nose seemed to list to the left like it got distracted along its route. With thumbs hooked into his belt loops and combat boots planted in a wide stance, he answered, "Told the man upstairs about your good behavior, and he's agreed to put you on the Hives."

"Hives, sir?"

"You know." Lacey seemed surprised I didn't know. "The housing project for the GeoPro Movement."

I'd heard of that before. The California-Annex's GeoProgressive Movement was launched before I was born. It was a massive undertaking where the outer Annex border was lined with ammonium nitrate (ANFO), blown up, dug hundreds of feet deep and three miles wide to make room for a massive housing project and transportation system. It was lauded as visionary, as progress for the Annex, and made everyone say *thank you for caring.*

Lacey pointed toward a wall lined with information on the working-prisoners program.

How had I never noticed this before?

With the yellow hardhat in hand, my eyes soaked in the details. The Hives weren't like normal housing projects. It was more like a vertical city soaring hundreds of stories above the surface and lining the California-Annex border. The name was inspired by the overall design—the structures were a polygonal shape so they fit together in a honeycomb pattern and had netted domicile bridging connecting them.

I could be a part of this?

Lacey put a hand on my shoulder. "But this is only if you continue to keep your class act up, yeah?"

"Of course, Gov', I won't let you down." And I wouldn't. I'd been lost since the library closed, and that feeling of wanting more than survival had started to creep back into my awareness. This was exactly what I needed when I needed it.

However, I first needed to be fitted with a T.O.M.S.I. before I could start work. So Lacey sent me up to the forty-sixth floor with Governor Saaki. I remember fighting back a yawn as the elevator ascended. I didn't want to be noticed by the governor, who stood centered in the metal box, watching the numbers tick up. Keeping my shoulders hunched, hands open, and palms visible, I made sure not to look in his direction. Instead, my eyes settled on the old bloodstain in the back right corner where Owusu had been beaten to death by four members of the Wah Ching gang. When the Lung Tao, the Wah Ching's leader, found out Owusu had provided fentanyl and shine to their rivals, the ABZ gang, he put a hit on him. Not long after, the short, stocky man was stomped and beaten so brutally that his jaw was nearly ripped off and his right eye ejected from the force—it rolled a few inches away from his face but was still connected by what looked like a pink string covered in blood.

Where had Saaki been then?

"BARBARIC," the nurse muttered as the doc moved in with my T.O.M.S.I. pinched by long tweezers. When the light was behind him and his face was dark, I could see his ocular insert glow in that Sensorium Biotech green color. I watched the mechanical rings twist for focus as he moved in closer and closer.

"These XYs are human beings, not test rabbits," she added.

With that, the doctor stopped, and I heard him sigh beneath his mask before he pulled it down.

"Mr. Callahan," he said as he straightened and lifted the tweezers up —the metal implant looked like sushi poised on the tip of chopsticks now. "You have been provided a choice due to your good behavior." His natural eye drifted away to settle on the pretty XX in lavender scrubs while the mechanical one stayed fixed forward on me. "Now you can stay confined to the prison walls, or you can go outside and contribute to GeoPro. Which would you prefer?"

This was an opportunity for me to be outside. No more bars. I'd be a hundred feet in the air with only a safety tether holding me back from freedom. More importantly, XYs like me didn't always get a chance to leave a good legacy. This was my chance.

"I've always been good with my hands, sir. I'd like to be a part of GeoPro."

The nurse looked at me as if I was the only thing to see, and she seemed to listen as if she was trying to hear the truth in each of my sylla-bles. I'd never had anyone give me their undivided attention like that before, so I tried to reassure her, but it almost felt like a burden to be seen so completely.

"It's okay, ma'am. I don't mind the idea of more metal." I lifted my left arm to show the steel knuckles and fingertips peeking through the e-skin I'd scraped off during a fight a few years back. It had messed with the somatosensory feedback, but I never consented to a fix—feeling less wasn't a bad thing in this place.

"All right, let's proceed," the doc said as he leaned in again. "You'll feel a fullness and then a sharp pain, but it's very quick."

The T.O.M.S.I. was placed into the crook of my ear and held down by those long stainless steel tweezers. I heard a mechanical whine before the sounds around me distorted. It was expanding, growing, stretching, reaching down into my ear canal. I tried to pull away, but the doc held his other hand flat against my cheek, holding me in place.

"You're doing well, Mr. Callahan. Just a few more seconds."

It was like a bug crawling across my skin, only deep inside. I needed to brush it away, get it off, pull it out, shake my head, shove a finger in my ear to dig it out, and then jiggle it loose. I grunted and squirmed but was held in place. Discomfort, violation, and then finally a pinch inside my brain. I yelped and shook loose of the doc.

"And there we go. You are all finished." He rolled back on his stool and yanked his gloves off with a latex snap. "You'll feel general discomfort for a few days, but that's completely normal."

"That's it?" I asked as I touched the device filling in my ear.

The doc was writing something down. "That's it," he answered without looking up. "Common side effects can include headaches, feeling light-headed, dizzy, confused, nauseous, tremors in your face or extremities, and increased thoughts of suicide. Just let us know if you feel like you are at risk of hurting yourself or others."

The nurse was looking at me with a broken smile and dark eyes. Why did she look so sad? All experimental technology had risks. Even if I had known other minds would slip into mine, I wouldn't have picked the alternative. I still had a choice, and I chose to be a part of the GeoProgressive Movement. I chose to build the future of California-Annex because it was my only chance to be more than what was summarized on my rap sheet.

———

IT WASN'T until I was hundreds of feet up and looking down I realized not everyone supported the movement. For months, protesters pooled below while their chants traveled up: *Is it safety or a cage? Global disaster has been staged. Don't fall for the wall! Don't fall for the wall!* Their handheld holo-pods projected similar messages onto the air molecules while the wind rippled the words.

It made me look at the cinder block wall just behind the Hives and wonder if it was the best way to ensure the future of California-Annex. I'd heard stories of war, disease, and devastation just beyond, but what if none of it was true? What if the chants were right to question the wall? The colossal structure came in from the west and peaked at Redding, followed the natural border of the Sierra Nevadas, cut east to include the tip of Death Valley, Mojave City and the prison city of Needles, where we were now. Eventually, it would make a sharp line to Calexico and then straight west to flooded-out San Diego—fully enclosing the Annex.

The protestors' question made me think of a block of words in my thin hardback: *Constrained by bars and chains? No, we are shackled by social contract, expectations, and conditioning. We think ourselves free because we are too blind to see the prison constructed around us, clad in fine finishes, fat-free, and eco-conscious, with amenities and extras bundled or a la carte. We don't touch the bars and acknowledge their names: Convenience, comfort, and security. Resistance should be a discordant choir, out of sync, out of tune, and yet the words are the same: Don't take our voices.*

Our hearts should be beating fast, blood pulsing and throbbing as we push against, push through, push past, push on. We were once survivors, warriors, innovators, and explorers, after all. But now our hearts sound out a panicked fluttering instead. Our minds whisper a persistent warning against discomfort, so we stay nestled inside, live by proxy, never even standing to take a stand, our causes like trends catered to our fluctuating morals by an algorithm.

No. No more. Rise up and fight, grab your rights by their intangible edges and pull them back down into your reality. No. A single word is all it takes to be free. Two letters, one syllable begins everything. No.

I'd heard the protesters say no for months now, but today was different. They weren't shouting and marching in circles. They had suitcases in hand, wagons stacked with boxes, while silent electric cars moved alongside them. I could see the few governors dotted along the build-sites stiffen as they looked down on the massive snake of people walking toward the border.

A mechanical blurt and *bwoop-bwoop* blared from a nearby drone before it tipped its nose and dropped down to ground level. Then another did the same. Then another. Eventually, all of them descended, and the few governors on the build-sites with us looked uncomfortable as their aerial support moved into action.

"Warning—" the drones blasted out their message in unison. "You are in violation of health and safety measures CoV-4 12.539. Be considerate of others. Please return for your safety and the safety of others."

I saw Governor Lacey looking over the edge with a hand pressed to one ear. He listened, then nodded, clutched his rifle to his chest, and followed the other governors to the elevator shafts. They were all descending on the exodus.

"Warning—" the drones repeated their message as they circled. I could hear screaming as people dropped to the ground when the drones swooped lower and lower. "You are in violation of health and safety measures CoV-4 12.539. Be considerate of others. Please return for your safety and the safety of others."

"This is wrong," I said more to myself just as Connors peered over the edge. Drones were herding people like cattle—isolating manageable-sized groups the governors could then arrest.

"I mean, what are they doing? I thought people were allowed to leave the Annex up until the end of next month?"

"Think about it," Connors said as he turned his back to the wind and lit a cigarette. "Why would they actually let them leave?"

I shook my head. "How can they get away with this?"

"Who's going to stop them?" The teardrop tattoo below Connors' eye twisted when he looked at me. "Who's going to tell?" With the smoking cigarette pinched between his index and middle finger, he pointed. "You?"

He was right. I continued to watch the chaos and fear spiral into a riot of tear gas and rubber bullets, screams and automated messages about safety protocols. I wondered about the words in my book: *A single word is all it takes to be free. Two letters, one syllable begins everything. No.*

Had dissent held more power once? Or was it a lie we always told ourselves? Did we ever have the power to say no?

———

NO, Javier, no. Please stop.

"Junior?" I looked up. "Junior?" I yelled his name again as I scanned our building. He wasn't there. I was hearing his mind call out in a panicked flutter like a bird beating its wings against a cage too small. His thoughts were falling into mine because he was scared, he was hurt, and the task at hand was to survive.

"Have you seen Junior?" I yelled to Connors, but he wasn't there either. Where was everyone?

My toolbelt slammed against my thighs as I ran across the build-site. The metal-and-wood scaffolding structure swayed as I climbed up and up.

As I searched for Junior, I heard the drones' messaging. "Warning: You are in violation of health and—" But the skies were eerily empty. All the workers must have taken advantage of the situation to meet up with other inmates.

Now I was actually hearing Junior's voice crack and pitch up into a desperate squeal. "Stop!"

There. I saw the kid writhing beneath a knee dug deep into his back.

"Hey, get away from him," I yelled. Jumping over stacks of material, wires, and tools, I could feel my heartbeat in my temples, my throat becoming drier with each ragged inhale of dusty air. I ran along the netted bridging to the next Hive top, then again made my way up, over, and across the jungle gym of metal and concrete.

Then my body pitched forward as I pulled back to a stop, my boots kicking up more white dust. *Where was the bridge?* I looked down at the gap between this Hive and the next, becoming dizzy from the deadly plummet.

Javier, the Calexico mafioso, bare-chested and slicked in sweat, taunted Junior in Spanglish, "Smile and *muerde, tarado*! Smile and bite! Bite! Bite!"

"Stop him," I yelled when I saw other workers flocked to the altercation like trash under a pier. But no one moved.

I was so close now I could see Javier's jawbone tattoo stretch into a howl and then clench into a snap like a rabid dog.

"Please. Stop," Junior was begging in a voice that quivered on the edges.

With both hands, Javier gripped Junior's face. He dug fingers into the corners of the kid's mouth and lifted his neck like a Pez dispenser. Junior's crooked teeth were exposed and positioned over a bump of concrete.

"Bite! Bite! Bite!" Javier repeated the command until the word *bite* devolved into a barking. Then his surrounding pack of thugs started to yap and howl alongside him in a frenzied group-think.

I had to jump the gap. It was only three feet wide, but the Hive wasn't the same level. I'd be jumping across and dropping down eight feet. I could make it, I just needed to land properly. I shook my hands and jumped up and down to get loose, but the fear from Junior was swirling into my reasoning. I smacked my cheek to snap me back into my reality. I needed to create a separation between Junior's mind and mine. That was when I noticed a light bleed across the surface—the swirl of particles in the air catching a glow of red.

"Warning—" an automated voice boomed out. "Subject 61629-098, you are in violation of—"

That was *my* number.

The drone hovered just out of reach, nose pointed at me as it throbbed its red light in a slow rhythm. I pointed across the way and kept my voice as level as I could, so as not to trigger its threat response.

"I'm reporting a crime. Assault. There's an assault taking place. There." I emphasized the direction, but the drone didn't turn its attention away from me. It simply hovered in place. How, through all of the chaos above and below, did it target me?

"You are in violation of safety protocol 502 D-16-3," the machine repeated. "Please clip a designated SSS rope onto your harness when in close proximity to the edge."

"There is a crime happening right over there." I was practically yelling now.

"Subject 61629-098, you are in—"

I moved back from the edge. "Yeah, yeah, yeah," I complained, keeping my hands lifted as a sign of compliance. "I'm away from the edge. Happy?"

Once the drone tipped its nose and its armored body turned, I ran toward the next Hive.

My feet left the ground, and I immediately felt choked by the tightness in my throat. My heart, which had been slamming blood into my ears, stopped after I cleared the gap and dropped down, down, down.

I gasped when a piercing pain shot through my side. *I'd been hit.* When I made contact with the ground, my ankles snapped, I pitched forward and my knees smashed onto the floor as I somersaulted across the surface. *I'd been hit.* Breath ragged from exertion and pain, my side now hot and buzzing, I lifted my shirt to see a burn mark. That damn machine, whose directive was to keep us safe, had tased me. And after it did, it descended back down, completely ignoring Junior's screams.

"Javier, stop. Please." Junior's words were distorted by the fingers pulling at his mouth.

"I'm coming, Junior," I said lamely as I attempted to stand.

That was when I saw Connors push past the crowd. Without stopping his momentum, he rammed a knee up into Javier's face. The thug's body was thrown back from the blow, but after he staggered and regained his balance, he dipped his head and charged like a bull.

Connors may have been older, but after a hard life of labor his body didn't recognize age. With biceps and deltoids condensed into a scrappy build and the muscle memory of an old boxer, he landed a jab that cracked Javier's nose. Blood sprayed across the onlookers as his neck twisted from the force.

Javier touched a hand to his nose and smiled. Then he moved his bifurcated tongue across his upper lip, licking at rivulets of blood. He was laughing now. Laughing in a way that made the inmates move a few steps back. Only Connors had a different reaction. He smiled and raised his guard.

This made Javier cut himself off and beat his chest with open palms. "You want to mess with me?"

I could feel the drip-drip of the T.O.M.S.I. make my mind swell with the mafioso's rage. A heat was spreading through my core as my mind toggled between self-loathing and anger, but there was a clarity to this burn. Truth sang to me in a violent melody, and I recognized it—I had hummed the same tune myself in the past. The only way to validate life was through pain. The only way to breathe, feel, or just exist was to hurt something outside of ourselves.

As these revelations unfolded, I saw Javier's crew move in on Connors. The old man wouldn't be easy to take down in a fair fight, but who fought fair here? It was four against one now. They threw sloppy punches and tried to tackle Connors to the ground. The more he resisted, the more I felt my anger rise up into a need to scream, pound my chest, and charge forward.

Nostrils flaring, grunting angrily, I began to stand. Who did I even want to hurt just then? I didn't know. The details weren't important. But before I could charge, Connors let out a gasp and dropped to his knees.

"*Puta madre*," Javier said before spitting a fat wad of mucus next to Connors. After that, the men walked off as if nothing happened.

"Connors?" I called out. The shock of reality made my mind snap back to being mine. My friend had been shivved. "Get out of the way," I said as I pushed past everyone to drop down. "Connors?"

"I'm okay." He reached out a hand—knuckles split, palm covered in red.

"Did they hurt you? Are you okay, Connors?" Juniors asked, taking the time to enunciate each letter like a schoolboy sounding out the words from a book.

I bit my tongue when the kid shuffled on his knees toward his friend, who continued to bleed out on the cracked concrete.

"I'm okay," Connors said again as he pulled Junior under his arm. "It'll take more than that to take me out. Are *you* okay?" He grabbed the kid's face and wiped the tears away only to smear blood on his cheeks. "Yeah you're fine," he reassured the kid. "You're an okay guy. I don't care what anyone else says."

"Where are the damn governors? Where are the drones?" I muttered angrily before turning back to Connors. "What do you need, buddy?"

———

"I NEED YOUR HELP," the pretty nurse said while peeking around the corner where Connors was lying. The chalky-green-colored scrubs she wore today seemed to make her caramel skin deepen in contrast. She was too pretty for this place. And too caring. After things had settled down with Connors and the doc left, I'd limped in and lifted my shirt for her to see where the machine had burned me. She adhered a healing patch over my side and wrapped a brace around my right ankle. I was struck by how methodical and caring her movements were—too damn caring for a place like this, filled with men like us.

"Callahan?" She called my name to bring me back to attention. Her big doe-like eyes had taken on a look of concern.

I nodded. "Of course, ma'am. What do you need help with?"

"I think the fight really rattled him. He's not acting like, well, he's—" She shook her head. "Well, you'll see. If he doesn't opt for the accelerated treatment, he could ride out his stay here in the infirmary until his release date."

Release date? What was she talking about?

"Can you help me convince him?" she asked.

"Ma'am?" I looked around the corner as if seeing Connors would give me more context. It didn't. "I'm sorry, what do you mean?"

"Connors. If he opts to heal the old-fashioned way, I can keep him here with me until his last day."

"Last day?" I was starting to understand what she was saying now.

The nurse tapped at her tablet now. "Yeah, he's due to be released in two weeks." She looked up and studied my expression.

"He said he'd always be on the inside," I said more to myself.

"I'm sorry, I thought you knew. You two have always been close."

I never thought about what Connors and I were to each other. *Close* probably wasn't a word I'd have used until this afternoon, but when I saw him fall to his knees, blood seeping between his fingers, I realized a closeness had been there for quite some time. I just never labeled it.

I nodded and smiled at the pretty nurse before saying, "I'll talk to him." Because I knew those who were scheduled for release were at risk of being targeted by inmates whose own date was never coming or too far away to feel real.

"You're a good man, Callahan," she said as she put her hand on my shoulder. Once again, she looked at me like I was the only person she saw, and it felt like a burden to be seen so completely because I knew she wouldn't like the real me.

I shook my head. "No, ma'am."

"We are the sum of our parts. Good and bad, pluses and minuses."

She may have been smarter than me in most ways, but people like her held onto hope like a kid with a popsicle in the summertime—too happy with the sun to notice how reality came running down her hands in bright, sticky streams.

"Maybe once," I said softly. "But now we're what we're remembered for, ma'am. We're our history according to whoever has the pen."

That was why I chose to be a part of the GeoProgressive Movement and build the future of California-Annex. It was my only chance to be more than what was summarized on my rap sheet.

———

"HEY, THERE HE IS." I put on a cheerful voice as I limped in. "How've you been?"

Connors sat up with a wince. "This"—he grabbed his side—"is nothing. The problem is this." He tapped his implant. "It's been b-buzzing like old s-static."

I'd never heard him stutter before.

"Did it get knocked during the fight? What did the doctor say?" I asked, but he wasn't exactly having a conversation with me.

"It's like having a dream." He started again and stopped. His speech hedged as if he was actively looking for his words. "W-w-where you're in your cell and, uh—" His eyes darted left-right-left before he smacked his palm against his temple. "Uh, something is, uh"—he smacked his head again—"out of place? Then when you wake up, nothing feels quite right?"

I nodded, but I'd never had a dream like that. "Something's out of place?" I started to realize I couldn't feel anything from him. Our implants were still on, but I heard nothing, felt nothing. Why couldn't I feel his thoughts?

"I just can't tell what's, uh"—his eyes darted left-right-left—"uh, real. This"—he gestured around him—"or somewhere else. Ya know?"

"Maybe the doc put you on the good stuff?" I joked, but I knew that wasn't it. The nurse was right, there was something wrong.

"No." He shook his head. "I can't do that shit because of my history, see? I hear this s-static sound in my mind, I just can't shake it out." He shook his head and smacked his temple again and again like a twitch until I reached out to grab him.

"Connors, hey, maybe you should do the slow re-gen. Stay in here with the pretty nurse for a week or two, ya know?"

"Yeah." He was nodding now. "Yeah, maybe. Hey, have you seen Junior? He okay?" His words were fluid now—no struggle, no twitching.

"Yeah, he's good," I reassured him. "Just some scrapes. He's good. Trust me. I'll keep an eye on him. I got him."

Connors nodded.

"So you'll stay here? Do the slow re-gen?" I asked.

Connors continued to nod like a bobblehead on a dashboard—no intent behind his eyes. But it must have been the confirmation the nurse needed because she rolled in a stainless steel tray with equipment laid out on top and said, "Okay, Mr. Connors, it's time to run some tests."

"INITIATE FILTRATION TEST," I yelled into the walky-talky crusted in paint and dust.

After a pause, a static-blurred response came back, and I could hear the cyclone filters start to purr.

The graphene foundations and supports were printed and then laid with enhanced Breathe Bricks to absorb pollution. Each time a level was completed, the filters kicked on for a test run, and I swear I could see the pollution reduced before my eyes. Then it was switched back off. After the exterior walls went up, we came in to run electrical and add interior finishes the brute 3D printers couldn't handle. Our skill level got better with each floor, so uneven molding and sloppy caulking leveled and righted more and more as we climbed up to the more luxurious domiciles. Even Junior got better. He actually thrived with the structure and expectations, but today he was a little lost. He missed Connors and kept making mistakes. I was running out of patience with him.

"Go on up to the next level while they run the filtration test," I said as I shooed him away.

"Where's Connors? Is he okay?" Junior asked for the third time today.

I wasn't in the mood to explain things again. "I said go up to the next level. I'll be up in a minute."

"Connors," Junior called out behind me.

"God damnit, Junior, I said—" I stopped myself when I turned and saw the grizzled man walk onto the build-site as if nothing had happened. "What are you doing here? Thought you were going to stay in the infirmary?"

"I wanted to get back to work," Connors answered with ease as he threw an arm around Junior's shoulders. "I don't care what people say about you, kid, you're an alright guy."

"You still hearing shit?" I asked as I tapped my own implant.

"Nah, doc gave me a tune-up," he said before giving a smile that made me uncomfortable. His cracked lips expanded beyond their natural stretch, exposing too much gums and teeth. It didn't look quite right.

"Seriously. You all right?" I asked again despite knowing he wasn't.

Without adjusting his smile or eyes, he nodded. Then he blinked and smacked his head a few times before walking to an uncovered outlet. His head ticked to the right, and he smiled again at nothing. "I'm completely fine. The doc fixed me up."

"I don't know, man. I think maybe you should go back to the pretty nurse and—"

"I ain't never leaving," he cut me off. "None of us are."

Goosebumps sprouted across my arms. He was not okay, but what could I do? The doc had cleared him. We just needed to get through the day and then talk to the pretty nurse tonight. Maybe he could be readmitted, maybe he could stay until his release date. So I ignored his twitches and smiles for the rest of the day.

When a distant banging sounded out lightly across the desert floor, I felt relieved. I eyed my watch unnecessarily because I knew it was six o'clock. Like clockwork, people would lean out their windows in solidarity, banging pots and pans, whooping and yelling *thank you* to all the essential workers while they remained in their homes.

When it first started, we joked it was for us. Junior would take a bow before wiping his nose, and Connors would yell back *you're welcome* from hundreds of feet up. But we got used to it. The timed aspect seemed to belie sincerity, like a man who only prayed at church. After five or six months, it felt like a clock tower tolling out a melody before knocking out the hours, or a whistle toward the end of our shift. It became a mark of time, nothing more.

"Why do they even bother anymore?" I said more to myself.

"Most people believe in this system. If people were to—" Connors stopped. His eyes flicked left-right-left, then he looked around as if trying to find his bearings. "I, uh, I was—" he started and stopped like his brain was buffering.

"You all right?" I asked.

Something's wrong.

"Something's wrong," Connors said as if speaking my thoughts. Then he started saying words he should not have known. "We think ourselves free because we are too blind to see the prison constructed around us—"

"How did you? Where did you hear this?" No one knew about my book, and I never quoted passages aloud.

He continued in a voice that wasn't his. "We don't touch the bars and acknowledge their names: Convenience, comfort, and security."

"Whoa, whoa, Connors, is my mind slipping into yours?" I started to panic. Was this why he had been acting so weird? "Where are you getting these words?" I asked as he paced back and forth. "I need you to focus, buddy." I tried to keep my voice calm.

"If people were to what, Connors? You didn't finish that sentence,"

Junior said as he walked toward us with laces still undone, always undone.

"Junior, I need you to hold on," I said as I raised my hand up. "Look at me, Connors. What are you hearing right now? I can help."

"Warning: Subject 10121-098," a drone projected out in a calm voice despite the underlying threat. "You are in violation of safety protocol 502 D-16-3." The machine hovered above us while its red lights throbbed out into the polluted air in that mesmerizingly slow rhythm.

"God damnit, Junior," I snapped. I felt a burn inside me rise into a scream. "Put your—"

"Damn clip on!" Connors finished my sentence as he jerked forward and shoved the kid. Almost immediately, I saw the old man's mind snap back to reality. His eyes widened in shock as he reached out, but it was too late.

As if in slow motion, Junior stepped back onto air, laces suspended as he tipped back. His childish voice pushed out the start of his friend's name before fear cut it short.

But I knew the word *Connors* was synonymous with mother in that moment of shock. Now the desperate need to be held wrapped around me and threw me down to my hands and knees. Falling, falling, falling into fear, I felt Junior's mind and mine scrambling for options. It was survival at its most pristine, but all overlaid with his simplicity. Like the slow tap-tap of two fingers hammering on a keyboard, I read as his brain spelled out S-A-V-E-M-E. Although I was breathing, it felt as if I was choking on myself, gasping for the memory of breath. My heart seemed to shudder while blindness seeped into me. An emptiness widened everything inside of my mind, and acceptance only blossomed with the finality of death.

Junior was dead.

"What the fuck did you do?" I screamed.

The patrol drone was now blaring an angry siren and flashing red lights.

"What did you do? What the fuck did you do?" I asked over and over, my hand wrapped behind my neck as I paced back and forth.

Why would he do that? Why would he push Junior? Did I make him do that? Was my mind slipping into his? But I didn't want to kill Junior. *Did I?*

Connors was on his stomach now, reaching down, grasping air while screaming. And for the first time since the hospital, I could feel his mind slip back into mine. A deluge of Connors' pain and confusion hit me.

"Stand up," I heard a familiar voice cut into the panicked scene. "Stand up, Connors. Stand up!" With weapons raised, Governor Lacey and two others moved in on him.

"Gov, don't shoot him," I begged.

"Stand up, Connors," Lacey barked again, but Connors could only scream out into the empty space. A desperate, pitiful scream that sounded almost inhuman as it bounced and shattered across the air molecules soaked in red.

"No. No. He wouldn't have done that, Lacey. He hadn't been acting like himself. The implant. Please." I kept my hands raised and my head bowed, but I couldn't stop shaking my head. None of this was right. "He was about to get out, and he loved that kid. He was like a father to the kid. Lacey, for fuck's sake, please listen."

Lacey put his gun away and moved in with a taser instead. After a quick zap, Connors' desperate scream was cut short.

"Grab his arm," one of the governors said as they positioned themselves around Connors' limp form.

"Lacey, please." I lifted my eyes. "You know he wouldn't do this. Tell me you know that. Tell me you—"

"Callahan," Governor Lacey cut me off. "I hear you, but he did what he did. You saw it."

"No. No, Gov', he wouldn't do that. Why would he do that?" I couldn't bring myself to tell Lacey about my suspicions. I didn't push the kid. I wasn't even sure I wanted to push the kid. Did I?

Lacey didn't look away. "Sometimes the prospect of freedom just scares the shit out of people who've been in the system too long."

"No." I continued to shake my head. "I don't believe that."

The Governor rested a hand on my shoulder and said in a voice too calm for the situation, "Thank you for caring."

I DON'T KNOW what they did to Connors after they dragged him off the build-site, but I no longer felt his mind in mine. I no longer got sour tastes in my mouth or felt the Gates meat being processed. And after I felt Junior die, I almost missed feeling like a whirligig frantically spinning in place, unable to gain traction.

The next day and the next, I did my best to forget their story, but I could feel a change in my mind begin to take place once I finally heard the silence. No more chatter between the old man and the kid, no more protests down below. My world and the outside world were silent until six at night, when the nightly chorus of gratitude started up like a mark of time.

"All right, Callahan. End of shift. Pack it up." I heard Lacey's voice cut into my thoughts.

"Hey, Lacey," I called out, making the governor stop and turn. "I think I'm done with this."

"Done with what?"

"Done with all of it," I said as I waved my hand over the Hives and the desert below.

For years I chose to be a part of the GeoProgressive Movement and build the future of California-Annex because it was my only chance to be more than what was summarized on my rap sheet. But after everything, I realized it wasn't a chance. My name would go on a placard no one would read. We were just the metal and meat needed to build up what was lauded as visionary, progress for the Annex, and made everyone say *thank you for caring*.

ABOUT ROSIE RECORD

From Southern California to Japan to Texas and finally back to SoCal, Rosie Record spent the remainder of her childhood in a sleepy mountain community with dreams of writing, pushing east, and exploring the world. After graduating with a BA in linguistics, she became entrenched in the world of corporate instead. It wasn't until she started her life over in NYC that she began to write again. Record believes books have the power to hold a mirror up to society and ask, *Do you still like what you see?* ...an important question she asks while exploring the concepts of control and what it means to be free in her gritty cyberpunk novel, Tronick.

TERMS AND CONDITIONS APPLY

MATTHEW A. GOODWIN

The price of freedom is high.

TERMS AND CONDITIONS APPLY

By Matthew A. Goodwin

"I want to quit." The words trembled out of Josh's mouth. He licked his lips, but his tongue was dry. His hands shook, and a sheen of sweat coated his brow.

"This division?" Mr. Greene asked.

Josh shook his head, steeling himself. "I want to quit ThutoCo."

"Oh." Mr. Greene leaned back in his large, comfortable-looking chair. "You want to *quit* quit?"

"Yes," Josh said before amending, "if that's okay."

"Of course it is. Has anyone gone over your options?"

"No. I read what little was available from my terminal, but it was hard to find, and what there was was pretty vague."

"Sure." Mr. Greene nodded slowly. "Well, you are free to quit anytime, and we can begin the process right now. I just have to ask again, are you sure?"

Josh had never been more sure or less sure of anything in his life. He knew he needed to quit, that he would never feel whole if he didn't, but he also couldn't picture life outside the burbs—outside his hex. He had lived in the corporate housing his entire life and had gone to company school and started working as soon as he was eligible.

"Yes," he croaked, his tone betraying his emotions.

"Okay, then," Mr. Greene said as though Josh had spoken with the surety of a much more confident man. "I will begin the process."

Josh wiped his shaking hand along his knee, leaving a trail of sweat on his linen pants.

"I have to ask," Mr. Greene began with a little smile. "Why are you leaving the company? Your parents were lifelong employees, and I expected you to be a lifer too."

"Oh, um," Josh said, trying to think of how best to explain that night. "I was struck by lightning."

"Up ahead is our last stop of the evening," the tour guide said as the bus landed slowly on the pad just off Polk Street. "I want everyone to stay close, and make sure you can see the other members of our group."

The driver put on a garish orange cap with ThutoCo City Tour projected in bright letters above.

"Make sure you can see this hat at all times."

"Could see that hat from space," Josh joked to himself as he stood, then he began filing off the bus. All the other stops had been to tourist attractions, but the final stop was their first taste of culture, if it could so be called.

BA City was a sprawl of juxtaposing wealth and poverty, chaos and conformity, and dark places under oppressive lights. The street they stepped out into was like a different world. Gone were the fluorescent lights, linoleum floors, and bleach scents he was used to. Instead, it was flashing neon, slick streets, and the smell of... Josh didn't even know. *Decay?*

Though it was only early evening, they were under so many layers of buildings and roads that it appeared to be night. People littered the streets, running between buildings and calling out to one another. The volume of the place was like nothing Josh had ever experienced. In the burbs, someone could be shushed for cheering too loudly when they finished their crossword puzzle. In the city, people standing a meter apart seemed to be shouting at each other, and Josh couldn't tell if they were friends or enemies—or perhaps both.

Josh sputtered and coughed as a man walked by, leaving a plume of smoke in his wake. He flicked his cigarette into a yellow puddle, and it hissed into death. Josh considered getting back on the bus. It was all too much. The unfiltered air was burning his lungs even before he had inhaled the acrid fumes, and as he looked down at the puddle in the street, he couldn't help but wonder if it was urine. They had passed any number of feral cats and giant skittering rats as they hovered over the city streets, but that amount of liquid was too much to have been produced by any animal.

The older woman standing next to him seemed to be having the same reservations. She was worrying her hands so much that it looked as though she were washing them in an invisible stream of water, and her eyes kept darting back to the door of the bus.

The tour guide stepped out in front of them. "I know the city can be intimidating," he said in a soothing voice. "But it's perfectly safe, and I'll be with you every step of the way. It's important to experience this at least once in your life, and when we get back to the burbs tonight, you'll be able to tell all your friends that you had dinner in a real BA City restaurant. If you have any questions, you can contact me, and I'll come right over, or you can just come find me at Shalimar Restaurant." He gestured to a little storefront across the street.

One by one, he began approaching all the tourists and handing them what Josh knew to be cash chips. Of course, back in the burbs, they were all paid in and paid with ThutoCo's corporate currency, but that was no good in the city.

He took the chip and looked it over as the tour guide explained, "There is enough on here for you to get something at any of these restaurants or, if you would prefer, a drink at one of the bars. Please don't leave this street and, again, feel free to reach out to me. The neural comms are private, and only the other employees in our party will be able to hear you."

Everyone nodded and began going their separate ways. Most people were taking the tour in groups of two or more, but Josh had come on his own, so he just started walking. The woman beside him had tried to make eye contact and, he assumed, would be more than happy for him to invite her to join him, but he didn't want to spend his only hour in the city with another employee. He had signed up for the trip to get a taste of the world outside, and he was going to do it, even if it terrified him.

Moving in the clothes he was wearing was difficult. He was so used to the company linens that the jeans and T-shirt that were recommended felt tight and scratchy. When he put the chip in his pocket, it felt like it was stabbing his leg, and he didn't know how people lived like that.

All the restaurants had names that, though they were written in English, he mostly didn't recognize as words. Reading the holographic display of the first menu he passed, he shook his head. "Served with a side of fries" was the only thing on the whole page he understood. He looked back at the bus longingly before shaking his head and continuing forward. He would see it through.

As he passed a large bar populated by attractive young people in professional attire, he turned and walked in. A drink would help.

There was a crowd at the front, by the door, and he stood for several moments, waiting for them to move. When he realized they had not noticed him and were clearly not going to move out of his way without prompting, he cleared his throat. The bar was loud, and his little sound evaporated before reaching their ears.

"Excuse me," he squeaked.

They all turned to look at him. He felt like he was being judged by the cool kids at school, but one of the guys just moved aside and allowed Josh to pass. He felt far braver than was warranted for simply asking a person to get out of his way, but he smiled and stepped up to a free spot at the bar.

The man working behind the bar was in a constant state of movement, pouring and mixing drinks and taking orders. He moved up and down the bar, attending to this person and that, but no matter how hard Josh stared, the man took no notice of him. Or if he had, he didn't care. Josh had no idea how much time had passed, but he kept trying to flag the bartender down with eye contact.

"You're gonna have to pull a tit out if you ever want him to notice you," a woman said from beside Josh.

He nearly leaped out of his skin, making a little yelping sound before turning to look at her. When he did, he was unable to speak for a moment.

His mouth opened and closed a few times like a fish's, and the girl holding the tray laughed. When she did, Josh felt like his heart was going to pound through his rib cage. She was the most striking woman he had ever seen. Where the people of the burbs were pale, the vitamin D lights not doing anything for their skin, the woman was dark with sun-kissed skin. Her large, bright eyes were highlighted by bright eyeliner and lipstick, and her microdyed hair shimmered like a waterfall when she moved.

When she smiled at Josh, his legs felt like they were going to give out.

"H-Hi," he murmured eventually.

She covered her mouth to keep from laughing at him. "Hi," she said, cocking an eyebrow at him. "Can I get you something to drink?"

"I'm Josh," he blurted in response.

Then she did laugh. "Hey, Josh. I'm Katy. Nice to meet you," she said through her bemusement. "Can I get you something to drink?"

"What do you suggest?"

She smirked. "You going to buy me one too?"

"Oh, um, yeah, sure!" he said excitedly. He didn't care if she was talking to him just to get free drinks and a big tip. He was happy for the conversation.

"Great," she said with a big smile, and he felt his heart flutter again. "I'll get us two."

She held out the reader for payment. Josh sheepishly reached into his pocket and fished out the cash chip.

"Oh my, you're a fucking bub!" Katy shrieked in amusement. "That explains the haircut."

"Hey, the AI at the BarberBot said it was the most 'in' hairstyle," Josh protested, and he was sure he had never seen anybody laugh as hard as she did. She laughed so long and hard that he eventually joined her.

"That sentence," she gasped when she had recovered some, wiping the tears from her cheeks. "That sentence was the most bub thing I've ever heard."

He thought he could extrapolate from context, but he had to ask, "What's a bub?"

Katy looked guilty for a second. "It's slang. Well, I guess it's more of a derogatory term. For people from the burbs."

Josh's face flushed. "Oh," he said. "It's that obvious?"

"Well, at first, I thought you were just a dweeb who couldn't talk to girls or whatever, but as soon as I saw that chip, it was as clear as day."

"Well, it's my first time in the city," Josh admitted.

"No shit?" Katy asked, unable to wipe the look of amusement off her face.

"It's true."

"Okay," Katy said. "Let me go get our drinks, and I want to hear everything."

Josh nodded. For the first time, he felt like she had seen him. Something about the fact that he was not from there and was new to the world obviously interested her.

He watched the Miners game on the massive holoprojected screen as he waited, and in no time, Katy was back with two steaming drinks whose colors shifted from yellow to green from top to bottom.

"What is this?" Josh asked in surprise.

"The most city drink I could come up with," she said with pride then pointed as two people vacated a standing table.

They moved right in and began chatting and drinking.

"So, what's your life like?" she asked with genuine interest as she blew on her drink and took a sip.

He copied what she did before answering. "It's really boring, actually. I'm an engineer at ThutoCo, so I use a neural uplink in my hex to control a robot who does a solar panel repair out in the betweens."

"That's less boring than you think it is," Katy said with a smirk. "Try saying you're an on-call waitress and sound interesting."

"That's less boring than you think it is too," Josh said with a little smile.

"So, what? You're here on some kind of tour? You're on safari here in the city?"

Josh's face heated. "Yeah, kinda."

"Well, that's fucked up," Katy observed.

"I mean, you're not wrong," he admitted.

As they had driven through the streets, and the tour guide had told them about the lives of the people in the city, it had felt a bit odd. It was as if the people were zoo animals, and the employees were the human gawkers. "But I had to see the world outside the burbs at least once in my life. The company provides this opportunity based on some old religious practice where these people lived in a society but got to go visit the world outside for a period of time before committing to their life. At least that's what I was able to glean. I'm not sure how true any of it is."

"Never heard of anything like that, but it makes sense. Plus, I'm sure the first time you stepped in a pile of dog shit, you probably wanted to run right back to your perfect vacuu-sealed life. ThutoCo has maintaining its worker bees down to an art form."

Josh hadn't thought about that, but what she said struck close to home. "It's funny. There was this woman standing next to me as we got off the bus, and I'm pretty sure she's probably already back on it at this point. I think you're spot-on that the company uses this as a way to keep us in rather than actually being an opportunity for us to get out."

"Oh man!" Katy exclaimed, clutching her hands to her chest, and Josh nearly jumped. "The evil megacorporation is an evil megacorporation!"

She laughed, but the words landed heavily for Josh. He had never thought about the company that way.

She read his expression. "Was it something I said?"

"Sorry," he said quietly then took another sip of his drink. His head was already swimming. He went to the bar occasionally with a friend from work but never had more than one beer before calling it a night. "This is all very new to me."

Katy put her hand on his, and it was like an electric shock to his system. "I'm sure that's true, and I was just joking around."

"But you weren't," he said. "It's just hard to realize that your sheltered life isn't the only reality and that the real world... I don't know... judges your very existence?"

"It's just jealousy," Katy told him. "It's different for the people out here. We have to bust our asses for a shitty coffin-size apartment where we pay for hot water by the milliliter and are lucky if we remember when our last meal was. It's a far cry from sitting in pajamas at a job you do via a chip in your brain. So, you know, we have a lot to be envious of."

Josh couldn't believe what he was hearing. He had taken his hex for granted his entire life. "Is that really true?"

Katy guffawed. "Dude, I'm pretty sure this is the sixth day in a row I've worn these pants."

He couldn't help but mutter, "Pretty sure...?"

"They passed the smell test." She shrugged.

She was so different from every other person he had ever met, and though they had only been talking for a few minutes, he was pretty sure he didn't want to have to talk to anybody else ever again. He felt heard by her in a way he never had at home. The other worker bees he buzzed at just buzzed back at him, but she seemed to actually hear him when he spoke.

"Hey," he said in a way to indicate that he was going to say something serious. "Thank you for coming over and talking to me. It... It means a lot."

"I'm happy that I did," she said, seeming sincere. "I actually clocked out when I went and grabbed these, so... I'm here because I want to be."

"Oh, wow," Josh said quietly. He'd never been happier in his entire life.

—————

"Love is a powerful motivator." Mr. Greene nodded after Josh had recounted the rest of the night—or as much of it as he remembered after a few drinks. "So, you plan to move to the city and find this girl?"

"That's the plan," Josh said, the knot of nerves in the pit of his stomach returning after nearly evaporating as he thought about Katy.

"Well, then who am I to stop you?" Mr. Greene gave a broad smile. "Between your accumulated productivity points and those of your parents, you should be able to leave here with a little bit of starter money. I should warn you—our currency's conversion rate is... not great."

"Oh," Josh said. That made him nervous. Nowhere on the company site or anywhere on the in-house search engine was the conversion rate listed. After one night in the real world, that didn't surprise Josh anymore.

"I am contractually obligated to offer you a little bit of extra starter money in exchange for a market research opportunity," Mr. Greene said quickly before adding, "but I don't think you want that, right?"

Josh was surprised by the second part. "No, I could use all the money I can get."

"I expect you'll get a job pretty quickly in the city, given your quali-fications," Mr. Greene said optimistically.

"Actually... Katy said it was pretty hard to get jobs in the city, and a little extra money at the onset could be pretty helpful. What would I have to do?"

Mr. Greene sighed. "You would simply be offered some 'targeted marketing opportunities to test which products might be of interest to somebody who just moved to the city,'" he read off his display.

"Oh, okay." Josh nodded. "I don't even need to know how much it is. I'm just excited for a little bit of extra money."

"Right, sure, well, I'll add that rider to your termination contract," he said. "Once we finish here, you will just have to go to HR and give them a thumbprint, and you will be on your way."

"Today?"

"Today," Mr. Greene affirmed.

And an hour later, Josh was on a shuttle with little more than a nearly empty backpack and a cash chip in his pocket.

Watching the city grow out of the window of the shuttle was very different from watching it as a tourist. As the shuttle banked and flew between buildings, Josh wondered if he had made a horrible mistake. Quitting was unbelievably rash, and he had no idea if he would even be able to survive.

Then he thought about Katy's face, and all his fears fell away. He could live anywhere, do any job, and survive anything as long as she was by his side. First, he would get a place, then he would go find her and tell her what he had done.

Rather than being intimidated by the city, he decided to be optimistic. The people walking the streets would be his new friends, and all the places would be new ones to explore. Katy could show him the ins and outs of the city, and they could be happy together.

That was the mindset he was carrying as the shuttle landed on the little docking pad and he stepped out the door. The sun was out, but it was cold, and a bank of fog had been moving in over the city. Josh had been dropped near where his tour had been, and he had seen a little shop selling hooded sweatshirts with the city's name emblazoned on the front. He made his way in the direction he thought he remembered the store being.

Then he heard a sound in his mind.

Looking for new clothes?
Look no further!
Comph brand apparel can be ordered through BA City and dronelivered to your location!
Terms and Conditions apply.
Wave hand to remove this ad for nominal fee.

The ad had obviously come from his neural chip, and the display of it was taking up his entire field of vision. It was translucent, so he could vaguely see the world, but he immediately waved his hand in front of his face to wipe the ad. He understood why Mr. Greene had been less than enthusiastic about it. But though it was annoying, he was happy for the extra cash, and it had actually been more than he'd expected.

Josh made his way over to the little shop and bought a hoodie. He asked where he might be able to find apartments for rent, and the man pointed and answered, but Josh wasn't able to understand him. He thanked the man and left the store, heading in the direction in which he had pointed.

Even with a sweatshirt, Josh was a bit chilly, and he realized that weather was something he was not used to. The lights in the burbs rose and fell in time with the sun, and there were a few windows throughout the building, but for the most part, he had no relationship with heat or cold, wind or rain, or seasons. Katy had used the term "sheltered" to describe him at one point in the night, and he realized that it was true both metaphorically and actually.

He thought about the little smile that crossed her lips when she had said it, and it reinforced his decision to be there. He continued down the street to the base of a large building that stretched up and disappeared in the fog. A holoprojected sign in front of the building had a large arrow pointing to the door and read Apartments for Rent.

It was kismet, and Josh knew it.

When he surprised Katy, he would already have his own place and be well on his way to an independent life.

He pushed open the door to Appletrees Apartments and walked up to the drudge, a humanoid robot that worked the front desk.

"I'd like to rent an apartment, please," he told the machine.

It had a plastic-and-metal body, and where the head should be was a screen displaying apartment names and rent prices. The various names like cozy deluxe one-room suite and ranch-house style, mansion-inspired loft were vague, meaningless, and confusing, and as Josh reached up, more words filled his vision and blared in his mind.

Looking for a room to rent?
Look no further!
The Appletrees Apartment complex is accepting applicants now!
Terms and Conditions apply.
Wave hand to remove this ad for nominal fee.

He waved the ad away, a bit irritated. He felt like he shouldn't be advertised to about the very building he was standing in, but Mr. Greene had said they were testing the ads, and maybe Josh's feedback would help them.

The drudge leaned an elbow on the counter in a surprisingly human-like move, and a voice came from a speaker beside the screen. "Which room style are you interested in?"

"The cheapest one would be fine," he said. He felt like he had a good amount of starting cash but knew that between rent, food, and life, it would disappear quickly.

"You have selected the grand legacy, nautical-themed luxury apartment," the drudge informed him, displaying a well-lighted image of a space that could hardly be called a room. It was a bed with a little table beside it and just enough room to hang your feet over. One wall had a small screen mounted on the side, and there was a tiny circular window at the back. Josh swallowed hard, and his hands began to shake.

He was oscillating back to fear and the feeling that he'd made a huge mistake. His hex was an estate compared to that. Even Katy's room had been palatial by comparison.

But remembering her room set his resolve back. He thought of her touch and how his breath had caught when her hands traveled to his belt line. His memories from that part of the night were strung together in loose, hazy snippets, but he valued them above nearly anything else.

"I'll take it," he said excitedly and let the drudge synchronize with his cash chip, watching the value displayed upon it plummet. He would have to be careful.

The machine printed him a digital key card before asking, "Do you have a neural implant? Would you like us to upload your apartment key?"

Distracted by the diminishing number on his cash chip, Josh simply nodded.

"Would you like a meal plan? One of our amenities is twice-daily meals that will be served on a tray and slid through your apartment door by a MealPod. It is a far less expensive option than purchasing every meal from a restaurant and is designed by a nutritionist."

Josh considered it for a moment but really liked the idea of not having to worry about where his next meal was coming from, so he simply said, "Sure."

He watched the cash run down again but reminded himself that he had everything he needed to get his life going in a good direction.

He quickly rode the elevator up and dropped his bag in his new room after finding it at the end of the labyrinthine series of hallways. It was even tighter in real life than it had appeared in the image, but Josh didn't care. Or he'd convinced himself he didn't.

He felt like a man on a mission. Back at the base of the tower, he began walking in the direction of the bar where he had first met Katy. He saw the same restaurants and, in some weird way, felt like the area was his old haunt. Everything in the city was so foreign in every way that a place he had been just once felt familiar and easy. Though the way people looked at him still made him uncomfortable. It was as if they knew he was a bub, that he didn't belong. Sweat poured all over the cash chip as he gripped it tightly.

Turning, he stepped into the bar. It was far less crowded than it had been over the weekend but not as empty as Josh would have expected for midday on a workday. The street in front of the place was littered with abandoned rent-a-scooters. His heart began to flutter, and he scanned the room for the woman he knew to be the love of his life.

He couldn't wait to see her reaction when she saw him.

Did you know you're close to one of the best restaurants in BA City?
It's true!

Josh quickly waved his hand and stepped up to the bar.

The bartender strode over and gave Josh a quick once-over. "What can I get you?" he asked.

The casual exchange and the fact that he hadn't been called a bub made Josh feel like the coolest kid at the party.

"I'll take a beer, and if you could send Katy over, that would be great," Josh said then leaned on the bar in an imitation of any number of badasses from movies.

"Who?" the bartender asked, his face contorting in confusion.

"What?" Josh asked.

"Who's Katy?" the man asked, slinging his rag over his shoulder before flipping over a pint glass to begin filling.

Josh looked at the man as though he were insane. He wanted to shout that she was the coolest, most beautiful human on the planet and worked in that very place. It was maddening that the guy was playing coy. Maybe he knew that she was in love with him and was jealous.

"Listen," Josh said, clearing his throat and trying to sound tough. "Just tell me where she is."

Josh waved his hand to see the man looking at him with a mixture of pity and annoyance. "You said Katy?"

"You know I did," Josh said, his retort impressing himself.

The man behind the bar chuckled. "Yeah, I think I remember her. She filled in the other night, right?"

The sincerity of the question made Josh realize for the first time that the man actually didn't know her.

"Oh… yes," Josh said.

The man set the beer down on the counter, and Josh took a long drink.

Oppressive images of beer glasses clinking filled his vision.

"Well, do you know how to get ahold of her?" Josh asked quietly before taking another sip.

"Not really. She was sent to us through an agency when we were short-staffed. We just alert them that we need somebody, and they dispatch a body. Might be a bit inelegant, but it works," he said with a shrug and took a drink of whatever brown liquid he was working on.

"Can I go to the agency?"

The man narrowed his eyes at Josh. "I mean, they don't have an office or anything. All businesses are decentralized. But I'm sure you could contact their support line or something."

The bartender was staring at Josh with an expression that he didn't quite recognize.

"What do you want with her?"

Josh felt a big smile pull at his cheeks. "I'm going to tell her that after our night together, I left the burbs for her. I moved to the city so that we could be together."

"Whoa," the man said and finished the rest of his drink. "You left your whole life behind after a one-night stand?"

Josh was appalled by the question. "It wasn't a one-night stand. It was the start of something beautiful."

The bartender stifled a laugh. "Whatever you say, man."

Josh's cheeks heated. He hated that a person who didn't even know their situation doubted that he was telling the truth. "Just give me the contact information for the agency."

"It's called Senda Tenda." When Josh just stared at him blankly, he added, "Like 'send a bartender' but catchier."

"But Katy's not a bartender," Josh said.

That time, the man did laugh at him. "Fucking bubs. Their whole business model doesn't revolve around just her."

"Right," Josh said, his annoyance replaced by shame for appearing so foolish.

"Drink's on me," the man said, tapping the bar beside Josh's beer before turning his back.

Need to make a call?
We can connect you!
Use Commitech Communication Services Now!
Terms and Conditions apply.
Wave hand to remove this ad for nominal fee.

That time, Josh reached out to tap the area of the overlay in his vision, selecting the option to use the service. Of course, he wasn't actually touching anything, but the neural link that allowed it to work recognized the motion and that he wanted the service.

In a moment, the displayed ad turned into a search box, and Josh inputted the name of the agency with his mind. Though he had never used that particular technology, it was the same functionality as his neural communication and, really, most of his job, so it was easy to utilize.

Several options appeared, and he chose the customer-support option. He heard a ringing almost immediately, then a voice came on a moment later, but Josh could tell that it was an AI.

"Thank you for calling Senda Tenda. How may I help you?"

"Agent," Josh stated. He finished the beer he had in front of him and a second one before he finally got a human being on the phone.

Hello? he heard in his mind.

"Hi, I was hoping you could point me in the direction of one of your employees," Josh said, and the woman at the bar beside him looked irritated that he was speaking aloud.

Oh, I'm sorry. We can't give out the personal information of any of our employees. For their safety. I'm sure you understand. Is there anything else I can help you with today?

Josh refused to let that be the end of it. Looking at the woman beside him, he communicated through his implant. *Listen, I met this girl the other night, and...* He paused, realizing that the person on the other end of the line would not be inclined to give the personal information of an employee out to somebody who might come off like a stalker. *She left her cash chip at the bar. I want to give it to her.*

He held up his cash chip and commanded his mind to send the image to the person on the other end. But as he saw it, he realized how little money he had left. He didn't remember the apartment and food being so expensive, but he only had a fraction of his money remaining. But no matter. Katy would help him find a job.

I'm sorry, sir, the person said.

It's not like I want you to give me her address. Just let me know where she's working tonight, and I can take it by there. Every little bit helps, and I know she would want it back.

After several moments, the woman finally said, *Okay. I'm not gonna tell you anything, but I've heard good things about the Dragon Lounge.*

Thank you! Thank you! Thank you! Josh said excitedly and disconnected the call immediately. He stood from his stool on wobbly legs before getting his bearings and rushing out the door.

"Good luck out there," the bartender called after Josh, who ignored the patronizing tone.

He saw the neon dragon across the street and went rushing toward it, unable to believe that she had been so close to him the whole time.

A horn blared, and a driver screamed as her car stopped short to avoid running over Josh, who had stepped into the street without looking. In the burbs, things were safe, but he had to learn to pay more attention in the city.

Injured in an accident?
We can help!
Contact Benjamin Paul, Esquire!
Terms and Conditions apply.
Wave hand to remove this ad for nominal fee.

It was terrifying that the ad showed up as he was still crossing the street, and he waved it away as quickly as he could. He felt like they were increasing in frequency, and it was becoming irritating. He had signed the contract without reading it carefully, and he wished he had. Though with how much the cash chip was already running down, he was still grateful for the money that he had been advanced.

Stepping back onto the sidewalk, he hurried as quickly as he could into the Dragon Lounge. It was a large bar and was crowded, since the workday had ended in the time he'd been on hold.

Josh felt his heart was going to beat out of his chest. He had never been more nervous or excited about anything in his life. He had made a monumental decision, and it was going to pay off.

Spotting her across the room, he began pushing past all the people to get to her. He had to wait a moment as she finished taking orders, but when she turned, they locked eyes.

He beamed at her.

Her mouth fell open. "Josh?" she asked in utter surprise.

He opened his arms for a hug, but she held up a hand to stop him. She was smiling, but he could see the worry in her eyes.

As he saw her face and remembered what the bartender had just said, his whole world crashed in around him. He felt like he had made a horrible mistake.

Josh waved his hand furiously. He felt like he was going to be sick.

"I moved to the city for you," he told her meekly.

She gripped his arm and pulled him into a quiet corner. The sound of chuckles followed from the table she had been waiting on.

"You did what?"

"I moved here for you," he said, but he could hear the defeat in his words. He'd been so excited for that moment—for it to be a grand romantic gesture and for her to leap into his arms, but he realized what a fool he had been.

"You moved here for me?" she asked, but that time, there was a different tinge to her voice. It was almost as if she was impressed. During their night together, she had told him that, in spite of everything she had seen and been through in her life, she was a hopeless romantic at heart.

Maybe his grand gesture had actually worked. Smiling, he said, "I did."

"That's… That's amazing," she responded, sounding nonplussed. "Insane. But amazing."

Josh waved his hands in rage. He didn't want anything blocking his view of Katy.

"What the hell was that?" she asked.

"A mistake," Josh snarled. "I agreed to some targeted marketing in exchange for a little starter capital when I left the burbs. But it's getting worse every second."

Katy's face changed then. Worry replaced happiness. Her eyebrows furrowed, and her lips tightened. "Oh, Josh," she said and reached up to touch his cheek.

"What?"

Having a hard time understanding others?
Consider a language class!
First session is always free!
Terms and Conditions apply.
Wave hand to remove this ad for nominal fee.

Josh waved his hand again, and that time, Katy took a step back. She was looking at him in a way that made him feel like a foolish child. The romance of the moment was gone, and she just seemed to see him for the dumb bub he knew he was.

Out of money?
Need a loan?
Come to an Opperistic Wealth Network bank now!
Terms and Conditions apply.
Wave hand to remove this ad for nominal fee.

Josh waved his hands, but he was worried. All the ads had been targeted toward whatever he was thinking about at the moment, obviously mining his brain for data. The latest one had been for a bank. He reached down and pulled out the cash chip. There was a minus sign before the numbers.

"What?" he asked in horror.

"You can't stay here," Katy told him, shaking her head. Her tone was firm and final. Whatever dream he had represented of her was gone.

The words flashed before his vision again.

Out of money?
Need a loan?
Come to an Opperistic Wealth Network bank now!
Terms and Conditions apply.
Wave hand to remove this ad for nominal fee.

HE WAS reluctant to wave his hand, but he did, and he watched the number on the chip grow. He was in debt. He could throw away the physical chip, but the debt would follow him.

"I don't understand," he said.

Need protection from debt collectors?
The Carcer Corporation can help!
Our officers are standing by now to help you!
Terms and Conditions apply.
Wave hand to remove this ad for nominal fee.

He couldn't bear to wave his hands, but he also could no longer really see Katy through the ad.

She closed his hand around the cash chip and said, "Josh, there's nothing I can do for you now. I can't pay off your debt, and neither can you."

He waved his hand so that he could see her, and to his surprise, she had tears in her eyes.

"But you feel the same way I do," he said.

Need protection from debt collectors?
The Carcer Corporation can help!
Our officers are standing by now to help you!
Terms and Conditions apply.
Wave hand to remove this ad for nominal fee.

"It doesn't matter how I feel. It doesn't matter how you feel," she said. "You're in the cycle now, and the only way to get out is to have the ads turned off. I've seen it happen to other people, and there's no escape. Maybe in another life, we could have been together, but it will take you years to pay back what you've already spent."

He wanted to see her, and he reached up to wave the ad away, but he felt her hand on his wrist.

"Don't do it," she said firmly.

"I have to see you," he said, but she wouldn't let go of his wrist.

"No, you don't. It'll only make this harder."

The ad became blurry as tears filled his eyes. When he could finally speak, he wailed, "What do I do?"

"Are you sure you want to do this?"

"Yes," Josh said miserably, unable to see Mr. Greene through the ad he had let sit in his vision all the way from the city back to the burb.

"Okay." Mr. Greene slid the tablet in front of Josh.

A single tear hit the screen as he pressed his thumb against it.

As soon as he did, the advertisement cleared, and he could see his new old life. His taste of freedom was over, and he would spend the rest of his days working to earn back all that he had lost. He had begged Katy to visit him, to consider moving to the burbs, but in his heart, he had known she wasn't the corporate stooge he was.

She had said no and kissed him on the cheek, and that was it.

Mr. Greene looked at Josh pityingly. "Welcome back to the company."

THE END

Terms and Conditions apply
Wave hand to remove this ad for nominal fee

ABOUT MATTHEW A. GOODWIN

Matthew A. Goodwin has been writing about spaceships, dragons, and adventures since he was a child. After creating his first fantasy world at twelve years old, he never stopped writing. Storytelling happened only in the background for over a decade as he spent his days caring for wildlife as a zookeeper, but when his son was born, he decided to pursue his life-long dream of becoming an author.

Having always loved sweeping space operas and gritty cyberpunk stories that asked questions about man's relationship to technology, he penned the international bestselling series A Cyberpunk Saga. His passion for the genre also inspired him to create and cofound Cyberpunk Day™, a celebration of all things high-tech / low-life.

For more information and *free* content, visit https://www.thutoworld.com/